L . D

MW01074299

J.D. Fairchild *(signature)*

THE LOST

THE PALUMBRA CHRONICLES: BOOK TWO

CITY

To Dave.

Dystopian fiction may not be your thing,

but loving and supporting me is.

CHAPTER ONE

Maeve toyed with her food unable to appreciate the fresh fruit and gruel on her plate. She should be ecstatic to be eating something other than protein paste. Six months after the overthrow of the World Government, life in Palumbra was slowly improving. Cleo, the former Resistance leader, had been elected as the new president, and Maeve and Gray had returned to their jobs -- her as a nurse and him as a soldier.

"You look awful," Gray said. He plopped a juicy orange slice into his mouth.

"More nightmares," Maeve mumbled.

"Again?"

Maeve nodded, feeling miserable. "Do you think they'll ever stop?"

Gray's gaze swept over her face. She was sure the dark circles under her eyes made her look as if she had been in a fight. He smiled at her. "I'm sure they will. It's only been a few months. Your brain is still trying to process everything."

"I just live the moment when I thought you were going to die over and over. Then I see the soldier I shot over and over. I don't know which tortures me more, the thought that you would die or the fact that I killed someone. How is my brain ever going to process that?"

"Time." Emma emerged from her bedroom and slowly made her way to the table. Maeve jumped up to make a plate for Emma, and Emma lowered her 86-year-old body slowly into the seat Maeve had just vacated. "It just takes time, honey."

After the WG fell, Emma left behind her life in the caves west of Palumbra to move in with Maeve. For the first time in 70 years, she lived in as much comfort as Palumbra could offer. It was Emma's help that had allowed The Resistance to uncover Arabella Laughlin's plan to use children and teenagers to power a weapon of mass destruction. With help from Maeve and some others, The Resistance had overpowered the WG and ousted Arabella from power.

"How much time? It's been six months."

Emma took a bite of her gruel. "It might take a lifetime. You need to understand that you sacrificed something, a piece of who you thought you were. You have to figure out who you are now."

Maeve let out a huff of frustration. "How do I do that?"

Gray pushed back from the table and gathered their plates and utensils. "I don't have Emma's years of experience, but I think you have to keep pushing forward. Don't stay stuck in the past and work to make a difference."

He placed the dishes in the sink and wiped the table with a wet cloth while Maeve ran a hand through her hair and grabbed her backpack.

"Are we making a difference? I feel like I'm spinning my wheels, that my life isn't that different than it was before we found out what the WG was up to."

"How can you say that?" Gray nearly shouted.

"We're working with the younger kids to make sure they understand the gift and responsibility of freedom. You help people every day at the hospital. Of course you're making a difference."

"I don't know," Maeve said as she twisted the strap on her backpack. "I just wish there was something more, something bigger. Am I going to go to the hospital every day for the rest of my life? Do I even like being a nurse?"

Emma studied Maeve silently. "Going back to a 'normal' life after a life-changing event is hard." She laughed. "Believe me, after 70 years in the wilderness, 'normal' seems weird. You have to figure out who you want to be now instead of yearning after who you were before." Emma's eyes took on a wistful look. "You have to let go of what you can't change."

Maeve gave Emma a hug and kissed the top of her head. "Thanks, Emma. I know this has been difficult for you, too, but I'm so glad you're here with me."

Emma smiled and patted Maeve's arm. "Now, you two get out of here. You're going to be late."

As soon as the door closed behind them, Gray took Maeve's hand and walked with her toward the hospital. "Do you really feel like you're not making a difference?"

Maeve shrugged. "Kind of. Since we helped Cleo and The Resistance get rid of the WG, no one seems to need us anymore. When was the last time we even heard from Cleo? We helped save Palumbra, but now we don't get much say in running it."

"Do you want to be in charge of those decisions? Is there something wrong with just living a normal life where we're not constantly worried about being caught or dying?" Gray gestured at the stores on the street. "Look around,

3

Maeve. All of this is because we helped remove the WG."

Maeve took in the activity on the street and thought about how much had changed since she and her friends had raced through these streets being chased by the WG. While change came slowly, the new government had loosened restrictions on who could own a business, and new enterprises were opening almost daily. They walked past a new clothing store, a shop selling flowers and gifts and a market where those with extra food could sell their excess.

Maeve sighed. "I know. It just seems like there's so much more to be done. Is it wrong to want to be a part of it? Don't you ever worry about Arabella being out there somewhere? And why haven't we found any sign of the city on the map? The Hub? I know they send out patrols every week. I just want to do something bigger than just go to work every day."

Before Gray could answer, Ginger ran up to them.

"Hey, Ginger," Gray said.

"Hey, guys. I'm late, but you two need to come by government headquarters after you get off work." Ginger worked at government headquarters in the computing department. She was brilliant with computers and was currently working to create a network for the remaining computers in Palumbra. The equipment was ancient, though, and as soon as Ginger fixed one problem, it seemed another popped up in its place. "Cleo called a meeting."

"Why?" Maeve asked.

Ginger shrugged. "I don't know. She asked me to tell you two and Tristan." She looked at the sun. "I really gotta go. See you tonight."

Maeve watched Ginger jog down the street. "What do you think that was about?"

Gray shook his head. "No idea. She could just want to know about our work with the kids."

It seemed like the most logical answer, but Maeve couldn't help hoping Cleo needed them for something more.

CHAPTER TWO

Maeve entered the tall, glass-walled building that served as government headquarters. It was the same building the WG had occupied when they were in power and the only building in Palumbra with consistent electricity and plenty of technology. After much discussion, the new government had decided it was the only logical place from which to run the government, although there was still some grumbling in Palumbra that not much had changed since the government took the best building. Maeve could see both sides, but she agreed with Cleo that for conditions in Palumbra to improve, someone had to be in charge and have access to the tools to make progress happen.

Maeve met Ginger inside the entrance and together they submitted to the security protocols. The security office searched Maeve's bag and checked them both for weapons, then quickly sent them on their way to Cleo's office. Despite much nicer spaces on the upper floors, Cleo had chosen an office on the main floor, saying she wanted to be as accessible to the people of Palumbra as possible.

"Why are we here?" Maeve asked.

"I don't really know. There was some commotion yesterday about one of the patrols that went out in the direction of where we think The Hub is. Maybe it has something to do with that?"

"But why are we involved?" Maeve asked as she quickened her steps to match Ginger's. "The New Government hasn't asked us to do anything since we defeated the WG."

They reached Cleo's office before Ginger could reply.

"No one's here. Where are they meeting?" Maeve asked.

Ginger shrugged. "No idea. I was told to come here."

"Finally," said a voice from behind them.

"Tristan!" Maeve whirled around in surprise. "You scared me. Are you here for the meeting, too?"

"Yep, I'm supposed to bring you guys to the conference room. We decided there were too many of us to meet in Cleo's office."

"Do you have any idea what this is about?" Maeve asked.

"Nope, but the sooner we get up there, the sooner we'll know. Let's go. Everyone is waiting."

"Glad you could join us," Cleo said as Maeve, Tristan and Ginger took their places around a rough, round wooden table. The government building looked shiny and new from the outside, but despite the technology around them, many of the furnishings were no better than what you could find in homes around Palumbra.

"But why are we here?" Maeve asked.

Gray winked at her as she took a seat next to him, and she took note of the rest of the meeting's participants. Cleo stood at the front with a young soldier dressed in a contamination suit that Maeve didn't recognize. Besides Maeve, Ginger, Tristan and Gray, the other seats were filled with high government officials, including John Shield, who had been something of a mentor to Gray and had helped them decipher the clues to The Lost Years that led to the downfall of the WG. A military general sat next to John.

"No one has more experience outside the borders of Palumbra than you four. I wanted you here in case you could offer some insight," Cleo explained. "Now, I want to introduce you to Corporal Shamus." She motioned to the young soldier standing next to her. "He has some interesting information to share with us." Cleo nodded at the soldier who looked down at his hands and began to speak.

"I was sent out on an extended patrol with five other soldiers three weeks ago. Our job was to patrol the area between here and the supposed city we've been referring to as The Hub."

"Wait, I thought we were staying away from The Hub," Gray interrupted.

Cleo smiled, her teeth gleaming white next to her coffee-colored skin. "We are. We have no idea what's there, but we decided there was no reason not to get close enough to take a look. We do need to know if it's even a city. All we have is the map you guys found, and it's 80 years old. For all we know, The Hub could have been destroyed a long time ago." Cleo motioned for the soldier to continue speaking.

"We never got close enough to see much, but from a distance, there's no sign of a city. We were setting up to snap some pictures and return to Palumbra when we were discovered."

"Discovered?" Maeve asked. "Discovered by who? We've been sending patrols out for months, and other than Emma, they've seen no signs of anyone. I was beginning to think the WG was right when they said we were the only ones left."

"Well, there are at least a few people left," Corporal Shamus replied. "Because they found us."

"Who was it?" Tristan asked.

Cleo stood and said, "Can we save the questions for the end, please? This will go much faster if we just let Corporal Shamus tell us what happened."

Cleo sat and Corporal Shamus began speaking again. "It was just a handful of people, only six -- a couple of teenagers and four adults. The teenagers were brother and sister, but the adults didn't seem to be related. They said they were the only survivors of an epidemic that wiped out civilization in The Hub."

No one interrupted, but a low murmuring began around the table.

Once again, Cleo stood. "Corporal Shamus has been decontaminated and tested for all known viruses. Doctors have assured me that he's not carrying anything that can contaminate Palumbra, but we're keeping him in the suit just in case. He will be quarantined for at least two weeks to be sure."

The murmuring quieted, and Corporal Shamus continued. "The survivors have been living in the desert outside where we think The Hub is for weeks. They asked for our help. Our team decided that one of us should head back here and let you decide what to do. The others stayed to help the survivors."

"Thank you, Corporal Shamus," Cleo said as she rose once again. Corporal Shamus moved to the empty seat next to General Crail, the leader of Palumbra's military. General Crail shifted his chair slightly away from the corporal.

"Now, we have some decisions to make," Cleo said from the head of the table.

"You're not actually thinking about bringing those people here, are you?" General Crail all but shouted at Cleo. "You could contaminate the entire population of Palumbra."

Cleo ignored his outburst and turned back to the rest of the group. "This is all the information we have. I don't think we have enough information to think about bringing the refugees into Palumbra." She crossed her arms over her chest. "But we can't just leave these people out in the desert to die, either."

"You're sure these people were from The Hub?" Tristan asked Corporal Shamus. The corporal nodded, and his contamination suit crinkled with the movement.

"Everything we know points to them being from The Hub," Cleo said. "Our most pressing issue is figuring out what to do with them. I think we're all agreed that leaving them out there to die isn't an option."

"I say we take them in," John said as he stroked his beard. "What choice do we have? It's the right thing to do."

General Crail stood. "Are you crazy? We have no idea what those people have been exposed to. We can't bring them into our city. If this thing wiped out whatever was left of civilization in The Hub, then it could do the same here in Palumbra."

Cleo turned from studying the map of Palumbra

that hung on the wall. "What do you think?" she asked Tristan.

"I don't know," Tristan said. He sat up straight in his chair and lifted his hands helplessly. "Neither of those options is acceptable. We can't endanger everyone in Palumbra, but we can't leave those people to die either."

Gray got up from the table and walked over to the map Cleo had been studying. "What about the caves?" He pointed to a spot on the map. "They could live in the caves until we're sure they don't have some crazy disease. Our doctors could test them, and they'd be quarantined from the rest of us. We could patrol the area with troops to make sure no one got out."

"I think that's a great idea," Maeve chimed in, getting up to stand next to Gray. "Emma lived out there for years. We know we can make those caves fairly comfortable."

Cleo looked around the table. "It's a good idea. Anyone have any other thoughts?"

"I still think it's too close to Palumbra," General Crail said. "But it's probably our best option."

"Anyone else?" Cleo asked.

Silence reigned as everyone looked around the table. "OK, then." Cleo clapped her hands once. "Let's figure out what to do next."

CHAPTER THREE

"Hi guys. Come on in," Emery said as she opened the door to Maeve and Gray. "Tristan is already here."

Maeve handed Emery the freshly baked loaf of bread she carried and turned to hang up her coat. After the meeting, they had all agreed to meet for dinner, something they did at least once a week.

"Hey, Emery," Gray said. "How's school?"

"Boring, as usual," Emery said with a grimace. "I'm not sure why I even go. I already know more than my teachers."

Gray grinned and patted her on the shoulder. "I'm pretty sure that's true. Maybe you can teach them something."

Emery was a slim, blond 12-year-old with a genius IQ. She had helped The Resistance defeat the WG, so it was sometimes easy to forget she was also a kid who had lost her mom and was adjusting to life with just her sister. It was one of the reasons Ginger insisted Emery continue to go to school even though she probably did know more than the teachers. They were doing everything they could to create a normal life.

"Hey, Gray," Tristan said from across the room.

Houses in Palumbra were small; most contained just one room and a loft. Ginger and Emery hadn't wanted to return to the house where their mom had been killed, so the new government had found them a house not far from where Gray lived. Since Ginger was 17, everyone had agreed that Emery would be best left to her sister's care. Ginger had moved several things from their old house, creating a homey atmosphere for her and Emery.

One side of the room held a couch and chair grouped near the fireplace, which was the only heat source for the house. The other side of the room housed the same kitchen appliances found in every home in Palumbra. An electric stove, refrigerator and sink stood in a straight line along the wall. A short countertop stretched between the stove and the sink.

A ladder leading up to the loft where Ginger and Emery slept on straw-filled mattresses stood next to the refrigerator. It was small, but it was home.

Maeve plopped down in one of the chairs thinking that she spent almost as much time here as she did at home with Emma, despite the fact that her home was larger. When the new government, which had taken on the name of The People's Government, had made a sweep of the caves where Emma hid, she had decided to give life in Palumbra a try. Since Maeve and Gray were the only people she knew, it made sense for her to live with Maeve. Housing was limited, but the new government had wanted to reward Emma's courage, and she and Maeve now lived in one of the larger houses in Palumbra, which meant they each had their own room.

"How's Emma?" Emery asked. Emma had quickly become one of Emery's favorite people, a stand-in for the mom and grandma she no longer had. "Why didn't she come tonight?"

"She decided she was tired and wanted to stay in," Maeve said. "She said to tell you to stop by tomorrow."

"I will," Emery said eagerly.

"What do you guys do when you go over there?" Ginger asked.

"I teach Emma all about computers, and she tells me stories about how she survived in the caves."

"I guess everyone learns something," Tristan said.

"We're ready to eat," Ginger announced.

They sat down to a typical Palumbran meal of vegetables and bread. Meat was still in rare supply as few people had weapons to hunt with. The New Government tried to make sure everyone got an allotment once a month, but it never lasted long. After bowing their heads to say a quick prayer, everyone dug in.

When they finished eating, discussion turned to the meeting with Cleo. "Do you think we could get Cleo to let us go with the rescue patrol?" Maeve asked.

"I doubt it," Tristan said. He knew Cleo the best, having served in The Resistance with her. Maeve had never heard the whole story of how Tristan had joined The Resistance, but she suspected Cleo had something to do with it. "She's determined to keep the five of us safe."

"So she made you and Gray soldiers? That's a safe job." Ginger rolled her eyes.

"We never get sent out on any patrol that might be remotely dangerous." Tristan's voice held a hint of resentment. "Mostly we patrol the perimeter of Palumbra."

"I want to be part of that rescue patrol," Maeve said. "I don't want to sit around waiting for them to get back to find out if we're all going to die from some plague. I need to do something more important than setting broken bones and talking to children. I bet we have more experience outside the perimeter of Palumbra than anyone else. Don't you guys want to get out there and do something?"

"I'm with Maeve," Emery piped up. "We should figure out how to go."

"Even if they go, you're staying here," Ginger said firmly. "One revolution before you're a teenager is enough excitement."

Emery pouted but gave Maeve a conspiratorial wink.

"Why is this so important to you, Maeve?" Ginger asked. They had been friends since early school, but Maeve knew it was unlikely that Ginger would understand how she was feeling. Maeve barely understood her own feelings. She just knew she was restless. Her old life no longer seemed to fit, and she itched to understand what had happened to The Hub.

"This might be our only chance to look for The Hub. Don't you wonder why we can't find it? And what about Arabella? She could still be out there, too."

Gray took Maeve's hand. "She could be," he said soothingly. "But don't you think Cleo and the rest of the government are looking for her? Most likely, she died in The Beyond."

"So what could be the harm in sending us on the patrol?" Maeve came back to her first point.

Tristan sighed. "I'll ask her, Maeve, but I'm sure the answer is going to be no."

Gray stood. "I need to get you home. Aren't you

teaching tomorrow?"

The new government had asked them to be part of an initiative to help the children of Palumbra understand their new freedoms, and they each took turns teaching an after-school class of 10-year-olds.

Maeve nodded. "Tomorrow's lesson is 'Making Good Choices,' you know like choosing to be a part of the government's rescue patrol." She smiled. "I don't know if you can really teach 10-year-olds how to make good decisions, though."

"Hey, I made good decisions at 10," Emery cried indignantly.

"Really?" Ginger asked. "So, writing equations on the wall was a good decision?"

"Of course it was," Emery said as she rolled her eyes. "Where else was I going to write it? It was way too long to write down on paper. I wouldn't have been able to see the whole thing at once."

Everyone laughed as they said their goodbyes.

"Thomas, what do you think a good decision would be in this situation?" Maeve asked a small boy in the back of the classroom.

Thomas thought for a moment, then said, "I wouldn't do either one. I'd take all the sandwiches and save them for a day when we had no food."

Maeve looked at the boy with black hair that just touched the collar of his shirt in the back. She shook her head. "But that's not one of the options. How would you keep the sandwiches fresh?"

"If they're protein paste sandwiches, they'll keep forever. That stuff never goes bad." Thomas made a face that had the other kids in the class laughing.

"But why do you think you need to save the sandwiches?" Maeve asked. "We have enough to eat now."

"But we haven't always, and you never know when the new government will decide to take away our food again." Several other children nodded in agreement with Thomas.

Thomas was an orphan whose parents had died when the WG rounded up Resistance fighters. Maeve also remembered when the WG had used food as a way to keep people under its thumb. If you followed the rules there had been just enough to survive, but if you defied the government, food often disappeared from your table.

Maeve glanced at Ginger and saw her shaking her head. Maeve decided to move on.

"Thomas, I don't want you to worry about the government taking your food," Maeve said gently. "The new government is different, but I understand your decision to keep the sandwiches for a different day. Does anyone else want to tell me what they would do with the sandwiches?"

"Thomas?"

"Yes, Miss Maeve."

"Just call me Maeve, Thomas. Can we talk for a minute?"

"Sure. I just have to be home by 5."

Maeve waved him toward a kid-sized table and chairs. "Thomas, you do know that things are different with the new government in charge, right?"

Thomas looked down and scuffed the ground with his foot. "I know we want to think they are, but what if that government goes bad, too? What do we do then?"

Maeve laid her hand on top of Thomas's smaller one. "Thomas, you're 10 years old. My friends and I fought so that you don't have to worry about having sandwiches tomorrow or the day after that or the day after that. We want you to embrace the choices you have for the future and not worry about whether there will be enough food or if your uncle is going to disappear."

Thomas looked hard at Maeve. "But you guys didn't have a lot of choices when you did that."

"Sure we did. We could have quit. We could have turned ourselves in."

"But the WG would have killed you!" Thomas exclaimed.

"Maybe," Maeve agreed. "But it was still a choice. That's the thing about choices, Thomas. Even when you're faced with two bad options, you still get to choose. I made some choices during that time that were tough, that weren't things I would normally do, but I made them so that my friends and I could survive. I made them so that you don't have to make them. My friends and I fought so that you don't have to worry about the government. There are good people in charge now, Thomas. They want people like you to be free to make choices about what you want to do when you grow up and even where you want to go."

"Go? Where is there to go?"

"Right now, we don't know, but there's a whole lot of land out there. Maybe someday we'll get to explore it." Maeve reached out and ruffled his hair. "Maybe one day we'll even get to explore the stars."

Thomas's eyes rounded and his mouth formed an O. "The stars, really?"

"Who knows?" Maeve lifted one shoulder in a shrug. "My friend Ginger thinks it's possible, and she's really smart. Way smarter than me."

"Wow," Thomas marveled. "I've never even thought about leaving Palumbra."

"It's one of those things that might be a choice in the future," Maeve said as she stood up. "That's why we want you guys to think about making choices and being smart about it now, when you're young. If you learn the value of freedom now, you'll be less likely to let anyone take it away from you."

Thomas stood up and gave Maeve a high-five. "Thanks, Miss Maeve. I can't wait to tell my friends we might one day go to the stars!"

Maeve turned to find Gray standing in the doorway as she watched Thomas rush out.

Gray smiled at her and said, "Still think you're not making a difference?"

CHAPTER FOUR

"No, absolutely not!" Cleo said to Tristan. "No way am I sending teenagers on this expedition. It's far too dangerous."

"Cleo," Tristan said calmly. "Why did you ask us to the meeting if you didn't want our help?"

Cleo threw up her hands in exasperation. "You guys know more about what's beyond The River than anyone else. I wanted your expertise, not to put you in danger again."

"That expertise makes us the best people to send," Tristan argued. "We have experience beyond The River, and we're the ones who discovered The Hub even existed. Maeve knows the most about the caves since she and Emma live together."

"No," Cleo repeated. "We're not putting you guys in harm's way again. You've done enough. Don't you all just want to have a normal life? Why do you even want to go out there?"

Maeve, Gray and Ginger watched the conversation intently from their spot along the back wall of the room. They had decided to let Tristan handle Cleo since he had known her the longest.

"We do want a normal life," Tristan said. "But how do we settle into 'normal' when we have no idea what's out there?"

Cleo paced back and forth. "You just let us handle it! We have soldiers and scientists who can deal with this. You don't need to."

Maeve stepped forward. "I think we do," she said quietly.

Cleo stopped her pacing and looked directly at Maeve. "Why?"

Maeve held Cleo's gaze without blinking. "I have nightmares. Every night."

"So you want to give yourself more?"

"No. I want to do something to chase them away. I want to find out what's out there so I can stop worrying about it. I want to protect what we've built here. I want the sacrifices we've made to mean something." Maeve stood completely still as she spoke, but her eyes burned with ferocity.

"She's right," Gray said, stepping forward and taking Maeve's hand. "This is something we need to do. We don't want to lead the team. We just want to be a part of it. Tristan and I are both soldiers, Ginger works for you and Maeve has proved she can handle herself. Let us go and see what's out there, so we can sleep at night."

Ginger walked over and stood next to Tristan. "What can it hurt? It's a quick trip into the desert. We'll be back in less than a week, and we might learn something that will make us all feel safe."

Cleo looked from one earnest face to the next then shook her head. "I'm sorry," she said with a touch of sadness to her voice. She looked at Maeve. "I know you think this will chase the nightmares away, but I can't send you out there. There's too much unknown, and you, all of you..." Her gaze swept over the others. "You've done enough."

"But," Maeve started.

Cleo straightened and all compassion fell from her eyes. Here was the strong leader that was moving Palumbra forward. "My final answer is no."

"She didn't listen to us, not really," Maeve complained to Emma as they cleaned up the dishes after dinner.

Emma slowly rose from her seat at the table to take her place drying the dishes that Maeve washed. Maeve noted that although Emma had plenty to eat and decent shelter now, her gait had noticeably slowed in the past few months. Living together had given Maeve a new appreciation for how hard Emma's life had been as Emma shared bits and pieces of her past. The two had grown close in the months they lived together, and Emma had become the grandmother that Maeve had never had. She hated to think that Emma might not be around that much longer.

Emma reached around Maeve to pick up the towel and patted her on the shoulder. "I know, dear, but Cleo has to think about bigger things than just the five of you. She has the weight of leadership on her shoulders." Emma picked up one of their two metal plates and began to dry it. "Imagine the outcry if she sent the heroes of The Resistance into the desert and they didn't come back."

Maeve stuck her hand in the soapy water, splashing it out of the basin. "But who knows more about what's out there than us?"

"Why do you want to go so badly?" Emma asked as she wiped a tin cup.

Maeve shrugged. "I need to know what's out there." She wiped her forehead with the back of her hand. "The WG believed that The Hub was dangerous enough that they were going to destroy it. The new government has looked for signs of the city and found none. Now we find people who claim to be from The Hub. If there are other people out there, shouldn't we work together?"

"And you don't think Cleo has the same goals?"

Maeve chewed on her lip. "I think she does, but what if The Hub does have dangerous secrets? Then what does she do?"

"Is that really the reason you want to go?" Emma asked gently.

Maeve shook her head. "I need to get away." Maeve's shoulders slumped. "I need to feel like I'm doing something." She turned defeated eyes to Emma. "There are things I just want to forget."

Emma put down the fork she was drying and embraced Maeve. "Running away isn't going to help you forget. I'm sorry to say you'll never forget what happened." Emma pulled back and pinned Maeve with a serious look. "And I don't think you really want to forget. Forgetting would mean everything that happened was meaningless, that who you've become isn't who you want to be. Do you really want things to go back to the way they were before?"

Maeve tossed the rag she was using into the basin with a plop, sank into her chair and dropped her head to her hands. "I just don't know what to do," she whispered.

Emma gently set her towel next to the basin and pulled her chair to face Maeve's. She pried Maeve's hands off her face and held Maeve's young, unblemished hands in her wrinkled and twisted ones. "You have to recognize that sometimes it's not the big things we do that change the world. More often, it's the little ones -- caring about someone, teaching others, living with compassion. Those are the things that make a difference, the things that change a generation."

"So you're saying I should just stay here and let others worry about the big stuff?"

"That's not what I'm saying at all," Emma said with a sigh. "Just don't forget the little stuff while you're chasing the big stuff."

###

"What are we going to do?" Maeve kicked listlessly at the ground the next day as she walked to the hospital with Gray.

"Tristan and I were talking last night," Gray replied. He looked at Maeve, drew his eyebrows together and frowned as he took in the circles under her eyes and the defeated slope of her shoulders. "We think we should just go anyway."

Maeve stopped and looked up. Her eyes sparked with interest. "Do you think we could?"

Gray cocked his head and gave her an incredulous look. "Are we not the people who braved the world outside of Palumbra and defeated the WG mostly on our own just a few months ago?"

"But we had no choice. We just did it. This would be much harder and a deliberate choice."

Gray took her hand and resumed walking. "You forget that you made a choice."

Maeve shook her head. "When? I feel like we were

just swept along in events. I didn't decide much of anything."

Gray stopped again and turned her to look at him. He swept a lock of her hair off her forehead and tucked it behind her ear. "Of course you did. Remember, in the tunnels with my uncle when he offered you a life of safety versus participating in The Resistance?"

Maeve looked at the ground and shrugged. "That wasn't much of a choice to make. I didn't want to live a life cut off from everyone else."

Gray tipped her chin back up so he could look in her eyes. "It was still a choice, one that changed our world."

"But think about how much we lost," Maeve said. "Silas, your uncle, Emery and Ginger's mom." She dropped her gaze again. "We're all forever changed. Was it worth it?"

"Do you think it was?" Gray asked.

Maeve chewed the skin on the side of her thumbnail, trying to come up with a truthful answer. Did she think it was worth it? She didn't even recognize the person she had been six months ago, living with her parents and blindly following the dictates of the WG. Did she really want to go back to that?

Finally, Maeve nodded. "I think it was. I just wish it hadn't cost so much."

Gray hugged her close and laid his cheek on the top of her head. "I know. I miss my uncle every day, but this is what he was fighting for. And I think he would want us to be involved in whatever mystery The Hub holds."

"I don't know, Gray. If we're not part of the official search party, how would we get out of Palumbra without being noticed? I'm sure Cleo will try to stop us since she's so determined to keep us safe."

Gray kissed the top of her head and stepped back, still holding her hand. "We're working on that. Tristan and I have some connections. We'll work it out."

She studied Gray's face. "Why do you want to do this? We could do anything we want. Cleo would make sure we got whatever kind of training we need for whatever we want to do. You could quit being a soldier. They would probably even let you study art." She squeezed his hand. "I know why I need to see what's out there, but what about you?"

Gray ran a hand through his hair and pulled her closer to the building on his left so other people could get around them. "I've discovered I like being a soldier, most of the time. I'm good at it. I can see strategy and tactics. I love art but mostly as a hobby."

"But why do you want to go out there?" Maeve waved her hand in the direction of The River.

"Part of it is curiosity. Part of it is not completely trusting the people in charge." He shrugged. "I think our recent experience has made us more wary of authority than other people, but..." He captured her face in his hands, and Maeve swore she could feel his gaze penetrate all the way to her soul. "The biggest reason is because you need to go."

"You would go just because I feel I need to go?"

Gray dropped his hands from her face and held both of hers between them, reminiscent of the way Emma had done the night before. "Do you really need to ask? We're in this together, remember?"

Maeve looked at their clasped hands and thought about Emma's words. "Emma said I needed to remember that the small things are what matters. What if I'm wrong and going out there doesn't accomplish anything?"

"Then we'll have had another big adventure, and we'll know what the government knows. And you..." He squeezed her hands. "Will have the answers you seem to need about what's really out there."

CHAPTER FIVE

"Get up, Maeve." Emma shook her shoulder.

Maeve opened one eye. "Huh?" Her eyes focused on Emma, and she sat up in alarm. "What's going on? Are you OK?"

"Shh," Emma said. "I'm fine, but you need to go."

Maeve shook her head. "Go where? It's the middle of the night."

Emma handed Maeve her pants and a shirt. Maeve rubbed her eyes and noted that the lamp on the table was unlit. The room was illuminated by the single candle that Emma held in her hand. While their home had electricity for appliances, it was not wired for lighting.

"The government search party is leaving. You need to be right behind them."

Maeve slipped on her clothes as she tried to make sense of Emma's words. She tied her shoes in the dim light, and said, "I really don't know what you're talking about."

Emma held out Maeve's coat, then shoved an apple and a protein paste bar into one of Maeve's hands and motioned toward a backpack in the corner. "You're all packed. Eat that on the way."

Maeve grabbed the backpack, sticking the apple

into the outside pocket. She nibbled on the protein paste bar as Emma opened the door and looked carefully up and down the street. While there was a lot more freedom in Palumbra now than when the WG was in charge, being out late at night was still a cause for questions. "Where are we going?" Maeve whispered.

"Your friends are waiting for you." Emma glanced over her shoulder as she hurried down the street. Maeve, in her sleep-disoriented state, struggled to keep up with the 86-year-old woman. "This is nuts. Why are they waiting for me?"

Emma stopped abruptly and stepped back into the shadow of a building entrance. Maeve heard footsteps and followed suit. Two men that Maeve recognized as members of Cleo's advisory committee walked by. Absorbed in conversation, they didn't notice Emma and Maeve.

"What do you think they'll find out there?" one man said. Maeve strained to hear the rest of the conversation.

"I'm hoping a few people and not much else," the other man replied. "We might be in trouble if there's a whole city of people out there. What if there are more of them than there are of us?"

Maeve leaned over to Emma and whispered, "Are they talking about The Hub?"

Emma held up a finger to her lips.

"What will we do if there are more people outside Palumbra?" the first man asked.

Maeve could barely hear the reply. "I don't know, but I hope they're friendly. The last thing we need is another battle. We're just rebuilding from the destruction of the World Government."

Maeve's eyes widened. Hadn't they just avoided war with people outside of Palumbra, and now the government, Cleo's government, was talking about it again? She turned to Emma, who was shaking her head.

"We never learn," Emma said. "Come on. Getting you on your way is more important now than it was before." Emma started to step back onto the street, but Maeve gently pulled her back and turned to face her.

"Emma, you need to tell me what is going on before we go any farther."

Emma glanced up and down the street. She nodded. "John and I are sending you, Gray, Tristan and Ginger out to follow the government team meeting the 'survivors' from The Hub."

"No Emery? I'm sure that didn't make her happy."

Emma shrugged. "She's too young. She's going to stay with me while you guys are gone."

Maeve nodded and mulled Emma's words over. "Wait, you and John? I didn't even know you two knew each other." The light from a lantern hanging on the other side of the street illuminated Emma's face just enough that Maeve could see her sheepish grin.

"Well, we've been spending some time together." Emma averted her gaze.

Maeve smiled. "That's great! You deserve someone, Emma, after all you've been through." Emma waved off Maeve's exuberance.

"Not the point right now. John got wind of when the team was leaving. After thinking it through, we decided you four need to go with them or at least follow them. John isn't convinced that everyone in the new government wants to make friends with people outside Palumbra."

Maeve chewed her lower lip. "But Cleo knows how hard we worked to avoid war with anyone who is out there."

Emma waved her hand as if swatting Maeve's argument away. "Oh, it's not Cleo, but there are people who wanted the WG gone so they could have power, not necessarily so everyone else could have freedom."

Emma took Maeve by the shoulders. "Listen, Maeve, we agreed that this would be the best way to keep an eye on the team heading out to meet the group from the Hub. No one is going to be surprised that the four of you went off on your own. You've done it before, and everyone knows you wanted to go from the beginning. Now, come on. We have to go."

Maeve followed Emma with her mind turning over everything Emma had said. It was true that she and Gray had decided yesterday to go on their own to see what was going on, so she shouldn't have been surprised that Emma, the ultimate rebel, had taken things into her own hands. However, it was still surprising that she had orchestrated everything so quickly. And with John. He was kind and gentle, nearly 10 years younger than Emma. The thought of him and Emma together made Maeve smile. After everything Emma had lived through, she deserved to find some happiness.

Lost in her own thoughts, Maeve bumped into Emma when she stopped in the shadow of a tree on the outskirts of town. Emma whistled three low notes spaced evenly apart. A moment passed in silence then Maeve heard a return whistle. Emma stepped out of the shadows, and Maeve watched another shadow, whom she assumed was John, move out from under the branches of a tree about 20 feet away. The two met halfway between the trees and whispered together before motioning to Maeve to follow.

As Maeve drew closer to the second tree, she saw other shadows beside Emma and John. When her eyes could finally make out features, she found the faces of her friends -- all four of them.

"Emery, what are you doing here?"

"I'm going too." Emery settled her hands on her hips as if daring anyone to argue with her.

"I thought you were going to stay with Emma," Maeve said, looking from Ginger to Emma.

"Please. You guys need me. I helped you save the world once." Emery hoisted the pack at her feet and slipped it on her back. "I'm not going to sit at home while you do it again."

Emma and Ginger exchanged a look, and Ginger shrugged. "She makes a compelling argument."

"It's your call," Emma said. "I think it would be safer if she stayed with me, but it's your decision."

Emery anxiously looked from Ginger to Emma and shifted back and forth. She opened her mouth to speak, then clamped it shut as she fixed her sister with a pleading stare.

Ginger placed an arm around Emery and said, "You can go, but you have to do what we tell you to."

Emery smiled in victory. "When do I ever not do what you say?"

Ginger just rolled her eyes.

While Emery and Ginger were sorting things out, Gray had moved to stand next to Maeve. "Did Emma fill you in?"

"Did you know about this?" Maeve swept her hand to encompass the group.

Gray nodded. "John found me yesterday after I dropped you off at the hospital. He and Emma had it all figured out."

"Why did they wait to tell me until the middle of the night?"

"I was the only one that knew. We sneaked Tristan, Ginger and Emery out, too. It was easier to keep it a secret that way."

Maeve looked doubtful, but she nodded. "I guess. I just hope Emma packed everything I need."

Emma looked up from the conversation she was having with Emery. "I didn't survive in the caves for 70 years without knowing what you need to survive, young lady."

"She has a point," Gray whispered. "I think you'll be fine."

A twig snapped from the direction of the tree Emma and Maeve had stood under, and everyone whirled around to look. Technically, they weren't breaking any rules, but there would be a lot of explaining to do if they were caught out in the middle of the night ready to travel. The group waited in silence, no one daring to move or even breathe. After a few minutes with no other sounds, their shoulders relaxed, and they began to talk again.

"So, what's the plan?" Tristan asked. "I assume we have one."

John stepped forward and laid out a map. "Is everyone up to speed?" he asked, the soft burr in his voice washing over them. John's grandad had come from a land far away, and the accent had been filtered down through the generations. "I filled this crew in on our suspicions while we were waitin' for you two." He turned to Maeve. "Lass, did Emma talk to you?" Maeve nodded and John turned his attention to the map. In the dim light from the moon, she could see it was similar to the map she and Gray had used when they had found Emma and the energy weapon machine many months earlier. She stepped closer.

"This is the caves." John pointed to a spot on the map next to a smudge.

"Wait," Maeve said. "Is that our map? The one we found in the time capsule?"

John nodded. "I may have liberated it from its hiding spot in the government headquarters." He shrugged. "You guys found it. I figure you should be the ones to use it."

Emma sent John a slight smile.

"Anyway, the government team is heading out into the desert to meet with The Hub survivors." He drew an imaginary line with his finger to a part of the map that none of them had been to. "But their final destination is the caves. You lot will have to decide whether to follow them into the desert or to just head to the caves. The group has about a three-hour head start."

"I vote we go to the caves," Ginger said. "It's safer, and we know how to get there."

"True, but we won't know what the group finds in the desert," Gray said. "It might be important to know what's out there."

Emery nodded. "I'm with Gray. If we don't follow them into the desert, we won't know what they know."

Ginger elbowed Tristan who glanced at her before

speaking. "I think if Emery is going, we need to head for the caves. We don't know what it's like out there or how far behind the government team we'll be. What if we end up in trouble and need help? Tactically, the caves are a better choice since it's known territory for at least some of us."

Everyone turned their eyes to Maeve. "You get the deciding vote," Gray said.

Maeve mulled her choices. She didn't want to disappoint Gray by voting for the caves, but she was concerned about Emery. The caves were a known quantity since she and Gray had spent time with Emma there, but something about going out into the desert and getting as close to The Hub as they could called to her. She couldn't pass up the chance to get some of her questions answered.

"We should go into the desert," she said with a nod of her head. "I want us all to be as safe as possible, but we need to know what the government team is going to know."

Maeve and Gray stood next to John and Emma as Emery, Ginger and Tristan gathered their packs and hoisted them to their shoulders.

"You ready?" Tristan asked.

"Not yet," John said as he stepped behind a tree. He returned with four rifles and a knife. "You might need these."

Gray shot a hasty look at Maeve who was stepping slowly away from John and shaking her head. She held her hands up in front of her. "No. Never again."

Gray stepped in front of her and took her hands. "Maeve, we can't go out into the desert without some protection. At a minimum there could be animals out there."

Maeve looked into his concerned eyes and

continued shaking her head like a wounded animal. "I can't, Gray. I can't carry a gun again."

Gray gave her a long look. Maeve lifted her chin resolutely as a tear leaked out of the corner of her eye. Finally, Gray squeezed her hands and turned back to John. "Do you have another knife?"

John nodded and handed Gray a sheathed knife like the one he had given Emery. Ginger and Tristan had already shouldered their guns and watched as Gray held the knife out to Maeve. "You have to have something to protect yourself with. If it's not going to be a gun, at least take the knife."

Maeve looked at the knife as if it was a snake that might bite her, but she blew out a long breath before reaching for it. "I'm not using this on a person," she said defiantly.

Gray nodded and stroked her arm. "Hopefully, you won't have to make that decision."

Maeve's eyes shot daggers at Gray. "The decision is made. I'm not hurting anyone else."

Gray said nothing, just nodded and turned back to take his own rifle and ammunition from John. Gray looked at Tristan who was shifting from foot to foot, clearly ready to go. "The government team has a big head start on us," Tristan said. "We need to get moving."

Gray nodded. "Give us a minute."

Maeve tucked the knife away in her pack and turned to embrace Emma. "Thank you for making sure we could do this."

Emma smiled slightly and nodded at John. "He was the one that decided there were good reasons for you five to follow the government team." Emma took Maeve's hands in hers and gave them a little shake. "Remember what we talked about. We make sacrifices for love, and those sacrifices change us. Focus on the little things, and the big things will take care of themselves."

Maeve looked down at their clasped hands and remembered all the nights that Emma had sat awake with her the past three months, nights when Maeve was afraid to go back to sleep and afraid to be awake alone. As she gazed at Emma's liver spotted and wrinkled hands, she wondered if she was wasting precious time on this trip that she could be spending with Emma. She looked up and caught Emma's gaze. "Am I doing the right thing? Will you be OK?"

Emma gave a short laugh. "Maeve, I lived for 70 years in a cave. I think I can handle a week or so without you."

Maeve grinned. "I guess you'll be fine."

Emma squeezed Maeve's hands again. "As for your other question, dear. Only you can decide if you're doing the right thing, and you might not know until after you've done it."

Maeve thought about that for a minute. She wasn't at all sure that this was the right thing to do; she only knew that right now, she needed to do it. She nodded and pulled her hand away from Emma's so she could embrace her. "Take care of yourself while I'm gone."

"I'll be fine. Get going. Your friends are getting anxious."

Maeve and Gray hoisted their packs and headed toward where Ginger and Tristan were huddled together over the map John had given them.

Gray tapped Tristan on the shoulder and said,

"We're ready. Do you want to lead?"

Tristan folded the map and nodded. "Based on this map, I have a pretty good idea of the route the government team will take."

Gray clapped him on the shoulder and said, "That's why they put you on the scout team." He fell into step next to Maeve. They walked silently through the woods, the miles passing quickly as they traveled through the darkness. Tristan led with a sure step, stopping periodically to consult the map and Maeve and Gray since they had traveled part of this area before.

"He's really taken to being a soldier," Maeve said, gesturing toward Tristan.

Gray nodded. "It suits him. He learned a lot about leadership in The Resistance, and he loves the strategy and planning involved."

"Do you?" Maeve asked quietly so the others couldn't overhear.

Gray shrugged. "It's OK. Right now, it's what I need to do. I feel like I'm making a difference, but if I'm honest, all that strategy and planning that Tristan likes aren't really my favorite. Sometimes it's a lot of sitting around and waiting. I prefer to be doing something."

"Yeah, you're not really one to sit around," Maeve said with a smile, thinking of all the times Gray had pulled her out of a chair to go "do something." "I definitely do more when you're around."

Gray grinned at her. "You would be so bored without me."

Maeve was so involved in her conversation with Gray that she didn't notice the others had stopped until she stumbled into Emery. Maeve furrowed her brows. Emery had been leading the way with Tristan, happily chattering about her newest school project. When had she dropped back behind Ginger? Maeve's hand crept toward her backpack, searching for her knife as she saw Tristan reach for his gun.

"Gray?" Tristan said quietly.

"I'm here." Gray stepped around Maeve, Ginger and Emery.

"I think we've got trouble." Tristan never took his eyes off whatever was in front of him. "Ginger, keep Emery between you and Maeve and find a tree to cover your backs."

Maeve shared a scared glance with Ginger over the top of Emery's head and began backing toward a large tree just off the path to their left. She gripped the knife in her right hand and Emery's arm with her left and watched as the boys slipped off the path into the trees on the far side.

"What is it?" Emery whispered.

Maeve shook her head. "No idea, but we need to do what Tristan says. Did you see anything, Ginger?"

Maeve could just make out Ginger shaking her head in the dim light of the moon.

Silence reigned as Maeve squinted into the darkness. She could feel the rough bark of the tree through the layers of her clothing and Emery trembling next to her. She leaned down to whisper in her ear. "It will be fine. Tristan sounded like he had a plan."

A terrible shriek rent the air. Maeve couldn't tell if it was human or animal.

"What was that?" Ginger asked as she frantically swiveled her head, looking for the unknown threat.

"I don't know," Maeve said, "but I'm going to find

out." She took a step away from the tree back in the direction they had come.

"Maeve," Ginger said urgently. "You don't even have a gun. You can't go back there on your own."

"I'll be fine. What if the boys are in trouble?"

The high-pitched shriek filled the night air again, followed by male voices shouting and the sound of running feet crashing through the woods.

"They might need help," Maeve said. "And you need to stay here with Emery. You'll need your gun to keep her safe."

"I don't think you should go," Emery said in a voice that quavered then held. "We should stick together." Her voice held more assurance. "What if you get separated from us?"

Maeve shook her head in frustration. "Fine. Let's all go." Another shriek and more shouting ensued. "I think Tristan and Gray might need more help than they think."

Ginger turned to Emery. "You do exactly what we tell you to, right?"

Maeve couldn't see well in the darkness, but it was clear Emery was rolling her eyes. "Yes, dear sister. You'd think I'd never done anything dangerous before. Not like I helped save Palumbra or anything."

Ginger began walking back the way they had come. "That may be, but you're still only 12. The rules of you coming on this expedition were that you would follow directions."

Emery jutted out her chin, and Maeve thought she was going to argue with Ginger, but she clamped her mouth shut and followed her sister just as a shriek followed by a large thud echoed through the woods.

CHAPTER SIX

The girls sprinted back up the path they had backed down when Tristan had told them to protect Emery. They no longer heard Tristan and Gray shouting.

Maeve skidded to a stop at the edge of a clearing where Ginger already stood staring open-mouthed at what lay in front of her. "What is that?" Ginger asked.

A large animal, its sides heaving and its breathing shallow laid on the ground. Blood streamed from a wound in its side. Maeve had never seen anything like it. Large animals were rare in Palumbra, and this one was more than large. It stretched at least seven feet from head to stubby tail. Covered in scales, Maeve decided its body shape looked like a photo she had once seen of a horse. She tore her gaze away from the creature and scanned the rest of the clearing.

"Where are the boys?"

Ginger shook her head. "No idea. But what *is* that?"

Emery stepped forward and peeked around Maeve's shoulder. "That's a plagoran. And it's hurt. We should do something for it." She took a step toward the injured animal, but Ginger placed a hand on her arm to stop her.

Maeve whipped her head toward Emery. "A what?"

"A plagoran," Emery said matter-of-factly, as if everyone had heard of it. "It's a reptile that can walk on two or four legs. No one knows where they came from, but they appeared after the Great Wars of 2090. They haven't been seen around here in probably 50 years."

"How do you even know that?" Ginger asked as she continued to scan their surroundings for any sign of Gray and Tristan -- or another plagoran.

"Oh, there's lots of things in the government database that we've never had access to before."

"Have you been hacking into the government system again?" Ginger asked with exasperation.

Emery vehemently shook her head. "No. You told me not to. The government made a whole bunch of stuff available to everyone, especially the history and nature stuff that was in the archives."

"OK," Ginger said. "What can you tell us about the plagoran?"

As Emery began to speak, Ginger moved around the creature and started walking across the clearing in hopes of finding Tristan and Gray. Emery and Maeve kept their distance from the injured animal but didn't move away.

"There used to be lots of plagorans. No one knows where they came from, but some people thought they were some kind of mutant experiment gone wrong -- maybe some government project to use as a weapon. Their scales act like armor, and they're hard to kill, but that's not the most interesting thing about them."

"Oh, what is?" Maeve asked.

"If you milk the venom from their fangs, it can actually help heal people."

Ginger stopped walking, turned to look at Emery and cocked a skeptical eyebrow. "So, I'm supposed to believe that this gigantic reptile has some kind of magical ability to heal people?"

Emery shrugged. "I'm only telling you what I read in the government files."

Maeve looked hopelessly around the clearing. "That's all great to know, but where are the boys?"

Ginger started to answer when she was interrupted by the sound of a twig cracking. She grabbed her gun and hurried back to Maeve and Ginger. Maeve shoved Emery behind her, then whirled to meet the threat head on. "Maybe it's the boys?" Ginger whispered hopefully.

A tree to Maeve's left began to shake and the ground trembled under her feet. Whatever was coming their way, it wasn't Gray and Tristan.

Maeve gripped her knife tightly in her right hand as the ground continued to shake. "Did you and Gray run into any of these things when you were out here before?" Ginger asked as they stepped backward toward the shelter of the trees.

Maeve shook her head. "No. Definitely not. I've never even heard of them before. Emery, how come we've never seen one of these before?"

"They're really rare," Emery answered as she clutched Ginger's arm. "I don't know anyone who has actually seen one. I didn't know they lived this close to Palumbra. They live in pairs but keep to themselves."

"Well, we've apparently disturbed them," Ginger said. "Where do you think the boys are?"

Maeve looked around the clearing again, as if willing Gray and Tristan to appear, but their whereabouts remained a mystery. "What are we going to do?"

Ginger stumbled. "No idea. No way this gun has bullets that will penetrate those scales. Emery, think. What do you know about these things?"

As they passed the injured plagoran, Emery stopped. The giant animal's eye blinked open and stared at Emery. Emery remained frozen. The ground shook.

"Emery!" Ginger whispered fiercely. "Let's go!"

Emery looked from the giant reptile's open eye to her sister, then back to the dying animal. The plagoran's sides heaved. She took a step toward her sister, hesitated then flattened her lips and turned back to the plagoran. The ground shook again. Emery hurried back to the plagoran, careful to avoid its long, curved claws.

"Emery!" Ginger screamed and aimed her gun.

Emery raised pained eyes to Ginger's and with a hitch in her voice said, "It's dying, and it's all alone." Ginger gripped her gun more tightly but didn't shoot.

Maeve stood frozen in horror as the plagoran slowly lifted its clawed arm that was as thick and tall as Emery's whole body. She lunged forward to snatch Emery out of the way, but Emery held up her hand and kneeled next to the plagoran's long, flat snout. The reptile lowered its claw back to the ground without harming Emery.

"It's OK." She stroked the plagoran's snout. "You're going to be OK."

Maeve shared a look with Ginger then went to stand next to Emery with her knife easily accessible.

"Can you help it?" Emery asked. She turned pleading eyes to Maeve.

"Emery, I'm a nurse for people. I've never even heard of a plagoran before today, and I think this one's mate is about to find us. This thing is dangerous if Gray and Tristan injured it." Trees swayed at the opposite end of the clearing, and the ground gave another shake.

"Please, Maeve. We have to try."

Maeve knelt next to the scaly belly of the beast and examined the wound. She frowned. She had assumed the plagoran had been shot, but the wound was jagged and torn in a straight line. "Did you hear gunshots when the boys were fighting this thing?" she asked Emery.

"No. Did you?" Emery looked up at Ginger who had taken Maeve's place next to Emery.

Ginger shook her head. "No. I just assumed they had shot it, but now that I think about it, I never heard a gunshot."

Maeve dug in her pack for a T-shirt and pressed it against the wound. She only hoped plagorans responded to the same first aid as humans. "Emery, I don't know how much good I'm doing. For all I know, whatever wounded this thing could have hit something important."

"Just keep trying," Emery said as she stroked the plagoran's snout again. "I think it knows we're helping it."

"How smart are these things?" Ginger asked.

Emery shrugged. "I don't know. I've told you everything I know."

Maeve worked frantically to stop the blood seeping from the plagoran's wound. She raised her head and swiped her hair out of her face with her forearm. "Emery, what is that?"

"What is what?" Emery asked as she continued to stroke the plagoran's snout.

"That yellow thing by its ear."

Emery shifted on her knees and moved her head to the side to see where Maeve was pointing. Her nose scrunched, and her eyebrows drew together. "I don't know. It looks like a tag." She rose up on her knees and reached a hand toward it, but the plagoran gave a low growl before she could touch it.

"Don't touch it, Emery," Maeve said quickly. "Just tell me what it looks like."

Emery returned to stroking the plagoran's nose and said, "I can't see all of it, but it's just a yellow tag with numbers on it – 56823. It looks like someone punched a hole in its ear to attach it." She ran a finger between the plagoran's eyes and down its snout. "You've had a tough go, haven't you," she said quietly. The plagoran blinked.

"Why would someone do that?" Maeve interrupted Emery's conversation with the plagoran.

"I read about some people who would do that when they were studying animals, so they would know they were looking at an animal they had already seen. It helps them to track the animals."

Ginger raised her eyebrows and kept her gun trained on the plagoran. "Who would want to mess with one of these guys?" Ginger asked.

Emery shrugged.

"Does it say anything else?" Maeve asked as she began working to tie a makeshift bandage on the plagoran. She didn't think the plagoran would be very cooperative if she tried to stitch the wound closed, and she wasn't willing to find out if she was right.

Emery cocked her head again. "It looks like the letters P.U.P."

Maeve snorted. "This thing is no pup."

Just then a loud shriek echoed through the clearing, causing the plagoran to raise its head a few inches off the ground and let out a small shriek that sounded more like a whimper. The second plagoran broke through the tree line and headed straight for them. Ginger aimed her gun.

"Don't shoot it!" Emery cried.

"Then, let's go," Ginger replied. "That thing is coming. Let's move, Maeve." Emery gave the plagoran's snout one last pat and rose to her feet. Ginger grabbed her by the arm and started running. "Maeve! Move it."

Maeve had created a makeshift bandage out of the T-shirt and quickly rose to follow Emery and Ginger. She glanced at the charging plagoran as another high-pitched shriek filled the air. She hesitated as she passed the injured plagoran's head and looked into its open, pain-filled eye. The plagoran blinked. She placed her hand on the plagoran's snout and looked it in the eye.

"I tried. I hope it was enough."

The plagoran blinked again. The ground shook as the its angry mate charged toward Maeve. She turned and ran for the edge of the clearing.

"Is it following us?" Maeve asked Ginger when she reached the edge of the clearing where Emery and Ginger were hiding behind some bushes.

Ginger shook her head. "It stopped to check on its friend."

"They live in pairs," Emery said. "I bet it would be really sad if its mate died."

"Emery, did you see that thing?" Ginger asked. "It

could have eaten us whole. Kneeling down next to that beast was a dumb thing to do."

Emery straightened, pulling her shoulders back and lifting her chin. "It wasn't dumb. That creature was hurt, and it needed help."

"Emery, it tried to kill Gray and Tristan."

Maeve stepped between the feuding sisters. "Emery is right, Ginger. Just because something or someone is a threat doesn't mean we have to kill it."

Ginger turned on Maeve. "It could have killed her," she whispered.

"But it didn't," Maeve said gently. "She gave it a chance, and it didn't. We might have saved it. Look."

They all turned back toward the clearing where the second plagoran was nuzzling the first with its snout. The injured plagoran raised its head and let out a small shriek as it struggled to its feet, Maeve's bandage still held in place on its underside.

The injured plagoran looked in their direction, let out another shriek and slowly led its mate to the other side of the clearing.

A twig cracked behind them, and all three spun quickly around. Ginger reached for her gun.

"Whoa," Tristan said, holding up his hands in a gesture of surrender. "It's just us."

CHAPTER SEVEN

"Where have you been?" Maeve nearly shouted.

"Shh," Emery said, pointing back toward where the plagorans had disappeared on the other side of the clearing.

"What were those things?" Gray asked. "We had a close call with one of them. Tristan managed to wound it with his knife."

"They're plagoran," Emery answered.

"Pla what?" Tristan asked. Emery filled them in on what little she knew about the creatures. When she was done, Ginger asked, "Why didn't you shoot at it?"

"We followed the noise and before we could grab our guns, it was pretty much on top of us," Tristan said. "Clearly I didn't do too much damage to it since it managed to leave."

"It had a little help," Ginger said gesturing to Emery and Maeve.

Gray turned questioning eyes toward Maeve, and Maeve pointed to Emery. "It was all Emery's idea."

Emery looked at the ground. "It was hurt. I didn't want to just leave it."

Tristan stared at her in disbelief. "You got close to that thing? It almost ate me for dinner. What were you thinking?"

Emery's lip trembled. "I was thinking that someone had wounded it and left it to die. I couldn't walk away, not again, not after what happened to mom."

Emery and Ginger's mom had been killed by World Government soldiers as she tried to protect Ginger and Emery months before. Emery had watched the shooting and seen her mother die.

Tristan hugged Emery. "It's OK, Em. I understand, but that was still a dangerous thing to do. Wounded animals don't always know you're trying to help."

"Maeve was the one who helped it."

Gray turned to Maeve. "You got near that thing, too?" His voice rose. "Tristan and I were trying to protect all of you from those things, and you three go waltzing up to play nurse?

"Hey, leave me out of this," Ginger said. "I kept telling them to leave it alone."

"What would you have done if that thing had decided to take a swipe at either one of you?" Gray asked Maeve. "How could you be so careless?"

Maeve gave Gray a long look and took a deep breath. "What would you have me do? Leave it there to bleed to death and have another life on my conscience? One that I might have been able to save?"

Gray rolled his shoulders and stared at Maeve then blew out a breath. "You can't save everyone, Maeve."

Maeve turned to follow the others. "No," she threw over her shoulder, "but I can at least try."

"We haven't seen any sign of the government group," Gray said. "Are you sure they went this way?"

They had been walking for several hours and had reached the edge of the desert beyond the lake at the edge of Palumbra. The river wound off toward the caves where Emma had lived for so many years, but to the east a barren desert stretched as far as the eye could see.

"No," Tristan replied. "But this was the most logical path to take." He stopped and pulled out the map, then knelt and laid it on the ground in front of him.

"Look." He pointed to a spot on the map in what seemed like the middle of the desert. "This is where Corporal Shamus said they found the 'survivors.' The route we're taking is the fastest way to get there. I think the government group just got a big head start on us, especially if they weren't waylaid by any plagorans."

Gray looked out over the desert. "Maybe. But I feel like we should be able to at least see their tracks at this point."

Maeve pointed to the trees at the edge of The River. "I don't know. The wind is blowing, so the sand could have blown over and covered their tracks."

"What do you want to do?" Ginger asked.

"I guess we keep going," Tristan said. "I just think it's odd there's no sign of them."

"Everyone fill up your canteens," Gray said as he knelt next to The River and dipped his canteen into the cold, clear water. "This is probably our last chance for a while."

Maeve knelt next to Gray to fill her canteen, and he placed a hand on her shoulder. She flinched away. They hadn't spoken since their exchange about the plagorans. Maeve looked up, and Gray sighed.

"I'm sorry," he said. "You scared me. When I think

about how big that thing was and how small you and Emery are in comparison..." He trailed off. "I got scared, and it made me angry."

Maeve capped her canteen and stood to be on level ground with Gray. She didn't want him towering over her as she spoke. "I know. I was scared, too." She gave him a long look. "But you have to trust me to make good decisions."

"But I do."

Maeve shook her head. "You don't. Not really. You wouldn't have jumped down my throat if you thought I could make decisions on my own."

Gray started to speak, but she stopped him with a look. "Gray, I'm not fragile. I have things I'm trying to work out, but I'm not going to break, and I'm not going to jump head first into trouble just because it's there. You have to trust me to figure things out and not always rely on you."

Gray took a step toward her. "Maeve, I think you're one of the least fragile people I've ever met. Look at all you've come through – the betrayal of your parents and overthrowing the WG." Maeve noted that he didn't mention the soldier she had killed. "You're strong and brave and usually level-headed. But you've been through a lot. You're trying to work through a lot, which means you might not be thinking everything through."

Maeve took a step back. Her voice rose. "Do you really think I didn't think that situation through? Do you really think I didn't know how much damage that plagorathing could have done to me and Emery? I knew, but I couldn't look into that girl's eyes and tell her I didn't care enough to try to save it. Could you?"

Gray scuffed the dirt of the riverbank with the toe of his shoe. "Maybe not," he allowed. He looked up and met her eyes. "I'm sorry I yelled at you. Will you forgive me?" he said simply.

Maeve eyed him warily and finally nodded. "Yes. Will you try to trust my judgment?"

Gray nodded without saying anything else. Maeve turned to finish climbing the bank back to the others but stopped and slowly turned back around. She held her hand out to Gray.

"Together?" she asked. He took her hand and intertwined their fingers. "Together."

CHAPTER EIGHT

Maeve watched as Emery looked over her shoulder. The desert stretched as far behind them as it did in front of them with no seeming end in sight. Small groupings of plants appeared every so often, but they hadn't seen any living creatures other than the small desert lizards since they had left The River. Emery wiped a trickle of sweat off her cheek as her shoulders slumped from the weight of her pack, and her feet began to drag. "How much farther?"

Ginger rolled her shoulders and put a hand on her sister's lower back, giving Emery a little extra help to propel herself forward.

"I don't know," Tristan replied from the front of the group. He had the map gripped in one hand and a compass in the other. "I feel sure we should have picked up the tracks of the government group by now. It's really odd."

Maeve tugged the band holding her hair back out of her ponytail and piled her hair on top of her head, quickly securing it with the same band. "Could they have taken a different route?"

"Maybe?" Tristan said. "But this is the most logical option."

"Maybe they didn't want to be this exposed and

decided to take a route with more cover," Gray suggested.

Ginger held her arms wide and turned in a circle. "Where? It's a desert. There isn't much cover anywhere."

"What about over there?" Emery pointed to where the sun was beginning to set in the west.

Ginger quit spinning in circles and stepped next to Emery, her eyes following Emery's finger. "What is that?"

Tristan cocked his head to the side and squinted. "Looks like a few trees. Maybe there's water as well. I'm getting close to empty." He held up his canteen and shook it then started toward the shadow of what could be trees on the edge of the horizon. With the sun blazing from behind the shadows, it was hard to make out what they were exactly.

"Wait," Maeve said. "What's that off to the left of the shadows?"

Gray raised his hand to his forehead to try to block the sun and peered toward where Maeve was pointing. "Is that a dust cloud?"

Tristan nodded. "Looks like it, but it seems to be headed away from us, not towards us. Could be the wind or it might be another group of people. It might be the government patrol, but we should still be careful." He once again started walking toward the shadow of what might or might not be trees.

Ginger dropped back to walk next to Maeve. "What do you think?" she asked. She spoke so softly Maeve had to lean closer to hear her.

"About what?"

"About all of this. No sign of the government patrol or the group sent out to find them. From what Corporal Shamus told us, I feel like we should have found the patrol and The Hub survivors by now, and we definitely should have run into the government group that was sent out to find them."

Maeve stared at the ground in front of her. "I agree, but this desert is big. Maybe they moved on or maybe they took a different route."

"Or maybe there's something wrong," Emery said as she came up behind them. "Look!"

Maeve jerked her head up to see a figure separate itself from the shadowy trees ahead of them and begin moving toward them. Gray, Ginger and Tristan reached for their guns. Maeve pulled Emery forward until she was sheltered between Gray and Tristan in front and her and Ginger in back. She reached for the knife she had strapped to her waist after the encounter with the plagoran but hesitated to pull it out. She could see Tristan and Gray frantically searching the area for a place to hide as the figure made its way toward them. Maeve just hoped it wasn't another plagoran.

Blinded as they were by the sun behind the figure, Maeve couldn't tell its shape until it got closer. She sucked in a breath then let out a relieved sigh. "It's a person."

"Don't be too relieved," Ginger said. "Some people are worse than plagorans."

Gray and Tristan stopped in front of them, forcing them to stop as well. "Who is it?" Maeve asked.

Gray shook his head without taking his eyes off the approaching figure. "No idea."

As the figure approached, Maeve could make out the outline of a person about as tall as Gray's six feet running toward them, puffs of sand exploding as each foot hit the ground. Maeve chewed the skin on the side of her thumbnail and shifted uneasily from foot to foot as the figure approached. With the sun still in their eyes, the person's face remained a mystery.

"Help!" came a decidedly male voice. "You have to help us!"

The boy skidded to a halt in front of them as he took in Tristan's and Gray's guns. Slowly, he lifted his hands. "I don't want any trouble," he panted. "We just need help."

Now that he was closer, Maeve could finally see the boy's face. His brown eyes were wide with fear as he took a few steps away from Gray and Tristan.

"Look," he said turning quickly in a circle with his hands still in the air. "I don't have any weapons. My sister and I just need help."

"Stay there," Gray said. "Don't come any closer, but you can put your hands down."

The boy was about the same age as Gray, and while they were close to the same height, the newcomer looked scrawny next to the other boys' muscular frames. His shock of curly black hair was covered with a white coating of sand from his run across the desert.

"Who are you?" Tristan asked.

"My name is Elton," the boy replied, lowering his hands. "My sister and I are lost out here. She's hurt. Please, help us."

"Where is she?" Gray asked, keeping his gun trained on the other teenager.

Elton motioned toward the trees. "Over there. I've been trying to keep her cool, and there's some water and shade under the trees."

"How did she get hurt?" Maeve asked. Gray gave

her a look that said he clearly thought she shouldn't be drawing attention to herself.

"She tripped and twisted her ankle. I think it's broken. She's in a lot of pain."

"How long have you been out here?" Maeve asked.

Elton looked at the sky and chewed on his lip. Maeve could see him calculating in his head. "Eight, no, nine days, now."

Maeve took a closer look at Elton and realized that his shirt was frayed on the bottom as if he had ripped a strip off of it. There was a tear across the knee of his pants and another at the neck of his shirt. His face had been cleaned, but there was a ring of dirt at the hairline. She noted a string of scratches on the olive-toned skin of his arm.

"*Why* are you out here is the better question. And who is with you?" Ginger asked.

Elton frantically shook his head. "No one is with us. It's just me and my sister. I swear."

"How old is your sister?" Tristan asked.

"14." Elton replied. He looked at Ginger. "Please help us. What would you do if it were your sister?"

Emery stepped from behind Tristan. "She'd already be pulling us toward those trees. But how did you and your sister end up out here?"

Elton blinked his eyes rapidly and shook his head. "Didn't I tell you? We were running away."

"From where?" Maeve asked, although she thought she knew the answer.

Elton pointed off to the East in the direction of what Palumbrians were calling The Hub.

"From Bellus. From the plague."

CHAPTER NINE

At the word plague, all five of the Palumbran teenagers quickly took a step backward, away from Elton.

Elton waved his hands and shook his head. "No, no. Don't worry. We're fine."

Gray stepped forward, motioning with his hand for the rest of them to stay back. "How do we know that? And why aren't you with the others?"

Elton looked around with an exaggerated movement of his head that seemed a bit too practiced to Maeve. "Others? What others? It's just me and my sister. If others got away, we haven't seen them."

Maeve stepped up next to Gray. "Are you sure? We know there were other people from, what was it you called it, Bellus out here in the desert. It's the whole reason we're here."

Elton gave another exaggerated shake of his head. "No. No. I don't know of anyone else who escaped. Please. You have to come help my sister. Do any of you know how to help her?"

Gray started to speak, but Maeve jumped in before he could. "I'm a nurse, but how do we know we can trust you? It seems highly unlikely that you haven't seen any of the others if you fled at the same time they did."

"Have you seen anyone else out here?" Gray asked. "Even people not from Bellus?"

Elton shook his head again. "I promise. I haven't seen anyone. Why won't you believe me?"

This time it was Tristan who answered. "Because we don't know you. And it's hard to believe you didn't see anyone else since we know this was the most likely direction for our people to have gone."

Elton threw himself to his knees in dramatic fashion. "I promise I haven't seen anyone else." His voice caught, and Maeve could see tears starting to form in the corners of his eyes. "Please just help my sister," he pleaded.

Maeve softened. Seeing how sincerely worried Elton appeared to be about his sister, she began to think she had misjudged him. Maybe he was just a kid caught up in circumstances beyond his control. She certainly knew what that felt like.

"OK," she said, reaching a hand down to help him stand.

"Maeve," Gray said with a lift of his eyebrows. "Can we talk for a minute?"

Gray moved to stand far enough away from Elton that they couldn't be heard. The others followed. Ginger kept her gun trained on Elton but listened intently when Gray began to talk.

"What are you doing?" Gray demanded. "Not only do we not know if he's telling the truth, he could be infected with something."

Maeve looked Gray in the eyes. "I agree that I'm a little skeptical of his story, but if he does have a sister who is hurt, we have to help. We can't just leave them out here."

"Why the sudden change of heart, Maeve?" Tristan asked. "You were the most skeptical when he started talking."

"Look at him." She motioned toward where Elton was brushing sand off his knees. "Whatever else he is, he is definitely a brother worried about his sister." She turned to Ginger. "C'mon, Ginger, back me up. How would you act if Emery needed help?"

Ginger never took her eyes off of Elton. "Probably just like he did. But his performance was almost too perfect. Did you see how he turned on the tears when he thought we weren't going to help him?"

"Wouldn't you have done that, too, if you were in his shoes?" Maeve asked.

"Maybe," Ginger allowed.

"So, what should we do?" Maeve asked. "I vote we help him." She held up a hand to ward off the objections from Tristan and Gray. "With utmost caution," she added.

Tristan and Gray still looked doubtful.

"I think we should go with him," Emery chimed in. Everyone turned to look at her.

"Why?" Ginger asked.

"Because if he really does have a sister and she needs help, we should help them." Maeve nodded, grateful to have at least one person on her side. "However," Emery continued, "even if he doesn't have a sister, it will give us time to learn more about The Hub, or Bellus, and start figuring out what happened there."

"What about finding the government group and the other refugees?" Tristan asked. "Do we just give up on our mission?"

"Said like a true soldier," Ginger said. "But maybe Emery is right. Maybe learning about The Hub from this Elton character can help us find the others."

Tristan and Gray exchanged a doubtful look, but they both nodded. "OK," Gray said. "Let's go help this guy's sister and hopefully learn something useful. Just stay alert."

"Tell us about your sister," Maeve said as they trudged across the hot desert sand. Sweat ran like a river down her back, creating a damp spot on her T-shirt at the small of her back. She swiped her arm across her forehead, pulled out her canteen and took a drink, noting that her canteen was less than half full.

"Her name is Shalara," Elton said. "She's 14, and she's the only family I have left."

"What happened to the rest of your family?" Emery asked.

Elton turned his head toward Emery, and through the fine sheen of sweat on his face, Maeve could see the torment in his eyes. "They were all killed by the plague – my mom and dad and my two youngest siblings. They were gone almost before we knew they were sick."

Tristan eyed Elton warily. "And you're sure you and your sister don't have this plague."

Elton shook his head, sweat drops flinging off the ends of his hair. "We don't. Everyone who got it died quickly. We left Bellus a week ago, and neither of us have been sick."

They trudged on in silence, the heat sapping their energy. Though the sun was setting, the heat had not yet dissipated. Maeve knew they were making progress toward the trees she had seen in the distance, but the shimmering heat of the desert made it difficult to see just how close they were. The trees seemed to swim before her eyes. The vastness of the desert stretched out in all directions, and she wondered whether the government group had found the other refugees or if they had been swallowed up into the sand-covered nothingness. It was hard to believe that Palumbra was only a day's hike behind them.

"Are we almost there?" Emery asked breathlessly. "I'm hot. And tired."

Ginger gave her an encouraging tap on the shoulder. "Almost there, Em. You can make it. See, it's just ahead."

Maeve lifted her gaze from the tips of her shoes. It seemed as if the trees had suddenly moved closer and were now no more than 100 yards away from them. Reinvigorated by the closeness of their goal, she began to pick her feet up a little higher and move a bit more quickly. She took another sip from her canteen and encouraged Emery to keep moving.

Gray slowed his stride to match hers and moved them away from the group a bit. "I want you to be really careful when you're looking at his sister's injury," Gray said.

"Careful, how?" she asked, drawing her eyebrows together and twisting her lips in confusion.

"We still don't know whether Elton is telling the truth, and we know nothing about this plague that hit The Hub. She could be sick and contagious for all we know."

"Do you really think he's lying?" Maeve asked. "I mean, I thought he was a bit over the top at first, but if they've been through everything he says they have then being a bit over the top is probably natural."

"I just want you to be careful. I don't think everything is as it seems. Tristan and I will be watching him and his sister closely. If things go sideways, grab Emery and Ginger and get out. And make sure to fill up your canteen as soon as we find water, just in case we have to run."

Maeve shrugged and nodded. "Better safe than sorry, I guess."

Gray took her hand and let the others move ahead of them then stopped and looked directly into her eyes. "I don't want us to be sorry. We've seen enough death and destruction. We don't need to see more."

"No more death and destruction. Will that day ever come?"

Gray gave her a quick hug and kissed her forehead. "I truly hope so, Maeve. We deserve it."

They stood there for a moment, then Gray gave her hand a squeeze and said, "Come on. We need to catch up with the others."

CHAPTER TEN

Gray glanced over his shoulder for the third time as they reached the shade of the first tree.

"What do you see back there?" Maeve asked.

Gray shook his head. "Nothing. I keep thinking I see a shadow, but it disappears when I look back. It's probably just the heat waves playing tricks on my eyes."

Maeve scanned the desert behind them looking for any sign of Gray's mysterious shadow. "I don't see anything."

"Like I said, it's probably just the heat waves. I'm sure I'm being paranoid."

"A little paranoia is probably good in this case," Maeve said with a small smile.

Gray grinned at her. "You like them crazy, huh?"

"A little crazy, maybe – not a lot," she said with a short laugh.

"We're almost there," Elton announced, and the smile left Maeve's face. She took a deep breath as her stomach did a backflip. She noticed Gray and Tristan gripping their guns more tightly and swiveling their heads constantly to monitor as much of the surrounding area as they could.

The landscape had suddenly changed from desert to shady oasis. Grass grew in clumps under their feet, and the shade from the stubby trees immediately cooled the air around them. Twenty feet in front of them, a clear, blue pool of water formed a large circle, and the breeze off the water cooled Maeve's hot face even more. Propped against a tree on the far side of the water was a girl dressed in loose white pants and shirt – at least they had once been white. Dust from the desert combined with the girl's sweat had turned much of the garments a dirty tan color. Maeve noted the look of misery on the girls face as she moved a cloth from her forehead to the back of her neck, leaving a swath of dirt across her forehead. She looked up and waved when she saw them.

"That's your sister?" Ginger asked.

Elton nodded. "It doesn't look like she's moved since I went to get you."

"Let's fill up our canteens," Gray said with a meaningful look at Maeve. "Then we'll go have a look at her ankle."

Maeve quickly knelt and filled her canteen. She stood as she twisted the cap back on, then said to Elton, "OK. Let's go."

They made their way around the pool of water to where the girl sat. Never shy, Emery was the first to greet Shalara.

"Hi! I'm Emery. Elton told us all about your ankle and how you escaped the plague." She pointed at Maeve. "Maeve's a nurse, so she can help with the ankle."

Shalara looked a bit bewildered at Emery's friendliness, and Maeve saw Ginger grit her teeth as Emery plopped down on the ground next to Shalara.

"Hi," Shalara said with a shy smile and a mellow voice. "I'm Shalara. I'm so glad you've come."

Ginger hastily moved to stand close to Emery and Shalara with her gun held down at her side. Shalara's eyes widened at Ginger's gun, but she didn't say anything. Maeve knelt near Shalara's legs and opened her pack.

"I'm Maeve. Like Emery said, I'm a nurse. Can I look at your ankle?"

Shalara nodded but remained silent. She pressed her lips into a small line as Maeve turned back her wide pant leg and touched her ankle. She looked up from the girl's ankle to see her hands digging into the sand.

"Hurts, huh?"

Shalara nodded and gave a little cough.

"I think it's broken," Maeve said. "I don't know whether I can set it or not. Ankles can be tricky since you have to get the joint aligned. I'll do the best I can, but it's going to hurt. A lot. I don't have anything to numb it with."

"You can hold my hand," Emery said.

Maeve looked at Elton, Tristan and Gray. "I'm going to need two of you to hold her down and one of you to help me set the bone."

Tristan and Gray exchanged another look of silent communication. Maeve wondered if it was something they taught them in the military – how to exchange information without talking.

Gray said, "I'll help you." He set his rifle nearby then knelt next to Maeve. Quietly, so only she could hear, he said, "You know I have no idea what I'm doing, right?"

"I'm not sure I know that much more," Maeve said. "I've only been a full-fledged nurse for a month. We'll just have to do the best we can."

Shalara was shaking her head and whispering fiercely to Elton.

"She doesn't want us to hold her down," Elton said.

Maeve leaned back on her heels. "Shalara, there's no way you'll be able to stay still while we do this. Not because you don't want to but because it hurts so much. There's no other way to do it."

Shalara shook her head so hard that she began coughing again. Elton knelt and whispered to her again. Maeve couldn't hear what they were saying, but after a short time Shalara nodded and waved her hand toward Maeve in a clear gesture to begin. Tristan and Elton knelt on either side of Shalara and gripped her legs, holding them still. Emery picked up the girl's hand and nodded to Maeve. Maeve took a deep breath, filling her lungs until they felt as if they would burst, then slowly blew the breath out.

"OK," she said to Gray. "You're going to pull on her foot to shift her ankle in place while I move her leg. It's going to hurt her. You have to block out the fact that you're causing pain. Can you do that?"

Gray nodded.

Maeve directed Gray to pull as she shifted Shalara's leg and braced herself for a scream, but the only sound she heard was a whimper. She spared a glance at Shalara's face and found her eyes closed, sweat beading on her forehead. Emery grimaced in pain as Shalara squeezed her hand with all her might, but only small whimpers escaped Shalara's firmly clamped lips.

Standing above her, Ginger's face had taken on a green cast, and she turned her gaze out toward the desert.

Maeve and Gray worked steadily for 10 minutes,

shifting the bones until Maeve was satisfied with their placement. Maeve stood and broke two sturdy twigs off a nearby tree and carried them back to Shalara. She quickly splinted the ankle with the twigs and some bandages from her pack. With a sigh, she sat back on her heels and wiped the perspiration from her face with the bottom of her T-shirt.

She nodded to Tristan and Elton. "You can let her up now."

Sometime during the procedure, Emery had shifted from holding Shalara's hand to hugging her around her shaking shoulders. Shalara's head rested on Emery's shoulder and her face and shoulders were drenched in sweat. Shalara lifted her head, and Maeve could see tear tracks through the accumulated desert dust on her face. She shifted her legs and grimaced but gave Maeve a wan smile.

"Thank you," she said quietly.

"You're welcome," Maeve said. "I'm sorry it hurt so much."

Shalara waved aside her apology. "It needed to be done. Elton." She turned to her brother. "We should offer them a chance to clean up and eat."

"Shalara is right. We don't have much, but what we do have is yours."

"We have our own food," Tristan said quickly. "But we would love a chance to wash up. Gray, you and Maeve go ahead, and Ginger, Emery and I will take our turn when you're done."

Elton gave Tristan a steady look, clearly understanding that Tristan was taking no chances at leaving him and Shalara alone, then shrugged. "That works for us. We can eat when you're done."

After everyone had washed, they gathered in a circle under one of the trees. Night had fallen, and Elton had lit a fire to ward off the chill of the desert at night. As hot as it had been during the day, as soon as the sun had slipped below the horizon in a blaze of orange and red, the temperature had dropped. Maeve shivered and moved closer to the fire. Gray dug in his pack and handed her a sweatshirt. She gave him a grateful smile and pulled it over head.

"What's your story?" Elton asked when they had finished eating. "Why were you out wandering in the desert?"

Maeve's gaze traveled across her friends' faces. She could almost see the wheels spinning in their minds as they tried to decide how much to tell Elton, but before any of them could make a decision, Emery started talking.

"We're trying to find a group of survivors from your city," she said from her place next to Shalara. Emery had been glued to the girl's side since Maeve had set her ankle, fetching things for her and keeping her company. "A patrol found them in the desert, and we sent a group out to find them. Have you seen them?"

"Emery," Ginger said in a warning tone.

"What?" Emery asked. "I just answered his question. It seems only fair that they know something about us since we know everything about them."

Ginger shook her head in exasperation, then gave Maeve, Tristan and Gray an apologetic shrug.

"It's OK," Maeve said. "We're all out here together, and what we're doing isn't really a secret."

Gray eyed Maeve but said nothing. She could feel the tension rolling off of him and had already noted that he kept both their packs near him and his gun always within reach. When she glanced over at Tristan, she saw he had Emery's, Ginger's and his packs nearby, and his gun sat at his feet.

The arrangement didn't escape Elton's notice either. "You guys can set your guns aside, you know. We're not armed."

"We'll just keep them nearby, thanks," Tristan said lightly. "You never know what's out there." He tipped his head toward the desert just outside the ring of light created by the fire.

Elton waved his hand toward Maeve. "How come you don't carry a gun?"

Maeve shrugged. "It's not really my thing. Doesn't mean I'm helpless, though."

Elton held up a hand. "I never implied you were. Just curious."

"Where are you from?" Shalara asked.

Ginger gave her a confused look. "We're from Palumbra. Surely you've figured that out."

Shalara shook her head. "I didn't know there was anything beyond the borders of Bellus until we fled. What is it like there?"

Ginger ignored the question and turned to Elton. "Did you know about Palumbra?"

Elton nodded. "I pay more attention in history class than she does. I knew Palumbra was the winner in the wars, and it was assumed there was nothing left of Bellus."

"How much *is* left of Bellus?" Gray asked.

It was Shalara's turn to look confused. She drew her eyebrows together, the flickering firelight illuminating her face and giving it an almost heavenly glow. Maeve was struck again by her fragile beauty and wondered how two siblings could look so different. Shalara had blonde, almost white, hair and a thin, almost skeletal, frame. Her facial features reminded Maeve of a doll she had once seen in a book. She transferred her gaze to Elton who was as dark as his sister was light. While her skin was pale, Elton's had more of an olive tone that set off dark eyes and midnight black hair. His facial features were broader and flatter than Shalara's but no less beautiful. Where Shalara's hair hung in straight lines around her face, Elton's curled uncontrollably. For a fleeting moment, Maeve wondered if they were really siblings but quickly shook the thought off. Siblings could look different, and the difference could easily be explained if they were half-siblings. She returned her attention to the conversation where Elton was expounding on the greatness of Bellus.

"But why haven't we been able to find any sign of Bellus?" Gray asked. "We patrol near where it should be, but we haven't seen any sign of it."

Shalara started to speak, but Elton cut her off. "That's weird. Maybe you're looking in the wrong place."

Gray shrugged and said, "Maybe," but Maeve could hear the skepticism in his voice.

Something didn't add up. Elton had definitely stopped Shalara from speaking, but Maeve didn't push the issue because Gray was also not revealing the World Government's plot last year to destroy Bellus. It probably wouldn't help their relationship with Elton and Shalara to announce that the WG had created a grand plot to kill them and everyone around them just a few months before.

Elton continued with his description of Bellus. "It's the greatest city in the world," he said with a far-off look in his eyes. "The buildings shine in the sun as they reach to the sky. Outside the city, there are rolling hills covered in trees. A lumber factory turns those trees into usable wood to create houses and furniture. Beyond the trees are the farms where food is grown – enough for everyone." Elton looked at the meager handful of nuts in his hand. He shook his head as if snapping himself back to the present.

"But it's all gone now," he said sadly.

"How do you know the disease hit everyone outside the city?" Gray asked.

Elton shrugged. "Maybe it didn't get everyone, but it got most people. When we fled, we first headed toward the farms, thinking that at least we would have food. But when we got there, everyone was dead. We headed for the desert because I thought we might be able to make it to Palumbra."

"But your sister didn't even know about Palumbra. Why didn't you tell her?" Ginger asked.

Elton's eyes widened as if surprised by Ginger's comment, but he said, "I didn't know she hadn't paid attention in history class. I assumed she knew where we were going."

Maeve thought it was odd that Shalara hadn't known and even odder that Elton had cut her off the one time she had tried to speak during their conversation. She looked across the fire to Shalara and noted the tired circles under her eyes and the lines of strain on her forehead, sure signs that she was in pain. She swept aside her concerns, chalking Shalara's silence up to her not even listening to the conversation as she tried to mask her pain. Maeve rose, wiping her hands on her pant legs.

"Shalara, let me look at your ankle again. Then,

let's find you some place more comfortable to sleep."

Maeve took a step toward Shalara when an unfamiliar voice said, "Stay where you are. No one is going anywhere."

CHAPTER ELEVEN

Maeve froze where she stood. In the dimness beyond where the fire's light could reach, she could just make out several figures. Out of the corner of her eye, she saw Gray inching his hand toward his gun, but before he could grab it, a man stepped into the pool of light provided by the fire.

The man was small, shorter than Maeve by several inches, but the gun he pointed at Gray was not. "Don't try it," the man said in a gravelly voice that Maeve would have associated with someone much older than he appeared to be. She wondered if something had damaged his vocal cords.

Gray had stopped moving his hand toward his gun on the man's command. Several other people stepped into the circle of light around the fire, all with guns pointed at Maeve's group. In the flickering light of the fire, the people looked as if they had stepped off another planet. Dressed identically in pants and shirts made of some kind of shiny, silver fabric, the newcomers, both men and women, all sported the same close-cropped hair. Maeve noted the hoods with clear plastic face shields that hung down their backs.

Slowly, Tristan raised his hands in a non-threatening gesture. "No need for guns," he said calmly. "We're not dangerous."

"Gather up their guns," the leader said in his gravelly voice. A younger woman hurried to obey. She gathered guns from Ginger, Tristan and Gray but stopped when she came to Maeve. "Where's yours?" she asked. Maeve shook her head.

"I don't have one."

The girl raised her eyebrows over eyes that shimmered with disbelief. She frisked Maeve. Satisfied she wasn't hiding a gun, the girl cocked her head and gave her a quizzical look. "You're with them, right?"

Maeve nodded.

"So why don't you have a gun?" She gestured toward Gray, Tristan and Ginger with the end of her rifle. "They all have guns."

"I'm not really a fan," Maeve said.

The girl cocked her head to the side and gave Maeve a quizzical look. "So you don't carry a weapon? Are you nuts?" Maeve shrugged and gave silent thanks that her knife was hidden on the ground under her canteen.

The girl shook her head and stepped back, handing the guns to a young man who was lingering at the back of the group.

"Everyone, over there," the man with the gravelly voice said, pointing to where Shalara was sitting. They complied and formed a horseshoe behind Shalara, Elton and Emery. Ginger and Tristan had placed themselves on either side of Emery, and Maeve saw them share a look that clearly indicated if things went south, one of them should grab Emery and run.

Gray edged closer to Maeve and gave her hand a quick squeeze. She was grateful for the reassurance.

"Who are you?" Elton ventured in a timid voice.

"Survivors," the man answered curtly.

"Survivors of what?" Tristan asked.

"The plague, boy. What else? Where are you from anyway?"

No one answered.

"The silent game, huh?" the man asked. "No matter. We don't need to know where you came from. We just need your provisions." He motioned to some of the people behind him to gather up their packs and begin rifling through them.

"Where did you come from?" Elton asked. "We escaped Bellus when the plague hit." He motioned toward Shalara but managed to encompass all of them in his wave.

"We did, too," the man said. "Ran into a little trouble with a group from Palumbra, though."

Maeve heard Gray suck in a sharp breath, but he remained quiet.

"Really?" Elton said. "What happened?"

"We thought they were going to help us, but what they wanted to do was quarantine us in some caves and study us. We're not lab rats." He shrugged. "We took care of it."

Maeve could feel Gray stiffen next to her. When she glanced down, she saw his hands were fisted at his sides. "How did you take care of it?" he asked in a slightly strained voice.

"Let's just say the vultures got a little extra dinner last night."

Emery let out a small whimper, and Maeve quickly

coughed to cover up the sound. The man spun on his heel toward her, pointing the end of his gun just inches from her face.

"You sick?" he barked.

Maeve shook her head. "No. Not sick. Just a tickle in my throat from walking through the desert all day. I'm not used to all the dust."

The man studied her intently then lowered his gun from her face but still kept it trained on them. "Can I have some water?" Maeve asked, motioning toward her canteen. She gave another cough for good measure.

The man relented and started to pick up her canteen. "Can I get it myself?" Maeve almost sprinted to where her canteen sat. "The cap is kind of tricky, and it leaks a lot. I wouldn't want you to get all wet." She prayed her explanation was plausible because it sounded stupid to her.

"Let me see that canteen." The man held out his hand. Maeve crouched down with her back to the man and quickly sloshed a little water out of the canteen as she picked up her knife and slid it up the sleeve of the sweatshirt Gray had given her earlier. She turned and handed the canteen to the man, then pulled her sleeves down over her shaking hands, hoping the man would think she was simply cold.

The man examined the canteen and handed it back to her then motioned for her to return to the others as he wiped his now wet hand on his pant leg. The shiny fabric crackled when he touched it. "Get back over there, and don't move again unless I tell you to."

"Sarge," shouted one of the men rifling through their packs. "I've found something."

"Don't move," the man said, giving Maeve an extra-long stare as she hurried back to stand next to Gray. The man spoke softly to one of the other men guarding them, then strode over to where the others in his group had begun to make piles from the things in their packs. Maeve saw a stack of food and a stack of clothing. The young man who had summoned "Sarge" held Emery's computer in his hands. Maeve groaned internally and grabbed Gray's hand. Tristan leaned down to whisper in Emery's ear. Emery nodded.

"No talking," said the man in charge of guarding them.

Sarge strode back over to where they sat near the fire. Despite his short stature, his legs ate up the ground and his broad chest gave the impression that he was much taller than he was.

"What have we here?" the man said when he reached them. "Who goes into the desert carrying a computer?"

No one said anything. "Still nothing to say, huh?" He pressed a few keys then drew his brows together and frowned. He called another young man to his side. "Bradley, you're the computer whiz. Can you get in this thing?"

Maeve hid a smile. Unless that kid was a genius, there was no way he was getting into Emery's computer. She had no idea what all Emery had on her computer, but she was sure it would identify them as being from Palumbra.

"No problem, Sarge." His voice oozed confidence. Bradley took the computer from Sarge and sat cross-legged on the ground. His fingers flew over the keys. Every so often he would pause and frown, then his fingers would once again tap out a new command. After a few minutes, the pauses and frowns became more frequent, and sweat began to bead on his forehead. Sarge watched him closely and impatiently, tapping his foot on the ground in an ever-increasing tempo. Finally, Bradley shook his head, took his hands off the keyboard and leaned back.

"I can't do it, Sarge. I don't know what kind of security they have on this thing, but it's too good for the likes of me." He set his palms on the ground next to him and braced his shoulders as if waiting for an explosion.

"What do you mean you can't do it?" Sarge bellowed. "I thought you were the best. That's why I picked you."

Bradley slowly stood to his feet and held out the computer to Sarge. "I am the best, but there can always be someone better – just not someone better in Bellus."

Bradley stood there with the computer stretched out in front of him as he waited for his words to sink in. Maeve cringed when Sarge's eyes widened, and he grabbed the computer from Bradley.

"Whose computer is this?" he said in a deceptively quiet voice. Maeve could see his hands shaking with rage.

No one spoke.

"Fine," Sarge said in a calm voice. "Shoot the blond one."

Shalara shrank back in fear at the same time Emery screamed "Nooo!" and threw herself in front of Shalara. "It's mine," she sobbed. "It's mine."

"Emery, no," cried Ginger, stepping in front of her sister and Shalara as three of the Bellus survivors raised their guns to shoot.

Sarge waved at the men and women to lower their guns and stepped around the fire until he was nose to nose with Ginger. "Get out of the way."

"No." Ginger shook her head defiantly. "You're not getting near her as long as I'm here."

Sarge raised his hand and lifted a single finger. Two of the Bellus survivors, a man and a woman appeared from behind Ginger and grabbed her by the arms, physically lifting her out of the way. Ginger kicked and yelled, and Tristan lunged toward the man holding Ginger's arm. The man raised his gun to Ginger's head, and Tristan froze.

Maeve and Gray stepped forward to intervene between Sarge and Emery, but the same young woman who had collected their guns quietly stepped between them, pointing her gun at Maeve. Sarge grabbed Emery by the arm and hauled her to the other side of the fire.

Sarge handed Emery the computer. "Open it up," he said. "And do it quickly. I can still have your friends shot."

Emery rubbed her arm where Sarge had drug her along, then nodded. She took the computer and dropped to the ground. With a few keystrokes, she handed it back to him and hung her head.

Sarge looked at the screen, then looked up at the rest of them. "Well, this is interesting."

CHAPTER TWELVE

Maeve chewed her lip. She had no idea what was on Emery's computer, but she knew there were any number of things that could identify them as being from Palumbra. She didn't think that would go over well with this crowd.

"What is it, Sarge?" Bradley asked, peering over Sarge's shoulder. The other two Bellus survivors near them kept their guns trained on Maeve and her friends. Maeve tried to catch Gray's eye, but he was staring intently at Sarge. The man and woman who had been holding Ginger had released her arms but stood with their rifles pointed at her back. Tristan stood as close to Emery and Shalara as he could, but Maeve knew they were trapped.

"Looks like we found ourselves some more friends from Palumbra," he said in a mocking voice with a sneering emphasis on the word friends. He looked pointedly at Elton. "Thought you said you were from Bellus?"

"I am. I am." Elton rose to his feet but stopped when all guns shifted to him. He held up his hands. "My sister and I fled from the plague, just like you. She hurt her ankle, and these guys were the only people around." He gestured toward Maeve's group. "We only just met them."

"Those two seem pretty close to have just met." Sarge pointed his finger at Emery and Shalara who were holding each others' hands tightly as they sat next to the fire with Tristan and Gray hovering over them.

Elton gave a small chuckle. "You know how it is with kids." Maeve raised her eyebrows, knowing that Elton was only a few years older than those "kids." "They form friendships with anyone their own age, especially if there's no one else their age around."

Sarge looked skeptical. Maeve thought he might be remembering how Emery had thrown herself in front of Shalara when he gave the order to shoot her. Sarge turned to Maeve.

"We haven't seen anyone from Palumbra in decades, and now we run into two groups of you in one day? Am I supposed to believe that's a coincidence?"

Maeve studied the ground trying to decide how to respond. Gray gave a slight shake of his head, which went unnoticed by everyone but her. She straightened her shoulders and raised her gaze to Sarge's, then shrugged. "We wanted an adventure. We knew the government patrol had found people, and we wanted to know who they were. We'd heard rumors that we weren't the only people left after the wars of The Lost Years." She gave Sarge her best grin. "We thought you might be interesting."

Sarge studied her thoughtfully. "Give me one good reason not to kill you like we did the others from Palumbra."

"We're just kids?" Maeve said hopefully.

"That one won't fly," Sarge said as he took a step toward her. Despite her height advantage, Maeve still felt intimidated. Sarge might be shorter than her, but he was definitely still stronger. She felt Gray stiffen beside her as Sarge took another slow step in her direction. "Try again."

"We mean you no harm?" she said as she fought to keep her feet still.

Sarge took another step. "How would I know you're telling the truth?"

Maeve thought frantically. Sarge was so close to her now that she could smell his breath, which carried the faint, unpleasant smell of onions. She didn't know what would happen when he reached her, but she did know Gray would intervene. He was like a tightly coiled spring beside her, just waiting to uncoil. Sarge lifted his foot for the final step. "We can show you the caves," Maeve blurted.

Sarge slowly set his foot back down in the sand. "Why would I want to go there? Isn't that where the other group wanted to take us?" The muscles in his legs moved as if he was readying himself to lunge at Maeve.

"But we know about places they don't," Maeve said quickly. "We explored them a couple months ago. Your group could take shelter there until you figure out what you want to do."

Sarge stretched his lips into a grin that looked more like a sneer. "Oh, we know what we want to do. We just need a place to do it from."

Maeve waited as Sarge seemed to consider what she offered.

"Why do I need more than one of you?" His eyes held hers. "Why should I keep all of them alive."

"Because I won't take you to the caves unless you do." Her voice trembled slightly. "Our safety in exchange for us leading you to the caves."

Sarge stared at her as if trying to decide if she was

bluffing. Finally, he nodded. "OK. Tomorrow you show us the caves."

Maeve blew out the breath she had been holding, and she heard Gray do the same.

Sarge grinned at her. "I can always kill you later," he said and walked away.

"What were you thinking?" Gray asked in a voice barely above a whisper.

Their captors had taken over their spot by the fire, and Maeve's group was now gathered underneath a tree outside the ring of firelight. Three of the Bellus survivors stood guard.

"I was thinking I didn't want him to kill us," Maeve retorted. "Did you have a better idea?"

Gray shook his head. "We can't take them to the caves. We don't know if they carry the disease, and I didn't like the way Sarge talked about knowing what they want to do. We can't let them get that close to Palumbra."

"But what if we do lead them to the caves?" Tristan broke into their whispered conversation. "It gets us that much closer to Palumbra, and maybe we can get some help."

Ginger scooted over to join them. "Guys," she whispered, "we have a bigger problem."

"What could be a bigger problem?" Maeve asked.

"I think Shalara is sick."

They lifted their heads and looked to where Shalara was lying on her side, sleeping. In the quiet of the night, Maeve could hear a rattle in her breathing. She raised scared eyes to Ginger. "When did you notice it?"

"When she laid down to sleep. She had been

coughing earlier, but I just thought it was the dust from the desert. But you can hear a definite wheezing when she breathes now. Her face is pretty flushed, too, but it shouldn't be now that we're away from the fire."

Ginger's gaze strayed to where Emery lay mere feet from Shalara, remembering how Shalara had been draped over Emery while Maeve and Gray set her ankle. "What do we do?" Ginger whispered anxiously. "What if Emery gets it?"

"She might not be sick, Ginger," Maeve said soothingly. "She could just be in pain from her ankle, and if she has an infection from her ankle, that could cause her to run a fever. Let's just keep an eye on her — and try to keep her and Emery apart."

"Why do you want to keep her and Emery apart?" Elton said from behind Maeve. Maeve jumped, startled by Elton's sudden appearance. She tried to mask the fear and concern on her face. Elton's eyes traveled from face to face, then diverted to where Shalara lay. "You think she's sick, don't you?"

Gray looked at the ground. Tristan picked at some dirt under his thumbnail. Ginger undid her ponytail and focused intently on retying her hair. Maeve chewed the side of her thumbnail and finally looked into Elton's scared eyes. "We're not sure. Her ankle could just be giving her trouble."

"You might know better than us," Gray said. "You've seen this before. What are the symptoms of this plague?"

Elton started to speak, then shook his head, his eyes straying to where their guards had taken interest in their discussion. "Not now."

"Hey," a female guard shouted as she took a step toward them. "Everyone spread out. No talking."

Elton returned to his place next to his sister, but Maeve noted he left a good distance between them. Tristan and Ginger scooted closer to Emery, leaving Maeve and Gray to lean against the tree. Gray said nothing but took Maeve's hand, rubbing his thumb soothingly over the back of her hand and wrist. "What are we going to do?" She whispered in a voice so quiet Gray had to lean toward her to hear it. He opened his mouth to reply, but whatever he was going to say was drowned out by a mighty roar.

The three Bellus survivors guarding the group whirled around to face the sound, their heads whipping back and forth, looking for the source. The roar sounded again. Maeve and the others jumped to their feet, and Emery huddled into Ginger's side. Elton helped Shalara balance on her good foot, but Maeve could see her sway unsteadily. A commotion ensued around the fire, and Sarge's voice bellowed, "Where is it? Take defensive positions! Shane, do you have any of the poison darts left?"

The sound roared again, and this time Maeve knew exactly what it was. "Plagoran," she said almost to herself.

"Get ready," Gray said as he took her hand and pulled her toward the tree they had been sitting against.

"Ready for what?"

"To run. This is our chance to escape."

"Where are we going to go? We don't have any supplies, and it's desert for miles out there."

Tristan jogged over to them followed by Ginger and Emery. "What have we got?"

Gray motioned to where a canteen lay on the ground, dropped by one of the guards in their hurry to confront the plagoran. Emery swooped in and gathered it up.

"Do we have any weapons?" Tristan asked. "We can't head out into that without some kind of protection."

Gray and Ginger scanned the ground as if hoping the guards had also carelessly dropped a weapon of some kind. Maeve reached up her sleeve and pulled out her knife.

"Way to go, Maeve." Gray pulled her in for a hard, quick hug and dropped a light kiss on her forehead.

"That's not going to be much defense against one of those beasts," Tristan said. "But it's better than trying to take it on in a fistfight."

"What do we do about them?" Ginger asked, pointing at Elton and Shalara who were slowly and painstakingly making their way toward the group. Shalara leaned heavily on Elton and moved forward with a kind of shuffling hop, every step making her wince with pain.

"We can't leave them here," Emery said decisively.

"Em," Ginger said calmly. "They'll slow us down. We'll never get away."

Emery folded her legs and sank cross-legged to the ground. "Then we'll just have to stay. I'm not leaving Shalara here."

Ginger looked helplessly from Emery to Shalara. Maeve knew from experience that Emery's stubborn streak meant they would have to carry her kicking and screaming from the camp, which would undermine their chances of getting away more than Shalara's slow progress.

"Em," Ginger tried once more. "We can't stay, and Shalara can't move fast enough. We..." She broke off and looked behind her, scanning the few trees around them and the dark desert beyond.

"What is it?" Tristan asked, but Ginger held up her hand for silence. Maeve could hear nothing except the commotion around them and the ever-closer roar of the plagoran.

"There's something out there."

"Yeah," Tristan replied. "A large reptile that wants to eat us."

"No," Ginger said, shaking her head. "Something else."

Elton and Shalara had reached the group, and Maeve noted Shalara's hands were shaking uncontrollably. She struggled to remain on her feet, and Maeve had no idea how they could take her with them and escape. "What are we going to do?" Elton asked. "They seem pretty distracted." He motioned to the guards who were now all grouped on one side of the oasis, leaving the area next to the trees unguarded. In the furor over the approaching plagoran, they seemed to have forgotten their prisoners.

"If we're going to go, we have to go now," Gray said as he hefted Maeve's knife in his hand and handed her the canteen. He nodded to Tristan. "You'll have to help them," he said with a glance toward Shalara and Elton.

"I'll help, too," Emery said, climbing to her feet once again.

"You'll stay with me and do what you're told," Ginger said. Emery shot Ginger a defiant glance but remained at her side.

Gray held up a hand for quiet and motioned that they should follow him. Ginger and Emery stepped into the space behind Gray, followed by Elton, Tristan and Shalara. Maeve brought up the rear. They hadn't gone more than

500 feet, when Gray abruptly stopped. The plagoran's roar sounded once again from off to their left. Maeve couldn't see Gray, but she could hear the murmur of his voice and another voice she didn't recognize.

"Maeve." Tristan turned to her and said quietly, "Gray wants you up there."

Fuming with the thought that Gray was being overprotective and not thinking through the need for one of them to cover the rear with injured people between them, Maeve made her way to the front of the group.

Gray's ice blue eyes met hers, and he gave her a quick grin. "There's someone here who wants to see you."

Maeve frowned, thinking this was a terrible time for jokes, when a young boy stepped out from behind Gray.

"Hi, Maeve," Thomas said with a little wave.

CHAPTER THIRTEEN

Maeve stood frozen with shock, her mouth hanging open.

"Hi?" Thomas tried again.

"Thomas," Maeve exclaimed as she pulled him into a hug. "How did you get here?" She looked around, scanning for other people, other adults. "Are you all by yourself?"

Thomas shook his head against Maeve's shoulder. "No, I brought Rufus."

Maeve turned confused eyes to Gray who shrugged his shoulders and mouthed the words, "No idea."

She stepped back from Thomas and said, "Who's Rufus?"

Thomas gave a muted clap with his hands, and Maeve heard a thudding sound before it was drowned out by another roar from the plagoran and more shouts from the camp. A large dog the size of a small horse came running up to Thomas. Just when Maeve thought he was going to knock Thomas over, he skidded to a halt, sending sand flying. Thomas laid a hand on the dog's neck and said, "This is Rufus."

Maeve opened her mouth to ask more questions,

but Tristan's urgent voice from behind her said, "We have to move if we're going to get away from here. Save your questions for later."

"He's right. We have to go," Gray said, moving forward once again. "Thomas, where have you been hiding?"

Thomas pointed to the south. "Over there. There's a set of dunes that are hard to make out from a distance. There are a few scrubby trees and a small pool of water."

"Can you take us there?" Maeve asked.

"Yep," Thomas said. "Follow me."

Maeve fell in next to Gray, and they followed Thomas across the barren desert, glancing frequently over their shoulders to watch for any of the Bellus survivors, but as the chaos from the camp and the roar of the plagoran grew fainter, it seemed that those left in the camp had their hands full. Maeve wondered if poison darts would do any damage against the scaly armor of the plagoran. While she wasn't a fan of Sarge and the other Bellus survivors, she didn't really want them to be eaten by a monster lizard.

"How much farther?" Elton's voice came out of the darkness behind them. Without a light, Maeve could barely make out Thomas in front of them and the vague outline of the rest of the group behind them.

"A little ways," Thomas said.

"Can you see where you're going?" Maeve asked. "Are you sure we're going the right way?"

"Rufus knows the way," Thomas said confidently.

"How long have you been out here?" Gray asked.

"The same as you. I followed you," Thomas said matter-of-factly.

Maeve shook her head as if to clear her ears, not

sure she had heard him correctly. "You followed us? Why?"

"I thought you might need me," he said simply. "Me and Rufus."

Maeve opened her mouth, then closed it, took a breath and opened it again. Still, no words came out.

Gray took pity on her and asked, "How did you even know to follow us? We didn't know we were leaving."

"I overheard Emma and John talking about your trip, so I packed some stuff, loaded Rufus up and trailed you. When you got caught, I looked for a place to hide until I could come help you."

Maeve finally found her voice. "Does your uncle know you and Rufus are out here?"

"He doesn't much care what I do. He's always saying I take up too much space and eat too much food, anyway." Thomas's voice trailed off. "He probably won't even miss me."

"I'm sorry, Thomas," Maeve said. "I didn't know."

"You didn't ask," Thomas said without accusation.

"Um, guys," Ginger said as she came jogging up from behind them. "We've got trouble." She pointed back the way they had come. "Anyone notice there's no lizard roaring? We're going to have company, I think."

"Guess poison darts do work on plagoran," Maeve said. She looked at Gray. "What's the plan now?"

Gray looked over his shoulder to where Tristan and Elton were mostly carrying Shalara along as quickly as possible. Emery was walking in front of them, encouraging Shalara to keep going. "What makes you think we're going to have company?"

"If you weren't busy finding out why kids are

wandering the desert unaccompanied..."

"Hey, Rufus is offended," Thomas jumped in, indignation coloring his voice.

"You would have noticed," Ginger continued "the plagoran had quit roaring, and there are faint voices behind us."

"I can't see them, though," Gray said. "Even in the dark, we should be able to make out their outline if they were close. Sound travels a long way in the desert."

"But that also means they can hear us," Ginger pointed out.

"Right, so we need to stop talking and just follow Rufus," Maeve chimed in.

Ginger nodded, and the group fell into silence, resting all their hopes on the broad back of the large dog leading the way.

The chill night air cutting through her thin shirt caused Maeve to shiver as she plodded along behind Thomas and Rufus. Their progress was hindered by Shalara's slow pace, but Maeve took comfort in the fact that the voices of the Bellus survivors weren't getting any closer. Maeve had checked on Shalara several times, but there wasn't much she could do while they needed to hurry. She hoped they could stay in one place for a bit, for Shalara's sake. Lost in her thoughts about Shalara, Maeve was startled when Rufus's head and back suddenly vanished. Maeve peered more closely, but the large dog was nowhere to be seen. She tugged on Gray's hand.

"What happened to Rufus?" she whispered.

"What? He's right..." Gray whipped his head from side to side in confusion. "Thomas," he whispered a little louder. "Where did you and Rufus go?"

"Right here," came the whispered reply, and a hand shot up just to the left in front of them. "The ground drops away here. It's why you can't see the dunes from the oasis where you were captured."

Gray took Maeve's hand, and together they carefully edged toward Thomas's hand. The sand under their feet turned into a steep slope, and Maeve's feet skidded as she tried to keep her balance.

"How is Shalara going to get down this slope?" Maeve asked Gray. "Even with Elton and Tristan helping her, this grade is too steep for her to manage with that ankle."

"Hey," came Emery's whisper. "Where did you guys go?"

Maeve popped her head back up over the edge of the dropoff. "Right here. The ground drops away. Be careful. Let Tristan and Elton know to stop before they get here. We have to figure something out for Shalara." Emery scampered back the way they had come to relay the message, and Ginger's face replaced Emery's.

"Yeah, that's not going to work for a broken ankle," she said.

"We know," Gray replied. "Got any ideas?"

Ginger toyed with the end of her ponytail. "Too bad we don't have any supplies. We could use a tarp or a blanket and use it as a litter and kind of slide her down."

"We have a blanket," Thomas said quickly. "Me and Rufus." He pointed from himself to the dog. "We share." Thomas turned and ran the rest of the way down the slope.

"They share?" Ginger whispered to Maeve. "How big is the blanket?"

Large. The blanket was large enough to cover a bed. "Where did you get that?" she asked when Thomas returned, dragging the blanket.

"My Gran made it for me and Rufus. Before she died." Thomas dropped his chin for a moment, and Maeve thought he might be trying to hold back tears. She wondered how long it had been since his Gran had died and felt a twinge of guilt for not getting to know more about Thomas. After a few seconds, he raised his head and grinned. "Rufus was always stealing my blankets at night, so she made us one big enough for both of us."

"She sounds like a fantastic Gran," Maeve said.

"She was, and she would be excited to know her blanket was going to be used to help someone. She was always helping people. Even when we didn't have much to eat ourselves, Gran would share what we had if someone else didn't have anything."

Maeve started to ask Thomas more about his life, but just then Tristan strode up to the edge of the dropoff. "How is this going to work?"

"We're going to use Rufus and Thomas's blanket to make a litter for Shalara and carry/slide her down the slope," Maeve said. "It was Ginger's idea."

Tristan shot Ginger a grin. "Good thinking. Let's get it done. Shalara's not in good shape, so the sooner we get her off her feet, the better."

CHAPTER FOURTEEN

"Is she going to be OK?" Ginger asked Maeve as the two of them sat with their backs against a stubby tree in the shelter of the dunes. They had maneuvered Shalara down the steep entrance to the dunes using Thomas's and Rufus's blanket, but the journey had been rough. Tristan and Elton had both stumbled once, nearly dropping Shalara, and Maeve could still hear her cries of pain ringing in her ears. She only hoped their captors couldn't hear them as well.

Maeve shook her head slowly. "I don't know. She was in pretty rough shape when I looked at her." Maeve picked at her thumbnail. "Her ankle looked OK. We did the best we could in setting it, but hopping across the desert, then being jostled around like that definitely isn't good for it. And I don't know why she has a fever."

Maeve was grateful they had some willow bark with them to help lower the fever, but there was no fire to make it into the tea that had saved Gray's life when they were on the run from the WG several months ago. She had done her best by sprinkling it into some water and giving it to Elton to force down Shalara's throat.

"Did you get close to her?" Ginger asked.

"I did my best to examine her from a distance," Maeve said. "And I washed my hands in the puddle over there that we're calling a water source."

Ginger glanced in the direction of the small pond off to her left even though it wasn't visible in the dark. "At least there's water. We'd be in big trouble without some kind of water source since we only have one canteen."

"True." Maeve fell silent. After a moment, she said, "Do you think we're really going to make it out of here? I mean, how long until Sarge and his group find us again? We didn't really travel that far."

Ginger looked over at where Emery slept, curled up against the chill underneath a second tree to their right. Thomas and Rufus lay wrapped in their blanket on the ground next to her. Gray and Tristan were keeping watch at the edge of the dropoff, and Elton was trying to make Shalara comfortable. "We'll make it out," Ginger said with confidence. "We haven't survived everything else to die out here in the desert."

Maeve gazed out toward the desert. "I wish I had your confidence." She draped her arms over her knees and put her forehead on her arms. "I just don't know how we're getting out of this one."

Ginger nudged Maeve with her elbow. "Come on. Are you the same girl who helped overthrow the WG or not?"

Maeve shrugged. "Not really." She raised her head and looked at Ginger. "I'm not sure who I am, Ginger. I'm definitely not the same girl who believed everything the government told her. But I'm also not the same girl who could shoot a soldier to save my friends. I don't know what I would do if I was in that situation again. And that scares me. What if something happens to one of you because I can't do what needs to be done?"

Ginger studied her intently. "Maeve, I know you're having a hard time forgiving yourself, but what else could you have done?"

Maeve shook her head again. "I don't know. I feel like I don't know anything – about who I'm supposed to be, about what I'm supposed to do. I don't know why the rest of you put up with me."

Ginger pulled Maeve into a one-armed hug. "We put up with you because you're our friend – and that's what friends do. We stick together, through the good times and the bad ones. You would never have abandoned us after our mom died, would you?"

"No, but that's different. That was horrible, and you didn't do anything to cause it." Maeve paused. "I created my own problem."

"By saving Gray," Ginger said patiently. "Would you rather he have died?"

"No!" Maeve vehemently shook her head.

"Then what else were you going to do? It was that soldier or Gray." Ginger's next words came out slowly as if she wanted Maeve to be sure to hear what she was saying. "Did you have to make a terrible choice? Yes. Was it fair? No. Do you have to live with it? Yes. Did it change you? Yes. But don't let that one moment define who you are, Maeve. Love requires sacrifice. My mom sacrificed her life for us, and I have to live with the choice that she made. I wish my mom could have found another way, but I have to accept what she did and live my life so that it wasn't in vain. You chose to do something you didn't even know you were capable of doing. And that's hard because it shows you a piece of you that you never knew existed. You need to make peace with who you are and move forward. You can't live it over and over again or you'll never heal."

"I know you're right," Maeve said. "But I just seem stuck. Emma said I should focus on the little things. And I know I never want to hold a gun again. But what if that decision puts you guys in danger? I'm beginning to think I shouldn't have come with you on this expedition."

Ginger started to respond, but whatever she was going to say was lost when they heard Tristan and Gray running down the path from the dropoff. They rounded the corner between the dunes and stumbled to a stop.

"We have to move," Gray said urgently as he leaned over and shook Emery and Thomas awake. Rufus growled in annoyance and rolled over, still asleep. Thomas shook the sleeping dog until he let out a large yawn and slowly rose to his feet. "Sarge and his crew are headed this way."

"How do you know?" Ginger asked.

Tristan helped her to her feet. "We can hear them – and see them. They're using lanterns to find us since they have us outnumbered and outgunned."

Gray helped Maeve to her feet, and she brushed the dust from her pants and hands. "Where are we going to go?"

The four of them looked at each other, indecision written on each face. "There might be a shelter in the dunes," Thomas said.

"What?" Gray spun to face Thomas who stood with one hand idly petting Rufus's head. Gray's abrupt movement startled Rufus who growled low in his throat.

"It's OK, Rufus," Thomas said quietly.

"What kind of shelter is it?" Gray asked.

"I'm not sure," Thomas said. "I only saw an indentation that could have been a hidden door. I didn't have time to look at it because you guys got yourselves caught."

"Well, show us where it is," Gray said impatiently. "We haven't got much time."

Maeve squeezed Gray's hand in warning and shot him a dark look at his impatient tone. "He's just a little kid," she said under her breath. "You don't have to be short with him."

Gray shook off Maeve's hand. "We don't have time to stand around. Sarge and his friends will be here soon, and we've got two kids, a dog and a sick and injured stranger. Our odds are terrible even if we do find someplace to hide."

Thomas gave Gray a hard stare, squared his shoulders and turned his back on them. "Let's go, Rufus." He looked over his shoulder at Maeve. "You coming?"

Maeve and Gray moved to follow Thomas while Tristan and Ginger gathered their things and Elton helped Shalara to her feet. Maeve noted with relief that Tristan and Ginger were keeping their distance from Shalara, but Emery was hovering closer than Maeve would like. Ginger's eyebrows drew together in a frown as she watched Emery, but she said nothing.

The group returned to the path between the dunes that rose high into the air. Maeve felt like she was in a canyon between mountains, and she guessed in a way that's exactly what this was. Maybe choosing to hide here wasn't the smartest idea. If Sarge found them, they would be easy targets with no way out. A shiver of fear ran up Maeve's spine.

"Here," Thomas said, pointing at the side of the dune. Maeve leaned forward for a closer look, but she couldn't see anything in the sand that looked like a door could be hidden there.

Gray and Tristan stepped up to the spot and began moving the sand with their hands. Sand cascaded down the side of the dune at a speed reminiscent of a waterfall. Maeve worried that the sand might bury Gray and Tristan as it pooled at their feet, covering their boots.

"There's nothing here," Gray said in frustration, shaking the sand off his boots and hands. "We've wasted precious time we could have used to get away."

"No, wait," said Tristan who was still digging through the sand. "There's something hard."

"Where?" Gray asked.

"Right here." Tristan guided Gray's hand through the sand to place it next to his. "It feels like wood."

Gray's eyes brightened and his shoulders lifted. "You're right. Let's get this sand shifted."

"Shhh," Maeve said suddenly as Elton and Shalara came up behind her. For a minute all was silent until a voice they all recognized as Sarge's floated through the night air.

"They have to be this way. It's the only way they could have gone."

"Hurry," Maeve said urgently. "They sound like they're near the dropoff."

Gray, Tristan and Thomas began digging madly. Rufus, thinking it was a game, began to dig next to Thomas, kicking up a spray of dirt that hit Maeve in the face. Sputtering, she stepped forward and gingerly stepped around Rufus to dig next to Gray. Ginger and Emery dug their hands in as well, but Elton and Shalara hung back.

After several minutes of digging and listening to the voices of their previous captors draw ever closer, Tristan said, "Stop. Everyone move back."

In the dimness of the night, Maeve could see Gray and Tristan lean into the hole they had dug in the side of the dune. She watched their muscles strain as they struggled to get the piece of wood they had uncovered to move. With a loud creaking sound, the wooden door opened just far enough for Tristan to slip through.

Less than a minute later, his head poked back around the door, and he motioned for them to follow him. Gray pushed the door open a bit more, and Emery, Thomas and Rufus ducked under his arm. Ginger followed. Maeve looked back at Shalara and Elton. They seemed to be having a heated argument, with Elton whispering urgently and Shalara vehemently shaking her head.

Maeve took two steps toward them. "Come on, you two. We need to go."

Shalara shook her head again. "I'm not coming. I'm sick. If we go in that room together, I could spread whatever this is to all of you."

Maeve noted Elton's grip on Shalara's arm tightened when she spoke. Shalara winced, but Maeve didn't know if it was from Elton's grip or the pain in her ankle. "You have to come, Shalara. I'm not leaving you out here."

A shout came from above them. Maeve assumed that someone from Sarge's group had stumbled on the steep dropoff. It wouldn't take them long to figure out how to get down to where Maeve stood.

"What are you guys doing?" came Gray's impatient voice. "Move it. They're going to find us, and then no one will have a chance to survive."

Maeve weighed her options. If Shalara stayed outside the shelter, Sarge and his friends would definitely kill her once they realized she was sick, but if she encouraged Shalara to enter the shelter, she would be exposing her friends to a potentially deadly illness. There wasn't really any choice.

"Come on, Shalara," Maeve said. "We don't even know for sure your fever is from illness. It could just be an infection in your ankle. If you stay out here, you'll definitely die. In there," Maeve nodded toward where Gray was holding the door open, "we all at least have a chance."

Shalara looked from Maeve to Gray who nodded at her and relented. "OK, I'm too tired to fight you on this. Let's go." She took a tired hop step toward the door. Maeve noticed that Elton's grip relaxed as soon as Shalara agreed to enter the shelter.

Shalara and Elton made slow progress toward the door, and Maeve could hear Sarge's voice coming down the incline. When Shalara and Elton reached the door, Gray motioned to her to hurry. Maeve ran to the door but stopped at the entrance.

"Won't they see the hole?" she asked Gray, with worry in her voice.

"Maybe, but I'm betting when I pull the door shut, sand will tumble over it, hiding it unless they look closer. It's dark, so we might get lucky. Come on. If we stand out here, they'll definitely find us."

Maeve stepped through the door, and Gray pulled it shut behind them. They could hear sand falling on the other side of the door, and both let out a sigh of relief.

Maeve stepped farther into the room and stopped. "What is this place?"

CHAPTER FIFTEEN

Maeve studied the small space made entirely of concrete and lit only by the dim light from a lantern. The only wood was the door behind them. Tristan, Ginger, Emery, Thomas and Rufus were sitting on the floor with their backs against the wall directly opposite the door while Elton and Shalara were huddled in the corner to their left. The rest of the room was filled with supplies – food in cans and boxes, water in bottles, blankets, lanterns and backpacks. Maeve noted flint and matches as well as canteens.

"Looks like a supply station of some kind," Gray said. "But why would someone build a bunker with supplies in it way out here in the desert?"

Before anyone could reply, muffled voices carried through the firmly closed wood plank door. Elton's eyes widened, and Tristan held up a finger to his lips in a request for silence. Thomas quickly made a hand motion to Rufus who had gotten to his feet and moved closer to the door. The dog looked from Thomas to the door, then returned to his spot and laid down next to Thomas. Maeve closed her eyes and prayed that the sand had covered the door again.

"Looks like they spent some time standing here." Sarge's distinctive voice came through the door. Gray grimaced, and Maeve hoped their tracks didn't give them away. "Look around. They might be hiding nearby."

They could hear sand falling outside the door, and Maeve only hoped it was more sand covering the door, not falling away from it. The sound of shuffling feet and muffled voices carried through the door. Everyone held their breath. Gradually, the sound of voices faded away, but still they sat without moving, barely breathing. Gray wrapped Maeve's hand in his own and gave it a squeeze. Despite his earlier impatience, she was glad he was here with her.

In the silence, she could hear the wheeze in Shalara's breathing. It sounded like it was getting worse. When Maeve looked to the corner where Shalara sat with Elton, she could see her shivering even though the temperature in the room was getting warmer by the minute. Maeve disengaged her hand from Gray's and quietly walked over to the supplies, picked up a blanket and tossed it to Elton. Elton fumbled it, and it fell to the ground with a soft thud. Everyone started as the sound echoed through the small chamber like a firecracker. He made a face and quickly grabbed the blanket, placing it around Shalara's shoulders. She gave him a small smile of thanks and closed her eyes as Maeve returned to her spot next to Gray.

Time ticked by, and still no one dared to say a word. Ginger and Emery whispered quietly, and Maeve strained to hear what they were saying. Maeve's curiosity won out over her caution, and she opened her mouth to speak when Gray gave her a hard elbow to the gut. Startled, she looked up to find him shaking his head with his finger over his lips. He tipped his head toward the door, and Maeve rubbed her side and listened intently. A faint murmur of voices wafted through the air.

Time ticked slowly by. Without any ventilation other than the cracks around the door, the air felt heavy and close. The back of her shirt was soaked with sweat, and Maeve wondered how much oxygen was actually in the room.

"They're not here, Sarge," came a voice that Maeve recognized as that of one of the female survivors who had been guarding them. "They must have run into the desert when they heard us coming."

"They can't have gone far," Sarge said in his raspy voice. "Let's head out. It's getting light, so it should be easier to find them."

Minutes ticked by as they waited to make sure Sarge and his crew were really gone. Tristan was the first to speak.

"We have to get moving. It's not going to take Sarge long to figure out we didn't go trekking off into the desert once the sun comes up." He picked up a backpack and began filling it with supplies. "We need to be long gone by then."

Gray surged to his feet and began handing out backpacks for everyone to fill. Maeve and Elton worked side by side for a few minutes before she felt a hand on her arm. She looked up into Elton's worried face.

"Maeve," he said quietly. "Shalara's definitely sick. I think it's the same thing that killed everyone in Bellus." Maeve looked at his hand on her arm, and her eyes widened in alarm. She stepped back, causing his hand to fall away. Gray shot her a questioning look but continued to pack supplies.

"Why do you think that?" she asked quietly.

Elton motioned her away from the others. "Look." He knelt down next to Shalara and pulled up her sleeve where a purplish rash had formed. Droplets of sweat fell from Shalara's hair onto Elton's arm, and she moved restlessly. She gave a weak cough.

"What do we do now?" Maeve asked.

CHAPTER SIXTEEN

"Right now," Tristan said urgently, "we're going to get out of here. Sarge will be back here before we know it. We have to move."

Gray took Maeve's arm and moved her gently back from Elton. "Keep your distance," he whispered in her ear. Maeve nodded and looked warily at Shalara.

"How are we going to move her?" she asked in a voice only Gray could hear.

"I don't know. She's too weak to walk, and we can't risk carrying her now that we know she's sick. We might have to leave her and Elton here."

Maeve turned horror-stricken eyes to Gray's face. "You'd just leave them here for Sarge to find?"

Gray couldn't meet her eyes, instead looking at the ground and scuffing his toe across the sand covering the concrete floor. "What choice do we have?" he said.

"Gray," Tristan called. "We have a problem." Tristan stood next to the open door, but a wall of sand stood in front of him. The dune had filled in the gap they had created. Gray grabbed two shovels from the stack that leaned against the wall, handed one to Tristan and began to dig. Rufus and Thomas joined in the digging while Maeve zipped up the full backpacks and distributed them to Emery and Ginger.

"Is Shalara going to make it? You can help her, right?" Emery turned hopeful eyes to Maeve.

"I hope so, Emery, but there's not much I can do. Elton thinks she has whatever plague killed off the people of The Hub."

Ginger looked startled by this news, but Maeve wasn't sure why. They had all talked about the possibility of Shalara being sick. "Are you OK?" Maeve asked as Emery went to see if she could help Gray and Tristan.

Ginger shook her head. "I think I had convinced myself she was just in pain from her ankle. What if we all get sick? Shalara cried all over Emery. What if she gets it? What then?" Ginger's voice rose in panic with every question.

Maeve ran her hand reassuringly across Ginger's shoulder. "All we can do is hope for the best. Emery seems fine right now."

Shalara started coughing violently just as a muted cry of victory came from Gray and Tristan. Sand cascaded from above the door opening like a gentle waterfall, but Maeve could see a clear path out of the shelter. "Maeve," Gray said loudly as he held the door open. "Get everyone moving."

"Thomas," Maeve said as she handed him a small pack for Rufus to carry. "You and Rufus go first. Wait just outside for the rest of us. Take Emery with you."

Thomas nodded, took Emery's hand and motioned for Rufus to follow him. Rufus rolled to his feet and loped after Thomas, with his pack securely fastened to his back. Maeve hid a smile as the large dog looked ridiculous carrying a backpack, but if he was going to survive the desert, then he needed his own supply of water.

"Ginger, Maeve, get moving," Tristan cried. "I don't like the way this sand is falling."

"What about them?" Maeve motioned toward Elton and Shalara.

"You're not going to leave us here are you?" Elton said, looking from one of them to the next with disbelief.

"Elton, you're going to have to get Shalara out," Gray said as he used his back to hold the door open against the wave of sand. "You've already been the closest to her, and we can't risk any of the rest of us getting sick. Come on, Maeve. You and Ginger need to get out of here."

Ginger walked quickly to the door, and with a glance over her shoulder at Maeve disappeared through the opening, getting a coating of sand on her dark hair as she left.

"Come on, Maeve." Gray made a come here motion with his hand.

Elton was trying to lift Shalara with no success. Despite his wiry frame, without Shalara being able to help, there was no way he could move her by himself. Maeve stood frozen, looking from Gray to Elton and Shalara. In her mind, she heard Emma's voice "sometimes it's not the big things we do that change the world." Gray's eyes widened, and he began shaking his head when he realized Maeve's intention. "Maeve," he said warningly. Maeve's gaze moved to Elton, watching the desperation in his struggle with Shalara.

"I have to," Maeve said. She grabbed a cloth off the pile of supplies and tied it around her face then picked up two more cloths and covered her hands. She sprinted over to Elton and lifted Shalara's arm over his shoulder. With a mighty heave, Elton grasped Shalara's hands with one hand and held her legs over his other shoulder, sprawling her across his back. Slowly, he stood and wobbled his way toward the door. Maeve grabbed his pack and followed, avoiding Gray's angry stare as she slipped through the doorway behind Elton.

Sand immediately filled Maeve's eyes and nose, and she was grateful for the cloth covering her mouth even if it didn't keep her eyes from tearing. Behind her, she heard the door slam shut as Gray and Tristan followed her. Elton joined Shalara's coughing as he stumbled toward where Ginger, Emery, Thomas and Rufus waited for them.

Just as Maeve moved to help Elton, a hand grabbed hers from behind. "What are you doing?" Gray's angry voice rose above the gentle whoosh of the falling sand. Tristan shot her a sympathetic look as he gave the two of them a wide berth. Maeve pulled the cloths off her hands and wiped the sand from her eyes.

"Trying to help," Maeve said calmly. "I can't believe you were just going to leave them in there."

"Maeve, you could have just infected yourself. We don't know anything about this disease. All we know is it's deadly. Why would you do such a thing?"

"Because it was the right thing to do?" Maeve said as she angrily pulled the cloth down off her nose and mouth.

"It was reckless," Gray said, taking a step back from her. "You're so busy trying to make amends for killing someone that you're willing to put yourself and all of us at risk."

Maeve stepped back as if she had been struck. "Is

that what you think?"

"Isn't that what it's all about? You don't owe Elton and Shalara anything. We barely even know them, but you're willing to throw your life away for them – even if it means killing the rest of us, too."

"It was the right thing to do," Maeve said, drawing each word out in a voice she might reserve for a particularly stubborn patient.

"For who?" Gray asked. "Because from where I stand, it wasn't the right thing to do for us. Elton told us it passes through contact, and you chose to touch her anyway."

"I covered my hands and face."

"Do we know that's enough? I just don't understand why you would sacrifice yourself for someone you barely know. Do the rest of us mean that little to you? Do I mean that little to you?"

Before Maeve could respond, Gray brushed by her without another word to join Tristan and the others. She stood motionless, unsure what had just happened. She and Gray didn't always agree, but he had never raised his voice to her before. Something warm and wet brushed Maeve's hand. Looking down, she found Rufus staring up at her with his soulful brown eyes. He whined, and Maeve sank her hand into the fur behind his ears. "Oh Rufus, what am I going to do?"

CHAPTER SEVENTEEN

"We can't take them," Gray said quietly to Tristan. "There's no way she makes it, and we can't help carry her. We can't expose ourselves even more."

Tristan shifted uneasily from foot to foot. "I know you're right, but it seems cruel to just leave them here."

A loud cough that sounded like air was being ripped from Shalara's lungs filled the air. Maeve, who had been standing next to Ginger, took a step toward Shalara, but Ginger laid a hand on her arm and shook her head sadly. Emery turned sad eyes to her sister, but Ginger once again shook her head.

"Please, Ginger," Emery pleaded. "Maeve could help."

"She can't, Emery. We hardly have any supplies, and we don't know what Shalara has."

"Maybe, maybe we could find that plagoran. Remember, I told you that the venom from their fangs can help heal people!"

Maeve smiled sadly at Emery, and Ginger crouched down so she could look her in the eyes. "Em, we have no idea where that plagoran is or even if it's still alive."

"We should at least try!"

Ginger pulled Emery to her side. "I don't think she has that much time." Emery said nothing, but her shoulders began to shake.

Elton sat next to where Shalara lay on the ground, holding her hand. He leaned over to whisper in her ear, and Maeve stepped closer. She thought she heard him say, "I'm sorry."

Maeve glanced over to where Tristan and Gray still had their heads together, talking, then took another look toward Ginger who was occupied with Emery. Thomas caught her eye and inclined his head toward Shalara. Rufus had taken it upon himself to play comforter and was stretched out next to Shalara on the opposite side from Elton. Thinning her lips in determination and knowing she was setting up another confrontation with Gray, she hurried over to Elton, knelt beside Shalara and handed Elton a canteen of water. She picked up Shalara's arm and felt for a pulse. It was thready and unsteady.

Elton gave her a hopeful look, but Maeve shook her head. "Shalara," she said. "Can you hear me?" Shalara nodded her head slightly. "It's going to be OK," Maeve lied as she brushed the hair back from Shalara's face. "Just breathe."

Shalara struggled for breath, then opened her eyes. Her lips worked to form words.

"I think she wants to say something to you," Elton said, his eyes never leaving Shalara's face.

Maeve leaned closer. Shalara wheezed in a breath, her eyes bulging with effort as she worked to push air out to create words. Elton's grip tightened on Shalara's hand, and Maeve thought she saw Shalara wince. Maeve noted

Elton's knuckles had turned white with the force of his grip. She felt sorry for the agony he was enduring as Shalara moved restlessly, still seeking enough air to talk. Another wheezing breath. Maeve hadn't treated many dying people, but she knew the signs. Shalara didn't have much time left.

Shalara used what little strength she had left to grip Maeve's hand where it rested on her wrist. She pulled herself up slightly off the ground and slurred, "He's not..." Maeve struggled to make out the words as Shalara fell back to the ground. The hand gripping Maeve's wrist went slack, and Shalara's eyes slipped closed. The air wheezed out of her lungs, but her chest didn't lift to pull any air back in. Maeve felt for a pulse, but the skin under her fingers was quiet and still.

She raised her head to find Elton watching her. She didn't know what Shalara was going to say, but she did know that Elton had just lost his only relative. "I'm sorry," she said quietly.

He nodded, and Maeve thought she saw relief flicker through his eyes. He set Shalara's hand on her chest, stood and offered Maeve his hand. She took it, and he pulled her to her feet. They turned to face the others. Emery had her face buried in Ginger's chest, sobbing while Ginger stroked her hands soothingly up and down Emery's back. Rufus had returned to Thomas's side, and Thomas stood silently with one hand absently stroking the dog's ears. Tristan had stopped talking to Gray and gave Maeve a look of pity. Finally, she turned her gaze to Gray's. His eyebrows were drawn together, and his fists were clenched at his sides. A muscle twitched in his cheek, and Maeve was sure he was gritting his teeth together in an effort not to shout at her. He stared pointedly at her hand clasped in Elton's, then turned away from her with a look of disgust. She quickly dropped Elton's hand and took a step toward Gray.

"Wait," Ginger said. "You need to at least wash your hands and face." She stepped forward with a canteen and held it out to Maeve without getting close to her.

Tristan had moved to stand a few feet away from Maeve and Elton. "I'm really sorry," Tristan said to Elton. Elton nodded and swallowed hard. Tristan's voice became businesslike. "Clean yourselves up, and let's get moving." He gave Elton an apologetic look. "We don't have time to bury her."

Maeve poured water over her hands and used a disc of soap from her pack to thoroughly scrub her hands, arms and face. When she was done, she searched for Gray, but he was nowhere to be seen. Thomas stepped to her side and said quietly, "He went to scout the route." Maeve's shoulders fell, and Rufus gave her palm a lick.

"Come on," Thomas said, taking her hand. "Everyone else is waiting for us."

CHAPTER EIGHTEEN

"Emery, there wasn't anything I could do," Maeve said quietly. The sun's rays were just peeking over the horizon, stretching out onto the golden sand before them. A brisk wind covered their tracks almost as soon as they made them.

"I know." Emery sniffed and rubbed her eyes. Maeve didn't know what to say.

"It just feels like everyone around me dies, you know," she said. "Why is that?"

Maeve put one foot in front of the other, sand filling her shoes with every step, and said wearily, "I don't know, Emery. I'm not much help on that front."

Emery's shoulders drooped further, and Maeve felt her own eyes filling with tears. Between Emery's despair and Gray's anger at her for doing what she thought was right, she felt helpless and alone. She swiped at her eyes angrily and searched for something comforting to say.

Before she could find the right words, Rufus came loping up next to Emery, gave her hand a quick swipe with his tongue and lightly leaned his bulk against her leg. Emery looked down in surprise but gave a small smile as Rufus licked her hand again. Emery rubbed his ears and walked on, comforted by his presence.

"Even the dog is more capable than me," Maeve muttered to herself.

"I don't think you're not capable," Elton's voice came from behind her. Maeve jumped. She had forgotten he was right behind her, close enough to hear her talking to herself. "Thank you for trying to help Shalara."

Maeve twisted her hands together. "I wasn't much help. I'm really sorry about your sister."

Elton stopped her with a hand on her arm and turned her to face him. He swallowed and rubbed his cheek with his finger. "She was a good sister. I'll miss her, for sure."

Once again Maeve tried to think of something comforting to say, but it seemed her well of comfort had run dry, for others and for herself. Elton, though, didn't seem to expect a response.

"You tried," he continued. "That matters. It mattered to Shalara. It matters to me." Maeve looked up into his handsome face framed by his curly black hair. Where Gray was ruggedly good-looking, Elton was more of a handsome nerd. Though it was early, his hair was already matted with sweat as the temperature rose with the sun. His dark eyes, so different from Gray's ice blue ones, bore into hers. "It means a lot that you tried. Unlike your friend Gray."

Maeve looked away. Somehow, standing here with Elton felt disloyal to Gray, but she didn't understand Gray's reluctance to try to help Elton and Shalara. His attitude coupled with his anger at her had left her feeling angry and confused. She started walking again without replying.

Elton fell into step beside her. "How do you guys

know each other anyway?"

"Ginger and I have been friends since early school. Gray and I helped spark a revolution in Palumbra together, but we didn't really know each other before then. Tristan was part of The Resistance that helped overthrow the World Government, and Thomas and Rufus are members of a class that we teach."

Elton didn't seem interested in Thomas as he focused in on Gray. "So, you haven't known Gray long?"

"I guess not, but we've been through a lot together." Maeve looked around for Gray, but he was still far out in front of them. They hadn't spoken since he stalked away from her. It wasn't like Gray to let things fester. He was usually the one who wanted to work out their differences while Maeve stewed on things for days.

"Does he get angry like that a lot?" Elton broke into her thoughts.

She shook her head. "No. That's what's so weird. I'm not sure why he's so angry."

Maeve tripped on a loose pocket of sand, falling to her knees. Elton reached down with both hands to help her up and glanced over her shoulder. When she got to her feet, he gave her hands a little squeeze and quirked the corners of his mouth up at the edges in a ghost of a smile. "Well, thanks for your help anyway. I'm sorry it made Gray mad."

Maeve squeezed his hands back and returned his smile. "It's OK. I'm sure he'll get over it."

"What exactly am I supposed to get over?" Gray's voice sounded from behind Maeve, the coldness in his voice making each word feel like he was throwing shards of ice at her and Elton. She quickly pulled her hands from Elton's and turned to face Gray.

"Where did you come from?" she asked. "I thought you were scouting out front."

"I came back to talk to you. You and Elton had fallen behind everyone else, and Tristan was getting worried. He thought one of you might be sick," he said pointedly.

"We're both fine," Maeve said quietly.

"I can see that." Gray mockingly raised his eyebrows. "Would you like to be alone?"

She let out a huff of exasperation. "Don't be stupid. I don't know what kind of grudge you're carrying or why, but I tripped and Elton helped me up. No need to throw snide accusations around."

Maeve turned her back on Gray and marched forward to catch up with the others but not before she saw Elton throw her a quick smile. She ignored him and focused on the desert in front of her. Let Gray catch up to her if he wanted to talk. Right now, she didn't have anything to say to him.

"We should make camp soon," Tristan announced.

The group had trekked on mainly in silence after Maeve and Gray's argument. Only Thomas and Rufus seemed unaffected by the pall that had fallen over the group, with Thomas talking merrily to the dog as they walked.

"Where are we even going?" Maeve asked. She had been following Tristan all day, assuming they were headed back to Palumbra. "This isn't the way that we came. We should be almost back to Palumbra."

"You're right," Tristan said. "We decided not to go back to Palumbra in case Sarge followed us. We're headed for the caves, in a roundabout fashion."

"Where are we going to camp?" Gray asked. "We need some kind of shelter – and water." He held up his near-empty canteen and shook it.

Thomas pointed to a spot in the distance. "That looks like some kind of tree over there."

Gray squinted and used his hand to block the sun. "Right. Then I guess we head that way. Lead the way, Tristan."

Gray dropped to the back of the group where Maeve was trailing behind, alone with her thoughts. She glared at him as he approached her, but he was undeterred and fell in beside her. Elton, who had been trudging along in front of her, gave her a questioning look and slowed his pace. It was Gray's turn to glare, and he sent the full force of his icy stare at Elton, who raised his eyebrows at Maeve. She shook her head and motioned for Elton to keep going, then slowed her pace to put some space between them.

"You don't have to keep glaring at him," Maeve said when Gray's gaze didn't leave Elton's back. "He's kind of had a rough day."

"I don't like him," Gray said, keeping his voice low so Elton couldn't hear him.

"He just lost his sister." Maeve gave him a disbelieving look. "I think you can cut him some slack."

"He doesn't seem real upset about it," Gray replied.

Maeve's jaw dropped, and she whirled to face Gray, spraying sand from under her feet. "I cannot believe that you, of all people, would criticize how someone else grieves. How long did it take you to cry over your uncle?"

Gray looked steadily at her. "A week. It took me a week, as you well know. But that was different."

"How? How was that different?" Maeve threw her hands up in exasperation. "You went through a traumatic experience and had to take time to understand it. Seems to me Elton is in the exact same situation."

Gray shook his head. "There's just something off about him. You'd see it, too, if you weren't so busy gazing into his eyes and trying to save everyone."

Maeve turned and started walking again with a brisk stride. "If you dropped back here to yell at me or lecture me, you're wasting your time. You don't get to treat me like you've treated me today, then think you have the right to continue to berate me – for helping someone."

Gray was silent. The wind blew gently, kicking up sand that swirled around them. Maeve felt like that sand – tossed around by the storm of Gray's emotions.

"You're right," he said finally. "I'm sorry. I may have overreacted, but I don't trust Elton. He's hiding something from us."

Maeve ignored his jab at Elton and said, "Why were you so angry that I tried to help?"

Gray shook his head. "I wasn't angry that you wanted to help. I was angry that you didn't think about anyone else before you did it." Gray tentatively took her hands in his and forced her to stop moving. "Maeve, you act like you're the only person who suffered any kind of loss or trauma when we fought the WG. I lost everything. I have no family left. Emery and Ginger lost their mom, and who knows what happened to their dad. I don't know all of Tristan's story, but I know the WG had something to do with the loss of his parents. And we all lost Silas."

Maeve's gaze dropped again to the swirling sand around them, remembering their friend Silas who had sacrificed his life to save Emery from being shot by WG drones. She raised her eyes back to Gray's and squirmed as his gaze burrowed into hers. "I don't think I'm the only one who lost things," she said quietly. "I just seem to be the only one who can't get past it."

"Do you really think we're all just over it?" Gray motioned in the direction of the others who were now far ahead of them. "You don't just get over stuff like that. It stays with you – forever. There's no magic wand you can wave to feel better. But you can't just make rash decisions, especially when they affect other people."

Gray tucked a strand of hair behind her ear, and Maeve's face tingled where he touched it. Even when they were upset with each other, she was still drawn to him. "Maeve, I've lost everyone I care about. Except you. When you put your life at risk, you put the person I care about most at risk." He brushed her cheek with his thumb. "And I don't think I could go on if I lost you, too."

A wave of sadness washed over Maeve as she realized just how much her actions had affected Gray. Suddenly, she understood just how much she meant to Gray, and how much he meant to her. He loved her. He had never said the words, but in this moment, as she gazed into those ice blue eyes, she knew. The knowledge made her grow warm inside, and she felt the heavy weight of responsibility settle on her shoulders. Being loved by Gray meant that she could hurt him in ways she hadn't considered. For a fleeting moment, Maeve wasn't sure she wanted that power. Then Gray leaned close and kissed her and all thought fled.

They had kissed before, but this kiss had a new flavor, as a new understanding flowed between them. She leaned into him, relishing the safety and love she felt in his embrace.

A loud woof and a cold nose broke Maeve and Gray apart. Rufus, tail wagging, wedged himself between them and barked again.

Maeve laughed. "I think he was sent back to get us."

Gray did a quick 360-degree scan of the area. "We probably should have been paying more attention. We should catch up to the others." He grabbed Maeve's hand and started to jog after Rufus who, job done, had already begun loping back toward the group. Maeve tugged on his hand, forcing him to stop once again.

"I'm sorry, Gray. I know you don't understand my need to make up for what I did, but I didn't mean to put myself or anyone else in danger. And I didn't mean to hurt you."

Gray nodded, gave her hand a squeeze and started jogging back to the group.

CHAPTER NINETEEN

"About time you two caught up," Tristan said from underneath a short, scraggly tree that could more correctly be called a large bush. "What were you doing out there – or do I need to ask?" He gave a short laugh and rolled his eyes in Ginger's direction. She rolled her eyes back.

A sharp cough caught Maeve's attention, and she scanned the area, looking for the source. Emery was picking up sticks underneath another one of the scraggly bush-tree things. "Are you OK, Em?" Maeve asked.

Emery coughed again and waved her off. "I'm fine," she said in a hoarse voice. "All that sand blowing around caused a tickle in my throat that won't go away."

Maeve gave her another concerned look, picked up her canteen and went to fill it in the small pool of water surrounded by the bush-tree hybrids. "What is Emery doing," she asked Ginger.

"Picking up sticks for a fire."

"Do we think that's wise? Sarge can find us if we light a fire."

Ginger shrugged. "Tristan thinks it will be OK. He seems to be doing a fair job of making decisions so far. I think we can trust his judgment."

Maeve was skeptical but decided to hold her tongue and finished filling her canteen. Emery's cough filled the air again, followed by a loud thump.

"Emery," Ginger cried, dropping her canteen and rushing to where Emery was doubled over on the ground, struggling to breath around the coughing. Maeve followed and dropped to her knees next to Emery, lifting her head to open her airway.

"Come on, Emery," Maeve said. "Breathe. Listen to my voice. In. Out. In. Out."

Slowly, the coughing stopped and Emery's breathing returned to normal.

"What happened?" Ginger asked, stroking the hair off Emery's forehead as Maeve held her.

"I just couldn't stop coughing," Emery said. "All that sand settled in my throat."

Maeve handed her the canteen she had just filled. "Drink this. Let's see if we can't soothe your throat a bit."

The rest of the group stood in a circle around Emery, Maeve and Ginger. Rufus nudged Emery's hand and whined. Emery rubbed his ears and said, "I'm fine, Rufus. Just a tickle." Rufus licked her nose, and everyone laughed. Maeve helped Emery sit up and announced, "Now that Emery is done scaring us, we should fix something to eat and get some rest."

Maeve threw another stick on the small fire they had made to heat up some of the canned beans in their packs. She had to admit it was nice to eat something warm and not just another protein paste bar. While the food situation in Palumbra had improved, protein paste bars were the food of choice for patrols in the desert.

Tristan sat down next to her. "Do you really think

she's fine?" He nodded to where Emery and Thomas were teaching Rufus to shake hands.

She considered Emery carefully. "I really don't know. She seems fine now, and she doesn't have a fever. We'll just have to watch her closely."

"Is there anything we can do if she is sick?"

Maeve shook her head. "We don't know much about this disease, and we have limited supplies. One thing I do know, though." Her voice became fierce. "I'm not losing her. No matter what it takes."

"She's still coughing," Ginger said to Maeve the next morning as they packed up camp.

Maeve stuffed a sweatshirt in her pack and picked up her canteen. "I know, but she doesn't have a fever or rash and says she doesn't feel sick. We just have to hope for the best."

Ginger wrinkled her nose in disgust. "I hate this. I just wish there was something we could do."

"Maybe there is." Elton looked up from where he was packing his own pack about 10 feet from them. Maeve hadn't spoken to him since her conversation with Gray the night before. She remembered Gray's concerns about Elton, but she shook them off. He had been quiet, but he had just lost his sister.

"Were you eavesdropping?" Ginger asked with some venom.

Elton held up a hand as if to ward off an attack. "Not on purpose. You guys weren't exactly trying to be quiet."

Ginger started to issue a retort, but Maeve motioned for her to be quiet. "What do you know?"

"There might be an antidote," Elton said without looking up from the protein paste bar he was shoving into his pack.

Maeve's eyes narrowed, and she could hear Gray's voice in her head saying, "I don't trust Elton."

"Why would you tell us this now?" she asked. "Why didn't you tell us when Shalara was sick?"

Elton still didn't look up, but his hands stilled. "There was no chance to save her." His voice was so quiet, Maeve and Ginger had to lean forward to hear him.

"We could have tried," Maeve said.

Elton shook his head. "She got too sick too fast, and Sarge was chasing us. We had no chance. She had no chance." He finally looked up with glistening eyes. "But we have a chance to save Emery."

"So, you think she's sick?" Ginger dropped the blanket she was folding. "Why do you think that?"

"The illness doesn't affect everyone the same. Some people get it and get really sick, really fast. Others get it, and it doesn't seem too bad at first. They have a cough for a couple of days before the illness sets in. But in the end, everyone gets the rash." Elton paused. "And everyone dies."

Ginger grabbed Elton by the shirt. "Emery is *not* dying. Whatever you know about an antidote, you need to tell us."

"Who's dying?" Thomas's young voice echoed through the camp as Ginger, Maeve and Elton fell silent. Thomas and Rufus ambled up to Maeve. "Who's dying?" he asked again. One hand tightened on Rufus's collar as he braced himself for the answer.

Maeve dropped to her knees, so her face was level

with Thomas's. She heard Gray and Tristan join Ginger. Emery walked up next to Thomas and took his hand. "Yeah, who's dying?"

Maeve remained silent, looking from Thomas's scared eyes to Emery's trusting ones. She took a deep breath, wiped her palms on her pants and said, "Thomas, Emery is sick."

"I'm not sick," Emery protested. "It's just a tickle in my throat. I feel fine."

Ginger stepped forward and looked Emery in the eye. "That's how it starts, Em. Elton says some people don't get sick right away."

Emery dropped Thomas's hand and stepped away from him, her eyes wide with horror. "But I don't want to die. And what if I infect all of you?" She continued to back away. When Ginger stepped toward her, she held up a hand. "No, you can't come near me. I ... I'll go. I can go out in the desert, and then you guys will be fine." She turned to pick up her pack, but Rufus blocked her way. Maeve hadn't noticed Thomas giving the dog instructions.

"You're not going anywhere, Emery," Ginger said. "We have another option."

Emery placed a hand on Rufus's back as if to shove him out of the way, but Rufus stood firm. She laid her forehead against Rufus's sturdy back. "What options?" she asked in a tear-filled voice.

Maeve stood and placed her hand on Thomas's shoulder to keep him from going to Emery. "Elton thinks there may be an antidote."

Gray and Tristan had been quiet, but at this pronouncement they both exclaimed, "What?"

"If there's an antidote, how did everyone in The

Hub die?" Gray asked with ice in his voice.

"And why are you just telling us this now? Didn't you want your sister to live?" Tristan asked.

Elton straightened his shoulders and confronted Tristan and Gray. "Of course I wanted her to live, and the antidote was just a rumor. Do you guys really think Palumbra was the only place with a corrupt government?"

Gray and Tristan had no response. Maeve knew they had all just assumed that life in The Hub was better than in WG-controlled Palumbra, but Elton's pronouncement gave them pause.

Thomas broke away from Maeve's grip on his shoulder and moved to stand between Gray and Tristan and Elton. "Can we focus? Emery is sick. She needs medicine. Elton thinks he knows where some medicine is. Shouldn't we just go get it? You can argue about bad governments later."

Rufus barked as if in agreement.

Thomas's words broke the standoff. "He's right," Gray said. To Elton, he said, "I'm sorry. I know you loved your sister. If you think you know where there's an antidote to help Emery, let's get moving." He held out his hand. Elton stared at it for a long moment, and Maeve wasn't sure he was going to take it for the peace offering it was. Slowly, Elton reached out and shook Gray's hand.

CHAPTER TWENTY

"Do you think we'll find anything?" Thomas asked Maeve as they once more trudged through the ever-swirling sand. Rufus loped ahead of them, his tongue lolling out of the side of his mouth as he panted in the hot sun.

Maeve looked down into Thomas's trusting face. "I hope so, Thomas." She turned at the sound of Emery coughing from several feet behind them, her face covered with a T-shirt so all Maeve could see were her eyes. Emery wouldn't allow anyone to get near her, terrified of infecting someone else. Sweat rolled down her forehead and disappeared under the T-shirt covering her nose and mouth.

Thomas took Maeve's hand. "She's going to be OK," he said with the complete confidence of childhood. Maeve wondered how much of that confidence was trust in her and how much was simply bravado. She didn't know much about Thomas other than his parents had died and he lived with his apparently apathetic uncle.

"What's your story, Thomas? How did you end up here?" Maeve spread her arms out to encompass the vast sea of sand.

Thomas kicked some sand and said, "I told you, I

followed you."

Maeve smiled and shook her head. "I didn't mean it literally. Tell me how you ended up living with your uncle."

Thomas's eyes went flat, and his voice became toneless. "My parents died."

The smile disappeared from Maeve's face, and she gave his hand a squeeze. "I know, and I'm so sorry. Tell me what they were like."

Thomas raised his head and searched her eyes. "Do you really want to know? My uncle never wants to talk about them."

Maeve nodded. "I really want to know."

Thomas's chocolate eyes lit up. "My mom was amazing. She worked at the factory, but she was an incredible singer. She sang all the time. I don't remember a day when my mom didn't sing something."

"Did she sing to you?"

"All the time. She sang me to sleep every night." Thomas paused. "I really miss that."

Maeve gave his hand another squeeze. "What did she sing?"

"It was a song she said was handed down through her family. I don't know how far back it goes."

"Do you remember the words?"

Thomas nodded. "I don't think I'll ever forget them."

"Can you sing it for me?"

Thomas looked around at the others spread out around them. "Here? Right now?"

Maeve followed Thomas's gaze then looked down at him. "Sure. Why not? What else have we got to do?"

Thomas gave her a look that said he clearly thought she was a little bit strange, but then he nodded. "OK, if you really want to hear it. I'm not that great of a singer."

"With a talented mom like yours, I'm sure your voice is great," Maeve encouraged.

Thomas dropped Maeve's hand, looked at the others, took a deep breath and started singing.

Sleep, sweet child, sleep, my love
Sleep in peace tonight
I love you so, more than you know
So sleep in peace tonight

Thomas's high, sweet voice pierced through the silence of the desert, and Maeve and the others stopped walking to listen. Thomas continued to sing.

When you're alone, be brave, sweet child
Always let love shine through
I love you so, more than you know
So sleep in peace tonight

Rufus, drawn by the sound of Thomas's voice loped over and nudged his hand. Thomas dug his hand into Rufus's fur and sang the last verse:

When I am gone, no need to fear
I'll always be in your heart
I love you so, more than you know
So sleep in peace tonight

The last note drifted off into the desert. Emery began clapping and started walking toward Thomas before remembering to keep her distance.

"That was beautiful," Emery said. Maeve could see tears mixing with the sweat on Emery's face. Despite their age difference, Thomas and Emery had a lot in common.

"It reminded me of my mom."

"I could teach it to you," Thomas offered. "That way we could both remember our moms together."

Emery nodded and said, "I'd like that."

Thomas gave Rufus another pat, reached again for Maeve's hand and addressed everyone else. "Don't we have some medicine to find?"

"How did you get Thomas to sing?" Gray asked. Despite the heat of the desert, Thomas had run ahead with Rufus to help Tristan and Elton lead the way, and Maeve now walked in step with Gray. Emery and Ginger were behind them, talking as quietly to each other as the forced distance between them would allow.

"I asked him about his parents."

"Did you find out his story?" Gray asked.

Maeve shook her head. "Just that his parents died, and he lives with his uncle, which we already knew."

"I don't know why, but I think there's a story there," Gray said. He lifted his canteen to his lips, took a big swallow, then wiped his sweaty forehead with his arm. He held the canteen out to Maeve, but she waved him off.

"He doesn't seem to want to talk about it much." She squinted ahead to where Thomas was now talking to Elton.

"I guess he'll tell us when he's ready," Gray said. "He's a resourceful kid. Just think, he made it out into this desert on his own, and he rescued us."

"Rufus helped," Maeve said with a smile as Rufus chose that moment to throw himself in the sand and roll around. Just as quickly, the dog jumped to his feet, the hair on his back standing straight up. A low growl began deep in his throat. They hurried to catch up to the others.

"What is it, boy?" Thomas asked Rufus quietly. Tristan slipped Maeve's knife from his belt; it was still the only weapon they had.

Rufus continued to growl, his usually wagging tail stiff and the rest of his body poised to pounce. Everyone scanned the horizon and listened for any unusual sound. Maeve noticed Elton's hands shaking and realized hers were shaking as well. No one moved. The only sound was their breathing and the occasional cough from Emery.

Then they heard it. A far-off cry they all recognized. A large shadow suddenly loomed on the horizon, moving quickly toward them. Rufus started to bark. Gray and Tristan frantically searched for cover. The cry came again, closer this time. Emery coughed.

"Run!" Tristan shouted and motioned for them to follow Elton.

"We're never going to outrun a plagoran," Ginger shouted.

"Do you have any better ideas?" Tristan shouted back.

Maeve had taken Thomas's hand and started running with Emery on her heels. She looked back to see Ginger closing her mouth and running after Emery as Tristan and Gray closed ranks behind her. Maeve's eyes scanned the barren desert landscape, looking for somewhere to hide. The plagoran cry rang through the stagnant air, closer than before.

A quick glance over her shoulder told Maeve it was gaining on them quickly, but that glance cost her. Her foot caught on an uneven stretch of sand, and she stumbled, falling heavily to her knees. Emery and Ginger flew past her.

"Come on, Maeve," Ginger said as she grabbed her arm. Maeve struggled to get her feet under her in the shifting sand. Without breaking his stride, Gray hoisted her by her other arm and hauled her to her feet. "Move!" he cried. With a last look at Maeve, Ginger stretched out her legs and sprinted to help Emery who was struggling to keep up with Elton, Thomas and Rufus. Maeve and Gray put on a burst of speed with Tristan hot on their heels. She could feel the vibration of the plagoran's large, lizard feet as they struck the ground with the force of a hammer. They were never going to make it.

Tristan had caught Maeve and Gray, but stayed behind them, wielding the knife. Maeve wasn't sure how much farther she could run, and she knew Emery had to be fading. She raised her eyes from the sand and tugged on Gray's arm. He turned his head and raised his eyebrows in a silent query.

"Where are the others?" Maeve asked.

CHAPTER TWENTY-ONE

Maeve was so shocked she almost stopped running. If Gray hadn't pulled her along, she would have been a tasty snack for the plagoran. Her eyes desperately scanned the horizon looking for any sign of her friends.

"Where did they go?" Gray shouted to be heard over the roar of the plagoran. The ground under their feet shook, and sand flew up every time the plagoran's feet hit the ground. Maeve was afraid to look back to see how close the giant lizard was.

"Keep running," Tristan panted from behind them. "They have to be up there somewhere. They didn't just disappear."

But they had. No matter how hard Maeve looked, she saw no sign of her friends. Suddenly, Gray veered off to the right. "There." He pointed ahead of him. Maeve saw nothing, but Tristan nodded, and they put on a burst of speed, lengthening the distance between them and the plagoran slightly. Maeve still had no idea what Gray and Tristan had seen; she only hoped it was something that led them to safety. Her legs and lungs burned, and she could barely see for the sweat dripping into her eyes.

Gray suddenly dropped to the ground in a slide

move Maeve had never seen. She did her best to imitate him and heard Tristan hit the ground behind them. She slid to a stop beside Gray, and Tristan piled in behind her. They were at the base of a small sand dune; it rose no more than four feet off the surface of the desert. Gray sat on the ground with his back to the sand dune and worked his arms like a snow angel to burrow his way into the dune. The falling sand buried his legs, and he was soon hardly noticeable from a distance. He motioned for Maeve to do the same. Sand coated Maeve until she felt like she was part of the dune. Grains of sand floated in her nose, landed in her mouth and covered her hair. She was sure she looked like a sand monster – she certainly felt like one. She turned her head slightly and saw Tristan lean to his right as if he was listening to someone next to him. Maeve squinted through the sand in her eyes and could just make out Ginger was on his other side. She had wrapped her dark hair in a gold T-shirt so it wouldn't stand out against the sand. The rest of her was covered in a thin layer of sand. Her eyes met Maeve's, and she held a finger to her lips.

The plagoran roared. The ground vibrated. Gray wrapped his hand around hers. Maeve held her breath as the plagoran approached. It turned in a circle, moving its large snout back and forth, scanning the ground at its feet. Its long neck moved up and down as it sought its prey. No one moved. The plagoran took three steps toward the sand dune. It was so close, Maeve could see the iridescent shine to its scales and pick out the different colors. The plagoran lowered its head so it was level with Maeve's face. She closed her eyes and prayed as she felt the beast's warm breath on her cheek. She gripped Gray's hand and used all her willpower to keep her limbs from shaking.

The plagoran sniffed once and turned its back. It slowly circled the sand dune, sniffed the air, let out a frustrated roar and turned back the way it had come. It set out at a loping pace across the hot desert. Maeve blew out a breath of relief, and the others did the same. She thought she heard a whimper that could have been Thomas or Emery. Still, she didn't move as the plagoran retreated into the distance.

Finally, when they could no longer see the plagoran, Tristan shook his arms free from the sand and leaned out of the dune, the sand cascading off his back. Maeve noted he had pulled his sleeves down on his shirt and had taken a page out of Ginger's book, using a T-shirt to cover the dark skin of his face and hands. While his clothing was covered with sand, his face and hair were relatively sand-free. Maeve only wished she could say the same. She felt as if she had bathed in sand and longed for a hot shower, even the short ones they were allowed in Palumbra since water was still rationed.

"Where's Rufus?" Emery asked.

Maeve looked around. The big, black dog was nowhere to be found.

"Rufus, rise," Thomas said.

The ground at his feet started to ripple, and a black spot appeared in the sand. That black spot quickly became a large, shaggy dog who shook his coat vigorously, showering the rest of them with sand. They held up their hands to ward off the onslaught.

"How did he hide himself so well?" Maeve brushed sand off her arms again.

Thomas shrugged. "It's just a trick I taught him. He's a great digger. The sand is so soft that when he laid down in the hole it covered him mostly up. I did the rest."

"But how did you get him to lay so still and be quiet?" Ginger asked.

Thomas looked at the ground and wrapped his hand in Rufus's fur. "Sometimes we have to be quiet at home."

No one knew what to say to that, and an awkward silence fell on the group. Maeve searched her brain for a way to change the subject and chose the most obvious topic.

"Why didn't it find us?" she said to no one in particular. The others, like her, were shaking sand from their hands, faces and hair. Emery coughed, and Maeve noted she was once again standing a distance apart from the rest of them.

"It has no sense of smell," Emery said.

"What?" Gray said. "That makes no sense. Reptiles have an excellent sense of smell."

"But this isn't an ordinary reptile." Emery unbraided her hair, combed her fingers through it to loosen the sand, then started to rebraid it. "Remember, I told you the going theory is that they were created in a lab during The Lost Years. For some reason, they removed its sense of smell."

"Why would they do that?" Ginger shook out the T-shirt she had wrapped around her hair. "How would that be a benefit?"

"Well, no one knows for sure," Emery answered. "But some people think they removed it so plagorans would be more useful in a battle."

"You mean they were weapons?" Thomas stood still while Maeve brushed the sand of his clothes. She handed him her canteen, then took a sip herself, trying to rid her mouth of the coating of sand.

Emery nodded. "With no sense of smell, they didn't get spooked as badly by fire, which made them a much more reliable weapon."

"Well, I'd like to shake the hand of the scientist that thought of that," Gray said, dusting sand off his knees. "That decision just saved our lives."

If she never saw sand again, Maeve would not miss it. Despite her best efforts, her hair and clothes still carried a coating of sand, and she was contantly pulling grit out of her eyes. The desert stretched endlessly in front of her and just as endlessly behind her. Though the sun was beginning to set, waves of heat rose off the sand in front of her.

"We're almost there," Elton said from the front of the group where he had returned to lead the way with Tristan.

Maeve raised her eyebrows in disbelief at Gray. There was nothing that looked like a city as far as the eye could see. "Is he hallucinating?" Maeve whispered.

Gray looked hard into the distance as if he could will the city into existence, then shook his head. "He must know something we don't."

"If we hadn't met Elton, I would believe our patrols that said there's nothing out here. I just hope Elton isn't lost." She focused her gaze on Thomas and Rufus. Thomas never complained, but she watched as he slid his feet along the sand, each step an effort. Rufus gave him a nudge from behind as if to encourage him to keep moving. "I'm not sure how much farther his legs will carry him."

Gray followed Maeve's gaze. "He's tough. He'll

make it. Something tells me he doesn't have an easy life with his uncle."

"I got that impression, too. We'll have to look into it when we get back."

Before Gray could answer, Tristan held up his hand in a silent signal for them to stop.

"We're here," Elton announced.

Maeve blinked.

"What is he talking about?" Ginger asked as she came up beside Maeve. "We're in the middle of the desert. There's no city."

"Elton, there's nothing here." Tristan fingered the knife on his belt and looked around for any sign of a threat.

Had they misplaced their trust in Elton, Maeve wondered. Had he led them into a trap?

"You just think there's nothing here," Elton said. "Put your hand in front of you." Elton demonstrated by holding his arm out straight and extending his hand up at a 90-degree angle to his arm, so his palm faced outward. Tristan rolled his eyes but did the same.

"Now step forward." Tristan took a tiny step with his arm still outstretched. His eyes widened in surprise, and he lifted both hands and ran them up and down in front of him, like a mime pretending to figure out the outline of a box.

"What is that?"

"It's the force field protecting Bellus," Elton said. "You have to live here to be able to get in."

"A force field?" Ginger exclaimed. "No way you have enough technology in Bellus to create a huge force field that hides the city from view. The amount of energy that would take is enormous."

Elton gave them a grin. "I think Bellus is a little different from Palumbra." He leaned down to examine a scrawny, dying plant that grew a mere six inches out of the desert. He took the top branch, if you could call it that, between his thumb and forefinger and squeezed, then pushed on the force field. The air in front of them parted, creating a hole in the force field.

Gray shook his head. "No wonder our patrols couldn't find it."

Elton disappeared through the opening then poked his head back through, "Are you guys coming?"

CHAPTER TWENTY-TWO

Maeve followed Tristan through the opening, marveling at how the force field looked just like the rest of the desert. She couldn't even fathom the technology that would be needed to accomplish that feat. To her knowledge, Palumbra had nothing this advanced.

Maeve stopped abruptly just inside the opening. "What is this place?" she said in an awed whisper.

They were perched on a hill of sand overlooking a huge city of towering glass buildings. The sun reflected off the buildings, forcing her to lift her hand to act as a shield for her eyes. She had never seen so many buildings and had certainly never seen any so tall. Government headquarters was the tallest building in Palumbra, but the shortest building in Bellus was twice the size of that building.

Maeve could see the distinctive layout of the city that had led Emery to nickname it The Hub. Six wide streets stretched out in all directions from a unique round, glass building in the center of the city, creating the impression of a wheel.

Thomas reached for Maeve's hand, and she looked down at him. "Are you OK?" she asked.

Thomas shook his head. "I don't know. This place

is..." He stopped and shook his head again. "I don't really know what it is."

Elton had closed the force field behind Emery and started walking, putting about a quarter mile of distance between them. He turned as if just realizing no one had followed him. "What are you guys doing? If we're going to find that antidote, we need to keep moving."

None of them moved to follow him, and he made his way back to where they stood frozen in awe. "You would think you guys have never seen a city before."

"Not one like that." Ginger motioned toward the sea of glass.

Elton quirked his eyebrow in confusion. "Does Palumbra not look like this?"

Gray gave a short laugh. "No. Palumbra definitely doesn't look like this."

Emery coughed, then said, "How does that force field work?"

"I don't understand it all," Elton said, "But in school we learned that it was made with magnets to deflect harmful energy weapons and lasers to create the camouflage aspect."

"But how did it know to let you in?" Tristan asked.

"Biometric data. The force field recognizes fingerprints and voice cadences. Some places use iris scans to determine whether you're cleared for admittance."

"Does everyone just give up their biometric data to the government?" Tristan asked.

Elton furrowed his forehead as if he had never encountered that question before. "As far as I know. Why wouldn't they?"

Gray and Maeve exchanged skeptical looks. They

knew all too well what could happen when you gave the government too much control.

Emery coughed again, and Elton motioned them forward with a wave of his hand. "Come on. We need to start looking for that antidote."

"How long will it take to get there?" Thomas asked, looking with trepidation at the steep incline down to the city.

"Not long if I can get the hovercar to work," Elton said.

"The what?" Gray asked.

"The hovercar." Elton spoke slowly as if he was talking to a young child. Maeve saw comprehension dawn in his eyes. "You don't have hovercars."

Gray shook his head.

"Does everything still work if everyone is gone?" Emery asked.

"It's only been a few days since we fled. The interface is designed to run on its own for at least a month."

Elton began leading them down the steep incline. Rufus took a few steps on the steep terrain and lost his footing, the large dogs gangly legs splaying out from his body as he landed with a thud on his broad chest. He whined and gave Thomas a reproachful look.

Thomas gave him a pat on the head and urged him to his feet. "You can do it, Rufus."

"He can just stay here if he can't make it down to the hovercar," Elton said.

Thomas turned with a look of fire in his eyes. "Rufus is coming. I'm not leaving him."

Elton held up his hands as if to protect himself from Thomas's words. "OK, OK. It was just a suggestion."

They picked their way down the incline to a plateau where two vehicles stood waiting. They were like nothing Maeve had ever seen. While there weren't a lot of cars in Palumbra, the few that existed had sleek lines and four wheels and stayed firmly on the ground. The hovercars, like their name implied, hovered about a foot off the ground, no need for wheels. They were clearly designed to carry a group of passengers with a boxier shape than the cars Maeve was used to seeing.

"We should go in one car, and Emery should go in one by herself," Elton said.

"What?" Ginger cried. "No way. What if something happens to the second car?"

"I'll ride with her," Tristan said.

"No," Emery said quietly from her spot at the back of the group. "Elton is right. Those cars are pretty small. I don't want to infect the rest of you."

Thomas leaned over and whispered in Rufus's ear. Rufus cocked his head as if to say, "Are you sure?" Thomas nodded and said, "Go."

Rufus trotted over and sat down next to Emery, waiting for his next instruction. "Rufus can go with you," Thomas said.

"Are you sure?" Emery asked even as her hand burrowed into Rufus's shaggy coat.

"You shouldn't have to travel alone. Rufus will keep you company."

"Thanks, Thomas."

"Don't thank me. Thank Rufus."

Getting in the hovercar was trickier than it looked. The car bobbed up and down on its cushion of air, making the surface unsteady even though it was just a foot off the ground. Maeve stepped up and wobbled, but Gray placed his hand on her back to steady her before she fell back to the ground. She gave him a grateful smile.

As Gray and Thomas climbed in behind her, she marveled at the interior of the hovercar. Where the outside was boxy, the inside was sleek and sparkling. She ran her hand across the back of one of the metal seats and squinted her eyes against the glare of the sun reflecting off the seat.

"What is this place?" she whispered to Gray.

Gray leaned his head close to her ear. "I don't know, but I'm not sure I trust it."

Ginger looked anxiously out the back window of the hovercar, watching Emery and Rufus board the one behind them.

"How will Emery's car know where we're going?" Ginger asked Elton.

"They have autopilot," Elton said. "I told her what to do to sync up with our car."

Maeve gave Ginger a one-armed hug. "She's good with technology. She'll be OK."

"Plus she has Rufus," Thomas chimed in. "He'll make sure nothing happens to her."

Ginger leaned into Maeve's hug, took a deep breath and straightened her spine. "She'll be fine," she said without conviction.

Tristan leaned down to look in Ginger's eyes. "She *will* be fine. She's smart and strong. And like Thomas said, she has Rufus. Her car will be tied into ours. Nothing's going to happen to her."

Ginger took another deep breath and straightened her shoulders. Looking directly at Tristan, she said in a strong voice, "You're right. She'll be fine." She sent a pointed look toward Elton and muttered under her breath, "She'd better be."

Elton ignored her and began to fiddle with the controls at the front of their hovercar. Gray watched him closely.

"Where are we going?" Gray asked.

"There's a building in the city center that was a research lab. We might find what we're looking for there."

Gray looked out the front window and surveyed the city below. "If there was an antidote, why didn't the government of Bellus use it?"

Elton's hands paused over the controls. "I heard rumors that some people had gotten it, but those people just disappeared. Everyone just assumed they had died from the disease, too."

"Should we be worried about touching things?" Tristan asked. "Are we going to get sick from using this hovercar?"

Elton shook his head. "That's what was so weird about the whole thing. They told us you could only catch it from someone else, and they had to touch you. It should have been easy to stop, but everyone died."

Tristan leaned against the side of the car. "How long did it take for the disease to spread."

"About a month. Some people got it and died quickly. Others got it and lingered for a week. No one knows what the difference was."

Gray watched Elton closely. "How did you and Shalara avoid getting it?"

Elton hesitated, then shrugged. "Just lucky, I guess. Our parents were some of the last ones to get sick. They were making preparations to leave, so they just sent me and

Shalara out into the desert, hoping we would make it to Palumbra."

Ginger continued to peer out the rear of the car. Emery gave her a quick wave from the console of her hovercar. "What about Sarge and his friends? How did they survive?"

"I don't know." Elton pulled on a lever with a red knob on top, and the car started to move. "It makes me wonder if other people survived, too. You guys might want to sit down. Sometimes there are air pockets on the trip down the hill, and it can be a little bumpy."

Maeve and Gray sat on one seat while Tristan and Thomas took the rear-facing seat. Ginger remained at the back window.

"Come on, Ginger," Tristan coaxed. "Sit with us. You can see Emery's car just fine from this seat, and you won't have to brace yourself to keep from falling."

Ginger gave Tristan a dubious look, but carefully made her way to the seat in the swaying car. They were quickly gaining speed as they plunged down the hill toward the city.

"Have you ever driven one of these before?" Gray asked Elton.

Elton didn't answer immediately.

"Elton?" Maeve asked.

"Um. Not exactly."

"What do you mean 'not exactly'?" Ginger jumped to her feet and quickly grabbed the back of the seat to keep from falling.

"Well, I've taken the training class, but you can't drive a hovercar until you're 18."

"That's my sister back there. She's sick, and you're

telling me you've never actually driven one of these?"
Ginger took a threatening step toward Elton. The gesture
lost some of its menace when she swayed and almost fell
as the ride got faster and bumpier. "You had better hope
nothing happens to her."

Elton gave Ginger a fearful look and went back to
working the controls. Tristan tugged on Ginger's hand and
motioned to her seat. "There's nothing we can do now. Sit
and let Elton do his best. You can beat him to a pulp when
we get there."

"Can you believe that guy?" Ginger sat with a huff.

"He did get us this far," Maeve said.

"Are you defending him?" Ginger asked in
disbelief.

Maeve crossed her arms in front of her chest. "I'm
just saying that he's doing the best that he can. We don't
have any choice now except to trust that he's going to get
us down this hill and into the city."

"Why exactly are we trusting him?" Gray asked in
a quiet voice. While the hovercar was fast and sleek, it was
also loud. Between the rumble of the engine and the air
rushing by outside, it was unlikely Elton could hear them.

"What choice do we have?" Maeve asked.

"We could let him take us into the city and then
part ways," Tristan suggested.

"How does that help us?" Maeve pointed toward
the hovercar behind them. "We need to find the antidote for
Emery – quickly. We don't know where to even start
looking." She gestured with her head toward Elton. "He
does."

"He says he does." Ginger's voice dripped with
skepticism.

"Like I said, what choice do we have?"

Gray opened his mouth to speak, but Thomas interrupted him when he jumped to his feet, grabbing Tristan's arm to stay upright. He pointed toward the back window. "That can't be right. What's going on with Emery's car?"

CHAPTER TWENTY-THREE

Ginger jumped up from her seat, stumbling against Tristan's legs as the hovercar made a swift turn.

"Stop! What is Emery's car doing?"

Elton frantically pushed buttons and twisted knobs on the hovercar's control panel.

"Where is her car going?" Ginger plastered both hands against the rear window and pressed her nose against the glass. She pounded on the glass. "Emery!"

The hovercar made another swift turn, and Ginger was thrown against the side of the car. Tristan and Thomas helped her up and all three peered out the back window where Emery's hovercar was moving away from their car. They could see Emery's face frozen in terror as she worked the controls, Rufus glued to her side.

Ginger pounded the window again. "Emery!" Her voice broke. "We should never have let her go alone."

Gray and Maeve were standing over Elton. "Get that car back, now." Maeve's voice and hands shook.

Elton looked up, and Maeve could see the panic in his eyes. "I'm trying. I don't know what's wrong with the tethering controls. It's like someone else is driving that car."

"Could someone else have taken control of the car?" Gray asked. His voice was so calm, Maeve had to look at him to see the muscle tensing in his cheek and the vein pulsing in his forehead to know he was angry. He clenched and unclenched his fist as if trying to decide whether to use it to punch Elton.

"I don't know. I guess. Maybe." Elton's voice faded away.

"Who could have control of her car?" Gray spaced out each word as if he were talking to a small child.

Elton continued to work the controls. "It would have to be someone with access to the transportation control center."

Ginger lurched her way to the front of the car. "I thought you said everyone was dead. How could someone have access to the control center?"

Elton refused to take his gaze off the controls. "I guess more people survived than I thought."

"Glad we figured that out now." Tristan's voice dripped with sarcasm.

"Turn around and follow Emery," Ginger demanded.

Elton's shoulders drooped. "I can't." His voice was little more than a whisper.

Ginger leaned forward. "What do you mean you can't?" Her voice seemed to rise an octave with each word.

"That's my sister. Of course you can."

Thomas tugged on Maeve's hand. "Don't forget Rufus."

Maeve gave his hand a reassuring squeeze and looked down into his face. "We won't forget Rufus, I promise."

"The controls aren't responding." Elton pressed another button and turned another dial. "We can only go to the location I programmed in."

"So, let me get this straight," Gray said. "Emery's car is driving itself, and our car is stuck on a single location? We don't know who's actually driving these cars, and we don't know where Emery is going to end up."

"And Emery's sick," Ginger interrupted.

"That's about right," Elton said. He gave a button on the console one last tap and turned to face the group. "I never thought this would happen. I'm sorry."

"We don't have time for you to be sorry." Tristan leaned over the console to peer out the front window. The city that had seemed so far away was fast approaching. "We need to figure out how to get out of this car before it gets to wherever you programmed it to go. Whoever has taken over the control of the cars knows exactly where we're going. Can you slow it down?"

Elton shook his head. "The controls are locked. Everything is on autopilot now."

"Do we know when it's going to slow down? It can't keep up this speed on city roads." Gray scanned the console looking for anything that might look like a brake.

"It might slow down when we turn the corner to get to the research facility, but it would be really close to the building." Elton glanced out the window to the buildings that were now flashing by then turned back to Gray. "We really need to get off this thing before then."

"What's that?" Thomas's voice rose from the floor where he had sat down to keep from falling as the hovercar raced through the city.

"What do you see?" Maeve asked.

"That thing sticking up from the floor under the console." Thomas pointed at a pedal on the floor that was protected by a plastic case. Across the top of the plastic case was the word Emergency.

Gray leaned down to look at where Thomas was pointing. He flipped the manual latch and lifted off the plastic case. The pedal was about a foot long, with rods that stretched from the bottom into the floor. "What happens if we press it?"

Elton leaned forward in his chair and peered at the pedal. "I don't know. I've never seen anyone use it."

"They don't cover the emergency protocols in the training class?" Ginger asked.

Elton looked sheepish. "Well, it might have been a stretch to say that I had completed the training. I went to a single class."

Ginger's entire body radiated anger. "You had better hope we find my sister safe and sound. Because if we don't..." Each word dropped from Ginger's mouth like ice, and Elton shivered.

"We'll find her, Ginger," Maeve said, stepping between Elton and Ginger.

"I think we should step on it," Tristan said, drawing their attention back to the emergency pedal.

"What other choice do we have?" Gray asked. "Hopefully, it's some kind of braking mechanism. You guys find something to hold onto, and I'll step on it."

The rest of the group backed away to the seats. Maeve and Thomas sat on one of the sleek, shiny seats. Thomas wrapped his arms around Maeve's waist, and she wrapped hers around the pole at the back of the seat. Tristan and Ginger sat on the seat facing them, with their arms wrapped around another pole. Elton sat alone in the driver's seat with his hands gripping the console. Gray wedged his fingers into the netting covering the window and stomped on the pedal.

Maeve gritted her teeth as the sound of shrieking metal pierced her ears. The hovercar slowed, and just when Maeve thought it would stop, it began a slow turn, the back of the car spinning toward the front as if in slow motion. The car tipped to its side and began to barrel roll. Glass broke and shards showered throughout the car, slicing her skin. She ducked her chin into her chest and squeezed her eyes shut. Her muscles strained with effort as she fought to maintain her grip on the pole. She could hear the others screaming as the hovercar rolled over and over again in a seemingly endless cycle. Finally, the car came to a halt with a thud.

Maeve took inventory of her bruised body and looked around. Her arms ached from holding onto the pole, and she only hoped the others were OK. She could feel Thomas still squeezing her waist, and she looked down to find blood streaming from his hairline into his eyes. "Are you OK?"

Thomas nodded, raising dazed eyes to hers. Gingerly, she removed her arms from around the pole and cautiously brushed glass from Thomas's hair. She unlatched his arms from around her waist, stood and took stock of the hovercar, or what was left of it. Glass from the windows covered the interior, making the floor look as if it was covered in crystals glittering in the sun. Tristan and Ginger were in a heap in the corner of the car, trying to disentangle their limbs without cutting themselves on the glass.

"Don't move," Maeve said to Thomas who nodded in response.

Stepping carefully, she crossed the car to Tristan and Ginger. She pulled Ginger to her feet as Tristan steadied himself with a hand on the side of the car as he, too, rose unsteadily to his feet. "Are you two OK?"

Ginger brushed glass off her shoulder and shook out her ponytail. Glass shards hit the metal floor with a clink. "I think so. You might need to look at Tristan. He's got a good bump on his head."

Maeve gave Tristan a quick once-over. "Can you walk?"

Tristan nodded, then winced and grabbed at the wall again. "I'll be fine, but you'd better check on Gray and Elton."

Maeve looked toward where Gray had pressed the emergency pedal but didn't see Gray or Elton. Tristan placed both hands on her shoulders and turned her the other direction, toward the back of the car. Gray lay sprawled face down on the floor while Elton was slumped motionless in the corner next to him. As quickly as she could, she made her way across the glass to Gray, ignoring the small cuts on her arms that were oozing blood. Unable to kneel next to his prone form, she crouched down next to him.

"Gray." She gently shook his shoulder. "Come on,

Gray. You need to wake up."

Glancing over her shoulder at Ginger, she said, "I need a jacket or blanket or something so I can roll him over on this glass."

Ginger looked around for their backpacks, which were strewn about the car. She grabbed the closest pack and pulled a blanket that was blessedly free of glass from it and tossed it to Maeve. Maeve laid the blanket over the glass on the ground next to Gray then as gently as she could rolled him onto his back. He groaned as she positioned him on the blanket. Maeve gasped when she saw the bruises and cuts that covered his face. A large cut across the bridge of his nose was pouring blood, making it almost impossible for Maeve to see the rest of his injuries. She used a corner of the blanket to apply pressure to his nose, and he groaned again.

"Gray?"

"Maeve?"

"What happened?" Gray slowly sat up, blinking his eyes like an owl.

"I guess that was the emergency brake. It may have done the job a little too well." Maeve pulled the edge of the blanket away, relieved to see that the blood flowing from the bridge of Gray's nose was stopping. "Here, hold this on your nose." She gave Gray the edge of the blanket and moved around him to look at Elton, who hadn't moved or made a sound since the car had rolled to a stop.

She felt along his neck with her fingers, letting out a sigh of relief when she found a pulse. "Elton?"

Elton remained silent, his chin slumped to his chest, and his body listing to the left. By the time Maeve had checked him over for broken bones, Gray was crouched next to her, still holding the blanket to his nose.

"What's wrong with him?"

"He must have hit his head." Maeve pointed to where his right wrist lay at an odd angle to his arm. "His wrist is definitely broken. I should probably splint that while he's still knocked out. It's not going to feel good."

She turned back toward Tristan and Ginger. Thomas had joined them at the side of the car, and Ginger was holding the edge of another blanket to the gash on his head. "What do we have that I can use as a splint?"

Holding onto the edge of the car to steady himself, Tristan gathered up the scattered backpacks. Ginger gave Thomas the blanket to hold on his head and began to rummage through the packs. "Will this work?" Ginger held up a couple of short sticks.

"Where did those come from?" Maeve asked.

"I threw them in my pack to use if we needed to start a fire," Gray said. Slowly, he used the back of the seat behind him to push to a standing position. He swayed slightly, then steadied. Ginger handed him the sticks, and he passed them on to Maeve.

"I'll need something to hold them on his arm. Maybe a sock or two?"

Ginger dug in the pack again and pulled out two socks. She passed them to Gray who again handed them off to Maeve.

Maeve looked at Elton and took a deep breath then reached for his injured arm. Holding her breath and wishing she could be gentle, she moved his broken bones back into alignment. Just as she slid his wrist so that it lined up with his arm bones, Elton let out a groan. "Someone needs to hold onto him," Maeve said quickly.

"I've almost got it, but if he moves, I'll have to do it all again."

Gray and Tristan moved with the speed of old men but managed to position themselves on either side of Elton and hold him still. "Tristan, I need the knife."

Tristan pulled the knife out of the sheath on his belt and handed it to her so she could use it to poke holes for Elton's fingers in one of the socks. She positioned the splints, then pulled both the splints and his hand through the sock. She took the other sock and tied it around his arm to hold everything in place.

"That's a terrible splint, but it will have to do. Now we just need him to wake up." As she said the words, Elton's eyes fluttered open. "Wh, what happened?"

"Um, guys." Ginger turned from the window with wide eyes. "We need to get out of here now." As she spoke, Ginger herded Thomas toward the empty window on the other side of the car. With the door a twisted mass of metal, the window was their only way out.

"What's out there?" Tristan asked, using one hand to brace himself as he moved to look out the side of the car Ginger had just moved away from. Tristan glanced out the window then handed Maeve and Gray their packs. He shouldered Elton's pack along with his own. "We're about to have company. Let's get moving."

Gray stood and hoisted Elton to his feet. "Questions later. We've got to go."

Maeve positioned herself on Elton's other side and together they helped him to the window. Ginger had already hoisted Thomas through the empty window frame and laid a blanket over the edge to keep the rest of them from cutting themselves on the jagged glass. Ginger clambered out of the car and held out her hand to help a still unsteady Tristan over the edge.

"Elton," Maeve said. "We have to climb over the edge of the car. Can you do it?"

Elton stared at Maeve with pain-glazed eyes that didn't seem to comprehend anything she said. "You go first," Maeve said to Gray. "I'll keep him steady until you can help him over the edge."

"I don't like you being the last one in the car. Why don't you go first?"

"There is no way I can help him over the side of the car. I'm not that strong. You'll have to go first. Together, you and Tristan can do it. I'll be fine."

Gray glanced over his shoulder. "Maeve..."

"Don't argue. We don't have time. Just go."

The muscle in Gray's cheek twitched, but he climbed over the edge of the car. Together, he and Tristan helped Elton out of the car as well. Maeve could see people approaching the opposite window as she supported Elton to keep him from falling backward. Finally, Elton was on the outside of the car.

"Your turn, Maeve. Let's go." Gray reached his hand back through the window for her. She grasped it and began to hoist herself up through the window.

"Halt!" came a voice from behind her.

CHAPTER TWENTY-FOUR

Maeve grabbed Gray's hand and hurled herself through the window, wincing as pain shot through her shins and knees as she hit the ground hard on the other side.

"Halt!" came the cry from inside the wrecked hovercar.

"Get moving!" Gray whispered with a hand on Maeve's back to propel her along. Ahead of them, Ginger and Tristan were helping Elton as Thomas sprinted ahead of them. Maeve and Gray quickly gained on the others.

Gray looked over his shoulder and urged the group onward. "We have to move faster."

Maeve chanced a backward look to see three men armed with guns gingerly climbing over the edge of the hovercar. One of them spoke into a microphone at his shoulder.

"I think they're calling for help." Every time her feet struck the ground, Maeve could feel the aches and bruises throughout her body from their roller coaster ride in the hovercar. She could only imagine how Elton and Tristan felt. Next to her, Gray's breath was coming in gasps, which surprised her since he and Tristan trained every day. She was easily keeping pace with him, which shouldn't be possible. She was a quick runner, but she wasn't faster than Gray. Usually, he slowed his steps to keep in stride with her, but she found herself shortening her stride to stay with him. Ahead of her, Elton was clearly struggling to put one foot in front of the other, and Tristan wobbled even as he tried to steady Elton. "We have to find some place to hide."

Gray nodded as he struggled to breathe and keep a steady pace. She looked at him with concern, chanced another glance over her shoulder, then sped up to reach Ginger, Tristan and Elton. As she drew alongside Ginger, they shared a worried look. "Elton," Maeve said. "We need a place to hide."

Elton's face was pale and drawn. Pain tightened his features, and he looked at Maeve as if he didn't understand what she was saying. "Elton," Maeve said again. "We have to get off this street."

When he still didn't respond, she scanned the buildings on either side of her, looking for any place that might offer them refuge, but all she saw was building after building of clear glass. Even if they could get into the buildings, the glass exterior would offer little in the way of protection from their pursuers.

"Thomas," she called. "Turn right." Thomas made a hard right onto the next street, and everyone else followed. She only hoped this street offered more possibilities for a hiding place than the last one. Elton, Gray and Tristan were getting noticeably slower, and Maeve could hear the men with guns gaining on them. Her gaze scanned along the buildings as she ran. Thomas looked back at her, and she saw his eyes widen at what she assumed were the men chasing them. As he turned his attention back to the street in front of him, he stumbled and fell. Maeve sprinted to him, reaching a hand down to help him up as she ran. But instead of grabbing her hand, he motioned at something on the side of the street.

"Maeve, look." He pointed toward a grate. Instead of getting to his feet, he rolled toward the drain and tugged on the grate. "Help me."

Not sure what Thomas was doing, Maeve took another look back to see the men had just turned the corner onto the street.

"What are we doing?"

"If we can get this grate off, we can get in there and hide." Thomas tugged on the grate again.

Understanding dawned, and Maeve crouched next to him and pulled with all her might. Ginger, Tristan, Elton and Gray caught up with them. When Gray saw what they were trying to do, he and Tristan added their weight to the grate, and their combined strength moved the grate out of the way. Before Maeve could stop him, Thomas quickly jumped through the hole, which was just large enough for a person to squeeze through.

"Oof."

"Are you OK?" Maeve called.

"Yes, hurry up. Be careful. It's kind of a hard landing."

Maeve pulled Ginger forward. "You next."

Ginger sat on the edge of the hole and, bracing her hands on the side, dropped through.

"Gray, Tristan, help Elton." Maeve leaned over the hole. "Ginger, help Elton drop down."

Gray and Tristan lowered Elton through the hole

then jumped through after him. Maeve took one last look at the men behind them. The drain was hidden from view by a curve in the road, and the men were slowed by their careful search through the windows of each building. Maeve sat on the edge of the hole and pulled the grate toward her, wincing at the noise the metal made against the pavement.

"Come on, Maeve." Gray's voice floated up from beneath her. With one hand on the grate, she pushed off and dropped through the hole, doing her best to pull the heavy grate over the hole as she fell. She landed with a thud on her already bruised knees in a pool of shallow water. She rose to her feet, feeling as if she had suddenly replaced her knees with Emma's eight-decade-old ones.

"Is everyone OK?" Maeve asked. She squinted as she waited for her eyes to adjust to the dim light.

"We're no worse than we were," Gray said from somewhere off to her right. "Do you think they'll notice the grate is off?" The shadowy figure Maeve assumed was Gray pointed up to the opening where despite Maeve's best efforts, the grate only partially covered the hole.

"Let's hope not." She shrugged. "There's not much we can do about it now. We should move away from the opening so if they look in, they don't see us."

"Everyone else went this way." Gray pointed at a passageway to his left, and they moved toward the opening to the passage. Now that her eyes had adjusted to the light, she could see that they were in what must be a storm drain. The walls were curved concrete, and three inches of water covered the ground, making the passageway slippery.

"Are you OK?" The cut on Gray's nose had opened again, making Gray look as if he was crying blood.

He waved away her concern. "It's worse than it

looks. I'll be fine."

"How's your head?"

"It hurts."

"We need a place to rest." Maeve abruptly stopped talking.

"What?"

"Shh." She held up her hand and stood still to stop her feet from splashing in the water. Faint voices filtered through the air, coming from behind them.

"Do you think they're in the tunnel?" Gray whispered.

She shook her head. The voices were too far away to make out the words. She and Gray waited silently for the sound of the grate being pulled away from the drain, but it never came. The voices gradually faded, and Maeve let out a relieved breath.

"Come on, let's find the others." She slipped her hand into Gray's and began sloshing her way down the passageway.

They found the others about 1,000 yards down the passageway, sitting in an alcove off the main passage where the ground sloped up enough to remain dry. Elton sat with his back against the wall and his eyes closed. Tristan leaned against the wall and talked to Ginger as Maeve and Gray approached. Thomas stood in the middle of the passageway keeping watch for Maeve and Gray, and his shoulders slumped with relief as they approached.

"Did the men follow us?" His eyes flitted from Maeve to Gray and back again.

"We don't think so." Maeve gave him a hug. "We heard them, but we never heard the grate move."

She moved into the alcove. "How is everyone?"

Tristan pushed himself away from the wall. "We're in rough shape. I think we need to take a minute and assess the situation."

Ginger began to pace back and forth in the small space. "We can't. We have to find Emery."

Tristan gentled his voice. "Ginger, we don't know where she is, and we can't keep going like this." He motioned to Elton and Gray. "None of us are able to move quickly or think well."

"Maeve, tell him we have to find Emery."

Maeve moved toward her friend and forced her to stop pacing. "Ginger, Tristan is right. If we're going to find Emery, we have to be able to think clearly – and move quickly. Let's just take a few minutes to look at everyone's injuries and create a plan."

Gray moved into the alcove and slid down the wall to a sitting position. "And let's eat something." He pulled off his pack and began rummaging through it.

Ginger backed away from Maeve. "I can't believe you guys. How can you want to just sit here and do nothing when Emery is in danger? She's sick." Her voice cracked. "She could be dying. And who knows what whoever took control of her car wants to do to her." She turned on Gray. "And you want to stop and have a snack?"

Elton opened his eyes. "I think I know where they took her."

Ginger whirled around to face Elton. "Why didn't you speak up before now?"

"Ginger, we're all worried about Emery," Maeve said. "But when would Elton have told us anything? The hovercar wrecked right after Emery's car turned away. Let's just listen to what he has to say now."

Ginger glared at Elton but motioned for him to speak.

"You guys were right when you said this city is built like a hub. There are six 'spokes' to the 'wheel'. Each spoke leads to the center." Elton paused and closed his eyes again.

Maeve rummaged in her pack and handed him a protein paste bar and a canteen. "What's in the center?"

"The Info Hub." At their perplexed looks, Elton took a bite of the protein paste bar and continued. "The Info Hub is the control center of Bellus. Surely you've noticed that Bellus runs on pretty advanced technology."

Thomas took a canteen from Maeve. "Yeah. This place is way better than Palumbra."

Elton took a sip of water. "The Info Hub is where the city leaders control everything. If someone got control of Emery's hovercar, I'm sure they took her there."

Ginger walked to the mouth of the alcove with a purposeful stride. "OK, if that's where she is, then let's go."

Tristan handed his canteen to Ginger. "Just a minute. We can't just waltz into the Info Hub and demand that they give us Emery. They have superior technology and guns. We have a knife."

"We can't just sit here and talk. We have to do something."

"Ginger," Gray said. "We have more than one problem to solve here."

"What are you talking about? We have to find Emery."

Maeve set a gentle hand on Ginger's arm. "We also need to find the antidote. Emery is still sick."

Ginger's shoulders slumped, and she stared at the ground. She swallowed hard. When she raised her head, defeat shone from her eyes. "She's going to die, isn't she? No matter what we do, we can't save her."

Thomas stood and slipped his hand into Ginger's. "My mom alway said, 'Hope only dies when you give up.' We're not giving up."

Maeve leaned her head against the wall of the passageway and closed her eyes. The conversation drifted around her.

"We have two problems." Tristan's voice came from across the small alcove where he sat next to a calmer, but still impatient, Ginger. "We need to find Emery, and we need to find the antidote. We're going to have to split up."

Gray shifted next to Maeve. "I don't like the idea of splitting up. We don't know the city. What if something goes wrong? How will we ever find each other again?"

"I know the city." Elton's voice was little more than a thready whisper. "I can get us where we need to go."

"You can barely move." Ginger's voice was filled with concern. "How are you going to lead us anywhere?"

Elton let out a sigh. "No one said anything about leading, but I can give you directions. I think it's best if I just stay here."

Maeve opened her eyes and leaned forward to look at Elton, who was sitting on the other side of Gray. She had done her best to treat all their injuries. Besides his broken wrist, Elton definitely had a concussion, and she suspected Tristan did, as well. Gray seemed remarkably unscathed other than the cut across the bridge of his nose and a twisted ankle that had slowed him down. Thomas's head sported a bandage from the meager first aid supplies Maeve had scrounged from the hidden bunker in the desert. "I don't think leaving you here by yourself is an option. What would you do if someone found you?"

Elton slowly turned his head to look at Maeve, wincing with the motion. "Tell them I fell into the open hole and broke my wrist and that I was waiting for someone to find me."

Gray leaned forward and looped his arms over his knees. "Honestly, that's probably the best option. We can leave him some food and water and come back for him when everything is safe."

Maeve narrowed her eyes at Gray. "Are you serious? You would just leave him here?"

"Keep your voice down. We don't want anyone to find us."

"Don't shush me. Why would you even consider leaving him?"

Gray put a hand on her shoulder, but Maeve shook him off. "Maeve, he can barely walk. His hand is useless. He's much safer here than he is with us."

Maeve started to speak, but Gray held up a hand. "Let me finish. What would happen to Elton if we had to run again? We barely made it here."

Tristan stood and dusted his hands off on his pants. "He's right, Maeve. We're not just worried about him slowing us down. We're worried about him. He's not up for running or even a lot of walking."

"I'll be fine." Elton's voice steadied a bit, as if he was trying to convince Maeve of his ability to fend for himself through the strength of his voice.

"I could stay with him," Thomas volunteered.

Maeve shook her head. "Uh, uh. No way. You're sticking with me."

Gray pursed his lips, and Maeve knew he was considering Thomas's statement. "It's a good solution."

"Gray, he's 10! You're going to leave the 10-year-old here to help the guy who only has one good hand and can barely walk. How is that logical?"

Thomas drew himself up to his full height. "This 10-year-old made it all the way across the desert and rescued you. I think I can hang out in a storm drain for a couple of hours by myself. Let me help. Please."

Maeve looked into Thomas's pleading eyes. She knew Thomas could take care of himself, but every instinct she had was screaming at her not to leave him behind.

"I'll look out for him, Maeve." Elton's voice was weak but confident. "We'll be fine. No one knows we're down here. We'll just wait for you guys to come back. If you don't show up by morning, we'll come find you."

Maeve chewed on the skin on the side of her thumb as she considered Elton's promise. Finally, she nodded and ruffled Thomas's hair. "OK. But you stay right here. No wandering off."

"Got it." Thomas grinned. "We'll be fine."

CHAPTER TWENTY-FIVE

"Don't move." Gray flattened himself against the side of the building and held out his arm to keep Maeve from going any farther. Maeve followed his lead and tried to shrink into the side of the glass building as well.

"What is it?" Maeve breathed out the words in an almost-whisper.

Gray shook his head and put a finger on his lips.

They were following one of the streets that made up the spokes that led toward the center of the city. Until now, they hadn't seen a soul. Either the plague had killed everyone or everyone was in hiding. The sun had set several hours ago and after grabbing a quick nap in the alcove, she and Gray had bade goodbye to Elton and Thomas and ventured back to street level with Ginger and Tristan. Elton had given them a quick overview of how the city was laid out and had provided specific instructions on how to get to the research facility. Tristan and Ginger had received similar instructions on how to get to the Info Hub, which was the most likely place to start searching for Emery. Once they reached the surface, Tristan and Ginger had headed east to use another spoke to reach the Info Hub.

Maeve opened her mouth to speak again but

snapped it shut when she heard footsteps marching along the street beyond the corner where they were hiding. Barely daring to breathe, she watched as a line of people marched in lockstep down the street. After they passed, Gray said, "I guess there are more people here than we thought. There are a lot of things about this place that don't add up."

Maeve thought for a moment. "You mean like the fact that they have all this advanced technology, and Palumbra isn't even close to this advanced."

Gray nodded. "And the story about the plague that Elton has been telling us. There's just something off about it. How did it kill everyone? And how did Elton avoid it? His parents and his sister died from it. If it's that contagious, why didn't he catch it? And why haven't we? We were all in that bunker together with Shalara, but only Emery got sick."

"You don't think Elton is lying do you?" Maeve's voice held a note of panic. "We left Thomas with him."

"I don't think he's a threat in his current condition, but I don't know what to think about him in general." He motioned in the direction the marchers had taken. "I do know that there's more going on here than we've been told."

Maeve worried the skin at the side of her thumb. "Maybe we should go back and get Thomas."

Gray pulled her into his side and gave her a reassuring hug. "We can do that, but it will take time away from looking for the antidote. What do you want to do?"

Maeve stared at the ground and let out a sigh. "I don't know." She looked up at Gray, her brown eyes troubled. "How do I choose between them?"

Gray pulled her hand away from her mouth, where she had chewed on the skin on her thumb until it bled. "Do you think Thomas can get away from Elton if he needs to?"

She stepped out of Gray's comforting embrace and considered his question. Finally, she nodded. "I do think that he can. Elton's injuries would make it impossible for him to move quickly." She leaned once again against the glass of the building behind her. "I guess our best option is to go forward, look for the antidote and get back to Thomas as quickly as possible." She nodded again, as if convincing herself. "Let's go."

Gray adjusted his pack on his shoulders. "You sure?"

Maeve took two determined strides toward the corner. "I'm sure."

Gray stopped so suddenly that Maeve bumped into his back. "What are you doing?"

He took her hand and pulled her up to his side. Her eyes widened. "What is this?"

Gray shook his head. "I have no idea."

Before them stood a crumbling stone structure, completely out of place in the middle of the sea of glass buildings that comprised the streets of Bellus. Maeve moved toward the building, running her hand over the remains of the front wall. "Why would they have left this here when everything else is so modern?"

Stone crunched under Gray's boots as he joined her in examining the structure. "Maybe it's a reminder."

"But a reminder of what?" Maeve ducked under the crumbling arch and entered what was left of the building.

"Wow," Gray whispered.

"What is this place?"

The interior of the building no longer had a roof, but three of the four walls still stood taller than Maeve's head. Those walls were covered with some of the most beautiful artwork she had ever seen. The paintings showed a man talking with children and feeding a crowd of people. While the colors had faded over the years, the attention to detail showed in the laugh lines around the man's mouth and the expressions on the children's faces.

Maeve traced the outline of the man's face with her finger. "Who would let this masterpiece just crumble to the ground?"

"Someone who is more interested in power than art," a soft female voice said.

Maeve and Gray whirled around to face the new voice, inching closer together to present a united front. Gray reached toward his waist, seeking a weapon that wasn't there.

A slim, almost ghostlike woman dressed all in white slipped from the shadows in the back corner of the building. She seemed to float across the ground, and Maeve fleetingly wondered how she managed to keep the hem of her dress from getting dirty as it dragged on the dirt floor. The woman held out her hands so they could see she held no weapon.

"Please," she said in a voice that reminded Maeve of music. "I mean you no harm."

"Who are you?" Gray asked.

"I'm the keeper of the sanctum, or I used to be."

"What happened here?" Maeve made a sweeping motion with her arm.

The woman shook her head. "This is not new destruction. When the invading army came to Bellus, this sanctum was a refuge for the city's defenders. Always before, the sanctum had been a place of sanctuary. Once inside its walls, no one could touch you."

"Even if you had committed a crime?" Maeve asked.

The woman nodded. "Even then. But you must understand Bellus was a peaceful place. Everyone had enough of what they needed. There was very little crime. Our sanctums were used mostly to escape unpleasant domestic situations or as a refuge for those needing time to themselves to sort things out. Never before had we faced a war."

"Things clearly didn't end well." Gray pointed toward the broken front wall.

The keeper of the sanctum folded her hands in front of her and took a deep breath. It was as if the retelling was physically painful to her. "No. The invaders had no respect for our sanctums. They broke down the walls and captured our defenders."

"But why did they leave this building when they rebuilt everything else?" Maeve glanced up at the glass skyscrapers towering over the roofless building.

"So that the people of Bellus would know that there is no refuge from the invaders."

"But that had to have been a long time ago. This building has clearly been in ruins for some time." Gray examined a protrusion from the wall that might have once held a candle or light.

"The invaders haven't forgotten, and neither did the people of Bellus."

"But why do they let you stay here?" Maeve asked.

"I have only recently returned here. My family have been sanctum keepers for five generations, but we have been in hiding. Then the plague hit. I'm the only one left." She turned her gaze to her hands and blinked back tears.

"But the people of Bellus and the invaders created a new society." Gray swept his hand to encompass the city outside the broken door.

The Keeper shook her head sadly. "The invaders did. The people of Bellus either went underground or they became slaves to the invaders. The people that took sanctuary in this room were the last of the Bellus fighters. They took the words on the wall to heart." She pointed at the gold lettering on the wall.

Maeve moved closer so she could read the elegantly inscribed words. "Greater love has no man than this, that he lay down his life for his friends."

The Keeper ran her hand over the word love. "Fifty Bellus defenders took sanctuary in this room, but when the walls were breached, none of them surrendered or ran away. Instead, they sent the children whose parents had left them here to safety through the back door. Then they returned to the fight. As others sought sanctuary here, the defenders made sure they were also sent to safety. The invaders whittled them down one by one. Each defender laying his life down for his friends." She turned her back on the wall. "In the end, there were none left, and the last sanctum lay in ruins."

Maeve read the words again, her lips moving silently in tribute to the brave defenders who so long ago had done their best to protect those they loved.

"But why are you here now?" Gray's voice interrupted Maeve's thoughts.

"I have nowhere else to go. This is my calling, to protect the sanctum for those needing sanctuary. Is that you?"

Maeve raised her eyebrows at Gray, wondering what he would tell this mysterious Keeper about their quest.

"No sanctuary for us, I'm afraid. We like to go looking for trouble." The corner of Gray's mouth quirked up in a half smile.

The Keeper returned Gray's smile, and Maeve felt a feeling of peace wash over her.

"May you find what you're looking for – even if it's not what you think you need." The Keeper's musical voice trailed off as she stepped back into the shadows and disappeared out the back entrance.

CHAPTER TWENTY-SIX

Gray tugged on Maeve's hand, signaling that she should stop as they approached the building Elton had identified as the research lab. After leaving the sanctum, they had jogged down the street toward their goal, trying to keep to the shadows of the buildings. While they hadn't seen any cameras, Maeve assumed that with all the technology they had seen so far, Bellus probably had a camera on every corner. She held out little hope that their approach had gone unnoticed.

Gray stood with his back against the window of yet another slick, glass building, scanning the street for signs of life. Nothing stirred except a lone piece of paper tumbling down the street in the first breeze they had felt all day. Maeve welcomed the cool brush of air across her sweaty face.

"What do you think she meant?" Maeve asked.

"Who? The Keeper?"

Maeve nodded. "Yeah. What do you think she meant when she said she hoped we found what we were looking for even if it's not what we think we need. Do you think she knows we're looking for the antidote?"

Gray looked back toward the sanctum. "I have no

idea. She couldn't know what we're doing here. That whole encounter was weird."

Maeve pulled her hair up to let the breeze cool her neck. "Would you do it?"

Gray drew his eyebrows together and shot her a quizzical look. "Do what?"

"Lay down your life for your friends."

Gray thought for a minute, then took her hand. His piercing blue eyes stared into hers, and Maeve felt her heart jump. "I'd lay down my life for you."

Maeve's eyes softened and she squeezed his hand. "And I'd do the same for you."

Gray gave her a quick, hard kiss, squeezed her hand and turned back to observing the research lab building. Maeve was silent as Gray completed his survey of their surroundings. "But would you do it for anyone else?"

He let out an exasperated sigh. "You want to talk about this now? We kind of have a job to do."

She shrugged. "I just think it's interesting to think about. Where is the line? Who would I die for?"

"Well, I don't want you dying for anyone."

"Are you going to answer the question?"

Gray gave up. "I don't really know. Definitely you. Probably Ginger, Tristan and Emery. Beyond that, it's probably a decision you make in the moment."

Maeve cocked her head. "Do you think those defenders made their decision in the moment or did they already know they would sacrifice themselves for other people, no matter who they were?"

Gray closed his eyes briefly and turned to face Maeve. "I really don't know, Maeve. I do know that we have a job to do here." He pointed to the front door of the research lab. "And I'd be really happy if neither of us gave up our lives to do it."

Maeve nodded. "That's my preference, too."

"Great, then can we get moving?"

Maeve nodded again, but her face remained thoughtful.

###

"Can you reach it?" Gray whispered. Maeve was standing on his shoulders, straining to reach an open window.

"Almost. Can you boost me a little higher?"

Gray grimaced and shifted to his tiptoes, his hands tight around her ankles. "Got it!" She wiggled, and he nearly lost his balance.

"Give me a push."

Gray loosened his grip on Maeve's ankles, put his hands on the backs of her feet and boosted her up so the top half of her body slid through the window. She kicked her legs, and the rest of her fell through with a quiet "Oof." After a minute she leaned back through the window and dropped a rope down the side.

"We're good. There's no one in here."

Gray breathed a sigh of relief and grabbed the rope. "Tie the rope to something sturdy."

Maeve disappeared again. When she returned to the window, she gave him a thumbs up, and he braced his feet against the side of the building and began to climb. His arm muscles strained to carry his weight, and Maeve took a brief moment to admire them. When he grabbed the window ledge, Maeve latched on to the back of his shirt and pulled him through the window. They untied the rope and looked around.

The room was exactly what Maeve expected to see in a research lab. Beakers of bubbling liquid sat on one counter while a computer with a large screen filled the desk in front of her.

Gray flipped one of the computers on, settling himself in the chair in front of it.

"Gray, what are you doing?"

"I'm going to see if we can find what we need."

Maeve looked over his shoulder. "Don't you think they're tracking the computers?"

Gray shrugged. "Maybe, but how else are we going to see if the antidote is here. We don't even know exactly what we're looking for."

Maeve chewed on the skin on the side of her thumb and looked anxiously at the door as Gray typed. A piece of paper next to one of the bubbling beakers caught her eye, and she moved over to the table and picked it up.

Her eyes widened as she read. "Gray, I think we can stop looking."

He spun the chair toward her, surprise written on his face. "What have you found?"

She waved the paper at him. "Look at this."

He leaned against the table and took the paper from her then shook his head in disbelief. "This can't be right. It means everything Elton told us about this disease is a lie."

Maeve pointed at a section of the paper. "It's not transmitted through the air or by touching someone. You have to be deliberately infected, either by ingesting the poison or through an injection."

"No wonder none of us caught it." Gray turned the

paper over, looking for more information. "But how did Emery get it?"

"Do you think Elton injected her or put it in something she ate or drank?"

Before Gray could answer, the door flew open. Two men in gray uniforms burst through the door and pointed guns at them. They slowly raised their hands. The click, click, click of high heels broke the silence.

A familiar form filled the doorway. "Hello, again, Maeve, Gray. I wish I could say it was nice to see you."

CHAPTER TWENTY-SEVEN

Maeve stood in stunned silence as she stared into the face of the woman she had hoped never to see again, the woman responsible for the death of Gray's uncle and Ginger and Emery's mom. The new government's forces had searched the desert for her for weeks after the World Government fell but had found no sign of her. The general consensus was that she had fled into the desert and died. The general consensus was spectacularly wrong.

Maeve recovered her voice. "Arabella." The word came out flat and disinterested. She gave the woman a slight nod.

Gray's eyes were still wide with shock. He opened his mouth, then closed it without saying anything. His hands clenched into fists at his side, and Maeve could feel him trembling with anger.

"I bet you're wondering how I came to be here." Arabella raised her arms to encompass the room, her blood-red fingernails sweeping through the air. Maeve had the impression that Arabella was in charge of a lot more than just this room. She stepped farther into the room, her heels making a staccato tap on the tile floor, echoing through the room like a gunshot.

She reached Maeve and Gray and studied them as if examining an interesting specimen under a microscope. "You two couldn't just leave well enough alone, could you? After all the work I've done, I'm not letting the two of you ruin it. Except this time, you've enlisted a few more friends."

Gray finally found his voice. "What do you know about our friends?"

Arabella laughed, a high, tinkling sound that made Maeve think of breaking glass. She ran one of her long fingernails down Gray's cheek. He winced and stepped back as if her touch burned his face. "Oh, Gray. I know everything about you and your friends. I've been watching you since you ran into Sarge."

Maeve stepped forward. The men in gray followed her with their guns. Arabella noticed and waved a hand at the men. "You can put the guns down. These two aren't going anywhere."

"Don't be so sure about that." Maeve struggled to control her shaking hands as she stepped forward again until she was toe to toe with Arabella. Arabella smiled as if amused by Maeve's show of bravado. "How have you been watching us? There are no cameras in the desert."

Arabella towered over Maeve, topping her by at least six inches. She tapped Maeve's nose and peered down at her. "You're right. Except for when someone is carrying one."

Gray took Maeve's hand. Arabella took note of the action, clapped her hands and took a step back. "Oh, that's fabulous. You two are a couple. That makes this so much better." Maeve shivered, wishing Gray hadn't given away their closeness.

Gray drew them back to the original conversation. "How could you know all about us? Sarge is clearly one of your people, but we ditched him in the desert."

Arabella tapped a fingertip against her chin. "Come now. You're both smarter than that. You can figure it out."

Maeve reluctantly said the name of the only other person it could be. "Elton. Elton is working for you."

Arabella clapped her hands together again. "Oh, you're a smart one. I knew you would get it. Would you like to talk to him?"

Arabella beckoned to a shadow in the doorway, and Elton, his arm in a cast and dressed in clean clothes of finer quality than Maeve could ever hope to own, walked confidently through the doorway. He grinned and raised his good hand in a little wave.

"Hi guys. Glad you could join us."

Maeve lunged toward Elton, but Arabella's guards raised their guns, and Gray's hand on her arm pulled her back.

"Ah, ah, ah." Arabella wagged her finger at Maeve. "We can't have that. Elton is injured. It wouldn't be a fair fight."

"Where's Thomas?" Maeve said through gritted teeth, still straining against Gray's restraining arm.

"Thomas?" Arabella pretended to think about Maeve's question, once again tapping that red-tipped finger against her chin. "Oh, your little friend with the dog? He's my guest, although he seems to have lost the dog."

Maeve raised her eyebrows at Gray. She had assumed that Arabella was behind Emery's disappearance, but if Rufus wasn't here, then maybe Emery was still free.

Arabella dashed Maeve's hopes with her next statement.

"The rest of your friends are enjoying our hospitality as well." She held up a hand and ticked their names off on her fingers. "Tristan. Ginger. Emery. And now you two. The old gang back together again. Isn't it wonderful?"

"What do you want with us?" Gray asked, still keeping his hand locked around Maeve's wrist. With every mention of their friends, her body had quivered with the need to attack the evil in front of them.

"What do I want?" Arabella laughed her glass-shattering laugh as if Gray had made the funniest joke she had ever heard. Abruptly, her face sobered, her eyes narrowed and she stepped close to Gray. In a voice filled with hatred she looked directly in his eyes. "I want the five of you dead. It's the only way to get you out of my way."

The guards raised their guns again, fingers on the trigger, ready to fire on Arabella's signal, but she once again waved them away. "Not yet, though. I have plans for you. Not only will the five of you be out of my way, but I can get rid of that pesky new government in Palumbra."

She stepped back and said to Elton, "Take care of them. Make sure they're not together or in the same cells as their friends." She turned her back on them and strode out of the room, the tapping of her heels fading as she moved down the hallway.

"Hello again, friends." Elton motioned with his cast for the guards to take hold of Maeve and Gray. In a flurry of motion, they struggled against their captors until Elton said, "If one of them gives you trouble, shoot the other one. We only need one of them anyway." They both ceased struggling and let the guards bind their hands and lead them out the door.

In the hallway, Maeve's captors marched her down the hallway in the opposite direction from Gray. "Maeve," Gray yelled. "I'll find you."

Before Maeve could answer, her guards turned her down another hallway. "Not if I find you first," Maeve whispered to herself.

Maeve studied the bare white wall of her cell as she sat on the uncomfortable metal cot's thin mattress, her back propped against an identical white wall behind her. She had already investigated every inch of the room, looking for anything that could be used as a weapon to aid in her escape. She moved her gaze to her hands, which she clenched and unclenched into fists and wondered about the fate of her friends. She knew Gray and Tristan could take care of themselves, and Ginger was smart and strong. But what had happened to Emery and Thomas?

She dropped her head into her hands, closed her eyes and took a deep breath. She blamed herself for their troubles. Her need to make amends for killing the WG soldier had drug them into this mess. Oh, Emma and John might have made it sound like they needed them to ferret out who in the government was still loyal to the WG, but she knew the driving force behind their mission was to give her a way to work out her issues. She tipped her head backward until the top of it leaned against the wall. She stared at the ceiling and let out a sigh.

How selfish she'd been. She wasn't the only one of her friends who had faced a devastating situation. Emery and Ginger had watched their mom die. Gray had lost the only family he had. Her problems were different but not more difficult than everyone else's. How had she gotten so caught up in her own problems that she had forgotten everyone else? She lightly tapped her head against the wall. When had she let her friendships become all about her?

And what about Gray? Maeve tapped her head against the wall again, letting the slight pain of hitting her head distract her from the turmoil in her soul. She couldn't believe that she had let him focus so much of his energy on her. After the initial shock of losing Night, they hadn't really talked much about his feelings and how he was coping. His concern had always been for her. And she had let him stuff all his grief away instead of helping him through it. Those were not the actions of someone who loved him.

And she did love him. Why hadn't she told him?

She shook her head in frustration. She had always thought there would be a better time. She wanted the first time she said it to be special, memorable. As she looked around the stark, white cell where she sat all alone awaiting whatever fate Arabella decided to dish out, she wished with all her being that she had told him that she loved him.

"I'm not waiting any longer," she vowed. "No matter the circumstances, I'll tell him if..." She paused, shook her head and continued, "*when* I see him again."

"But I'm not going to see anyone again if I can't get out of here," she muttered as she got to her feet.

She began pacing the 10-foot-by-10-foot space again. She already knew from her previous circuits that it was twelve steps from the back wall to the door. The scuffed, white tile floor was broken up only by the bed and a steel toilet. A steel sink protruded from the wall. The walls were smooth and white, and the expanse of the door was broken only by a slot through which the guards pushed a protein bar every few hours. Maeve had no idea how long she had been in the cell, only that she had been there long enough to have been given four protein bars. She had eaten none of them as she couldn't be sure they were safe. Every time the guards pushed a protein bar through the slot, she tipped her head under the sink faucet and drank, knowing that water was essential to her survival.

As Maeve completed what seemed like her 7,000th lap around the room, no closer to an escape plan than she had been on lap one, a key turned in the lock on her door.

CHAPTER TWENTY-EIGHT

The door opened and two men in gray pointed guns at Maeve. She held her up hands and walked backwards until her back touched the wall.

"What do you want?"

Neither man said a word, but the one on the left looked over his shoulder and motioned to someone with his head. The sharp staccato of high-heeled shoes echoed through the room as Arabella appeared in the doorway. With a flick of her wrist, she dismissed the two men who backed out of the door, closing it behind them.

"Hello, Maeve," Arabella said in her musical, tinkling voice. She took a seat on the bed.

Maeve said nothing.

"Oh, come now, we can't have a conversation if you're not going to talk."

She considered launching herself at Arabella, her eyes flitting to the door, wondering how long it would take the guards to come crashing back through it. Arabella seemed to read her mind.

"I wouldn't try it if I were you. You would be dead in seconds and would miss out on the amazing opportunity I'm about to lay out for you. Why don't you have a seat?"

Arabella smoothed the bed next to her with her long, red fingernails.

Maeve shook her head. "I'd rather stand."

"Suit yourself. Don't you want to know why I'm here?"

Maeve shrugged. "Do I?"

"I'm about to offer you the chance of a lifetime. Granted, if you take it, yours will be a short lifetime, but it's a pretty good offer considering the circumstances."

Maeve crossed her arms over her chest and widened her stance. "If you're just going to kill me anyway, why would I take your offer?"

Arabella scanned her from head to toe and back up. She crossed her legs and dangled one high heel from her toes.

"Why indeed? What if I told you you could save your friends?" Arabella's eyebrows arched above eyes as hard as stone.

Maeve let out a bark of laughter. "Why would I believe you?"

Arabella shrugged. "You make a good point. I've not given you much reason to trust me, but you might just have to take your chances." She uncrossed her legs, leaned forward and said in a loud whisper, "It's the only chance you've got."

Maeve stood motionless, her mind whirling. Several minutes passed in silence, during which Arabella examined her fingernails and Maeve considered her options. Finally, Maeve said, "What would I have to do?"

"Ah. I knew you'd come around."

Maeve just stared at her.

"We would inject you with the virus, of course,

then drop you on the outskirts of Palumbra. You infect the government leaders with the virus, and Palumbra is back in my control." Arabella clapped her hands together, the sound echoing in the small chamber. "Simple, yet effective."

"But the virus isn't contagious unless you're injected on purpose."

Arabella gave her an assessing look. "Figured that out, did you? You might have been in the lab too long before we found you." She grinned. "No worries. Just today we created a special formulation that is much more contagious than the one we used here in Bellus. So, what do you say?"

Maeve stood silent and motionless. Arabella wanted her to trade her own life and the lives of the people in Palumbra for the lives of her friends. She closed her eyes and wrestled with the impossible choice. Finally, she opened her eyes and said, "Emery gets the antidote."

"What?"

"Emery gets the antidote," Maeve repeated. "I won't do it unless Emery gets the antidote. And you let my friends go before you inject me."

Arabella stood and shook her head. "Now we can't do that, sweetheart."

Maeve refused to give up. "Then it's a no go. I won't do it. Kill me now."

Arabella's eyes narrowed, and Maeve could feel the hatred emanating from her. She huffed and said, "Fine. You can watch us drop them off in The Beyond."

"The Beyond?" Maeve stared at Arabella. "They won't last two days in the Beyond. No one even knows what's out there."

Arabella smirked. "Well, not no one. It's the best offer you're going to get. At least your friends will be alive."

She stared into Arabella's emotionless eyes. "Take Emery and Thomas to the oasis before you inject me. They're kids. What kind of trouble are they going to cause?"

Arabella threw her head back and laughed, a high-pitched screech that hurt Maeve's ears. "Are we talking about the same Emery that almost single-handedly took down the WG? No chance."

"Emery gets the antidote. Thomas gets left at the oasis. My friends get dropped off in the Beyond. Before you inject me."

Arabella tapped her blood red fingertip on her chin. "Why would I give you anything? I hold all the cards."

Maeve shook her head. "You obviously need me or you wouldn't be making this offer. My guess is you've created a virus, but you don't want to shoot a missile at Palumbra. Either you don't have missiles or you want this to seem like it just happened. Then you can swoop in with the antidote and be the hero. With the government in Palumbra gone, the people will once again look to you to lead them."

Arabella's eyebrows drew together, and her forehead creased. "Well, aren't you the smart one. I could, of course, just inject one of my men with the virus and send them to Palumbra. But that would be such a waste of good personnel, and there's something poetic about using you since you were so involved in my fall from power."

"Emery gets the antidote, and the others go free."

Arabella stood silent then threw up her hands. "Fine." She tapped on the door, a signal for it to open.

"Let's go tell your friends, shall we?"

Maeve stood next to Arabella, her hands bound behind her, in a large, open room with a high ceiling. The floors and walls were the same stark white as her cell, but the walls were decorated with art, although Maeve thought it was a stretch to call the shiny, twisted pieces of metal art. The room was empty except for Maeve, Arabella and Arabella's two guards, who stood with their guns pointed at Maeve. The door at the other end of the room opened, and Emery stumbled through, her face pale.

Sweat dotted her forehead. She struggled to put one foot in front of the other then fell to her knees where she stayed, unable to push herself off the floor with her hands bound behind her back. Maeve took a step toward her.

"Ah, ah, ah." Arabella held out her arm in front of Maeve to stop her from moving. "She'll be fine in a few minutes."

Maeve glared at Arabella but made no further attempts to go to Emery. Ginger and Tristan came through the door next, accompanied by two guards, one of them sporting the beginning of a bruise around her eye. Ginger hurried over to Emery, and Arabella raised her eyebrows at the guard in a silent question.

"That one." The guard pointed to Ginger. "Took a swing before we could get her hands bound."

Arabella nodded. "You can punish her later."

The guard grinned. Maeve's head swiveled toward Arabella. "But you said..."

Arabella cut her off. "I didn't say what condition I

would leave them in."

Maeve let all the hatred she felt for Arabella show in her eyes and gritted her teeth. She worked the bonds binding her hands.

"Oh, come now." Arabella waved her hand in the direction of Tristan and Ginger. "I promised to leave them alive. You should be happy with that."

"Where are Gray and Thomas?" Maeve said through her gritted teeth.

"They're coming."

Gray stumbled through the door next, shooting a glare at the soldier who had given him a rough shove from behind. His shoulders slumped in relief when he saw Maeve standing next to Arabella. "You OK?" The soldier gave him another shove for talking.

Maeve simply nodded, not wanting Gray to draw the ire of the soldier again.

Finally, Elton walked through the door with his hand on Thomas's shoulder. Thomas winced as Elton gave his shoulder a squeeze, then shook his hand off and ran to stand next to Gray. To Maeve's relief Thomas's hands were unbound. Arabella really didn't see him as a threat. Thomas looked back toward the door as if waiting for someone else. She wondered if he was looking for Rufus. She hadn't seen the dog since he had stayed with Emery, and Arabella hadn't mentioned him. Maeve hoped at least he had gotten away.

The guards moved Tristan, Gray, Thomas, Ginger and Emery to a spot a few feet from where Arabella and Maeve stood. Emery leaned against Ginger who supported her as best she could with her hands tied behind her back. Arabella clapped her hands like a child who had just been told she could have a second helping of dessert.

"I'm so glad you could join us. Maeve and I have come to an agreement."

Gray's worried eyes met Maeve's. "What kind of agreement?" he asked, his eyes never leaving Maeve's face.

"I have agreed to let the five of you live. Isn't that nice of me?"

"You've never been known for being nice," Tristan said derisively. "What's the catch?"

Arabella stuck her lower lip out in a pout. "You think so poorly of me. Why I've agreed to give Emery the antidote and to let the rest of you live. What's not nice about that?"

Ginger straightened at the news that Emery would get the antidote. Then she swung terrified eyes to Maeve. "What did you promise her?"

"Go on, Maeve." Arabella stepped back as if to let Maeve have the floor. "You should be the one to tell them."

Maeve's hands trembled behind her back. She prayed her friends wouldn't do anything rash and make her sacrifice worth nothing. She took a deep breath and straightened her shoulders as her gaze passed over her friends: Emery who was so sick and had suffered so much already; Ginger, her best friend; Tristan who had become a leader and a friend in such a short time; Thomas, whose life she had changed without even knowing it; and Gray. Her eyes glistened. They had had so little time together, but they had meant so much to each other. Maeve gave a little nod as if verifying something for herself, sucked in a breath and blew it out slowly to calm her racing heart.

She held Gray's gaze without blinking. "Gray." Her

voice broke. She heaved in another breath and started over. "Gray, I love you. I want you to know that." Gray blinked and started forward, but the guard roughly pushed him back into line.

"Maeve, why are you telling me this now?" he asked warily. "What have you done?"

Maeve took another deep breath. "Arabella is going to give Emery the antidote."

Emery pushed herself upright and swayed. "I don't want it if you're going to do something stupid to get it."

Maeve ignored the interruption and continued. "She's also going to let Thomas go to the oasis."

Thomas moved closer to Gray at the mention of his name. "Alone?" he asked. "I don't want to go alone."

Gray leaned down and whispered something in Thomas's ear. Thomas nodded and looked back at Maeve.

Maeve lifted her chin and attached her gaze to Gray's once more. "Last, she's going to drop the four of you in the Beyond." Gray's eyes widened. Ginger's mouth dropped open.

"No one knows what's out there," Tristan said quietly.

Maeve nodded. "I know." Her voice trembled. "But at least you'll be alive."

Gray's blue eyes pierced Maeve's brown ones. She knew what was coming next. "What happens to you, Maeve?" His voice was calm, but a muscle in his jaw twitched and his body vibrated tension.

Maeve refused to blink. "She injects me with the virus and sends me back into Palumbra to infect the new government."

CHAPTER TWENTY-NINE

Gray struggled with his bonds and rushed forward. Arabella's guards moved forward, guns pointed at Gray, but she motioned them back. Gray stood just inches from Maeve.

"Now, that's not gonna happen." Gray pinned Maeve with an icy stare. "Why would you agree to something like that?"

Maeve stepped toward him, close enough to feel the heat, confusion and rage rolling off his body, her eyes pleading with him to understand. "What choice do I have? It's the only way Emery gets the antidote and the rest of you survive."

"But what about you? What about us?" Gray's voice broke.

She moved forward until she was right in front of him. "I love you. This is the only way." Her voice got even quieter. "Greater love has no man than this, that he lay down his life for his friends. Remember?"

Gray leaned down until his forehead touched hers, and Maeve closed her eyes. She could feel his breath on her face, and she savored the feeling, knowing it was probably the last time she would ever be this close to him.

Tears prickled her eyes. "Surely there's another way. Let her inject me. Why does it have to be you?"

Maeve leaned just a little closer. "Because she sees me as the root of her downfall. For her, it's poetic justice. For us, it's the end."

Gray breathed through his mouth as if in pain. Maeve opened her eyes and looked into his gorgeous blue eyes. The agony in them pierced her soul. "I love you," she said again as if saying it over and over would make up for all the times she hadn't said it and would never get to say it in the future.

"I'm not giving up. We'll find you." His eyes blazed with intensity. "Don't you dare give up!" He shifted slightly so his mouth now covered hers in a searing kiss. Maeve threw her heart and soul into the kiss, trying to convey all the joy she had felt in her relationship with him and all the sorrow that it would be over far too soon. Finally, one of Arabella's guards nudged them apart, and Maeve thought she saw a hint of compassion in the guard's eyes.

"Don't do this for me." Emery's weak voice broke the silence.

"Or me." Thomas's voice echoed with frustration.

Maeve, still standing as close to Gray as the guard would allow, turned toward Emery. She missed the feel of Gray's skin against hers. She took a tiny step closer so their sleeves brushed. "Emery, I would gladly sacrifice myself so you can live. Just be amazing, OK? Live a fantastic life and show the world how brilliant you can be."

She turned to Thomas. "And you. You are one of the bravest people I have ever met. Stay strong. You can do this. Find your way home." She stepped away from Gray and walked to where Thomas stood next to Tristan. She leaned down so her eyes were level with his. "You can do this. I promise."

Thomas sniffed, wiped his nose with the back of his hand and nodded. She straightened and looked at Emery again. "Take care of your sister, OK?"

Still leaning against Ginger, Emery nodded her head as tears leaked down her cheeks followed by a gut-wrenching cough. Ginger leaned her head against Emery's and whispered something in her ear. Emery nodded and turned her face into Ginger's shoulder.

"Thank you." Ginger's voice caught. "This shouldn't be a choice. She shouldn't force you to make this choice." Ginger's eyes burned with hatred as she looked at Arabella, who gave her a tiny wave with her red-tipped fingers. "You've always been my best friend, but this..." Ginger broke off, unable to continue. Tristan stepped closer to her, trying to offer comfort with his presence.

"Maeve," Tristan said. "You don't have to do this. We can find another way."

Maeve smiled sadly. "How? You know this is the only way. Sacrifice me to keep all of you safe. It's not a bad trade, not really."

Her gaze swept over her friends. "And how lucky am I? To have all of you as my friends, my family. I wouldn't trade you for the world. Just make good use of the rest of your lives, please. Make all of this worth it. Don't let things go back to the way they were. Keep fighting for what matters. And always remember that I love you all."

As Maeve finished, Arabella began to clap. "Oh, bravo. That was touching. I'm so glad I could be a part of your sad goodbyes. But, time's up. We have so much to do.

Take them away."

She motioned to the guards to return everyone but Maeve to their cells. "Wait." Maeve marched across the room until she stood in front of Arabella. "I get to see Emery get the antidote."

Arabella glared at her.

"We had a deal, Arabella."

Arabella said nothing. The guards had stopped prodding the others in the direction of the door, waiting to see what Arabella had to say. Arabella's face tightened, and a muscle twitched in her cheek. Finally, she nodded. "Fine."

Arabella held her hand out to Elton. He used his good arm to reach in his pocket and hand her a small packet.

"Wait," Maeve said. "You knew where the antidote was the whole time?"

Elton smirked at Maeve. "Of course. You don't think I'd take any chances of accidentally getting the disease, do you?"

Maeve's mouth dropped and her eyes narrowed. "But why didn't you get it to save your sister?"

Elton gave a short laugh. Maeve and Gray shared a horrified look.

"You guys are quite easily fooled." Elton laughed again. "She wasn't my sister. She was just a girl from the slums."

Emery gasped. "You killed her," she said in a whisper. Tears rolled down her cheeks. "She was my friend, and you killed her."

Maeve shook her head in disbelief. "But why did she go along with the lie? We could have helped her."

It was Arabella's turn to laugh. "She was beyond help. We had her family, so she did what we asked. Kind of like you, Maeve."

Maeve winced. "What happened to her family?" Even as she asked the question, she wasn't sure she wanted to know the answer.

Arabella waved her hand carelessly. "Dead, of course. They died before she and Elton even left Bellus."

"Did you kill them?"

Arabella shook her head. "We didn't have to. They were infected."

Ginger raised her head and stared at Arabella with hatred burning in her gaze. "How can you be so callous? All those people died, and for what?"

Arabella's perfectly manicured eyebrows rose to her forehead. Her voice took on a menacing tone. "For what? For a better future for humanity."

"And you're going to provide that future?" Tristan chimed in.

"Of course. Can you think of anyone better?"

"I can," Gray muttered under his breath.

Arabella's eyes blazed with passion. "What does that future look like?" Maeve asked.

Arabella's eyes became distant as she stared into a future none of them could see.

"It's a future of peace where everyone agrees on how things should be run. A future where I lead the people of Palumbra into an era of plenty."

"The people of Palumbra you're trying to kill off with a disease?" Derision dripped from Maeve's words.

Arabella seemed to come back to herself and stared at Maeve with displeasure. "Not all of them. Just the ones

that threw me out of power. We plan to target our weapon
– that's you, dear – well so as not to infect all the people of
Palumbra. We don't want to repeat the mistake we made
with Bellus."

"So, you didn't mean to kill all the people?" Gray
asked.

"Of course not." Arabella's voice took on a
defensive tone. "Do you think I'm stupid. We could have
used some of those people. We thought we had the virus
targeted to simply take out half the population – the
weakest half. But someone messed up and added it to the
main water supply instead of putting it into the water
station that served the poor side of the city." She waved her
hand dismissively. "That person is no longer with us."

"So, by the weakest people, you mean the poor
people?" Maeve asked.

Arabella tapped her chin. "Of course. The ones that
contribute the least to society. Who would you have gotten
rid of?" She cocked her had as if it had never occurred to
her that there was another option.

"None of them." Maeve was nearly shouting.
"Why did you need to get rid of any of them?"

Arabella looked at Maeve as if she had just
dribbled something on her shirt.

"Because there aren't enough resources for all of
us. The water and food supplies will run out in 10 years at
our current rate of population. But with the technology of
Bellus and the weapons cache hidden in Palumbra, we can
conquer the other survivors out in The Beyond and
survive."

Maeve's eyes widened at Arabella's
pronouncement. She shifted uncomfortably from one foot

to the other. Her arms were starting to hurt from being bound behind her. She shook her head in confusion. "What weapons cache? There are no mass weapons in Palumbra. We destroyed them."

Arabella smiled. "Oh, honey, do you think the weapon you discovered was the only one? We have secrets that you and that silly new government will never find."

Maeve struggled to take in this piece of information. She scanned the faces of her friends, and they all wore the same look of shocked disbelief that she knew was mirrored on her own face. She opened her mouth to ask another question, but Arabella cut her off.

"Enough of that. We have work to do."

She took the packet from Elton who had stood wordlessly while Arabella outlined her mad plan to rule Palumbra again and marched over to Emery.

"Open your mouth."

Emery shook her head and looked at Maeve.

"Oh, little girl, not taking the antidote won't save her. It will just kill you."

Emery's eyes glistened as she held Maeve's gaze. Maeve nodded, and Emery opened her mouth. Arabella poured the contents of the packet into her mouth.

"Swallow that, and it will deactivate the virus. You should be good as new in a couple of hours."

Arabella motioned to the guards. "Take them back to their cells. We have work to do." She turned to Maeve. "Rest up. You'll need it."

CHAPTER THIRTY

Waiting to die was boring. Maeve lay on the bed in her cell, her head cushioned on her arms, and stared up at the ceiling, which was dotted with tiny holes. She had counted all 182 of them – twice. It had been hours since Arabella's guards had marched her back to her cell and shoved her in. Her stomach grumbled.

She had thought she would be anxious as she waited for her impending death, but she simply felt hollow. She didn't want to die, but she knew that given a choice between her friends and her own life, she would make this choice every time. The only thing that worried her now was how to avoid infecting her friends in Palumbra and whether Arabella would keep her word and not go after Gray, Tristan, Ginger and Emery after Maeve was dead.

With nothing to do but think, she let her thoughts wander. She thought about her parents and wondered how they would react to her death. While their relationship wasn't great, she did love them, and they loved her. She knew her dying before they had time to fully repair their relationship would be devastating to them. It was devastating to her. She wished she had been quicker to forgive them and had worked harder on restoring their relationship.

Her thoughts turned then to Emma, who would be distraught at having sent them into this kind of danger. Maeve had no doubt that Emma thought they would go into the desert and meet up with the patrol. Their job was supposed to be easy – spy on the patrol and see if they could figure out who was undermining the new government. Instead, they had found Arabella. Thinking of Emma gave Maeve new strength as she remembered just how much Emma had endured in her life. Emma would be OK. Maeve sent up a prayer that she could be half as brave as Emma had been in her life.

She rolled to a sitting position and pulled her knees up to her chest, resting her arms on top of them as her thoughts turned to Gray. She wrinkled her nose and sniffed, determined not to cry. They had had so little time together – and so much of it they had lived in danger. She smiled when she thought about how they had met and their first fishing trip. She still wasn't sure what it was about her that attracted Gray, but she was grateful for it.

She closed her eyes and envisioned the rugged lines of his face and those crystal blue eyes that pierced her soul. She remembered the tingle she felt the first time their hands had brushed, the tingle she still felt every time they touched. She touched her lips as she relived their first kiss and the many kisses after that. Her sorrow turned bittersweet as her mind slipped back to the kiss where she knew everything had changed, where she knew she loved him.

She opened her eyes and grimaced as she thought about telling him she loved him while they were both prisoners held to the whim of Arabella. They widened a bit when she realized he hadn't said those words back, but she shook off the doubt quickly. He loved her, but his artistic soul wouldn't have wanted to share that moment with their enemy. She knew she might never get to hear him say it.

She began to pace the room, wondering how long it would take Arabella to be ready to implement her plan. On her fourth circuit of the room, she heard a key in the lock. She took a deep breath and braced herself.

The door opened.

"What are you doing here?" Maeve said, disgust dripping from her voice.

"Bringing you some food." Elton motioned toward the tray he was holding. "It's a last meal of sorts. Wish it could be more than a protein bar and some water." He set the tray on the bed.

"You can leave now." Maeve stood against the back wall of the room as far from Elton as she could get.

Elton ignored her dismissal and sat on the bed next to the tray.

"I want you to understand why I did what I did."

"What's to understand? You've thrown your support to an evil woman, and you betrayed us. And used an innocent girl to get us to sympathize with you. How do you possibly think you could convince me you had a good reason for that?"

Elton looked at his hands and shrugged. "From your point of view, I understand that things look bad."

"Look bad?" Maeve stared at him in disbelief. "I'm a prisoner. My friends are also prisoners, one of them could be dying for all I know. I'm about to let myself be injected with a deadly virus so they can live, and you think that 'from my point of view' things look bad?" She shook her head and began pacing again. "From my point of view things look about three levels worse than bad."

"Please, just hear me out." Elton gave her a pleading look. "We made a decent team out there in the desert. For Shalara's sake, for her memory, just listen to what I have to say."

Maeve stopped pacing. "Don't even say her name." Maeve's voice was deadly quiet. "You killed her. You don't get to claim her."

Elton nodded. "I understand your feelings. But listen to what I have to say. Then I'll go."

Maeve stopped pacing and leaned against the wall with her arms crossed in front of her. "Fine. But make it quick."

He fidgeted on the bed and finally raised his eyes to Maeve's. "My family really did die of the plague. That much is true. And while Shalara wasn't my sister, she was my friend."

"I'd hate to be your enemy." Maeve shifted her shoulders against the wall.

"We went to school together. Both of our families died of the plague. One day they were fine. The next they were dead." Elton looked down at his hands and shook his head. "I don't know why she and I didn't get sick. I guess we just missed out on drinking the water that day."

Elton pinned his gaze on Maeve again. "We were part of that group that Arabella wanted to get rid of, the working poor. We barely scraped by. Not much to eat, and we owned little. It was a hard life, but at least we had family. And then that was gone. Shalara and I were all that was left."

Despite herself, Maeve was intrigued. "What did

you do?" The words left her mouth grudgingly as she tried not to be moved by Elton's story.

"We didn't know what was causing people to die, so we took to the streets and hid. We would move from place to place, sleeping in abandoned homes. The plague was over in just a few weeks. There was just a small handful of survivors left. One morning we woke to guns pointed in our faces."

"Let me guess. Sarge."

Elton nodded. "He brought us here to Arabella. She knew that Palumbra had been patrolling the desert and it was only a matter of time before they found the force shield. She wanted to trap a patrol."

Maeve pushed herself off the wall and strolled over to the bed where she picked up the protein bar then returned to her place on the opposite wall. "But why? If she had control of Bellus, why did she need Palumbra?"

Elton shrugged. "I don't know. She's a bit mad when it comes to Palumbra, and especially you and your friends. She wants revenge. She also wants Palumbra's weapons."

"What weapons? We destroyed the energy weapon. What else is there?"

Elton looked at her in disbelief. "You don't know?"

"Know what?"

"It wasn't just energy weapons that were developed in Palumbra. There are plans for laser weapons as well. Arabella wants to get her hands on those plans."

Maeve began to pace again. "But how does she even know they exist? We certainly haven't heard anything about laser weapons."

Elton gave her a pitying look. "Do you really think

they would tell you if they had access to laser weapons?"

She stopped and pinned Elton with a steely-eyed gaze. "Yes." She paused. "Maybe."

"And maybe not. Your government probably isn't as clean as you think."

"What does that mean?"

Elton went back to studying his hands. "Nothing. Just an observation."

Maeve chewed the side of her mouth and decided not to pursue it. Anything Elton said was suspect anyway. She already knew from what John had told them that not everyone was on Cleo's side.

"Finish your story. You still haven't explained how you could kill your friend."

Elton raised his gaze, and Maeve saw anguish flit through his eyes.

"Arabella threatened to kill us both. We didn't fit her profile of useful people. But then she decided we could be used to trap the Palumbran patrol. We agreed." He twisted his hands together. "What else could we do?"

Maeve said nothing.

Elton sighed and continued. "We worked with Sarge to come up with a plan, and it worked beautifully. Shalara and I played the poor, lost surviving souls from Bellus. The patrol took the bait. It was easy for Sarge and his crew to come in and kill them. What we didn't plan on was you."

"Was it so surprising that Palumbra would send out a second group to help the first patrol?"

Elton shook his head. "No. We expected that, and we took care of them. But we were surprised when you and the others showed up. Arabella had told us about you and your friends. She was very specific that if we saw you, we should capture you. She didn't care about the other patrols. She just didn't want them getting close to Bellus."

Maeve pushed away from the wall and stood straight. "I don't understand how all this led to Shalara's death. Why did you need to kill her?"

"Your boyfriend."

"What? Gray?"

"He was too suspicious of me. Our story had huge holes. And Shalara liked Emery. She wanted to share our story with her. Arabella had been clear before we left that any deviation from her plan would result in our deaths. Shalara was going to tell Emery the whole story. I had to stop her."

Maeve whirled on him in disbelief. "So you killed her? You couldn't come up with any idea other than that?"

Elton stood. "I didn't mean to!" he shouted. "I thought we would make it back in time to get the antidote! I didn't mean for her to die. I just wanted you to stay away from her so she couldn't tell you our story."

"And how did you infect Emery? Surely, she would have noticed you sticking a needle in her arm."

Elton shrugged. "I did it while she was sleeping. It's a small needle, and she's a deep sleeper. She probably just thought it was a bug biting her."

Maeve sighed heavily. "You are despicable. What did Arabella offer you?"

"How do you know she offered me anything?"

"I know how she works. Was it power? Wealth? Safety?"

Elton sat back down. "All of it." He looked up at her. "Do you know what it's like to be really poor? To have no one looking out for you? To be looked down on by everyone in society? To be so unimportant that your own government wants to kill you?"

Maeve shook her head.

"You'll do anything to get out of that situation. Anything. Betray your friends. Lie. Cheat. Steal. Kill. No one else matters. It's survive or be destroyed."

Maeve looked Elton up and down. "I don't believe that. Those are choices that you made. Choices that you now have to live with. You could have chosen to tell us your story and let us help you. You could have saved Shalara and never infected Emery. You could have turned your back on Arabella and chosen your friends over your own need for power and wealth."

It was Maeve's turn to give him a pitying look. "But you chose yourself over everyone else. You may have power and wealth when this is over, but you won't have what really matters. Friends. Self-respect. Peace."

Elton acted as if he hadn't heard her. "But now, I'm important. I have power. I'll never go hungry again. I can help Arabella build a new order." He paused. "And you can too."

Maeve's eyes widened, and her eyebrows rose as if she hadn't heard him correctly. "What?"

He nodded vigorously. "You can. Just choose one of the others to be injected. You and I can work with Arabella and create a new and better world. Just think, we could make it so no one is ever poor again. So no one suffers injustice. We could make it better."

"And you think that would justify killing one of my friends?" Maeve's voice shook. "Just pick one to sacrifice and all will be well?"

Elton's eyes burned with passion. "It would be for the greater good. You liked me once. You could again. Just imagine all we could do together." He held out his hand to her.

Maeve looked from his hand to his face and wondered how she had ever thought him handsome. "No."

Some of the fire left Elton's eyes. "You're willing to give up the opportunity to create a new world just to save your friends?"

Maeve nodded. "You see, Elton, what you fail to understand is that it isn't wealth or power that makes us strong. It's loyalty, love and fighting for what's right. You may have power and the illusion of safety, but that's all it is, an illusion. What makes you think Arabella won't eventually decide you're not worth keeping around?"

Elton stepped back, and Maeve could see her words had shaken him.

"With friends like Arabella, who needs enemies?" Maeve continued. "No, I'll take my chances. Even if I die, at least my friends will live on to fight another day."

Elton regained his composure and looked at her with sadness in his eyes. "It's a shame, Maeve. I really like you. We could have built something together. But your high principles won't mean much when you're dead."

He rapped his knuckles on the door. When it opened, he motioned to the guards and said, "Take her away. We're done here."

CHAPTER THIRTY-ONE

"Thomas will be delivered to the oasis." Maeve was once again standing with her hands bound before Arabella.

"I want to see him dropped off." She stared defiantly at Arabella.

"Why would I allow that, dear?" Arabella's voice contained a hint of laughter. "You'll just have to take my word for it."

Maeve shook her head. "No. That's not how this works. I need proof that my friends are safe before I go along with your plan."

"How are you going to stop me? Once I inject you with the virus, there's not much you can do. How sweet that you thought you could bargain."

"We had a deal, Arabella."

"And I'm changing the terms since you really have nothing to bargain with."

"Really?" Maeve gave her an innocent look. "Do you actually think I'm going to just waltz into the government headquarters and infect everyone?"

Arabella walked over to Maeve and studied her like an insect under a microscope. The muscle in her jaw

Maeve had noticed earlier twitched again. "I remember not that long ago when you were a good little girl, following the edicts of the WG."

"I haven't been that little girl in a long time thanks to you." Maeve lifted her chin. "I get to see my friends dropped off, and I'll do whatever you want. If not, I'll just sit down in the woods and wait to die."

"Why should I believe that?"

"Because I'm not like you. I'll do whatever it takes to save my friends."

Arabella paced away from her, tapping her red-tipped fingernail on her lips. "You know, I actually believe you." She chuckled. "That integrity is going to get you killed."

Maeve tried to look defeated. It wasn't hard. She felt defeated, but her only concern now was to save her friends. She could figure out what to do about Palumbra later.

She searched frantically for a better bargaining chip. She didn't trust Arabella to keep her end of the bargain and release her friends.

"What if I could tell you where the plans are for the laser weapons?"

Arabella looked at her in disbelief, then gave a full-throated tinkling laugh. "Nice try, but how would you know where they are? You didn't even know they existed until Elton told you."

Maeve gave a start of surprise.

"Oh, yes, I know all about his visit to you." She laughed again. "Who do you think sent him to you? I watched the whole thing." When Maeve's eyes widened, Arabella chuckled. "Didn't you know about the cameras?

You're a star. That was a touching speech you gave about loyalty and love. Too bad those things won't save you."

Maeve scrambled to recover from Arabella's pronouncement. "But I've had time to think since Elton told me about them, and I'm pretty sure I know where they keep those plans. I have had access to a lot of the government buildings, and I know a lot of the people."

Arabella tapped her chin with a fingernail and narrowed her eyes. "Let's hear what you have to say."

Maeve straightened to her full height. "When you release my friends."

Maeve swore she heard Arabella growl as she whirled on her heel and took several steps away from Maeve. She turned back with a glint of anger in her eye.

"Once I control Palumbra, I can find those plans myself."

"But can you? Remember, the government is controlled by members of The Resistance. They had hiding places you never knew about."

Arabella studied Maeve with narrowed eyes, persistently tapping her chin with that blood-red fingernail. Maeve felt the weight of her friends' lives hanging in the balance.

"Fine," Arabella finally announced with a huff. "I'll release your friends. They're of little use to me anyway. You can watch on video. Then you tell me where the plans for the laser weapons are, and we inject you with the virus."

Maeve let out a sigh of relief and nodded.

"One more thing. I want to see Thomas first."

Arabella gave her a pitying smile. "I think not." She walked away, then turned back to Maeve. "But I'm not a complete ogre." She nodded at one of the guards. "Give her a pencil and some paper. You may write him a note." When she smiled this time, it held a hint of malice. "But keep in mind that I will be reading whatever you write."

The guard walked forward and loosened Maeve's bindings, keeping her gun pointed at Maeve the entire time. Another guard handed Maeve a small piece of paper and a pencil. Maeve flexed her hands, which had gone numb from being bound, until she could grasp the pencil. She knelt on one knee, and using the other knee as a desk, began to write.

Thomas,

Don't be afraid. You're not alone. Your friends are always near. Be brave. Make good choices.

Love,

Maeve

She handed the paper to Arabella who read it and threw back her head and laughed. "You are amusing. Why give the boy false hope? His friends are going to be far away from him. He'll be lucky to survive two days in the desert." She shrugged. "Better to die with hope than in utter despair, I guess."

Maeve rose to her feet and stepped toward Arabella, her brow drawn and her eyes burning with anger. Both guards prodded her with their guns to keep her from moving any closer to Arabella. Another guard rushed to bind her hands.

"He's a 10-year-old kid, and you want him to die in despair? What kind of monster are you?"

Arabella brushed aside Maeve's criticism. "He's of no use to me. I've already used him to get what I need."

The anger seemed to leave Maeve in a rush. Her

body relaxed, and she unfisted her hands. "You know, Arabella. I pity you."

Arabella looked startled but quickly recovered. "You? Pity me? That's laughable. I have no need of your pity or anything else. You'll soon be dead."

She gave Maeve one last withering look, turned on her high heel and walked out of the room.

Maeve looked around yet another stark white room. The guards had brought her to this room containing only a TV screen and a chair. Her hands were unbound. Arabella apparently felt the two guards by the door and the locked cell were enough to keep her contained.

A light tap sounded at the door, and one of the guards opened it and stepped out. Maeve eyed the other guard, considering her chances.

"Why do you follow her?"

The guard stared straight ahead and didn't speak. His hands tightened on his gun, the only indication he had heard her speak. This guard was one Maeve hadn't seen before. He was a young man, not that much older than Maeve with dark hair and freckles on his cheeks.

"You have to know she's evil. She killed an entire city, for Pete's sake."

The young guard remained silent.

Maeve cocked her head and eyed the guard thoughtfully. "What's your story? Did your family die in the plague, and she recruited you to be part of her team. What did she promise you? A better world? The promise of plenty for everyone? No more senseless death?"

The soldier's eyes shifted slightly toward Maeve, and his knuckles were now white where he was gripping his gun.

"Have you ever even fired that thing?" Maeve nodded toward his gun. "Do you have any idea what it's like to kill someone?"

The guard lowered his eyes.

"No? Well, I do. You fire that gun without thinking. No, that's not true. You're thinking it's the only thing you can do to save your friend, protect your property, follow orders. And that might be true. But it will never change the fact that you killed someone. You'll live with that for the rest of your life."

The guard's hands trembled slightly on his gun, but still he remained silent.

Maeve rose from the chair and took a step toward the guard.

"You'll wonder if the person you killed had a family who grieved for him. You'll see the moment over and over again in your dreams, wondering if you had another option, any other option." She took another step toward the guard who remained silent and motionless. "You'll grieve, not just for the person you killed, but for the person you were before you fired that shot." Another step. "Because you'll never be the same person again." One more step.

The guard seemed to come to life and pulled the rifle around to point it at Maeve. She stepped closer. The gun shook as the guard's hands trembled. His finger lay on the trigger. Slowly, Maeve grabbed the barrel of the rifle and pointed it away from her. "Is that who you want to be? Someone who has to live with knowing that you killed someone – and you didn't even know why?"

The guard finally spoke. "Y-y-you're an enemy of

Bellus. You're here to destroy what's left of the people of Bellus."

Maeve chuckled. "Is that what she told you?" Maeve shook her head. "We're not here to destroy anything. We were sent to save the survivors from The Hub."

The soldier gave Maeve a blank look.

"That's what we've been calling Bellus. We didn't know the city's name."

"B-but Arabella said Palumbra wants to kill us all."

Maeve shook her head. "We want to live in peace. Arabella used to lead our city. She controlled everything and everyone, but people in Palumbra banded together and overthrew her and her government. Now, we live in peace, and people are building new lives."

The guard shook his head in confusion. "That can't be true. That's not what she told us."

Maeve looked him straight in the eye. "I promise you, it's the truth."

The door started to open, and in a swift move, Maeve used her hold on the gun to pull it away from the surprised guard. She hit the guard on the head with the butt of the rifle, knocking him out, then pointed the gun at the door as Arabella stepped through.

"Oh my. This is a surprise." She glanced at the unconscious guard and lifted her hands. "I guess leaving your hands free was a mistake. As was leaving him in here alone with you."

"Close the door." Maeve motioned with the barrel of the rifle. Arabella pushed the door shut behind her. "Lock it." The lock snicked into place.

"What are you going to do now?" Arabella asked

in a bored tone. She studied her fingernails for chips in the polish. "Kill me?"

"I should." Maeve's voice trembled.

"Yes, that would go well for you. Shoot me and dozens of guards will come through that door. You'll be dead in seconds."

Maeve shrugged. "I'm going to die anyway. Then the world would be rid of you."

"Do you really think that would stop things?" Arabella dropped her hand to her side and looked Maeve in the eye. "Another would just step in and take my place. Are you going to kill them, too? Besides, your little friends are already on their way to their final resting spots." She motioned to the monitor that had sprung to life with a split screen image of two hovercars. On one side of the screen, Thomas sat huddled on a seat by himself surrounded by three guards. He looked smaller than Maeve remembered – and scared. On the other side of the screen, Gray, Tristan, Ginger and Emery sat with their hands bound in front of them. Maeve squinted at the screen and noted with satisfaction that Emery looked much better.

"At least they'll be free."

Arabella laughed her high, tinkling laugh. "For about three days until they die of thirst."

Maeve kept her gun trained on Arabella and her eye on the door as she watched the screen. Thomas's car stopped first. One of the guards nudged him with the gun, and he got to his feet and moved slowly toward the door. With a vicious shove, the guard pushed him out of the hovercar. The door closed, and the camera panned to where Thomas stood in the yellow sand of the oasis, looking small and alone in the vastness of the desert.

"He'll be OK," Maeve said to herself, wondering again what had happened to Rufus.

"You have a lot of confidence in a 10-year-old kid," Arabella said in a mocking tone.

"He's smarter than your average 10-year-old. He makes good choices."

"You mean like getting tangled up with you? Yeah, that was clearly a great choice."

Maeve shrugged and checked the door, where she could hear a commotion on the other side. She turned her attention back to the screen, being careful to keep part of her attention on Arabella. Thomas was resourceful. He had made his way to the oasis once. He could find his way back to Palumbra.

The hovercar on the screen stopped, but the soldiers made no move to release her friends.

"Why aren't they letting them go?"

"You owe me something."

Maeve tightened her grip on the gun. "The rules have changed. Let my friends go or I'll kill you."

Arabella laughed. "How will that help?" She held her hand out, palm up, showing a device with a single button on it. "They won't release them until I press this button and the light in their hovercar turns green. If the light doesn't turn green in 10 minutes, they'll shoot them. So, you see, my dear, killing me will change nothing."

Maeve ground her teeth together.

"Where are the plans for the laser weapons?"

Maeve didn't answer. Instead, she took a step toward Arabella, the rifle just inches from Arabella's face. "Give me the button."

"Well, I can do that, but as soon as this device

leaves my hand, the light in that car will start flashing red, a signal for the guards to shoot your friends. So, I ask you again, where are the plans for the laser weapons?"

Maeve was stuck. She couldn't kill Arabella and risk having the device fall from her hand, but she had no idea where the laser weapon plans were. She quickly sifted through plausible answers in her head. Finally, she said, "In the tunnels. I'm not sure where."

"How do I know you're not lying?"

"You don't. Now let my friends go."

"I guess that's plausible."

"You won't have a chance to find out if you don't push that button. I have nothing left to lose."

Reluctantly, Arabella pushed the button, and Gray, Tristan, Ginger and Emery were roughly shoved from the car. "Aren't they going to cut their bonds?"

"Of course not. Why would we make it easy for them? They could turn on my guards like you did. No, the agreement we had was to drop them in The Beyond. We've done that."

The hovercar doors slid closed. Maeve got one last glimpse of her friends standing on what looked like hostile, rocky terrain before the camera went dark.

"So, you see, it's too late to renegotiate." Arabella waved at Maeve's gun. "Now put the gun down because we both know you're not going to use it."

Maeve looked at the gun in her hands. It would be so easy to squeeze the trigger and end Arabella's evil scheme. She knew it would be the last thing she ever did. Her vow to never use a gun again flitted through her brain. But didn't this situation merit a rethinking of that vow? She could rid the world of Arabella and all her plans to destroy

Palumbra. She tightened her grip on the gun.

Images flooded Maeve's mind of the last time she had held a gun. Gray in danger. Blood blooming on the soldier's chest. The thud of him hitting the floor.

She looked at Arabella. Sweat broke out on her forehead, and her hands were damp with it. She readjusted her grip on the gun.

"Well, if you're going to do it, I'd do it now." Arabella inclined her head toward the door. "They won't wait much longer to break it down. I'm only supposed to be in here for 10 minutes."

Maeve blinked and took a deep breath. Her finger closed on the trigger. She tried to convince herself this was the best way to end it. She would willingly sacrifice herself for her friends – and take Arabella out with her. But this would be murder, not a shot in the heat of the moment to protect Gray. It would be a choice, one she couldn't undo. But it would be worth it, right?

She pictured Gray's face when he found out she was dead. She knew he would be sad. But would he be proud? Would he think her choice had been the right one?

And what about Emma who had always been so wise? What would she think? She heard Emma's voice saying, "You have to learn to forgive yourself and recognize that sometimes it's not the big things we do that change the world. More often, it's the little ones – caring about someone, teaching others, living with compassion. Those are the things that make a difference, the things that change a generation." Killing Arabella would be a big thing. Would it change the world? Would it be more valuable than those other little things Emma had talked about?

Thomas's scared face flashed before her eyes. She remembered her conversation with him about choices, about making good choices. She pictured his face when he discovered what she'd done.

Maeve lowered the gun. "I'd rather die knowing that there are ways to achieve what you need without killing others than die with a gun in my hands." She tossed the gun to the floor.

Arabella threw back her head and laughed. "You naive fool." She opened the door, and two guards came in and restrained Maeve. "You never let your enemies go when you have a chance to get rid of them." She stuck her head out the door and called "Bring in the injection."

Turning back to Maeve, she smiled. "You wasted your chance, and you're still going to die."

CHAPTER THIRTY-TWO

Maeve stood in the empty room, the silence echoing against the stark, white walls.

So, this is how it ends, she thought. Alone and in silence.

She sat back down, leaning back and crossing her feet at the ankles, her bound hands resting on her stomach. She studied the wall in front of her, noting that the crack in the wall looked a bit like a tree, and wondered how long it would take them to bring in the injection.

Would it hurt, she wondered. Shalara suffered while she was sick, but the end had been quick. Emery had been miserable once she had been injected. Maeve smiled. At least Emery was well again. If nothing else, her sacrifice had saved Emery.

Her thoughts turned from wondering about her own death to concern for her friends. How long could they last in The Beyond? And what about Thomas? What chance did any of them have? What would keep Arabella from just picking them up again? Had Maeve sacrificed herself for her friends to simply die in a hostile landscape where no one would find them?

She should have killed Arabella when she had the

chance. Maybe she could have reasoned with the guards and found her friends. Had she made the wrong choice?

Maeve shook her head, forcefully flinging the thoughts from her mind. No. She had done the only thing she could. If she had killed Arabella, she would already be dead, with no chance to warn Cleo and the others about the danger Arabella posed. Alive, she had a chance, albeit a slim one to still save Palumbra.

Arabella might have the technology of Bellus behind her but without the plans for a laser weapon, she could only do so much harm. Her attack only worked if Palumbra was unaware of her existence. Maeve intended to change that.

The door opened again. Two guards stepped through, along with Elton and a short, bald man with a mustache carrying a syringe. Maeve sat up straight in the chair.

"Back again?" Maeve asked Elton mockingly.

"I came to give you one last chance to join us. You don't have to die." Elton looked sincere.

Maeve gave him a grim smile. "I admire your persistence, but I'd rather die than be a part of Arabella's schemes."

"But she just wants to make it better for everyone, where everyone has enough."

Maeve felt sorry for Elton. He wanted so badly to believe Arabella had a plan that would benefit everyone that he ignored her cruelty and taste for killing.

"I've seen what she thinks is enough, and I'm telling you, Elton, it's not the same as what you think."

Elton shrugged. "It has to be better than how I was living before."

"Maybe," Maeve allowed. "But what will you give up to get it?"

"Enough," snapped Elton. "She's had her chance." He motioned for the mustached man. "Get on with it."

He turned to leave.

"Not staying to watch?"

With his back still to her, Elton said, "I gave you a chance, Maeve. I have no need to watch." He opened the door and let it slam behind him.

While Maeve was still staring at the door, the mustached man lifted her arm and sank the syringe into it. He removed the syringe and left the room without a word, the door closing quietly behind him.

She had no idea how long she sat alone in the room, waiting for the signs of illness to set in. She was still feeling fine when the door opened and two guards dressed head to toe in protective gear hauled her out of the chair and through the door. They forced her down a corridor and out into the sunlight. Maeve blinked and squinted, the sunlight blinding her after so long indoors. The guards shoved her into a waiting hovercar, causing her to land hard on her knees. The door slid closed behind her as she struggled back to her feet, using her bound hands for leverage.

She was alone in the hovercar, but as soon as she seated herself, the video screen at the front burst to life. Arabella's face filled the screen.

"Can't you leave me alone?" Maeve asked, unsure if Arabella could hear her.

Arabella tilted her head back and let out her high, tinkling laugh. Maeve wanted to cover her ears.

"Oh, my dear, I'm going to be with you every step

of the way. We wouldn't want you to be all alone when you die, now would we? I'm not a monster."

"Your actions say otherwise."

"Now, Maeve, you had plenty of opportunities to avoid this. Why you could have even killed me. Your current situation is simply a consequence of your own choices. And, may I say, I don't think they were very good ones."

Maeve stared at the screen and remained silent.

"Nothing to say? Oh, well. I have a few things to tell you."

Maeve's nose itched like she needed to sneeze, and a tickle started in the back of her throat. She twitched her nose trying to avoid giving Arabella the satisfaction of seeing the symptoms of the virus start.

"First, the virus we injected you with is much stronger than the one Elton used on Shalara and Emery. We released it on a timed delay so you should just be starting to experience symptoms. They will get worse over the course of your ride to the outskirts of Palumbra."

Maeve twitched her nose again and tried to suppress the need to cough.

"When you get to the outskirts of Palumbra, you will be escorted into the woods. My guards will form a perimeter around the edge of the woods, so don't even think about trying to escape. You are to make your way into Palumbra. Anyone who gets within a few feet of you will get infected."

Maeve swallowed the urge to cough. "Do you really think no one in Palumbra will notice a hovercar approaching or your men standing guard?"

"We disabled the surveillance system on the edge

of Palumbra, and the patrols won't be back around to that side of the town for a few hours." Arabella smiled. "You see, we have it all worked out."

Maeve swallowed. Her throat burned. "What makes you think I'm going to just walk into town and infect people?"

Arabella pointed at a screen behind her, and Maeve stifled a scream. Thomas's face filled the screen. He was at the oasis, but Sarge stood next to him, holding a gun to his head. Thomas's eyes were wide and terrified.

"Checkmate, Maeve. Do what I say or I'll have Sarge shoot him. If you want him to live, you'll follow instructions."

Maeve gave in to the urge to cough, and a wracking cough shook her body. "How do I know you won't shoot him anyway?"

Arabella gave a dainty shrug. "You don't. But I give you my word, Maeve. Do what I say, and we'll let him go."

"How will you know what I do after they drop me off?"

"Do you really think I haven't thought of that? We put a tracker under your skin when we injected you with the virus."

Maeve looked at her arm where the needle had entered. Just under her skin, she could make out the faint outline of a square. Her shoulders slumped. "What about the others?"

Arabella laughed and waved her hand at another monitor behind her. It showed Emery, Gray, Tristan and Ginger climbing over rocks, trying to balance with bound hands. "I'm not worried about them. They'll be wandering out there for days, and with no supplies, The Beyond will take care of them quickly. Who knows what's out there? I'm sure they'll make a tasty snack for some large creature."

Maeve's thoughts strayed to the plagorans they had encountered on their way to find The Hub days ago. What if there were more creatures like that in The Beyond? Her friends didn't stand a chance. Maeve's head dropped; she closed her eyes and fought back tears. She had lost. She would die and so would her friends.

She raised her head and met Arabella's gaze. "Fine." Defeat echoed in her voice. "Just let Thomas go when this is over."

"You have my word, Maeve." For a fleeting moment, Maeve thought she saw compassion flit through Arabella's eyes. "You know, it's a pity you refused to join us. You could have become my protege, and all of the power could have one day been yours." She tapped her red-tipped finger on her chin. "Maybe I'll just adopt Thomas and make him my protege."

The screen went black. Maeve stared at it in disbelief. In trying to save Thomas, she had sentenced him to a life under Arabella's thumb. She sneezed. A wracking cough caused her body to tremble. She sank, shivering, to the floor of the hovercar, curled into a ball and tried to hold back the tears that threatened to fall.

The hovercar came to an abrupt halt, causing Maeve to lurch forward even as she was curled on the ground. Her body burned with fever. Her throat felt as if it were on fire, and her eyes watered. Every few minutes her body felt as if it were being torn apart by the force of her cough. She brushed her hair out of her eyes and struggled to sit up, her limbs shaking. She had no idea how she would walk anywhere.

The door of the hovercar slid open, and guards covered in protective gear pulled her forward with a vicelike grip on her arm. They gave her a rough shove toward the forest.

She looked around, trying to get her bearings and almost laughed. They were at the end of the path that led to Gray's back yard, the path where this nightmare had started. For a moment, Maeve wondered what would have happened if she had never noticed the flapping corner of the note on the time capsule. If she had just left it there, would she be kissing her parents good night and climbing the ladder to her loft or would revolution have happened in Palumbra without her? Was there a single choice that had led her to where she stood now or was it just a series of choices that all added up to this colossal failure?

A searing cough shook her body, and she felt as if her lungs might burst. She didn't remember Shalara and Emery coughing this hard, but Arabella had said this version of the virus was not just contagious but more powerful. She wondered how much time she had left. Probably more than she wanted.

The guard pushed her again and motioned with the end of his gun for her to start walking. She focused on putting one foot in front of the other. Her feet felt like lead, and the path in front of her wavered as if it were an ocean wave. She dutifully moved her feet forward, feeling as though she were walking underwater. What would happen if she just lay down and stayed here? Thomas's face flitted through her mind, and she continued the effort to move toward Palumbra.

Slowly, she stumbled toward Gray's backyard, less

than half a mile away. It seemed more like 300 miles. She felt as if she would collapse long before she made it. Was that good or bad? If she died in the woods, then no one would be infected, but Thomas would die. Maeve no longer knew what the right choice was. All she knew was that Thomas had risked himself for her, and she would return the favor.

Her knees gave way, but she steadied herself on the branch of a nearby tree. She stood panting and coughing, trying to muster up the strength to go on. Finally, she took a step forward and caught her foot on a root. Too weak to catch herself, she tumbled to the ground.

CHAPTER THIRTY-THREE

Maeve lay where she fell, struggling to catch her breath. Her arms and legs trembled and sweat trickled down the side of her face. She closed her eyes and attempted to draw in a deep breath. A cough violently shook her body. When the coughing ceased, she rolled over to her back and stared at the trees above her. It would be so easy to just stay here, to never open her eyes again. She could just see the sun through the tree branches above her. Thomas's face appeared in her mind, and the memory of their last conversation in Palumbra drifted through her thoughts.

"Maybe one day we'll even get to explore the stars," she had said.

His face had lit up. "I can't wait to tell my friends we might one day go to the stars!"

Maeve smiled at the memory then rolled over again. She knew Arabella was watching her progress. She slowly pushed herself to her knees, put one hand on a nearby tree and drug herself to her feet. Looking around to make sure she was headed in the right direction, she continued her slow trek along the path.

She made steady progress, lurching from tree to

tree. She could barely make out the outline of Gray's house when she stumbled and fell again, this time hitting the ground hard. Tears of pain and frustration sprang to her eyes. She raised herself to a sitting position, resting her back against a nearby tree. The tears spilled over and joined the sweat rolling down her cheeks. She shivered even though the day was warm, laid her head against the rough bark of the tree and closed her eyes again.

A twig cracked behind her. Her eyes flew open, and she half rose to her feet before falling back to the ground. She could hear something shuffling in the forest beyond the tree. She scrambled backward on all fours, facing the sound as it grew closer, feeling around on the ground for something to use as a weapon without taking her eyes off the tree. Her breathing was heavy and raspy, and she struggled not to cough. Finally, her hands closed on a large stick about an inch thick and two feet long. It wasn't much, but it was all she had. She forced strength into her legs and shakily rose to her feet, one hand holding the stick and the other braced against a tree.

The shuffling sound came closer. Maeve squinted into the gathering darkness of the woods, straining to see the source of the noise. In the shadows, she thought she could see an outline of an animal moving toward her. She gripped the stick more tightly and prayed she had enough strength to fight off the wild animal. Thomas's life depended on it. She took another deep breath – and bent over at the waist, coughing heavily. The animal, drawn by the noise, rushed toward her. Maeve screamed and tried to swing the stick at it, but the beast was too large and powerful. Two large, hairy black paws hit Maeve's shoulders driving her backward toward the ground. She raised her arms to protect her head and tried to curl into a ball, waiting for sharp teeth to tear into her body, but all she felt was a wet tongue trying to get at her face. What kind of beast licked you to death?

Slowly, she rolled to her back and lowered her arms. A large, rough tongue licked the side of her face. Maeve opened her eyes to stare into Rufus's big, brown eyes. She started to laugh as Rufus continued to lick the sweat and tears off her face. "Oh, Rufus, where have you been?"

She pushed herself to a sitting position, wrapped her arms around the huge dog and buried her face into his soft fur. Rufus whimpered and nudged at her arm, urging her to rub his ears. Maeve obliged and reveled in the feel of his fur against her face.

"Guess we'd better get moving. Huh, boy?" Using his sturdy back to steady herself, Maeve regained her feet, feeling a bit stronger. She was still sick. She had no idea what she was going to do. But she was no longer alone.

Maeve and Rufus approached Gray's dark house. Despite the fact that they had only been gone a few days, the house held an air of neglect. The grass had grown longer than normal and dust from the hot, dry summer had gathered on the windows. To be honest, Maeve knew it could have looked like that before they had left. Gray spent more time at her and Emma's place than she spent at his.

Maeve stepped around the corner of the house, hoping she could avoid seeing anyone on this street. This was where she had grown up. She didn't want to be the reason that her friends and neighbors died.

"OK, boy," she whispered to Rufus. "Let's be careful. We don't want to get close to anyone."

Luckily, the street was deserted, and Maeve and Rufus stumbled toward the city center. Maeve knew she had to keep moving in that direction to keep Thomas safe, but as long as she didn't get too close to anyone, things would be fine. She could let someone know what was going on, then go somewhere to be alone and die. It was a good plan, she thought.

Her toe caught on a twig that had fallen to the dirt road. She stumbled and reached grasping fingers toward Rufus to steady herself, but her fingers came away with nothing but air, and she hit the ground face first. She lay there unable to move. Her body was sore and achy. A cough once again wracked her entire being. Rufus nosed at her, urging her to rise, but her strength was gone. The sky seemed to shimmer and wobble. She blinked. Once. Twice. Then closed her eyes and didn't open them again. Rufus's cold nose pressed against her arm, then her head. Then it was gone.

She was alone again. Maybe that was best. She wheezed in a breath, struggling to breath without coughing. She was so cold, yet sweat droplets dripped off her face and hair. There was a reason she needed to get up and keep moving, but she no longer knew what it was.

She heard slow, purposeful footsteps and turned her head toward the sound. They were coming nearer. But they shouldn't. There was a reason no one should get near her. What was it? A cool hand touched her face. Maeve turned her face toward it. Something warm covered her. Rufus's nose was back, pushing at her head and her hands.

"Maeve, Maeve, can you hear me?"

Maeve knew that voice, but she shouldn't be near her. There was something about Maeve that would be dangerous to her. Maeve struggled to open her heavy eyelids. She caught a glimpse of the woman kneeling next to her, the woman who had covered her with the blanket and touched her face. Her eyelids slid closed and a silent tear rolled down her face.

"Maeve, it's me. Emma." She patted Maeve's cheek. "You need to wake up."

CHAPTER THIRTY-FOUR

"Get away." The words were barely a whisper. Maeve tried again and managed to add some strength to her voice. "Get away, Emma."

Emma continued to examine Maeve, running her hands over her arms and legs, looking for the source of what ailed her. Maeve feebly pushed her hands away.

"You have to get away from me." Maeve struggled to draw air into her lungs. "I'm sick. It will kill you. Please. Get away."

Emma ignored her and placed her hand on Maeve's forehead.

"You're burning up. We have to get you inside. Come on, John."

Hands lifted Maeve to her feet, her arms were placed over others' shoulders, and she was half-dragged down the street.

"We have to get you into bed and get some willow bark into you."

Maeve struggled to stop her forward progress. She couldn't go into the house with them. She needed to get to the city center. Her thoughts were jumbled. She pulled her arms away from their shoulders and crumpled to the ground again.

"I can't. Don't want to infect you." Maeve's words came out in a rush, leaving her breathless. Emma crouched next to her.

Maeve tried to scoot backward. Emma drew her eyebrows together and studied Maeve thoughtfully. Maeve tried to scoot away again, putting more distance between them. Rufus stood patiently at her side, and Maeve leaned her head against his flank.

"Please, Emma. Get away from me."

Emma heard the urgency in her voice and took two steps backward.

"Fine." She turned to John. "Go get the willow bark and some water. Hurry."

Maeve heard John's footsteps retreat.

"What's going on, Maeve? How did you get sick?"

A fit of coughing shook Maeve's body from head to toe. When the coughing subsided, she just shook her head. "It's too much to tell, Emma. I can't sit here long. Thomas's life depends on me moving toward the city."

Emma's gaze took in Maeve's prone form. "You're not going anywhere under your own power right now, so you might as well tell me what's going on." She took a step toward Maeve.

"No! You can't get near me."

Emma held up a calming hand and stepped backward. "OK, OK. I'll stay here. You start talking."

Between coughing fits, Maeve gave Emma a short version of all that had happened since they left. She had just finished when John returned with the willow bark mixture.

"Take this, Maeve." John held out a tin cup filled

to the brim. He stepped toward her.

"Stay back," Maeve said weakly.

"OK. I'll set it right here." He set down the cup and backed away to where Emma stood. Maeve scooted forward until she could reach the cup then raised it with shaking hands to her lips, a few drops spilling on her leg. She drained the cup, then leaned her head against the wall of the building behind her. Closing her eyes, she sat in silence, listening to Emma quietly fill John in on all that Maeve had told her.

Maeve began to struggle to her feet.

"What are you doing?" Emma said with alarm in her voice. "You're too weak to go anywhere. Let John go get Cleo, and she can come to you."

Maeve looked at her with pleading eyes. "I have to keep moving, or Arabella will kill Thomas."

"How does she know where you are?" John scanned the sky, looking for anything watching her.

"There's a tracker in my arm."

"Where?" John took a step closer. "Show me."

"Stay there." Maeve pushed up her sleeve and pointed to the barely visible square below the flesh in her upper arm. John studied her arm from a distance.

"We could take it out."

"What?" Maeve's brain was sluggish.

"We could take it out." John continued to study her arm. "Then I could carry it with me when I go to get Cleo. Arabella will never know the difference, and you won't infect half the government."

Maeve shook her head as if to clear it. It seemed too easy. Wouldn't Arabella have thought of that?

"Are you sure it will come out, that it's not, I don't

know, grafted into me somehow?"

John shrugged. "There's only one way to find out." John pulled a small folding knife out of his pocket. "We're going to need some water and a fire. Can you make it to the house?" John pointed toward Maeve's and Emma's house 100 yards away. The distance looked like a mile to Maeve. She wasn't sure she could make it at all, but she pushed away from the house she was leaning against and commanded her brain to put one foot in front of the other. She began to move in a slow, painful shuffle, stopping frequently to rest as a coughing fit tore through her body. John and Emma walked about 10 feet in front of her. Every time they stopped to wait for her, she motioned them onward. She didn't want them any closer. The ground in front of her wavered before her eyes. As she struggled to get her legs to do what her increasingly sluggish brain told them to do, she wondered how John was going to get the tracker out without getting near her.

The 100-yard distance took Maeve 15 minutes to navigate. She knew she was going too slowly and Thomas's life was on the line, but what did Arabella expect? Arabella had made her almost too sick to move.

Finally, they reached the house, and Maeve sat heavily on the front step. "Hurry," she said in a hoarse voice. "Get the tracker out."

John entered the house and after a few minutes returned with a bowl full of water, holding his knife out away from his body. Maeve assumed he had sterilized it in the fire inside. When he got to the top of the steps, Maeve held up a hand.

"How are you going to do this?" She shook her head wearily. "You can't get near me or you'll get sick, too." She turned her head and coughed into her arm. When the coughing fit had subsided, John was sitting next to her on the step.

"No, you can't do this!" She grabbed the railing and tried to pull herself up to get away from him.

John placed his hand gently on her arm and eased her back to the sit on the step. "Maeve, I'll be fine. I promise. Let's get this done."

"You can't know that." Maeve's voice rose hysterically. "You'll get sick. You'll die. I need to protect you."

John patted her soothingly on the shoulder. "Maeve, listen to me. I promise I will be fine. I am not going to get sick, and I definitely don't plan on dying."

His calm, measured voice broke through Maeve's panic and she stopped struggling to get away. "You can't know that," she said in a more normal tone.

John nodded his head. "I can. I'm pretty sure I can't catch the virus."

Maeve's fevered eyes studied his face, looking for signs that he was lying to her. "How? How do you know that?"

"Because he's been injected with the vaccine," Emma said from where she was standing near the door of the house.

Maeve looked from Emma to John. She knew she couldn't have heard Emma right. "What vaccine?"

John took Maeve's arm and raised his knife to begin cutting out the tracker. "Focus on what I'm saying, Maeve. This is going to hurt a bit." He cut into her skin with the tip of his knife, and Maeve bit her lip to keep from making a sound.

"I used to work for Arabella – a long time ago before I joined The Resistance. Back when I believed in her ideals of making Palumbra a haven of peace and plenty. Before power became her only goal. I was in the process of making arrangements to leave the government and go into hiding with The Resistance when Arabella insisted that all of her top advisors receive this vaccine."

"Didn't that worry you?"

John shook his head. "I was naive. I had no idea what the vaccine was for. We got shots to keep us healthy all the time. I just assumed this was another one, but when I went to get the shot, there were only about 10 of us in the room. Usually, everyone in the government got the shots, and the line would stretch through the building."

Maeve winced as John's knife dug into her arm. Through gritted teeth, she asked, "How do you know the vaccine was for this virus."

"Because I asked the nurse administering the shot. She said it was for a new virus and was just precautionary. My suspicions were great enough that I started investigating this new virus and found it was something Arabella's scientists had created in a lab."

Maeve clenched her hands into fists as John made another cut on her arm. "Why didn't you do anything about it?"

"I did. We did. When the WG fell, we went to the lab and destroyed all the samples. She must have taken a vial or two before we got there. While we were able to round up nearly all of Arabella's supporters, some got away. They must have followed her to The Hub. Got it."

John placed a small chip on the towel he had laid next to his leg. "Let's get you fixed up. I can't do stitches, but we'll bandage you up and it should be fine. You might have a bit of a scar."

"If I live that long," Maeve said.

John patted her on the shoulder again. "We'll figure it out, Maeve. Have faith in your friends."

John handed Maeve another tin cup filled with a greenish mixture. "Drink this. It will help with the pain."

Maeve's arm had begun to ache where John removed the tracker, so she drank the vile-smelling mixture without complaint. John picked up the tracker and rose to his feet. "I'm going to get this to Cleo." He smiled at Maeve. "You let Emma take care of you."

Maeve shook her head weakly. "She can't come near me. I may have already infected her." She slumped back against the step. "I'll just sit here."

John hoisted her to her feet. "Come on. You can't sit out here where anyone can see you. I'll help you up to bed." John cut her off before she could protest. "Emma will stay outside your room, but you'll be more comfortable."

John settled her into her own bed, plumping the pillow behind her. Emma hovered in the doorway. As he moved to step away, she grabbed his hand. "I'm going to die, aren't I?" she whispered softly so Emma couldn't hear.

John leaned lower to hear her whispered words. "Not if I can help it," he said fiercely. He squeezed her hand. "You hang in there until I get back."

CHAPTER THIRTY-FIVE

"This is never going to work." Ginger adjusted the rock in her bleeding fingers. "We'll be here until next week trying to get these things off our hands." She held up her still-bound hands to show what little progress she had made on cutting through the thick, leather ties holding her hands together. Blood from her raw fingers dripped down onto the leather.

"Keep working at it," Gray said through gritted teeth. "We have to get back to Maeve." Gray sawed at the leather ties with his own rock though he hadn't made much more progress than Ginger.

"Hey, guys." Emery's voice echoed through the cavern where they sat. Gray looked at where Emery had been sitting, sawing at her bonds like the rest of them but didn't see her. "Where are you, Emery?"

"Over here."

Gray turned to look behind him. The cavern was lit by the sun shining in through the high entrance, but the shadows hid Emery. All he could see was her outline. "You need to see this." Her voice drifted from the shadows.

Tristan walked over to where Emery stood. "How did you... Oh, wow. Great job, Emery. Get over here, you two."

Gray and Ginger scrambled to their feet and hurried over to Tristan and Emery.

"What is it?" Gray asked. "How did you get your hands free?"

"Ta-da!" Emery waved her hand as if presenting something. "Our key to freedom."

Gray squinted in the shadows and made out a piece of rock protruding from the wall of the cave. "It's razor sharp." Emery held up her newly freed hands as if to prove that it worked. Tristan was already sawing through his bonds that came away with a soft snap as he broke through the last strand of leather. Ginger and Gray quickly removed their own bonds.

"Well, that's one problem solved." Tristan shook his hands to return circulation to his fingers. "On to the next one. Where are we going to find food?"

They looked at each other, no one sure where to begin. "We've been out here too long already." Gray began to pace then raised his head with an agonized look. "She could be dead already."

Ginger rubbed his arm. "Or she could still be alive. She's smart, and she's tough. We have to focus on finding our way back. We can't help her if we're stuck out here."

"Do we even know the way back?" Gray ran his hands through his hair in frustration.

"I do." Emery tapped her head. "Photographic memory, remember? And I'm pretty good with directions."

"How far do you think it is, Em?" Ginger asked.

"Well, those hovercars don't have a really long range."

Ginger sent her a questioning glance. Emery

shrugged. "I didn't really have anything else to do in the hovercar all by myself except for Rufus, so I checked it out."

"What happened to Rufus?" Tristan asked.

"I don't know. He made a run for it as soon as the hovercar doors opened. I was surprised Arabella's guards didn't shoot him. I think he must have surprised them."

"Back to where we are," Gray said impatiently.

"Right. The hovercars have a very short range, and they needed to get back to The Hub. I figure we can't be more than fifteen to twenty miles outside of Bellus."

"Fantastic." Sarcasm seeped from Gray's voice. "It will take us a day to get back to Bellus and another two days to get back to Palumbra. How does that help Maeve?"

"But we don't have to go back to Bellus," Emery said. "Look." She picked up a stick and began to draw in the dirt floor of the cavern. "This is Palumbra." She pointed at an X she had drawn in the top right of the space. "This." She drew another X to the right of the first one. "Is Bellus." She drew a third X below and midway between the two X's. She pointed to it with her stick. "This is where I think we are." She drew a line between the third X and the one representing Palumbra. "We can just go straight to Palumbra, cutting off at least a day."

Ginger moved so she could study Emery's crude map. "Are you sure, Emery? We don't want to wander around out here forever."

Emery nodded decisively. "I'm sure. We go straight from here to Palumbra. We should be there in a couple of days."

"What about Thomas?" Tristan asked quietly. "Where's the oasis?"

Emery considered her map for a minute, then drew an X midway and slightly to the right of the line between Palumbra and their location. "I think it's there."

Tristan eyed Gray warily before speaking. "It's right on our way."

Gray said nothing but continued to study the map on the ground. Ginger came to stand next to him. "It's your choice, Gray."

"Why?" He raised tortured eyes to her. "Why is it my choice? Do I condemn Thomas to save Maeve or do I give up on Maeve to save Thomas?" His eyes glimmered. "How do I make that choice?"

Maeve woke with a start. Sweat dripped down her face, and her hair was plastered to her head. She moved her head restlessly from side to side. There was something she should be doing. She couldn't lie here in her bed. People were counting on her. But who? Her fevered mind couldn't quite grasp any one thought, and her eyes slipped closed again.

"Maeve," a voice broke through the fevered fog surrounding her brain. "Maeve, drink this."

Maeve struggled to open her eyes, but they felt like someone had glued them shut. She knew that voice. She needed to reach it to keep the speaker safe. Finally, Maeve pried her eyes open. She squinted against the sunlight and saw a figure leaning over her, holding a cup to her lips. Maeve began to struggle to get away. Arabella. Arabella had done this to her and was trying to finish her off. With what little strength she had left, Maeve knocked the cup out of Arabella's hand, and she heard it clatter to the floor.

"Shhh." Maeve felt a cool cloth on her forehead.

"It's OK, Maeve. It's just me. Emma."

The name penetrated Maeve's fever-induced delusion, and she stopped struggling and closed her eyes. Almost immediately, they opened again in alarm. "Emma," Maeve croaked. "Why are you in here? Get away. You'll get sick."

Emma slowly straightened from where she had leaned over to pick up the cup. "I think I get to make that choice, Maeve."

"But we don't have the antidote. Why would you do this? We don't both need to die."

Emma clasped Maeve's hand with both of her own. "Do you really think I could just let you suffer without trying to help?" She plumped the pillow behind Maeve's head and refilled the cup. "Drink this. It should help with the fever."

Maeve allowed Emma to lift her head and tip the cup's contents into her mouth. She no longer had the strength to fight, and she had to admit that it was nice not to be alone.

"How long have I been asleep?"

Emma looked at the clock on the wall. "A couple of hours. John should be back soon. Do you know what Arabella's plan was after she dropped you off here?"

A coughing fit consumed Maeve's body. When it stopped, she dropped her head weakly back onto the pillow. "She was going to let everyone get too sick to fight back, then swoop in with the cure and retake power." Maeve turned her head to look at Emma. "The cure, of course, would only be available to those who swore allegiance to her."

"Which the current leaders would never do."

Emma rose and moved to look out the window. "It's almost a perfect plan."

Maeve laughed weakly. "I like your optimism."

Emma turned back to Maeve. "You are not going to die. And we are not going to let Arabella regain power in this city. We've worked too hard and come too far. I've spent my whole life fighting this battle. I'm not about to stop now."

Emma gave a weak cough. Maeve looked at her in alarm.

"Don't worry about me. Let's focus on keeping you comfortable." She coughed again.

"Emma, you need to rest. If you've been infected, your body won't be able to fight it. Forget about me," Maeve pleaded. "Take care of yourself."

Emma patted Maeve's hand as another coughing fit wracked her body. "I'll be fine, dear. You go back to sleep."

Exhausted, Maeve's eyes slid closed.

"Give it to her."

"Emma, be reasonable. What if we split it? Half to her and half to you. Surely that would be enough to keep you both alive until the lab can make more."

"John, you know that's not how it works. Give it to Maeve. She's going to die if you don't."

Maeve heard the whispered voices but couldn't make sense of the conversation. It sounded like someone was going to die. She wheezed in a breath. Why was it so hard to breathe? She tried to open her eyes, but her eyelids were too heavy. She sank further into the pillows and blankets and focused on breathing. Breathe in. Breathe out.

254

Breathe in. Breathe out. Breathe... A cough tore through her body, and she thought her lungs might exit her body through her mouth.

A cool hand raised her head, and she felt a syrupy liquid in her mouth. She tried to swallow, but her throat felt thick and closed, and she began to splutter and cough. "Come on, Maeve. You need to drink it." Maeve turned her head away from the cup like a child refusing her dinner. The cup returned to her mouth. Too tired to fight, Maeve allowed the liquid to flow down her throat and tried to swallow without coughing.

"That's great. A little more."

Maeve opened her mouth for more liquid. She heard a loud cough from the other side of the room. Her eyes were still too heavy to open. She knew she should be concerned about that cough, but she couldn't hold onto a thought for more than a second. She swallowed another gulp of liquid before the hand holding her head gently settled her back on the pillow.

She struggled to breathe once more. A hand clasped hers. "Come on, Maeve. Just breathe. You'll feel better soon."

Maeve focused on breathing and drifted once more into oblivion.

CHAPTER THIRTY-SIX

"Let's pick up Thomas on the way to Palumbra." Gray heaved a sigh. "It's what Maeve would want us to do. We can't just leave him there all alone."

Tristan gave Gray a thoughtful look. "Do you really think Arabella just left him there?"

Gray walked to the entrance of the cavern and looked at the barren, rocky ground outside their shelter. "What do you mean?"

"She threw us out here because she figured we couldn't survive very long with no food or water and our hands bound. But I doubt she left Thomas at the Oasis by himself." He walked over and stood next to Gray. "It wouldn't make sense. How do you think she was going to get Maeve to actually infect people in Palumbra?"

Gray's eyes narrowed as he processed what Tristan had said. Ginger and Emery joined them at the entrance to the cavern.

"Arabella's smart. Crazy. But smart," Ginger said. "It only makes sense that she would hold Thomas as leverage over Maeve. Otherwise, Maeve would just hide somewhere until she died without infecting anyone else."

Gray stared off into the distance. "That's what I'm

afraid of. That she would just give up on living to avoid hurting anyone else." His voice broke. "If she thought she was responsible for harming anyone else, it would break her. She would rather die."

Ginger slipped her hand into his and squeezed. "She's stronger than you think, Gray. We'll find her and figure out how to make her well. But we're of no use to her here. We have to get moving."

Gray swallowed hard and nodded.

"Emery says we need to move Northeast." Tristan looked at the sun then pointed slightly to their right. "We need to go that way."

"What about water?" Emery asked as they made their way out of the cavern and down the rocky slope, sliding and stumbling on the loose rocks.

"There has to be some water somewhere." Tristan surveyed the barren landscape around them. "We'll just have to hope we find something before we reach the desert."

Maeve woke to a darkened room and the faint sound of coughing, but it was not hers. Her muscles ached as if she had run a long way, but her mind was clear. She looked around the dim room and realized it was her own. She searched her memory for how she had come to be in her own bed. The last thing she remembered was stumbling into Palumbra and meeting Emma.

Emma. Maeve's eyes widened, and she struggled to push herself to a sitting position. She swung her aching legs to the floor and pushed herself to her feet. She swayed but remained upright. With one hand on the wall, she crossed the short distance to the door and quietly opened it.

Steadying herself on the hallway wall, she followed the sound of voices and coughing. At the doorway to Emma's room, she stopped. John was sitting next to the bed, talking quietly to Emma. The look of love and sadness on his face held Maeve's attention. Emma smiled at something John said, then noticed Maeve.

"Maeve. Come on in." She coughed weakly after she spoke.

Maeve slowly entered the room, and John offered her his chair.

"What happened? Did I get you sick?"

Emma patted her hand. "No, Maeve. I chose to take care of you. You didn't cause this."

"But I did. I brought this disease to you." Maeve turned stricken eyes to John. "Isn't there anything we can do?"

John gave her a sad smile. "The government scientists are working to recreate the antidote, but it requires plagoran venom, and we don't have any. No one has seen plagorans in years."

"But we have," Maeve said excitedly. "We saw two plagorans on our way to The Hub. We helped one of them after Gray and Tristan wounded it."

John's sad eyes brightened slightly. "Where did you see it?"

"Just outside the outskirts of Palumbra, to the West, toward The Hub, before you get to the desert."

John hurried over to the other side of Emma's bed. "Did you hear that? It's our best hope. I have to go tell Cleo and the others." He kissed Emma's forehead. "You stay alive. I love you." Maeve turned her head away to give them a moment of privacy. John straightened and hurried toward the door.

"Wait." John stopped at Maeve's words. "The plagoran had some kind of tracking tag in its ear. It might help you find it."

John nodded and turned to go again. "Please don't hurt it," Maeve pleaded.

"I'll do my best, but we need that venom." He gave Emma one last look and walked out the door.

Maeve turned back to Emma. "Why are you so stubborn?"

Emma gave a slight shrug. "Guess I was born that way. Nice to see you looking better, though."

Maeve wrinkled her forehead. "How did that happen? And why isn't John sick?"

"You don't remember?"

Maeve shook her head. "The last thing I remember is Rufus getting you. Where is Rufus anyway?"

"Downstairs, sleeping. He looked like he'd had a rough few days. We cleaned him up and fed him. John says he's been sleeping ever since."

"But why do I feel better? And why isn't John sick?"

"A long time ago, John worked for Arabella." Maeve's shock must have shown on her face. "It was a long time ago, Maeve. There was a time when Arabella had ideals that John thought were worth pursuing. When her goal became the pursuit of power, he walked away."

"But that doesn't explain why he's not sick."

"There was a vaccine for this virus, and Arabella gave it to her top advisors."

Maeve sat in stunned silence. "She's had this virus plan for that long?"

Emma raised an eyebrow. "She's a smart lady. She always has a plan."

"But why do I feel better, and you're still sick? I thought this virus was 100% deadly."

The edge of Emma's mouth quirked in what could have been a smile or a grimace. "It is. John gave you the antidote."

"How did he have the antidote? Why didn't he give you some, too?"

Emma captured her gaze with a strong, steady one of her own. "When the WG was disbanded, all of their research was set aside to be looked at. The new government hasn't had a chance to go through everything, so John and some others went through the research to find anything related to this virus. They only found one dose of the antidote, Maeve. I told him to give it to you."

Maeve stared at Emma in stunned silence. "Why would you do that?" Her voice was strained. A lump formed in her throat.

Emma picked up Maeve's hand. "Because you have so much more life to live."

Maeve pulled her hand away and struggled to her feet. "So do you," she shouted. "Why would you choose to give it to me when I was the one that made you sick?"

"Maeve, sit down," Emma said in a calm but firm voice. "Shouting isn't helping anyone."

"But how could you do this?" Maeve returned to the chair. "You've survived so much. Why would you choose me?"

Emma scooted herself up a bit in the bed, and Maeve adjusted her pillow. "Maeve, it's because I've survived so much that I made that choice. I've lived my life. I've done my part." She began to cough, and her whole body contorted with the effort. When the coughing fit had passed, Maeve passed her a glass of water.

"Now, it's your turn. You have so much life left, Maeve." She smiled a weak smile. "Look at what you've already accomplished. Imagine how much more you can do."

Maeve shook her head. "What have I really done? Walked my friends into trouble because I was ridden with guilt. Infected you with a deadly virus. That's not a really great track record."

"Overthrew a corrupt government. Saved Gray's life. Taught kids like Thomas that freedom means something." Emma patted Maeve's hand. "I'd say you've done pretty well for only being 17."

Maeve gave her a doubtful look, then picked up Emma's hand. "But you can't die. I need you." Her eyes glimmered with tears, and she could speak no more.

Emma's body was once again wracked by a coughing fit. Maeve gripped her hand tightly until it passed. Emma took another sip of water. "You will be fine when I'm gone." Maeve shook her head but said nothing, still holding tightly to Emma's hand. "I've lived way longer than I expected to when I was your age. I've seen and done so many things. But my time is over."

"Don't say that. John and the others will make some more antidote now that they know where to find the plagoran."

"Maybe. And that would be great. But, honey, if they don't get it made in time, it will be OK. I don't want you to blame yourself."

"But I did this to you. I brought this virus into our

house."

"No," Emma said fiercely. "Arabella did this to us. You did what you had to do to protect someone who was defenseless. You made the right choice."

Tears spilled over out of Maeve's eyes. "But I didn't," she sobbed. "I had the chance to kill Arabella, and I didn't. I could have prevented all of this."

"Tell me what happened."

Haltingly, Maeve told Emma about holding the gun on Arabella and choosing to set it aside rather than kill her. By the time the story was told, Maeve had laid her head on the bed, weary to the bone.

Emma gently stroked Maeve's hair. "Why did you make that choice, Maeve?"

Maeve sniffed. "I couldn't do it. All I could see was that soldier dying when I shot him." She raised her head. "I would do it again to save Gray, but I couldn't just kill her in cold blood. I couldn't." She wiped her nose on the back of her hand. "But I should have. If I had..."

Emma stopped her with a raised hand. "What would have happened if you'd shot her?"

"Her guards would have killed me." Maeve continued talking before Emma could stop her. "But that would have been OK. At least you would have been safe."

"What about Ginger, Tristan, Emery and Gray? What about Thomas? What would have happened to them?"

Maeve stared at the frayed edge of the quilt before speaking. "The guards would have killed them, too," she said quietly.

"And what happened next?"

Maeve looked at her in confusion. "They injected

me with the virus."

"So instead of making the choice that would assure you and your friends died, you chose to lay down your life and gave your friends a chance to live. Is that right?"

Maeve's eyes widened at Emma's choice of words. "Those were the words at the sanctuary."

Emma wrinkled her nose in confusion. "What sanctuary?"

"In Bellus, Gray and I ended up in a sanctuary, and the keeper told us this story about these men who had saved the people of Bellus at the cost of their own lives. Inscribed on the wall were the words 'Greater love has no one than this that he lay down his life for his friends.' I don't think I really understood them until I had to make a choice." She raised her eyes to Emma's. "But if you die, was it the right one?"

"Maeve, look at me." Maeve raised her eyes until they met Emma's wise gray ones. "You made the right choice."

Maeve started to interrupt, but Emma held up her hand again. "You made the right choice. In both instances, the soldier and Arabella, you protected your friends. That's never wrong. You gave them a fighting chance at life."

Maeve still looked skeptical.

"All we can do in this life is make the best choices we can, guided by what we know to be right and true. Is killing ever right? In a perfect world, no." Emma let out a short laugh that ended with a cough. "But this world is far from perfect, and sometimes there are no good choices. You can only pray that the outcome of the one you choose causes less harm than the other option."

Maeve considered Emma's words. "But how do

you live with the knowledge that you picked a bad option simply because it was less bad than the other one?"

Emma shifted in the bed. "No one can tell you that. You have to make peace with it however you can. You pray for forgiveness, and you learn to forgive yourself. And, Maeve, if I don't make it, remember, I made a choice, too. And I know it was the right one."

Emma's eyelids began to drift closed. "I'm tired. Why don't you get some rest, too?"

Maeve helped Emma lay back down in the bed and returned to the chair. Emma's breathing evened out, but it contained a worrisome rasp. Maeve knew she should return to her own bed, but she stayed in the chair for a long time.

CHAPTER THIRTY-SEVEN

"Come on, Emery. You have to keep up." Ginger stopped to wait for her sister. Emery stumbled on the rocky ground and slowly made her way up the hill everyone else had already climbed. Her face was pale and her hair lank and sweaty. Her breath came in short pants.

"I'm trying, Ginger," she huffed. "But I'm so thirsty." Emery finally reached the top of the hill and leaned against Ginger, struggling to catch her breath.

Tristan glanced over his shoulder at them. "We have to find water soon," he said in a low voice to Gray.

Gray nodded as his eyes scanned the horizon, looking for any sign of water. In the distance, he could see the edge of the desert. Without water, they would never make it to the oasis. Emery was still recovering from being infected with the virus. She needed water and rest. Gray's stomach growled. Some food wouldn't hurt either. He turned to continue toward the desert when a shimmer to the west caught his eye. Slowly, he turned his head to get a better look, hope rising inside him like a fountain. He squinted into the distance and raised a hand to shield his eyes from the afternoon sun as a smile broke over his face.

"Water," he cried.

Tristan looked in the direction Gray pointed, and he, too, broke into a grin. "Did you hear that, Emery? Water ahead."

"But that's the wrong direction," Ginger said. "It will take hours to reach it and get back on course."

"What choice do we have?" Tristan asked. "It's the only sign of water we've seen. We can't hit the desert without water."

Ginger looked at the shimmer of the lake or pond in the distance and back at Emery's wan face. "I guess we'd better get moving then."

Maeve didn't know how long she sat in the chair next to Emma's bed. She must have nodded off because when she woke, the thin rays of afternoon sun coming in through the window had disappeared into darkness. After her conversation with Emma, she felt the weight of the guilt she had been carrying start to lift. Emma was right. Maeve couldn't change the things she had done. She had to forgive herself and move forward.

Careful not to wake Emma, she rose from the chair on shaky legs and went back to her room. Her stomach rumbled. She couldn't remember the last time she had eaten. Once in her room, she pulled on some clean clothes and made her way slowly down the stairs to the kitchen. She put together a protein paste sandwich with a side of carrots from their garden and a glass of fresh milk. John must have taken care of the animals before he left.

When she sat at the table, Rufus's head appeared in her lap.

"Hey, boy." She gave him a piece of her sandwich. He swallowed it in one gulp and looked up at her with his pleading brown eyes. "I know it's not great, but it's what we have."

Maeve finished her meal, sharing the rest of her sandwich with Rufus, although he turned his nose up at the carrot she offered him. The food did Maeve almost as much good as the antidote. She drained the last of her milk and walked to put her dishes in the sink on legs that were weak but no longer shaking. She rinsed her dishes and left them to dry. Wiping her wet hands on her pant legs, she said, "Well, Rufus, what do we do now? I can't leave Emma here alone, but I need to do something to find my friends." She sat back in her chair at the table at rubbed Rufus's ears.

"What do you think, boy?"

Rufus whined.

"I know you miss him. We'll find him, I promise."

Rufus's ears perked up at a noise at the door.

"I hope that's John."

The door opened and John walked through, his shoulders slumped and his steps slow. Maeve rose from her chair.

"John?"

John jumped, startled at the sound of her voice. "Maeve. What are you doing out of bed?"

"I needed something to eat." She motioned toward the drying dishes in the sink. "I'm feeling much better, but you look exhausted."

John sank wearily into a chair and dropped his head into his hands, massaging his scalp with his fingers.

"How's Emma?"

Maeve returned to her chair. "Not good, but she's hanging in there."

John lifted his face from his hands and looked at Maeve in the dim light of the lamp she had lit. "There's no antidote coming, Maeve."

Maeve stared at him with horror-struck eyes. "They can't get the plagoran venom," he continued.

"But I told them where to look," Maeve said in an unsteady voice.

"They sent out a team, but they haven't come back yet." Tears pooled in John's eyes. "I don't think they're going to find it in time."

"What are we going to do?" Maeve whispered.

John heaved a sigh. "Cleo really needs to talk with you about everything that happened. I put her off saying you were too sick to be of help, but if you really are feeling better, then you need to go down to government headquarters and talk with her."

Maeve nodded slowly. She knew this summons would be coming. Her eyes drifted to the ceiling. "What about Emma?"

"I'll stay here with her. I'll let you know if there's any change."

Maeve nodded and got to her feet. "Come on, Rufus. You can go with me."

Maeve and Rufus slowly made their way through the streets of Palumbra. Though nothing had changed since she left, the once familiar buildings looked strange to her. In just a week, she had changed, and the trappings of her old life no longer seemed to fit. They passed her parents' house, and Maeve's feet slowed. She remembered her resolve to make things right with her parents when she was sitting alone in a cell, but she knew Cleo was waiting. "Later," she told Rufus. "We'll stop later."

When they reached the modern glass building that served as the government's headquarters at the city center, Maeve paused to look up and down the street. This area had been at the heart of the destruction caused by the WG. Bombs had ruined businesses all along the street, but people were rebuilding.

At the doors of the building, a guard stopped them. "No dogs in the building."

Rufus looked at Maeve with his sad, brown eyes, and Maeve scratched his ears before turning back to the guard. "We're here to see Cleo. She'll want to see the dog, too."

At Cleo's name, the guard raised his eyebrows. "What's your name?"

"Maeve Jackson." She gestured toward the dog. "This is Rufus."

At the mention of her name, the guard's demeanor changed. His eyes took on an awed look, and his mouth formed an O. After a week of running for her life, Maeve had forgotten that she was semi-famous in Palumbra. "Just a minute, Miss Jackson. I'll call right up." He walked briskly to the wall and picked up a black phone. After a minute, he hung up the phone and motioned to her.

"President Cleo says you can go on up. She's on the top floor." He held the door open for her, and his eyes shifted to Rufus. "The dog, too."

Maeve smiled at him and walked into the lobby. Unlike the rest of Palumbra, this building held all the modern conveniences, including shining tile floors and glass walls that rose into the air. A chandelier hung from the high ceiling, its crystals sending shafts of sunlight throughout the building like fairy lights. While the new government had tried to cut down on the obvious differences between the government building and the dwellings in the rest of Palumbra, there was no hiding that the people who worked here enjoyed a much nicer work environment than most other Palumbrans. Maeve knew it would be a waste not to use the building, but she shook her head at Arabella's monument to her own power. Cleo had converted the lower levels of the building into housing for some of the older residents of Palumbra, a kind of community for those who could no longer work or needed help getting around. Maeve waved to a few residents who were out for a stroll around the lobby then took Rufus over to the bank of elevators. They stepped in and Maeve pushed the button for the top floor.

Rufus gave a start when the elevator lurched into motion, pressing himself so hard against Maeve's leg that she had to put a hand on the wall for balance. She scratched his ears and said, "It's OK, boy. We're just going up."

When the doors opened, Maeve stepped out into the large open space that served as the meeting space for the top government officials. A large glass table took up the center of the room, and desks were situated around the edge of the room. Cleo didn't like the idea of having walls between the government leaders, so no one had an office up here. While Cleo had a ground floor office, she rarely used it. They all worked in the same common space. Cleo sat at the table, engrossed in some papers, but she looked up when Maeve and Rufus exited the elevator and gave Maeve a quick smile.

"Maeve, you look like you're feeling better." She held out her hand for Rufus to sniff. When he sat in front of her, she ruffled his ears and looked at Maeve. "This must be Rufus. I hear he saved your life."

Maeve gave a grim smile. "He got Emma and John. I think John did the actual saving – at the expense of Emma."

Cleo's face took on a sober look, and she kept her gaze on Rufus. "I know, Maeve. I'm sorry. There wasn't enough antidote for you both. We all agreed you should get it." She gave Rufus a final pat and straightened, looking Maeve in the eyes. "Our scientists are working around the clock to figure out how to make a new batch, but..." She trailed off.

"I know. No plagoran venom."

Cleo shook her head, and her shoulders slumped slightly. "Our team is out looking for plagoran, but they haven't found any yet." She walked over to the table and pulled out the chair next to her own. "We should talk." She gestured to the chair. "Maybe you'll be able to tell me something that will help point us in the right direction."

CHAPTER THIRTY-EIGHT

Maeve slumped gratefully into the chair. Until Cleo had offered her a seat, she hadn't realized how tired she was from the walk to the building. A protein paste bar and some water appeared in front of her.

"You look exhausted. Eat."

Rufus settled himself at Maeve's feet, and she picked up the protein paste bar, broke off a piece for Rufus, and took a bite herself. When she had finished the snack, she set down her cup and turned to face Cleo.

Maeve noted the worry lines on Cleo's face and the fine streaks of gray around her temples that hadn't been there six months ago. The weight of leadership had aged her in just a few months, although Maeve reminded herself that Cleo had been leading The Resistance long before she had taken over as leader of Palumbra. She compared Cleo's tired eyes and plain clothes to Arabella's continually youthful appearance and extravagant fashions. Cleo felt the pain of the people; Arabella caused it.

"Why don't we start with you telling me what you know about the plagoran." Cleo tucked a stray wisp of hair back into the braid on the side of her head.

Maeve shrugged. "Not much, really. We ran into a

couple on our way to the desert and then another one in the desert."

"Plagoran are dangerous. How did you get past them?"

Rufus shifted and laid his head on Maeve's feet. "Tristan and Gray wounded one of them. Emery insisted that we stop and help it." Maeve silently wondered where her friends were and if she would ever see them again. She closed her eyes against the tears that threatened to leak out. Cleo squeezed her shoulder and said nothing. Maeve sniffed, took a deep breath and opened her eyes again to find Cleo looking at her with a mixture of impatience and sympathy.

"I told John that the one we helped had a tag in its ear. I thought it might help in tracking it."

"It would if we knew the frequency." Cleo tugged a piece of paper out of the stack in front of her. "These are all the frequencies we've tried, but so far we haven't found anything."

Maeve picked up the paper and scanned the five-digit numbers on the sheet. "I wish Emery was here. She could probably remember the numbers on the tag."

Cleo leaned forward. "Think, Maeve. Even if you can only remember a few of the numbers, it will help speed things up."

Maeve leaned back in her chair and closed her eyes. The weight of Rufus resting on her feet reminded her of the urgency of getting this right. She sent her mind back to the moments when she and Emery were trying to stop the plagoran's bleeding and Emery had told her the numbers on the tag.

"The tag was yellow." She spoke without opening

her eyes. "Emery said it had been punched through the plagoran's ear. She talked about the numbers on the tag." Maeve scrunched up her nose, desperate to remember. "Maybe 568 were the first three numbers?" She opened her eyes and shook her head in defeat. "I'm sorry. So much has happened since then. That's the best I can do."

Cleo patted Maeve's arm, wrote the numbers on the piece of paper and handed it to a young man about Maeve's age who was working at the desk closest to her. "That helps, Maeve. It narrows down the search." She returned to her seat and gave Maeve a serious look. "We'll find it, Maeve. We'll do everything we can to save Emma."

"I know you will," Maeve said quietly. "But will it be enough?"

Silence fell between them until Maeve finally spoke.

"What did John do with my tracker?"

"He walked around with it for a bit, then put it in an empty office. We figured they expect you to get really sick and die, so you're not going to walk around forever. Plus, they had to expect we would isolate you."

Maeve nodded. It was a good idea.

"What are we going to do about Thomas and the others?"

Cleo averted her eyes. "We're working on a plan." She began to shuffle the papers in front of her.

Maeve leaned forward. "We are going after them, right?"

Cleo sighed. "Maeve, I've got a team trying to hunt down the plagoran and another team trying to figure out how to repel the invasion Arabella is going to send our way. I don't have a lot of people to spare to go find Thomas and the rest of them. We don't even know where they are."

At Thomas's name, Rufus lifted his head and whined. Maeve felt like doing the same. She couldn't believe what she was hearing.

"We risked everything, and you can't spare people to find them?"

Cleo rose and walked to the window, looking out over Palumbra.

"Maeve, you went on an unsanctioned mission, and you got caught. You brought a plague back to the city that simply by the grace of God didn't annihilate us."

Maeve rose, too. Rufus gave her a disapproving look as he moved his head out of her way. "We discovered Arabella is still alive and plotting against Palumbra. We went on the mission to try to uncover who was still loyal to Arabella within your own government. And you just want to leave my friends out there to die? Thomas is 10! And he's all alone. Haven't we done enough for Palumbra to warrant being rescued? Tristan is out there. Didn't you practically raise him when his parents died?"

Cleo fell silent for a moment. "Did you find out who they were?"

"What are you talking about?"

"The people trying to undermine my government. Did you find out who they were?"

Maeve shook her head then realized Cleo couldn't see her. "No. We never got close to the patrol before they were killed by Sarge."

"Sarge?"

"You know him?"

Cleo turned from the window. "If it's who I think it is, he used to be my friend, a leader in The Resistance. But he sold us out for money and power."

Maeve thought of Elton. "I know the feeling."

Cleo studied the floor. "A lot of people died because of his greed. I can't let that happen again."

Maeve joined Cleo at the window where they could just make out the edge of the desert. "You can't just let them die out there."

Cleo turned from the window to face Maeve. "It's not that I don't want to send people after them, Maeve. I simply can't spare the number of people it would take to mount a rescue mission for Thomas and a search mission to find the others. I have to protect the people of Palumbra. That's my job."

"How many can you spare?"

"What?"

"How many people can you spare to look for them?"

"Not many. Three, maybe four?"

"I'll take them."

"Maeve, you can't go traipsing back through the desert. You're recovering from being sick. Think of how tired you were when you got here."

"Think of how tired my friends are. Think of how scared Thomas is. I have to go back and find them."

"What about Emma?"

Maeve winced. Thinking about Emma hurt.

"I can't let you go, Maeve. You're too weak, and Emma needs you." She placed a hand on Maeve's shoulder and looked straight into her eyes, her chocolate brown eyes intense in her dark face. "I promise we'll find Gray and Thomas and the others as soon as we've met the immediate threat from Arabella."

Maeve saw the determination in Cleo's eyes and knew she was beat. She would have to find another way to get to her friends.

"Are you sure we're going the right way?"

Tristan rolled his eyes at Ginger's question. "Yes. Believe it or not, Gray and I actually trained to become soldiers who can survive in the wilderness. We can tell north from south."

Ginger rolled her shoulders to ease the discomfort of carrying her own weight plus half of Emery's. Emery was valiantly trying to stand on her own feet, but a few miles back she had started using Ginger for balance.

"No need to get snippy." She moved closer to Tristan. "She's not going to make it much farther."

"I can hear you," Emery said without much emotion. "I'm fine."

Ginger gave a short laugh. "You're not fine. You need rest and water."

Tristan unlooped Emery's arm from Ginger's shoulder and scooped her up.

"I can walk."

Tristan grinned down at her. "Sure you can, but right now you don't need to."

"You can't carry her all the way to Palumbra." Ginger toyed with the end of her long ponytail. "You're going to have to leave us behind."

"Now that's not gonna happen," came Gray's voice from behind them. "Tristan and I will take turns carrying Emery until we find water. Hopefully, we'll find some food, too. That should give her the energy to go on."

Gray pushed between Tristan and Ginger.

"Now, let's get going. We don't have time to waste."

Tristan and Ginger followed him across the endless rocky ground. Despite having walked several miles, it felt as if they hadn't moved. The scenery was the same everywhere. Rocks of all sizes with the occasional small growth of vegetation, no trees, no large bushes, nothing to relieve the never-ending sameness of the horizon. Ginger was beginning to wonder if they had really seen water or if it was just an illusion.

"How is he holding up?" Ginger nodded toward Gray whose long legs were eating up the ground about 10 yards ahead of them.

"Gray?" Tristan grimaced. "He's beating himself up that he's not already on his way back to Maeve, but he won't leave us out here. It's tearing him up inside."

Ginger kicked a rock, and it rolled forward and dropped into a small crevice in the ground. "I wish we could move faster."

"I'm sorry," Emery said in a small voice.

"Oh, Em. It's not your fault. No one blames you."

"Listen to your sister. Definitely not your fault." Emery looked skeptical. "If you want to blame someone, blame Arabella. She's the one that did this."

"And Elton," Ginger said bitterly.

"And Elton," Tristan agreed.

They trudged on in Gray's wake, stopping occasionally to reorient themselves as the sun moved across the sky. Ginger's feet were sore and on their way to having blisters, and her stomach felt as if it were chewing on itself. She licked her lips trying to moisten them with what little saliva was in her mouth. The world had narrowed to the small patch of ground in front of her. If she could take just one more step, she would be one step closer.

Gray stopped abruptly, and Ginger raised her head. For the first time in their journey, the landscape ahead of them had changed. Trees rose from the ground, and the endless rocks gave way to dirt.

"I think the water is on the other side of these trees." Gray pointed needlessly toward the trees in front of them.

Ginger looked at Emery's wan face as she lay in Tristan's arms. She tugged on his arm and began to run. "Let's go."

"Wait, Ginger!" But Ginger ignored his call, intent on getting to the water that would revive her sister. She ran through the stand of trees, pushing branches out of her face with her hands and ignoring the brambles that snagged her shoes and pants. She broke through the other side of the trees at full speed. She tried to find purchase on the loose stones on the ground, windmilling her arms and backpedaling frantically. The ground beneath her feet disappeared.

"Ginger!" she heard Gray's cry as she toppled over the edge of the cliff.

CHAPTER THIRTY-NINE

"You can't," John said for what Maeve thought must be the hundredth time.

"We've been over this. I have to." Maeve shoved a sweatshirt into the backpack on her bed.

"Why?"

Maeve stopped packing and looked at him in disbelief. "Are you really asking me that?" She waved her arm at the window. "My friends are out there. They need help, and no one is helping them."

"I know that, Maeve. But what help do you think you're going to be if you go out there all alone? And what about Emma?"

Maeve moved closer to John. "John, I love Emma. But she would want me to go. You know that."

John hung his head. "I know. I just don't want to lose both her and you."

"You won't." Maeve pulled John into a fierce hug. "We're going to find that plagoran venom, and I'm going to find my friends." She pulled back, still holding onto his arms. "I'll come home. I promise."

John gave her a long look, then nodded. "I'm going to see Emma. Say goodbye before you leave."

Maeve finished packing, threw her pack over one shoulder, then looked around her room. It was much nicer than the loft she had grown up in. Maeve hadn't wanted to take over this house when Cleo offered it to them because it was better than most of her friends' houses, but Gray had convinced her that it was time for Emma to enjoy some of the comforts of life after living in the caves for so long. Now Maeve wondered if Emma would even be here the next time she came home. Shaking off the morbid thought, she closed the door to her room and walked down the short hallway to Emma's room. She poked her head into the darkened room. At first, she thought Emma was sleeping and debated whether to wake her, but Emma weakly waved her into the room.

"You're leaving." It was a statement, not a question. Emma knew her too well.

Maeve nodded as she set her pack on the floor and sat in the chair next to Emma's bed. "Yes. I'm going to help find the plagoran."

Emma let out a chuckle that quickly turned into a coughing fit. Maeve waited for the coughing to ease before helping her take a sip of water from the glass on the bedside table. "You're going to find Gray and the others, aren't you?"

Maeve nodded again. In the weak sunlight coming through a crack in the curtains, for the first time in Maeve's memory, Emma looked old. The wrinkles in her well-lined face were more pronounced, and black circles rimmed her eyes. Maeve bit her lip to hold back the tears. She picked up Emma's hand. Her skin reminded Maeve of brittle paper as she ran her thumb over the veins on the back of her hand. Emma gave Maeve's hand a weak squeeze.

"You go on. Don't worry about me."

"How can I not worry about you? You've been the grandmother I never had." Maeve gave Emma a watery smile. "I wouldn't have made it through the past few months without you."

"That's nonsense." Emma strengthened her grip on Maeve's hand. "You listen to me. You are stronger than you think. You've got a good head on your shoulders, and you know what's right. You would have done just fine without me."

"But I don't want to do just fine without you." Maeve shifted closer to the bed. "Who else is going to call me honey and tell me when I'm being stupid? Who else is going to love me anyway?"

"Oh, honey. There are plenty of people who love you regardless of what you do." Maeve looked at her skeptically.

"Your parents, for one." Maeve shook her head. "They do, Maeve. Did you know your mom comes over here sometimes when you're still at work?"

Maeve sat back in her chair, stunned by this news. "Why?"

Emma cleared her throat, and Maeve helped her to drink more water. "Because she loves you. She wants you to forgive them. Don't you think it's about time?"

Maeve shifted uncomfortably. She had vowed to work on her relationship with her parents, but their actions still stung. "They betrayed me."

Emma coughed once and shifted restlessly in the bed. "Yes, they did. But they thought they were looking out for you. Walk a mile in their shoes, Maeve. They were trying to protect you."

Maeve started to protest, but Emma raised a hand to cut her off. "They went about it the wrong way, but they really were trying to protect you. Give them a chance, Maeve. We all need people who love us no matter what. You're going to need them when I'm gone."

Maeve stood up. "You're not going anywhere," she said fiercely. She picked up her pack and slung it over her shoulder with more force than necessary. "I'm going to find that plagoran, and we'll have the antidote. Then I'll find Gray and the others, and we'll be able to defeat Arabella."

Emma gazed at her with calm, sad eyes. "If determination is enough, you'll definitely succeed. But if it's not, Maeve, then know this: You are loved more than you know. It has been the great pleasure of my life to be your friend. Don't let guilt and hatred rob you of the life you were meant to live." Emma motioned weakly with her hand. "Come here."

Maeve returned to Emma's bedside and leaned over to hear her words. "Do great things, Maeve. But always remember to forgive yourself and others. No one is perfect. Not you. Not them. When we forgive each other, love always wins in the end. Never forget that."

"I love you, Emma." Maeve leaned down and kissed her cheek. "You hang on until I get back, OK?"

Emma nodded and wiped a tear from Maeve's face. Maeve turned to go and found John leaning against the wall next to the door. He nodded to her and said, "Good luck, Maeve," then pulled the chair Maeve had vacated closer to the bed, sat down, picked up Emma's hand and began talking to her in a low murmur. Maeve watched for a moment before she turned and walked out the door.

###

Tristan and Emery rushed out into the open as Gray struggled to comprehend what had just happened.

"Where's Ginger?" Tristan asked at the look of horror on Gray's face.

Unable to form words, Gray pointed at the edge of the cliff.

"No!" Emery shouted and rushed to the edge. Tristan grabbed her and pulled her back before she could follow Ginger over the edge. She pounded her fists on Tristan's chest. "We have to help her." Emery sobbed hysterically.

Tristan gripped her by the arms. "We will. But you stay here. The edge isn't safe." Tristan waited for Emery's sobbing to die down. "Do you understand?" Emery nodded.

Gray was already laying on his stomach, peering over the edge. Pieces of dirt and rock crumbled away from where he lay.

"Tristan! Get over here."

Tristan gave Emery one last warning look, then crawled over to where Gray lay. "What do you see?"

"Look." Gray pointed slightly to his left. "She fell to a ledge down there."

"Ginger," Tristan yelled, his voice echoing through the canyon. "Can you hear me?"

When the echoes of Tristan's voice had died down, they heard nothing but silence.

"Can you see if she's conscious?" Tristan asked Gray, straining to see around him to the ledge where Ginger was.

"It doesn't look like it." Gray shifted to give Tristan a better view of Ginger, who lay sprawled on her stomach with one leg cocked at an awkward angle.

"Is she even alive?" Tristan asked in an anguished whisper to keep Emery from overhearing.

Gray shook his head. "I don't know. We need to get down there to find out."

Tristan looked frantically around for something they could use to rappel down the side of the cliff.

"There!" Emery pointed toward the trees to their left, next to the shimmering pond full of precious water. Tristan squinted. Something black was hanging from one of the trees. He sprinted to the trees and stared at the gift they'd been given. A black rope dangled just out of reach from a branch above his head.

Gray blew out a breath as he joined Tristan at the tree. "Guess one of us needs to go up."

Tristan walked to the base of the trunk and reached above his head to grab the nearest branch.

"Are you sure that will hold you?" Gray eyed the thin branch then looked back to Tristan's tall, fit frame.

"It's going to have to." Tristan grabbed the branch with both hands and began to pull himself up. He flung one leg over the branch. The branch bent ominously under his weight. Emery joined Gray at the base of the tree, and they exchanged worried glances before gluing their eyes back to Tristan.

"Can you see where the rope is tied?" Gray peered through the web of branches, straining to see where the rope ended.

Tristan tilted his head for a better view. "I think it's about 10 feet up."

"Do the branches get bigger as you go up?" Gray asked as the branch Tristan stood on dipped even lower.

Tristan shook his head. "No. Unfortunately, they

get smaller."

"They're never going to hold you."

Tristan looked up toward the top of the tree again. "We have to get the rope." He reached for the next branch, but before he could grab it, an ominous crack rang through the air.

"Tristan!" Emery yelled.

The branch cracked again and fell away beneath Tristan's feet. He reached for the next branch but missed and crashed to the ground.

Emery and Gray rushed to his side. "Tristan?" Emery said as she and Gray moved away the pieces of the branch so they could reach Tristan.

Tristan rolled to his back and groaned as he sat up, rubbing the back of his head. "That didn't feel so good."

Gray quickly checked Tristan over to make sure nothing was broken. "Do you know your name?"

Tristan stared at him. "Of course I know my name. It's Tristan." He wobbled as he rose to his feet but steadied himself quickly. "The better question is how are we going to get that rope if the branches won't hold our weight."

Emery walked over to the base of the tree. "It might not hold your weight, but I'm sure it will hold mine."

"That is not happening," Gray said. "Your sister will kill me if anything happens to you. And 10 minutes ago you could barely hold yourself up. What are we going to do if you pass out while climbing that tree?"

Emery examined the tree then turned to Gray. "My sister isn't going to be around to be mad at you if we don't get that rope." She pointed at the pond. "Grab me some water, and I'll be fine. Adrenaline is an amazing thing."

Gray rushed to the pond, looking on the ground for

something to use as a cup. A large piece of bark curved like a cup lay next to the pond. He hurried to fill it with the clear pond water and handed it to Emery. She drank deeply, then said, "Give me a boost. I'm going up."

Gray still refused to give her a boost. Tristan limped over to where Gray and Emery were arguing. "She's right, you know. Those branches won't hold our weight. They should hold hers. Unfortunately, she's our only hope of getting down to that ledge and helping Ginger."

Gray still made no move to help Emery reach the next branch. "Ginger and Maeve are going to kill me."

Emery shifted impatiently from one foot to the other. "We're wasting time. You know there's no other option. Give me a boost."

Gray sighed then stepped forward and cupped his hands. "Don't you dare fall."

Emery grinned at him and placed her foot in his hands. He boosted her upward, and she successfully grabbed the next branch and pulled herself up.

"Be careful," Tristan admonished.

Emery gave him a thumbs up, reached for the next branch and disappeared into the thick leaves. Gray and Tristan stared into the dense thicket of branches above them, unable to see much of Emery. Occasionally, leaves and small twigs would fall to the ground.

"How are you doing?" Gray yelled.

"I'm fine. Almost to the rope."

Gray found it hard to stay still at the base of the tree and began pacing back and forth. Tristan leaned against the tree trunk.

"What's up with the leg?" Gray asked.

"Nothing. It's fine."

"Who are you kidding? I saw you limp over here." Gray stopped pacing and pinned Tristan with his icy blue stare. "Be honest. You know the first rule of tactics. Know your weaknesses."

Tristan dropped his gaze to the ground. "It's my knee. It took the brunt of the impact."

Gray nodded and resumed his pacing.

"Um, guys?" Emery's voice floated down from the top of the tree.

"What is it, Emery?" Tristan asked.

"The knot is stuck. I can't get it undone."

"Is there a small branch you can break off and stick it into the knot to give you leverage to loosen it?" Gray asked.

"I'll try."

Tristan pushed himself away from the tree. "I'm going to check on Ginger."

Gray nodded, and Tristan limped back toward the edge.

"How's it going, Emery?" Gray yelled toward the sea of leaves and branches above his head. He thought he could see Emery's shoe far above his head. The rope next to him swayed as Emery worked on loosening the knot.

"I think I've got it." The thick, black rope swayed again then began to drop and coil around itself as it hit the ground.

"Great job, Emery! Now, get your feet back on the ground."

He could hear Emery scrambling her way back down the tree and kept his gaze glued to where he thought he had seen her foot. He let out a relieved sigh when her skinny leg appeared through the branches and leaves. Her foot felt for the next branch, and she gently lowered herself down, using the trunk to keep her balance. She repeated the process until she was on the branch Gray had boosted her to.

"Am I glad to see you," Gray said, not taking his gaze from her.

"Me too." Emery grinned as she moved to sit on the branch to let herself down. Her foot slipped. Gray watched in horror as Emery threw out her arms, frantically looking for a handhold. Her hand brushed the trunk but failed to gain purchase. Off balance, she hit her shoulder on the trunk. Her other foot slid out from under her, and she tipped off the branch. At the last moment, her right hand grabbed onto the branch, and she dangled just over Gray's head, holding on with one hand.

Gray broke out of his paralysis and rushed over to where she swayed precariously. "Hold on, Em! I've got you." He grabbed her legs just as the strength in her hand gave out, and they both tumbled to the ground.

"Are you OK?" Gray sat up and ran his hands over Emery's arms and legs to assure himself nothing was broken.

She pushed him away. "I'm fine. Grab that rope. We need to help Ginger."

CHAPTER FORTY

"Absolutely not." Cleo faced Maeve with her hands on her hips. While her words were stern, her eyes were soft and conveyed compassion. "You just got out of bed. No way are you going on an expedition to find a deadly creature that we're not even sure we can find. You need rest, not a trek across the countryside."

"I need to help Emma." Maeve's eyes remained locked on Cleo's. "I'm the only person who has even seen a plagoran in the past 30 years. You know I'm your best hope of finding it."

Cleo dropped her gaze. "How can I let you go? You already almost died because you decided to go off on your own. How do I know you won't take off on your own again?"

Maeve took a deep breath. Had Cleo read her mind? "Where am I going to go and how could you think I would ever abandon Emma? She needs that antidote."

Cleo turned to look out over Palumbra. She let out a sigh and her shoulders slumped. "I know you would do everything you can for Emma." She stared out past the edge of the city. "I would go myself, but I have to prepare Palumbra for Arabella's attack." She shook her head. "I know I'm going to regret this, but fine, you can go."

Maeve smiled and released the breath she had been holding. She was going on this expedition to find the plagoran whether Cleo approved it or not, but it was much easier with Cleo's approval. Maeve started to speak, but Cleo held up her hand.

"You stay with the expedition, and you are not to go near the plagoran. Do you understand me?"

Maeve nodded.

"Get out of here. The team came back, but a new one is gathering in the conference room on the first floor."

Maeve turned to go but stopped when she placed her hand on the door handle and turned back to Cleo. "Thanks, Cleo," she said softly. "I appreciate it."

Without turning from the window, Cleo nodded.

Maeve returned to the first floor. She paused outside the conference room door as a wave of loneliness swept over her, weighing her down with fatigue. Was Cleo right? Did she have the stamina for this? Images of Gray flitted through her mind: fishing together, meeting for breakfast, walking to work, talking late into the evening. If she closed her eyes, she could almost feel his arms around her and his kiss on her lips. Despite her tiredness, she squared her shoulders and opened the door. Emma, Gray and the others were depending on her.

Conversation stopped, and all heads turned toward Maeve as she entered. She lifted her hand and gave a little wave and a small smile before slipping into an open seat. Rufus once again settled at her feet. She was surprised to see Corporal Shamus leading the meeting. The screen at the front of the room contained an image of a map of the area surrounding Palumbra. The place where Maeve had helped the injured plagoran was marked in red.

"I thought you might be joining us," Corporal Shamus said. "Everyone, this is Maeve Jackson. She's the only one of us who has seen a plagoran. What can you tell us, Maeve?"

All eyes turned to Maeve, and she took stock of the small group around the table that was mostly made up of young soldiers. Maeve remembered Cleo saying she couldn't spare many people for this mission, and it appeared she had chosen the least experienced soldiers in the ranks. Five soldiers, all around Maeve's age, looked at her as if she had all the answers. She recognized two soldiers, a guy and a girl, as classmates of hers in school. Corporal Shamus was the most experienced soldier in the room, and he was probably only a couple of years older than Maeve.

Corporal Shamus raised his eyebrows, indicating she should say something. With a start, she realized that in this group, she was the experienced one. She looked around the table once more, then walked to the map. She pointed to the red area.

"This is where we saw the plagoran the first time."

Corporal Shamus drew his eyebrows together in confusion. "The first time? You saw the plagoran more than once?" He shuffled through some papers on the desk. "There's no mention of that in the briefing."

"Well, we didn't actually see it the second time, but we heard it."

Corporal Shamus continued flipping through his papers. "Where was that?"

Maeve turned back to the map and studied it for a moment before pointing to a spot in the desert. "Maybe in this area? It was dark, and we never saw it. But there's no mistaking its roar."

She had Corporal Shamus's full attention, and the other soldiers were looking at her with something akin to awe. "When was this?" Corporal Shamus asked.

"A day or two after we saw the first plagoran."

A skinny soldier with skin pale enough that Maeve wondered if he ever went outside raised his hand. Corporal Shamus nodded at him.

"What are they like?"

"The plagoran?" Maeve asked. "They're big. And their skin is tough, but they're not invincible. Tristan and Gray were able to wound one with a knife. But they travel in pairs, so if you see one, be on the lookout for another one."

Another soldier, a young woman with dark hair pulled into a bun and a scar on her cheek, raised her hand. Corporal Shamus motioned for her to speak. "Who are Tristan and Gray?"

Maeve paused before answering as thoughts of her friends flooded her mind. Were they even still alive? She shook off the morbid thought and answered the question. "They're my friends who were out there with me. We were captured. I got away, but they were sent into The Beyond." It was a simplified version of what had happened, but she didn't know how much this group had been told about what had happened beyond the borders of Palumbra.

The soldier's eyes widened at her response. "Are they still out there?"

"I hope so," Maeve said quietly. "I definitely hope so." She turned back to Corporal Shamus. "Any luck with the frequencies?"

He shrugged. "Maybe. We may have gotten a transmission from around here." He pointed to an open space on the map. "Since we aren't sure of the entire frequency, it's just a guess. But it's a place to start."

Corporal Shamus took over the meeting, and Maeve returned to her chair. "We have one mission." He looked at Maeve when he said it, and she wondered if Cleo had told him to keep an eye on her. "We need to find the plagoran and extract the venom from its teeth." He looked around the table, assessing his young, inexperienced team. "Let's get to it."

Gray tied the thick rope to a large tree near the edge of the cliff then tied the other end around his waist.

"What do you think you're doing?" Tristan demanded.

"Going to get Ginger," Gray said evenly.

"I'm going over the edge, not you."

"How are you going to rappel down to the ledge and get Ginger back up here with a bum knee?" He pointed at Tristan's pant leg where the fabric was torn. "You can barely hold your own weight. There's no way you can hold Ginger's as well."

"I should be the one to go."

"Tristan, I know you and Ginger are close, but you can't. You need to stay up here and make sure the rope holds and Emery stays safe. Remember our training: always choose the best person for the job."

Tristan sighed and nodded. "You're right."

Gray clapped him on the shoulder. "Let's rescue Ginger; then we can rescue Maeve." Gray tried to push thoughts of Maeve out of his mind before they overwhelmed his ability to think.

They walked to the edge where Emery was kneeling talking to Ginger. "She still hasn't moved. Do you think she's alive?" Gray could see the panic in Emery's eyes as she asked the question.

Gray hugged Emery. Her face was pale, and it was clear the adrenaline she had used to climb the tree was wearing off. "She's going to be fine, Emery. She probably hit her head when she fell. She'll wake up soon."

He nodded at Tristan, then moved to the spot they had chosen as the best option for rappelling. With a final wave, he eased himself over the side as Tristan fed out the rope and Emery continued her one-sided conversation with Ginger.

Gray pushed off from the cliff face with his feet, praying that the rope held. He and Tristan had checked it over, but Gray worried that in their rush to get to Ginger, they might have missed a small cut or fray that could turn dangerous. He looked down as he pushed off again. His stomach lurched at the sight of how far it was to the ground, and he quickly returned his eyes to the cliff face. The small ledge where Ginger lay was the only one Gray could see sticking out from the sheer cliff face. Gray noted he had moved too far to the right and adjusted his angle of descent with the next push of his powerful legs. He swung back to the cliff face and gave one last push. His foot touched the ledge next to Ginger, but the ground crumbled beneath his toe.

Tristan's head appeared over the edge of the cliff as Gray dangled in mid-air, his momentum stopped by his attempt to land on the ledge. "You OK?" Tristan yelled.

Gray gave him a thumbs up. "Don't let out any

more rope," Gray yelled back. "I'm going to try to swing over to the ledge."

Tristan returned Gray's thumbs up, and his face disappeared back over the edge of the cliff. Gray stretched out his feet and leaned back as if he were on a playground swing, trying to create some momentum. Slowly, he began to swing back and forth, his arc widening with each swing. After a few short swings, he once again reached the ledge. This time, he landed his whole foot on it. He quickly brought his other foot down, but his momentum caused him to stumble. Stretching out his arms for balance, he scrambled to find a handhold on the cliff face, breathing a sigh of relief when his hand landed on a rocky protuberance and his feet found purchase on the ground below him.

He dropped to his knees next to Ginger, felt quickly for a pulse, letting out a whoop of relief when he found one, beating steadily. He examined her for obvious injuries besides her oddly bent right leg. Besides a bump on the back of her head, he didn't find any other external injuries. He could only hope she wasn't bleeding internally.

"Ginger." He shook her gently. "Ginger."

Tristan's head appeared over the edge of the cliff once again. "How is she?"

"She's alive but unconscious. I can't wake her up."

Tristan turned his head and yelled, "Emery, she's alive." Turning back to Gray, he said, "How are we going to get her up?"

Gray eyed Ginger's leg and wished Maeve was beside him. Beyond some basic first aid, he didn't have the training to deal with injuries, and Ginger's leg looked like it needed more than basic first aid. Standing, he began to untie the rope from around his waist.

"What are you doing?" Tristan asked.

"Give me a little more rope."

Tristan disappeared, and the rope went slack in Gray's hands. Tristan's head reappeared. Gray peered up at him, trying to judge his strength.

"Can you lift both of us at the same time?"

Tristan assessed them. Together, they would weigh close to 300 pounds. He shook his head. "Even with Emery's help and using a tree for leverage, I don't think so."

Gray nodded. "That's what I thought. I'm going to tie the rope around Ginger. If I can't get her to wake up, it's going to be difficult to raise her to the top without hurting her even more."

Tristan grimaced. "What choice do we have?"

Gray looked at Ginger's prone form. "None. Let's get it done."

He took the rope and fashioned it so two lengths of rope hung from a central knot. Gently, he slipped one length of the rope under Ginger's shoulders, brought it around and tied it at her sternum. He gave the rope an extra tug to make sure it was tight. He tied the other rope around Ginger's hips, in the hopes that the two ropes would keep her more stable as she rose and limit the chance for more injury. As he slipped the rope under her hips, Ginger groaned. Gray moved quickly to her head, ignoring the ground at the edge of the ledge that crumbled under his foot.

"Ginger!" Gray lifted her head as she let out a weak cough. Her eyes fluttered open, and her face contorted with pain. She raised a hand to her head.

"Ooh. What happened?"

"You fell. I think your leg is broken."

Ginger strained to look at her leg. "That might be why it hurts. What happened to my head?"

"You must have hit it when you fell."

She slowly lowered her head back to the ground and closed her eyes. "Emery?"

Gray jerked his head toward the top of the cliff even though Ginger couldn't see him with her eyes closed. "At the top with Tristan."

Ginger opened her eyes again, squinting against the sunlight. "That's kind of a long way up. Do you have a plan?"

Gray nodded. "It's not a good one."

"I assume it has something to do with the rope?" Her eyes followed the rope to where it vanished at the top of the cliff.

"It's a better plan now that you're awake, if that helps."

"I don't know how much help I'm going to be."

"You can do this, Ginger. You have to. It's the only way off this ledge." His eyes scanned the edge of the ledge where the ground had crumbled away.

"Tristan can't lift both of us, so you're going to have to go up on your own. If you can grab the rope, it will be much easier than lifting you unconscious. But it's going to hurt. I'm sorry."

Gray quickly fashioned the second length of rope into a loop. "You can sit on this and hold onto the rope as Tristan pulls you up. Ready?"

"No, but I don't think I have a choice. I'm not sure I can stand."

He helped Ginger to a sitting position and tried not to worry as more ground fell away from the edge of the ledge. "I'm going to put my arms under your arms and pull you to your feet."

"What's going on down there? Are you ready?" Tristan's head appeared once more at the top of the cliff. His face broke into a smile when he saw Ginger sitting up. "Ginger! Fine time to take a nap."

She gave him a weak wave. "I knew you had it under control, and I was tired."

"What's your plan?" Tristan asked Gray.

"When I give you the signal, raise her up." He placed his hands under Gingers armpits and lifted. She cried out as her injured leg protested the change in position. "Sorry, Ginger. This is the only way."

"Hey, Ginger," Tristan yelled. "Quit whining and let's go."

"Quit whining," Ginger muttered. "I'll give him something to whine about."

"He's just trying to help," Gray said as he carefully maneuvered her body into the loop that was serving as a seat for her. "If he makes you mad, maybe you won't notice the pain as much."

"I know. It's not really helping, though."

He gave her a sad smile. "I know. Sorry Maeve isn't here to mend the break."

"Let's just get this over with."

Gray nodded and gave the rope a final tug then placed Ginger's hands around the rope. "Hold on tight and try to protect that leg."

She nodded.

"OK, Tristan. She's ready." He gave Tristan a

thumbs up, and Tristan's head disappeared once again. Emery's head popped over the edge instead. Gray could hear Tristan admonishing Emery to be careful.

"Hi, Em," Ginger said gamely.

"Are you OK?"

"I banged up my leg and head, but I'll be fine."

"OK. Tristan is going to pull you up now."

Ginger nodded and closed her eyes, bracing herself as the rope tightened and she started to rise off the ledge.

CHAPTER FORTY-ONE

Maeve watched Rufus trot on the path in front of her and wished for a hovercar. Her body, still weak from the virus, protested the prolonged march to find the plagoran. The others walked ahead of her, and she took stock of the group. Corporal Shamus led the group, his back stiff, and his eyes scanning the area around him. She wondered how he was dealing with the loss of his team in the desert and if any of that team had been on Arabella's payroll. How many more traitors were in their ranks?

Maeve set that worry aside as something for John and Cleo to worry about. She had her hands full. Her gaze traveled from Corporal Shamus to the youngest member of the group, Private Thompson. At 16, he was just old enough to have started his career training. Tall, thin and lanky, he hadn't yet achieved the filled out look of most soldiers. His wide eyes stood out from his olive-toned skin as he took in his surroundings. Judging from the look of wonder on his face as they reached the outskirts of Palumbra, she didn't think he had ever left the city before.

Next to him, marched Private Campbell, a short, stocky, dark-haired girl of 17. What she lacked in size, she made up for in personality. During the meeting, she had not been shy to speak up and voice her opinion about their plan. Even now, she was saying something Maeve couldn't catch to Corporal Shamus; Maeve thought she was probably still trying to tell him how to lead the expedition.

Directly in front of Maeve and Rufus marched the pale, skinny soldier who had questioned Maeve during the meeting. She knew him slightly as they had been in the same grade at school. Private Allen was not much taller than Maeve; he looked as if a strong wind could blow him over. His eyes flitted nervously, scanning the area around him as if he expected a plagoran to jump out of the trees and attack. Something about him reminded Maeve of Silas. She only hoped he was half as brave as Silas had been.

The last soldier in line was Private Javan, the girl with the tightly wound bun and the scar on her cheek. Maeve thought her first name was Amelia. Other than Corporal Shamus, she was the only one who held her gun like she had ever fired it before, and she walked with a quiet confidence on nearly silent feet. Maeve wondered how she had come by the scar since she knew it hadn't been there when they had been in school together.

Private Javan dropped back to walk with Maeve, keeping a watchful eye on their surroundings.

"Tired?" she asked quietly.

Maeve nodded.

"But too stubborn to stop?"

Maeve nodded again. Private Javan looked Maeve over from the top of her head to her toes then shook her head. "You know, if I was going to pick someone from our class to save the world, it wouldn't have been you."

Maeve gave her a small smile. "Amelia, right?" Private Javan nodded. "Me neither."

"How did you end up here?" Amelia gestured to the woods around them.

"Just lucky, I guess." She nodded toward Amelia's scar. "How did you get the scar?"

"Just lucky, I guess," she said with a smile as she echoed Maeve's words. She sobered. "I got it fighting against the WG. Just because their weapons didn't work didn't mean they forgot how to fight. One of them got me with a knife."

"I'm sorry."

"Don't be. I hit him with a mean right cross. He fell like a brick." Amelia smiled, but it didn't reach her eyes.

They walked on, Amelia slowing her steps to match Maeve's pace. Only Rufus's snuffling in the brush at the side of the path broke the silence.

"Have you ever killed anyone?" Maeve wasn't sure what prompted her to ask the question.

Amelia shook her head. "I hope I never have to. I didn't become a soldier to kill other people."

Maeve gave her a quizzical look. "Then why did you become a soldier?"

Amelia shrugged. "The WG told me I had an aptitude for it and placed me to be part of the army. When the new government gave us all a choice, I decided to stay. It's not about killing other people. It's about standing up for what's right and protecting the people I love. We do so much more than just fight."

"I know," Maeve agreed. "Gray is always talking about the ways the soldiers are helping to rebuild Palumbra." She motioned to Amelia's gun. "I hope you never have to use that."

"Me too," Amelia said. "But I know how to defend

myself if I have to."

Amelia scanned the forest around them as Corporal Shamus turned them onto a different path. "Why don't you carry a gun?" she asked without looking at Maeve.

"I don't like the result when you fire one."

"But don't you want to be able to protect yourself?"

"There are other ways to protect yourself." Maeve paused. "I killed a man, a boy, really, during the fight with the WG. I'm finally coming to terms with that, but I don't ever want to do it again. So, I choose not to carry a gun."

"But aren't you scared to be out here without one?" Amelia asked, still scanning the area around them. They had reached the lake at the edge of Palumbra. The river ran for a few miles, then the desert began.

Maeve shrugged. "I've been out here before without one. I survived. Hopefully, I can do it again."

Amelia was saved from responding to Maeve by Corporal Shamus's order to gather around. They formed a loose circle with Corporal Shamus at the center.

"OK, we're approaching the area where Maeve said they encountered the plagoran and where we may have picked up its signal. We'll take a 15-minute break here before we head out. Keep your eyes and ears open for any sign of the plagoran – tracks, broken branches, anything that looks like a large creature could have done it. Any words of wisdom, Maeve?"

"Do your best not to kill them, please."

Corporal Shamus raised his eyebrows. "How do you expect us to get the venom from its teeth? It's not like it will just give it to us."

Maeve thought for a moment then said, "I don't know, but I'm sure we can think of something."

Ginger cried out as her leg hit the side of the cliff, and Gray winced. Hampered by her broken leg, Ginger was unable to use both feet to push off from the cliff face, resulting in more bumps than Gray had anticipated. Emery kept up a steady stream of encouragement as Ginger slowly rose to the top.

"Not much farther, Ginger," Emery said. "You're almost there."

Gray could see the tears streaming down Ginger's face as she tried to hold back her cries of distress. Just as Ginger reached the top of the cliff, a strong gust of wind forced Gray to take a step backward. He flattened himself against the cliff face to keep from being blown off the narrow ledge. He heard Tristan say, "I've got you" and glanced upward again to see Emery leaning over the edge of the cliff, grabbing one of Ginger's hands while Tristan held the rope and grabbed the other one. Gray watched until Ginger's feet disappeared over the edge of the cliff top. His gaze continued up to the sky as another gust of wind hit. Clouds skidded across the sky, covering the sun and turning what had been a hot, sunny day into a windy, gray one. The clouds roiled into tall towers, and Gray knew they would soon be soaked. They didn't get a lot of rain in Palumbra, but the little they did get came from storms like the one brewing. He just hoped he was off this ledge before it hit.

"Throw me the rope," he called to Tristan.

"We're working on it," Tristan replied. "We need to get you up here before that storm breaks."

As if on cue, lightning flashed across the sky, and Gray wondered if this day could get any worse. A large drop of rain splattered on his nose.

"Hurry it up. We're about to get wet."

The rope appeared over the edge of the cliff and was quickly lowered to the ledge, swinging wildly in the increasing wind. Gray tried to grab it, but a wind gust sent it careening to his left. He waited patiently for the wind to die down. Rain began to fall in earnest, and the ground beneath his feet quickly turned to slippery mud. Finally, the wind lessened for a moment, and he squinted through the rain to see the rope dangling just off to his left. He stretched, but the rope remained just beyond his fingertips. Holding onto the side of the cliff and planting his feet as well as he could in the mud pit on the ledge, he stretched again, his fingertips just brushing the rope. The slight contact with the rope set it swinging once again. Still squinting through the ever-increasing rain, he waited until the rope's momentum brought it within range and grabbed it, the motion causing his foot to slip. He fell to his knees on the ledge, causing chunks of ground to fall away.

With hurried motions, he wrapped the rope around his waist. His wet hands struggled to knot the now soaked rope. He hoped the knot would hold his weight as he gave the rope a tug to let Tristan know he was ready and held it tight. The rope drew taught, and he placed his feet on the cliff face, planning to walk up the side as Tristan pulled. Another gust of wind forced Gray away from the cliff face where he began swinging wildly. He thought he heard Tristan yell something, but he couldn't make out the words over the roar of the wind and rain in his ears. He winced as his shoulder hit the rocky cliff face. He twirled in the air, his back slamming into the cliff.

The rope around his waist shifted, and he peered

through the rain, trying to assess the condition of the knot. Another gust of wind forced him hard against the cliff once again. The rope around his waist shifted. Unable to see the knot, Gray released the rope with one hand and felt the rope at his waist. The once tightly cinched knot had loosened enough for him to slip his hand easily between the rope and his stomach. He tried to tighten it but only succeeded in getting rope burn on his hands. He considered wrapping the rope around his wrist but worried that if the knot gave out, the tension in the rope would sever his hand. Instead, he gripped the slippery rope as tightly as he could with both hands, turned his face upward to see how much farther he had to go and got a face full of water for his efforts. He quickly turned his face back toward the cliff to avoid drowning in the deluge.

The next gust of wind sent the rope spinning, and Gray worked his legs desperately to find purchase on the cliff while his hands turned white as they gripped the rope. The rope at his waist loosened even more as he hit the cliff feet first and was, for a moment, able to lessen the weight he was putting on the rope knotted around his middle. After two steps up the cliff face, the wind sent him spinning again. The rope was now so loose that it shifted around his waist as he twirled in the air, leaving his tightly clenched hands as the only thing keeping him from plummeting to his death. His hip bumped the rocky face of the cliff. He winced but retained his grip on the rope.

"Tristan!" he screamed into the wind.

He heard nothing in return, but he continued his slow rise to the top. His arms began to ache as they now held his full weight. He tried to pull himself up so he could wrap his legs around the rope as well, but the wind made it impossible. To take his mind off his aching arms, he thought of Maeve – her laughter when he splashed her with water on one of their fishing trips, her desperate search for redemption after killing the WG soldier, her saying 'I love you' when Arabella held them captive. He wondered now why he hadn't said it back. When Maeve had said it, he was in such shock at her decision to let Arabella inject her with the virus that he hadn't said anything, and the moment had passed. But he did love her. Even when she was stubborn and put herself in danger. He hoped she knew. His hands slid on the slick rope, tearing into his hands. He hoped he got another chance to tell her.

Another strong gust of wind sent him slamming into the cliff, shoulder first. His left hand lost its grip. The wind sent him spinning again as he struggled to keep his right hand anchored on the rope. His arm felt as if it was slowly being pulled from its socket, but he gritted his teeth and held on, trying desperately to get his other hand back on the rope. His right hand slipped. The knot around his waist had come completely undone, and the rope flailed in the wind below him. His hand slipped again. He closed his eyes and conjured up Maeve's face in his mind. If he was going to die, he wanted her to be his last thought.

"Gray!" Tristan's voice seemed to come out of nowhere. Gray opened his eyes and squinted upward through the rain. He could just make out Tristan's extended arm. "Grab my hand."

Gray threw his left arm upward, grasping Tristan's hand as his right hand slipped farther down the rope. Their rain-slickened hands clasped together for a fleeting moment, then slipped apart. Gray dangled helplessly, then gritted his teeth and threw his left hand toward Tristan again. This time, Tristan grabbed him around the wrist just as Gray's right hand lost its grip on the rope. Tristan hauled backward with all his might and slowly pulled Gray over the edge of the cliff.

They collapsed on the ground with the wind blowing around them and the rain beating steadily down on them. Gray sucked in several deep breaths and said, "Let's not do that again."

CHAPTER FORTY-TWO

Gray lifted his head from the ground and pushed to his knees. "Where are Ginger and Emery?"

Tristan stood and leaned into the wind, moving until he could untie the rope from the tree and begin winding it up to carry with them. "I carried Ginger into the cover of the trees. Not that it's much cover from this rain."

The wind gusted once more, driving sheets of rain into their faces. Once under the canopy of trees, the rain lessened enough for Gray to make out Ginger and Emery sitting at the base of a tree. As he drew closer, he could see Emery had gathered two small, but strong branches and laid them next to Ginger's leg, which was bent at an odd angle below the knee.

Tristan knelt next to Ginger. "How are you?"

"Oh, I'm just great. I really only need one leg, and I always wondered what it would feel like to have someone beat my head with a hammer."

Tristan sat back on his heels. "OK, dumb question."

Ginger looked up at Gray. "Any problems making it to the top in this wind?"

Gray and Tristan exchanged a glance, and Tristan

shook his head slightly. "Nope," Gray lied and hid his hands behind his back so she couldn't see how raw and ripped they were. "No trouble at all."

Emery had seen the silent conversation between Tristan and Gray and eyed him skeptically but stayed silent. She pointed to the branches.

"I don't know how to set the bone, but I thought we could use these for splints."

Tristan ran his hands down Ginger's leg, trying to feel where the bones should go. Ginger winced but didn't cry out. He looked at Gray with rain still streaming down his face. "Do you know how to do this?"

Gray shook his head. "That's Maeve's department."

At the mention of Maeve's name, they fell silent. Gray watched a raindrop slide off a leaf and plop to the ground. He felt a gentle hand in his. Ginger's grip was surprisingly strong.

"We'll find her. She's going to be fine." Ginger squeezed his hand and released it.

Gray gave a short nod and dropped to his knees on her other side. "We know a little first aid, but neither of us have ever done this before. It's going to hurt."

Ginger looked from Gray to Tristan and nodded. "Just get it over with. Emery, come hold my hand." Ginger had Emery face her, so she didn't have to watch the boys slide her bones back in place. Tristan and Gray worked together to move her leg back into a more normal-looking position as Ginger did her best not to cry out, and Emery talked tirelessly to keep Ginger's focus on her. When Tristan finally reached for the rope to tie the make-shift splints to Ginger's leg, Emery's voice was hoarse from talking, and Gray couldn't tell whether rain or tears had made Ginger's face wet. Her eyes were closed, and she lay limply against the tree. Gray gently laid his hand on her shoulder. "I'm sorry."

Ginger wiped her nose on the back of her hand and cleared her eyes of the rain/tears. "It's OK." It wasn't, but Gray got to his feet anyway, brushing his hands off on his wet, muddy pants. "I'll be right back."

"I won't go far," he added when Emery looked at him in panic.

"It's fine," Ginger said to Emery. "Let him go."

Emery peered over at the splint. "How are we going to move her?"

Tristan scooted up to sit next to Ginger. "You can hop. How does that sound?"

Ginger didn't open her eyes or lift her head from where it rested on the wet tree trunk. "Sure. Sounds great. Let's get going."

"How about we use this instead?" Gray held up a long branch that looked like a Y. "It might not be the most comfortable crutch, but it should work."

Ginger eyed the crutch. "I'm going to walk across the rocky ground of this place with that crutch?"

"Yep," Gray said with confidence.

"Yeah, no chance."

Tristan picked up Ginger's hand and gave it a squeeze. "You can do it, Ginger. We'll help." Determination glowed from his eyes. "We don't have any choice. And no one is dying out here."

"We need to find somewhere to get out of this rain," Gray said. While not as much rain made it through the canopy of the trees, it was still coming down steadily, making the muddy, rocky ground slick and shiny. Tristan and Gray helped Ginger to her feet while Emery held the crutch. As Ginger took her first step, setting the crutch firmly on the slimy ground, a faint, high-pitched whine echoed through the trees.

"Is that..." Emery cocked her head as if to hear better over the wind and rain. "Nah, it couldn't be."

Ginger's crutch slipped, and Tristan hurried to steady her.

"What do you think it is?" Gray asked.

Emery didn't answer. Instead, she hurried past Gray, back the way they had come before Ginger had tried to walk on the sky. Gray had to jog to keep up with her. About halfway down the hill, Emery stopped, listened and turned right. Sliding on the muddy terrain, Gray struggled to keep his balance as he trailed her until Emery stopped so quickly, he almost ran into the back of her. She walked slowly to the edge of the trees but remained under the cover of the forest, peering into the murky gray of the storm and straining to see through the falling rain. Gray came up beside her, struggling to make out the source of the noise.

"There." Emery pointed to the other side of the clearing. "I thought so."

Gray's gaze followed her finger. "What is a hovercar doing here?"

"I don't know," Emery replied. "But I think that's our ride out of here."

Maeve's feet felt heavy, and every breath seemed to contain less oxygen than the one before as she continued to put one foot in front of the other. Amelia kept shooting her concerned glances but said nothing. Corporal Shamus set a grueling pace, anxious to finish his mission and return to the pending fight with Arabella. Though they had entered the area where Maeve had last seen the plagoran, they had yet to see any sign of the large beasts.

"Does anyone even know whether these things stay in one place?" Private Thompson asked.

Maeve took a swig from her canteen. Rufus trotted wearily by her side, and she stopped to offer him a drink. He lapped up the water eagerly. She ruffled his ears, and said, "I know, Rufus. We'll rest soon."

When no one answered Private Thompson, Maeve said, "I'm guessing they travel pretty far. No one had seen a plagoran in decades before we came across the ones here."

"Don't you think that's odd?" Amelia asked.

"What's odd?" Maeve took another drink of water and tried not to stumble.

"That all of a sudden you saw a plagoran after no one seeing them for decades? I just think that's odd. Like someone released them recently."

Maeve studied the horizon and the swiftly setting sun. "I hadn't really thought about it, but that makes some sense."

Amelia's voice took on a tone of urgency. Her next words confirmed to Maeve that Amelia had been thinking about this for a while.

"No, think about it. No one sees a plagoran anywhere near Palumbra in decades, yet when we're about to make discoveries about The Hub, suddenly some appear not too far from Palumbra." Amelia's dark eyes danced as she spoke, animating her entire face. "These things were made in a lab, right?"

"According to what Emery told me, that's right."

314

"So, what if they had died out or been kept contained since the wars of The Lost Years? And what if someone decided to bring them back?"

Maeve felt some of the tiredness leave her bones as she considered Amelia's new theory. It seemed like just the sort of thing Arabella would do.

Amelia took her silence for doubt. "Look, you said The Hub has way more technology than we do. What if Arabella created new plagoran?"

"But why? She has plenty of weapons. Why would she need the plagoran?"

Amelia's face lost some of its animation as she pondered Maeve's question. "The virus!"

Maeve wrinkled her forehead. "You're right. She would need the plagoran venom for an antidote, just in case she or one of her lackeys accidentally contracted the virus. You don't build a weapon you can't control."

Amelia's eyes began to sparkle once again. "Sending the plagoran out here was just a bonus to try to keep you from making it to The Hub."

Maeve eyed Amelia thoughtfully. Before she could respond, Corporal Shamus called out an order to halt. Maeve noticed for the first time that the sky had begun to darken.

"Let's set up camp here." A clearing opened up within a circle of trees just behind Corporal Shamus. "We're not going to find them in the dark." He struck some flint and used it to light a lantern, then hung it on the nearest tree branch. The rest of them hurried to set up camp. Maeve and Amelia gathered firewood while the others started the fire and laid out their bedrolls. When Maeve returned to camp with an armful of wood, a fire was blazing, and several members of their group were sitting on their bedrolls eating protein paste bars. She dropped gratefully to her own bedroll and pulled out a protein paste bar, just as lightning flashed across the sky.

"Looks like we're going to get wet," Corporal Shamus said as he dropped to the bedroll next to hers.

Maeve eyed the dark sky warily. "Don't we have some kind of shelter we can build?"

Corporal Shamus looked up. "We could, but I've been watching these clouds, and they're building into a storm. Any shelter we build won't stand up to the wind." He motioned to the trees that circled them. "Hopefully, the trees will break most of the wind, but it's going to be a wet couple of hours." He raised his voice then and said, "We're going to need to hunker down. That storm is about to break, and we're going to get wet. Pull out your rain coverings and plan to stay put. Try to get whatever sleep you can."

He dug in his pack and pulled out his military-issued rain covering. "Do you have one?"

Maeve shook her head.

He raised the corner. "Scoot over here then."

Maeve looked at the small rain covering, then eyed the dark sky again. Deciding some protection from the rain was better than none, she shifted her bedroll closer to Corporal Shamus, squeezing up next to him and tucking the corner of the rain covering around her. An awkward silence filled the small space.

"This is cozy, isn't it?" Corporal Shamus said with an awkward chuckle.

"Just a bit," Maeve replied. "Maybe it would be less awkward if I knew your first name."

In the dim light, Maeve saw him smile. "It's Patrick." He stuck out a hand.

Maeve ignored the confined space, took his hand and smiled back. "Nice to meet you, Patrick."

"Never thought I'd be snuggled up with the famous Maeve Jackson."

Maeve heard rain begin to hit their rain covering and felt a few drops on her exposed feet. "I don't know that I would call this snuggling, and I'm certainly not famous."

"Face it, Maeve. Whether you like it or not, every kid in Palumbra will know your name for centuries to come. You're the girl that unraveled the mystery of The Lost Years and started a revolution in Palumbra."

Maeve shook her head. "I had a whole lot of help."

Shamus shrugged. "Maybe, but it's your name that will be remembered."

"I hope they remember that I'm not perfect. No good comes from putting someone on a pedestal. They'll just fall off, causing disappointment all around."

"Why do you say that?"

Maeve looked at him to make sure he was serious. "Did you notice that I brought a plague to Palumbra?"

"From what I hear, you did that to save your friends. Sounds pretty brave to me."

"Sounds more like I had no choice. It was the only option to keep my friends alive." Maeve shook her head wearily. "It could have gone horribly wrong." She stopped. "What am I saying? It did go horribly wrong. The woman I admire more than anyone is sick and dying because of me." She let out a frustrated sigh as the rain began to pick up, and the ground beneath their bedrolls soaked up the moisture. She noticed Rufus curled up against the trunk of the tree, trying to stay dry and clicked her tongue to get him to join her under the rain covering. Rufus raised his head, gave her a look as if to say, "I'm quite comfortable here," and laid back down. She left the dog to his own devices and clutched the edge of the rain covering tighter as the wind tried to tear it out of her grasp.

Patrick picked up her hand and gave it a squeeze. It felt weird to have someone other than Gray hold her hand, but there was comfort in it as well. "We'll find the plagoran, Maeve. We'll save Emma. You have to hold onto that."

Maeve nodded wearily but said nothing else. Patrick kept her hand in his. "Try to get some sleep."

Maeve retrieved her hand from Patrick's grasp and pulled the rain covering closer around her shoulders. She closed her eyes not expecting to sleep. But to her surprise, she did.

CHAPTER FORTY-THREE

"Let me go with you." Tristan ran a hand through his hair in frustration. "We can leave Emery here to look after Ginger."

"We're not leaving a 12-year-old to look after Ginger," Gray whispered fiercely.

He glanced over to where Ginger and Emery were huddled together for warmth. He could barely see them in the gathering darkness. With the hovercar nearby, they didn't want to try to light a fire even if they could have forced the wet wood to light.

"But you're going to take the 12-year-old to steal a hovercar?" Tristan pinned him with a hard stare. "Somehow that's safer?"

Gray acknowledged Tristan's point with a nod. "At least her skills will be useful. I have no idea how to drive a hovercar. Do you?"

"No. But does she have any chance of defeating the owners of the hovercar?" Tristan started to pace. "Our best chance is for the two of us to go overpower anyone who is near the hovercar, then bring the brains of the operation," he motioned toward Emery and Ginger, "when it's safe."

"What if we miss one of the people who came with that hovercar? What if they find Ginger and Emery? What then?" Gray glanced toward Emery and Ginger and noticed Emery watching them closely. "One of us has to stay with Ginger. And we need that hovercar. She isn't going to make it if we don't get some faster transportation."

Tristan stopped pacing and stared at Ginger and Emery for a minute. A swarm of emotions crossed his face. Gray touched his arm.

"Look, I know you want to be in on the action. But protecting Ginger is important, too. She needs you."

Tristan's face softened slightly. "You're right, I know. I just want to prove that I can lead, that I can save the day."

"Did you not pull me over the ledge? As far as I'm concerned, you've done your share of saving for today." He slapped Tristan's shoulder. "Ginger needs you. Keep her alive while we get our wheels."

Tristan nodded, and they rejoined the girls.

"Are you done talking about us like we aren't here?" Emery asked.

"Emery," Ginger admonished in a weak voice.

"Well, they were over there acting like we can't make up our own minds about what to do. Here's my plan. You three stay here while I go hotwire the hovercar."

Gray gave a short laugh. "Like that's ever gonna happen."

Emery got to her feet and planted her hands on her hips. "You know I can do it."

Gray gave her a serious look. "I know you can, and I'm going to let you do it."

Emery grinned and started walking toward the

hovercar. Gray grabbed her gently by the arm. "But not by yourself. I'm going with you."

Emery looked from him to Ginger. "Who's taking care of her?" She pointed her thumb at Ginger.

"I am." Tristan stepped forward. "I'll make sure she's still in one piece when you get back."

Emery nodded, and Gray could see her mask of bravado slipping. Tristan stepped forward and leaned down so he was face to face with Emery. "I promise to make sure nothing happens to her while you're gone. Deal?" Tristan stuck out his hand.

Emery pondered his outstretched hand, then shook it with her own. "You'd better keep that promise."

Tristan nodded solemnly.

Emery turned back in the direction of the hovercar. "Let's go, Gray."

Gray followed Emery through the trees. He caught up with her in a few steps and motioned for her to fall in behind him. When she started to protest, he gave her a hard stare. With slow steps, she let him pass.

When they reached the clearing, they could see fire and hear voices. Gray and Emery crouched behind some bushes while Gray counted four men gathered around the fire. Only one had a visible gun. He leaned close to Emery and whispered, "We're going to wait for them to go to sleep, then steal the hovercar. Hopefully, they won't know we're there until we fire up the hovercar."

They settled down to wait. Before long, Emery's weight shifted to lean against him, and he heard the deep sound of her breathing as she fell into a restless sleep.

Several hours later with the moon high in the now clear sky, Gray shook Emery awake. She looked blearily around and opened her mouth to speak, but Gray placed his hand over her mouth to keep her from giving away their presence. Awareness of their situation returned, and she nodded her head to let Gray know she understood. He removed his hand, and they slowly got to their feet.

Gray skirted the edge of the clearing until they were on the same side as the hovercar. He motioned for Emery to go in front of him before they ran to the side of the hovercar opposite where the men lay sleeping near the embers of the fire. The man who was supposed to be keeping watch sat with his back against a tree, his head drooping to his chest as he let out a soft snore.

Emery pushed the door of the hovercar open and stepped up into the vehicle with Gray close behind. She quickly made her way to the controls and studied them.

"Can you do it?" Gray whispered.

Emery dropped to her knees and pulled off the front of the console, exposing a mass of wires. "I think so, but it's going to take a few minutes."

Gray's eyes roved over the sleeping men outside. "Just do it as quickly as you can. And stay low so no one can see you if they wake up."

Emery nodded and set to work.

"Are you almost done?" Gray's anxious voice echoed through the hovercar despite his attempt to be quiet.

"Almost," Emery answered. "One more wire ought to do it."

Gray peered out the hovercar window, struggling to make out the sleeping forms of the men now that a cloud had drifted across the moon. "Can you even see what you're doing?"

Emery made a noncommittal noise and continued fumbling with the wires. Several minutes passed before she said, "Are you ready?"

Gray covered the short distance across the hovercar with quick strides. "You're sure?"

Even in the darkness, Gray could see the incredulous look Emery gave him. "Of course I'm sure. Child genius, me, remember?"

"And so humble about it, too." Gray grinned at Emery through the darkness then sobered. "When you start this thing, those men out there are going to wake up and most likely start shooting." He motioned to the floor. "You need to stay as low as you can and get us out of here as fast as you can."

Emery's eyes widened. "Gray, I've never driven anything before. Just because I can start it, doesn't mean I can drive it."

Gray's blue eyes took in Emery's startled face and did a quick sweep of the sleeping camp outside. He lowered himself until he was eye level with Emery. "What happened to the child genius of a few seconds ago?"

Emery gestured at the mess of wires in front of her. "This is mechanical. It's technology. I understand that. I live in that world." She motioned to the scene outside the window. "This is real-world stuff. Driving. Shooting. I don't do either of those things. This is where the child part of child genius comes in."

Gray scanned outside the windows once more then turned his attention back to Emery. He placed his hands on her shoulders and captured her gaze with his. "You can do this. You only need to drive long enough to get us out of range of their weapons. Then I'll take over. I believe in you. You just have to believe in yourself."

Emery nodded and looked outside once more. She straightened her shoulders and said, "OK, I'll do my best."

Gray gave her a friendly slap on the back and said, "That's all anyone can do. Now, what's the best way out of here?"

They discussed their exit strategy for a few minutes before Gray returned to his post crouching at the opposite end of the hovercar. "Remember, stay low."

Gray heard Emery inhale deeply. She whispered, "Ready?"

"Ready."

The hovercar rumbled to life. The sound startled awake the men in the camp. As they struggled through the fog of sleep to identify the sound, Emery slowly scooted the car forward.

"We need to go faster, Em," Gray said, keeping his eyes on the camp. Two of the men had pulled themselves from their bedrolls and were scrambling for their weapons.

"I'm working on it. It's hard to see in the dark. Can I turn on the lights?"

"No lights. That will make us a target. Just head around the camp toward Ginger and Tristan."

Emery worked the controls, hunching as low as she could over the control board.

The first bullet thunked into the side of the hovercar. Gray crouched next to the window, wishing for a rifle. A large thump came from the front of the hovercar, and they stopped moving.

"What's going on?" Gray ran to the front of the car, keeping low, until he was at Emery's side.

"Sorry. Tree stump."

"Emery, get us moving." The delay had allowed the men to gain on them, and one reached out to grab the outside handrail just as Emery lurched the hovercar forward again. The man fell and another stopped to help him up. More bullets struck the side of the hovercar.

"Can you give us more speed?"

The hovercar gave another thump and shuddered to a stop, the engine dying. "Emery!"

"I'm trying!"

Gray took a deep breath. The window behind him shattered from the impact of a bullet. Another man had reached the hovercar. Emery re-fired the engine, and the car lurched forward but not before the man had grabbed onto the handrail, dropping his gun when the hovercar moved. His feet found purchase on the outside step, and he used his free hand to begin prying open the doors. A bullet shattered another window.

"Emery, wiggle from side to side. We're about to have company."

She jerked the hovercar from side to side, but the vehicle wasn't built for maneuvering; it was designed for straight line transportation. Her efforts did little to knock the man off. The doors to the hovercar opened slightly, and the man pushed his arm through. Gray's gaze swept the hovercar, landing on an ax handle the men had left in the vehicle. He brought the ax handle down hard on the man's arm and heard the sickening crunch of breaking bone. The man screamed and fell from the car.

Emery put on a burst of speed, and the men from the camp fell into the distance behind them. Gray pushed the doors shut, then joined Emery at the controls.

"You can drive now." Emery made to move out of

the way.

"You've got it all figured out now. Sure you don't want to keep going?"

Emery stepped back. "I'm good. Child, remember?"

Gray stepped up to the controls Emery had vacated and studied them. They seemed fairly straightforward and reminded him of some training they had received from an old text about technology-driven vehicles. At the time, he was sure he would never use it. He wondered if the training had been created by someone who knew about The Hub. He shook away the unanswerable question and focused on piloting the car back to Tristan and Ginger in the dusky gray of dawn.

CHAPTER FORTY-FOUR

Maeve woke to a wet nose nudging her face. Her head leaned against Gray's shoulder, and she snuggled closer, not wanting to open her eyes. Rufus's nose nudged her face again, this time followed by a whine. The shoulder under her cheek shifted, and she opened one eye, tilting her head to kiss Gray on the cheek. She jerked herself away from Patrick, embarrassed that in the fog of sleep she had mistaken him for Gray. Rufus sat in front of her and whined again. Patrick gave her a rueful smile, and asked, "How do I work as a pillow?"

Maeve's cheeks reddened, and she avoided his gaze. "Sorry. I forgot where I was for a minute."

Patrick rotated his shoulder, working the kinks out after having stayed still for so long. "No problem. It's been a rough week for you. I'm just glad you got some sleep."

Rufus whined again, and Maeve finally gave him her full attention in the dim light of pre-dawn. "What is it boy?"

He sniffed the air, whined and paced to the edge of the clearing where he whined again.

"He wants us to follow him." Maeve removed the rain covering from around her shoulders. The storm had passed during the night, but the humidity remained. She stood, pulled two protein bars from her pack and handed one to Patrick.

Patrick took a bite and said, "We should wake the others and see what Rufus has found."

In minutes, everyone was awake and eating protein bars as they shouldered their packs. Patrick and Amelia gathered the canteens and refilled them in the stream they had found last night. Rufus waited impatiently at the edge of the clearing, occasionally letting out another whine.

"OK, boy. Lead the way." Maeve gave Rufus a quick scratch on the ears, and he took off into the forest, crashing ahead of them then waiting impatiently for them to catch up. Once, he stopped, sniffed the ground, started one direction then doubled back to go the opposite way.

"Does he know where he's going?" asked Amelia, who had fallen into step next to Maeve.

Maeve shrugged. "He hasn't led me astray so far. He helped keep a 10-year-old kid safe in the desert, so he's earned my trust."

"Has Patrick also earned your trust?" Amelia asked with a touch of bitterness.

Maeve gave her a bewildered look. "I trust him. Don't you?"

"You two seemed pretty cozy over there for just knowing each other a short time. I thought you had a boyfriend."

Maeve gave short laugh. "That was nothing. He offered to share his rain covering since I didn't have one. I fell asleep. I actually thought he was Gray when I woke up this morning."

"So, there's nothing going on between you?"

"Not on my part." Maeve moved a branch out of the way and carefully picked her way around a prickly thornbush. She turned so Amelia could see her face. "I've already given my heart away. I only hope there's still someone to give it to when this is over."

Amelia gave her a long, hard look then nodded. "If he's half as determined as you, I'm sure he's fine and trying his best to get back to you."

They followed Rufus in silence for a few minutes before Maeve broke the silence. "So, you're interested in Patrick?"

Amelia blushed. "Maybe. I don't really know him very well, but he's strong and capable and a good leader." She glanced over her shoulder to where Patrick was guarding their rear. "I'd like to get to know him better."

"Maybe when this is over, you will."

"I don't think he knows I exist as anything other than a faceless soldier."

"When this is over, seize the moment, Amelia. You don't know when you're going to get another chance."

Before Amelia could answer, Rufus let out a round of sharp barks and stopped at the base of a tree. Maeve hurried over to him. "What is it, Rufus?"

The dog continued to sit at the base of the tree, looking at Maeve with his large, brown eyes as if asking for praise for a job well-done. She looked around the area in confusion. She could see and hear nothing except the forest and the animals in it. Had Rufus led them out here to chase a squirrel?

"Well," Patrick said when he reached her side. "What did he find?"

Maeve looked around again. "I don't see anything."

She knelt down next to Rufus and scratched his ears. "What are you trying to tell us, boy?"

"You got us up before dawn to follow a dog on a chase to nowhere?" Private Campbell's voice split the silence. "So glad we've got you on our team."

"Rufus wouldn't just bring us out here for no reason. There has to be something here." Maeve walked a circle around the tree but still saw nothing.

"He's a dog," Private Campbell said. "He probably got distracted by some wildlife. And now we've lost sleep and will have to backtrack."

Maeve moved closer to Private Campbell. "This dog saved my life. I'm never going to ignore him when he's trying to tell me something. If he says there's something here, then there's something here. We just have to figure out what it is."

Private Campbell let out a snort. "Who put you in charge?"

"No one," Patrick said. "I decided to wake you and follow the dog." Patrick put a hand on Private Campbell's shoulder and sent her a warning look.

"There has to be something here," Maeve repeated.

"I know you think Rufus is amazing," Patrick said. "And I'm not saying he's not," he added quickly before Maeve could object. "But is it possible he's just being a dog? That he smelled or heard something and wanted you to chase it with him?"

Maeve's gaze traveled across the tree canopy and around the forest floor. Birds chirped and leaves rustled in the breeze. The forest was filled with the sounds of its inhabitants waking up, but nothing out of the ordinary struck Maeve. She opened her mouth to admit defeat when an ear-splitting roar filled the air.

The roar echoed through the forest, and the hair on Maeve's arms stood up. The soldiers immediately reached for their guns. As quickly as it had started, the roar ended, but Maeve could feel the ground vibrating through her boots as the trees swayed.

"Is that the plagoran?" Amelia whispered to Maeve.

Maeve nodded. "That's it."

"Remind me how big these things are again," Patrick said. The ground vibrated again.

"About seven feet tall, scaly, with some big teeth." Maeve felt a smidge of satisfaction when she noted the tremble in Private Campbell's hands. "And they usually travel in pairs."

At that pronouncement, the group of soldiers shifted slightly closer to one another.

"And how do we get this venom out of their teeth?"

"We kill it, of course." Private Campbell gripped her gun more tightly. Maeve glared at her.

"I'm not sure, but if we can somehow restrain it, we can probably do it without killing it."

"You want to put it on a leash like a dog?" Private Campbell's voice dripped with disbelief. "Are you crazy?"

Maeve turned on her. "I just don't think our first option should be killing a creature that has done nothing to us just because we need something it has."

Patrick stepped between Maeve and Private Campbell, holding up a hand in each direction. "We'll try it Maeve's way first. But," he continued when Private Campbell started to protest, "we *will* shoot it if it tries to harm anyone. Fair?"

Both girls nodded but continued to glare at each other. Maeve turned her back on Private Campbell and marched forward, following Patrick deeper into the forest with Rufus trotting at her side.

They followed the periodic roar of the plagoran through the forest until a second, softer roar joined the first.

"I guess you were right about them traveling in pairs," Patrick said.

"This is one time I would have been happy to be wrong." Maeve turned her attention back to the ground in front of her and stopped short, reaching out to grab Rufus. She stumbled into Patrick, pushing them both slightly forward into a large clearing. At the opposite edge, a long, scaly neck and head protruded from the trees, and Maeve could see the yellow tag in its ear. Rufus trembled beneath her hand and let out a whimper.

"Shh." Maeve stroked his back as she tugged him back into the cover of the trees.

Patrick's eyes were wide.

"I told you they were big."

He motioned with his arm. "But not that big."

Amelia came up behind them. "Why are we stopping?"

Maeve pointed.

"Oh. Wow. That thing is huge." She turned to Maeve. "You think we're going to get venom from that thing without killing it?" She swiveled her body to face Patrick. "And you think we *can* kill that thing?"

Both Maeve and Patrick nodded. She looked from one to the other, her mouth open. "You guys are crazy."

The other soldiers had joined them, forming a half

circle at the edge of the clearing.

"I say we take them out," Private Campbell said.

Maeve glared at her. "We're going to try this without gunfire first."

Private Campbell snorted. "You really think you're going to milk the venom from that thing's teeth without killing it. You're delusional. I'm not going anywhere near that thing without a loaded gun."

"You'll do what you're told," Patrick told her in a tone of command.

Private Campbell sank into a sullen silence.

"I think these might be the same plagoran we encountered before," Maeve said. "Maybe it will remember me."

"What good will that do?" Amelia asked. "Are you going to just ask it for some venom?"

Maeve shrugged. "Maybe. What harm can it do to approach it without weapons first? We have no idea how intelligent it is."

"And what if it's not the plagoran that you saw before? What then?"

"Run?" Maeve said with a grim smile.

"I think Maeve is right." Private Thompson's voice could barely be heard over the noise of the plagoran entering the clearing. "Animals always respond better to kindness than to pain."

"And what do you know about it?" Private Campbell sneered.

Despite his height, Private Thompson seemed to shrink in on himself. Then he took a deep breath, straightened his shoulders and raised his head. "I grew up helping my dad breed cows and pigs for Palumbrans."

Private Campbell's lip curled. "And you think that makes you an expert on plagoran?"

Private Thompson stared at the ground and settled into silence. Maeve thought he might have used up all of his bravery in confronting Private Campbell.

"Leave him alone, Campbell." Amelia jumped to Private Thompson's defense. "He knows more about animals than you do."

Private Campbell pointed toward the plagoran. "Those are not animals. Those are monsters."

"A-a-are we really going to take those things on?" Private Allen spoke for the first time. "We've been trained to fight men, not monsters. Why do we need to do this?"

Maeve stared at him open-mouthed. "People are going to die without this venom. Do you want that to happen?"

Private Allen refused to meet her eyes. "Well, only one person is sick, right? If she doesn't pass it on to anyone else, then the virus dies, right?"

"You're willing to sacrifice Emma just so you don't have to do your job?" Maeve's voice rose, and the plagoran in the clearing raised its head. She stepped closer to Private Allen, stopping when she was toe to toe with the soldier. She could feel him trembling, and a fleeting spark of compassion ran through her. "Look, I know you're scared. Those things are scary, but it's not just Emma's life that is at stake here. Do you really think that Arabella won't hesitate to use this virus again? We need to be able to protect everyone in Palumbra. To do that, we have to get the venom."

Private Allen nodded and took a step back from Maeve.

Patrick moved to the center of the group. "Has everyone had their say?" Heads bobbed all around. "Great. Because none of you get a vote. That's not how this works. We have a mission, and we're here to complete it. We're a team. We either work together or we fail. So, no matter what your personal feelings about this mission are, you have a job to do. Let's get it done."

CHAPTER FORTY-FIVE

Emery pushed the button to open the hovercar doors before Gray had stopped the vehicle. She jumped down to the ground and stopped at the sight of Ginger's head laying in Tristan's lap, her face drained of all color. "Is she?" Emery couldn't bring herself to finish the question.

Tristan shook his and eased Ginger's head off his lap so he could stand. "She's still alive." He pulled Emery in for a comforting hug. "But we need to get her help. Soon."

Gray jumped down from the hovercar, his eyes quickly taking in the situation. With a curt nod, he strode over to Ginger and motioned for Tristan to help him lift her. "We've got to get moving. The owners of this hovercar weren't exactly happy that we took it."

"I've got her." Tristan leaned down to Ginger and gently lifted her in his arms. Her breathing hitched as he lifted her but resumed its shallow rhythm as he strode toward the hovercar. Gray grabbed the rope that had saved Ginger, and he and Emery returned to the hovercar. He took his position at the controls, and the hovercar began to move once more. Tristan settled Ginger on the bench seat along the side of the hovercar, cushioning her head once more in his lap. Emery sat at Ginger's feet. Ginger began to shiver as the air rushed through the shattered windows, but the hovercar held no blankets.

"Rub her legs, Emery." Tristan blew on his hands to warm them, then began to briskly rub her arms. Ginger's clothes had mostly dried from the previous night's storm, but they were too thin to offer much in the way of warmth.

"She's in shock. We really need to get her warm." Emery looked around the hovercar once more, but it held nothing in the way of supplies. It was a vehicle to get from place to place, nothing more. Any supplies that the original owners had carried to their camp, they had taken with them. Tristan pulled his shirt over his head and laid it over Ginger's torso, providing a tiny bit of warmth. Gray removed his shirt as well, handing it to Emery to tuck around Ginger's shaking shoulders.

Emery looked up at Tristan with fear-filled eyes. "Is she going to be OK?"

"She will be if we can get her some help," Tristan promised.

Emery faced Gray. "How fast can we get back to Palumbra?"

Gray scanned the horizon. "This thing can go pretty quick since it just skims over the rough terrain. Arabella's people didn't take us too far into The Beyond." He pointed. "We can see the desert right there. So, maybe half a day to get all the way to Palumbra – assuming we don't get lost in the desert."

Emery looked startled. "Do you think we'll get lost?"

Gray shook his head. "I'm pretty sure I can get us

back to Palumbra. The question is do we make a stop in the desert or not."

"What?" Emery drew her eyebrows together in confusion. "Why would we even think about stopping? We have to get Ginger some help."

"Do we just forget about Thomas?" Gray did not turn around to see Emery's expression, but he heard her sharp intake of breath.

"Thomas," Tristan said with an air of defeat. "What do we do?"

Gray took a last look at the open expanse of land in front of him, set the hovercar to continue in a straight line then turned around. Tristan's shoulders drooped as he sat shirtless and continued to rub Ginger's arms. "Exactly. What do we do?"

"We go back to Palumbra and get help for Ginger." Emery stood, bracing her legs against the sway of the hovercar and placed her hands on her hips. "How can we do anything else?"

Gray and Tristan shared a look of misery then Gray said, "So we abandon Thomas?"

Emery looked defiantly from Tristan to Gray, then dropped her hands from her hips and closed her eyes. "No. Yes. I don't know." She slumped back down at the end of the bench seat next to Ginger's feet. She looked from her sister to Gray with tortured eyes. "How do we choose?" she whispered.

Gray raised an eyebrow at Tristan. "Any thoughts?"

Tristan's hand smoothed Ginger's hair away from her face. "She's not going to make it if we stop. And what if we have to fight? We have no weapons. Someone would have to protect Ginger, and Emery's not a trained fighter." He looked at Gray. "What do you think?"

Gray leaned against the control console. "I think our options are all bad. No matter what we do, we abandon someone. I hate the thought of leaving Thomas behind." He stared at some peeling paint on the floor. "Maeve will kill me," he said softly.

Emery's and Tristan's eyes met over the prone form of Ginger. Emery raised her eyebrows as if questioning whether he thought Maeve was still alive. Tristan shrugged.

"But she'd kill me if something happened to Ginger, too," Gray continued, ignoring Emery and Tristan's silent communication. He stopped talking and began to pace in front of the control console. "But, what if." He fell silent and stared out the front window.

"Want to fill us in on what's going on in your brain?" Emery asked.

Gray turned back around, his eyes gleaming with determination. "We have to go through the desert anyway, right?"

Tristan and Emery nodded.

"Let's make a sweep by the oasis. If it looks like Thomas is there, then I'll stay behind and see if I can rescue him. If not, we'll continue on to Palumbra."

"We can't split up," Emery said heatedly. "How is Tristan going to fight if we run into trouble if he has both me and Ginger to defend?"

Tristan looked thoughtful. "No, that could work. We have the hovercar, which means we can outrun anyone on foot, and it offers some protection. We should be able to make it without stopping." He looked up at Gray. "It's a good plan. Let's do it."

Gray pushed the hovercar to its top speed, skimming over the rocky ground like a skater gliding across ice. Every so often, he would take his gaze off the desolate view outside his window and glance back at Ginger and the others. Ginger's breathing remained shallow but steady, and her eyes stayed closed. Bruises had begun to appear on her face and hands, which was all Gray could see of her skin since they had swaddled her in his and Tristan's t-shirts. Tristan kept her head in his lap and made the occasional comment to Emery who had moved to the bench on the other side of the hovercar. Emery's gaze never left the rise and fall of her sister's chest.

"We've reached the desert," Gray announced.

Tristan flicked his gaze to the window as if to confirm Gray's announcement, then went back to watching Ginger and stroking the hair off her face.

Emery joined Gray at the console. "Do you know where we're going?"

Gray nodded. "I think so." He pointed slightly to his right. "We should run into the oasis if we angle in that direction."

"Do you really think Thomas will still be there? Do you think Arabella actually let him go?"

Gray said nothing.

"Gray, tell me the truth."

He shook his head. "I don't think she ever had any intention of letting him go, not when she can use him as leverage over Maeve."

"So, you don't think he'll be at the oasis?"

"I don't." He adjusted one of the controls. "But we have to look."

Emery nodded and returned to her seat, but her gaze now alternated between the view outside and Ginger's unconscious form.

No one said anything else. Gray glanced over his shoulder to find Emery's eyes slowly closing and her head slumping to her chest. He concentrated on driving as the low murmur of Tristan's voice carrying on a one-sided conversation with the unconscious Ginger broke the silence.

He slowed the hovercar in what seemed to be the middle of the desert. Emery's eyes popped open. "Are we there?" she asked as she wiped her eyes. Gray nodded and noted that the short nap had done nothing for the dark circles under Emery's eyes.

"How is she?" Gray asked Tristan.

Tristan shrugged his shoulders. "OK, I guess. She's still breathing, and her pulse is weak but steady. There's not much else we can do for her except get her to a doctor. Why did we stop?"

Gray turned to gaze out the driver's window. "The oasis is just up there."

Emery hopped off her bench and ran to stand next to Gray. "Where?"

Gray pointed at a shadow on the horizon. "Those are the trees of the oasis."

Emery squinted. "Are you sure?"

Gray nodded. "I'm positive. It won't take us 15 minutes to get there at top speed."

"So why are we sitting here?"

"Because we can't just drive up and announce ourselves, Emery." Tristan shifted slightly, trying to move and not jostle Ginger.

"Exactly," Gray said. "We need a plan. It would be better to wait until it gets dark."

Tristan was shaking his head before Gray finished speaking. "Ginger can't wait that long. We need to be in Palumbra by the time it gets dark."

"I know. That just makes it a bit harder to get in and out without being seen."

Tristan looked around the barren interior of the hovercar. "Do we have any supplies at all?"

Emery kneeled down and crawled under the driving console. "There's this."

Gray took the piece of gray fabric from her. "What is it?"

"I don't know. I just noticed it out of the corner of my eye."

Gray shook out the lightweight fabric. It had holes at the top and was a rectangle about seven feet long and four feet wide.

"Look up." Tristan pointed to a rod above Gray's head. "I bet it's a curtain to set the driver apart from the passengers. But we can use it as a disguise and a blanket for Ginger because we're going to need our shirts."

Gray had almost forgotten he had given Ginger his shirt. "How are we going to tear the fabric?"

All three looked around the car, seeking a sharp point to rip the fabric.

"There." Emery ran to the back of the hovercar where a strip of metal had come loose where it met the door. "We can use this."

Gray took the fabric over to the sharp metal piece, placed a corner of the fabric against the sharp edge and tugged. A small rip appeared in the fabric. "How do we want to cut it?"

"Cut enough to make a cloak-like thing to cover someone's head. Leave the rest for Ginger. We can double it over and keep her warmer."

Gray slung the fabric around his shoulders and flipped it up over his head like a hood. He grabbed the fabric where it touched his knees and placed that spot on the sharp edge and tugged. A two-inch rip appeared. By carefully sawing the fabric against the sharp edge, the tear slowly grew to about four inches.

"This is going to take forever," Gray announced, wiping sweat from his forehead. With the hovercar stopped, the heat in the metal vehicle was rising quickly.

Emery motioned for Gray to stop and took the fabric from him. "Don't you know anything about fabric?" She stood on the bench and let the fabric drop to the floor. She placed her hands on either side of the rip Gray had made and pulled her hands apart. The fabric tore in a long strip, and she continued tearing until she had two pieces of fabric in her hands. The whole process took two minutes.

Gray took the smaller piece from her. "Glad one of us is smart."

Emery shot him a grin as she laid the other piece of fabric over Ginger. "Genius, remember?"

"OK, genius," Tristan said. "What's next?"

"No idea." Emery tucked the side of the fabric under Ginger, being careful not to jostle her. "You guys are the mission planners."

Tristan tossed Gray his shirt as he shoved his arms into his own. Gray raised his eyebrows at Tristan. "You seemed to have an idea when you told me how to cut the fabric."

Tristan smoothed the fabric surrounding Ginger. "We get a little bit closer, then one of us uses the fabric to conceal our face and heads toward the oasis on foot. Because the fabric is close to the color of the desert, we'll be harder to see. We should be able to get close enough to at least see if anyone is there without being spotted."

Gray nodded. "It's a good plan. You've learned a lot in the past few months."

Tristan shrugged and looked down at Ginger. "I feel like we'd be better off if I knew more first aid and less about mission planning." He took the fabric from Gray. "I'll be the scout."

Gray shook his head. "You should stay here with Ginger and Emery."

Tristan motioned to Emery to take his place cradling Ginger's head. They carefully switched places, and Tristan stood, stretching his back and shaking out his legs.

"Remember how we decided who got to go steal the hovercar?"

Gray nodded.

"Let's use the same logic here." Tristan held up a finger. "One, you know how to drive the hovercar. I don't." He held up another finger. "Two, you're exhausted. You've been driving us for hours after staying up all night to steal this thing. I've been sitting on a bench, and I was able to doze lightly last night while we were waiting for you." He held up a third finger. "Three, it's my turn."

"You were doing great until that last one," Gray said. "There are no turns out here. We pick the best person for the job." Tristan started to interrupt. Gray ignored him and continued. "Normally, I would argue that I am that person, but you make good points." Gray looked at

Ginger's motionless form. "Get suited up. I'll get us closer."

The trees of the oasis grew larger as the hovercar raced across the desert. Gray slowed the car to a stop when they were still about a half mile away.

"This is as close as I think we can get without being seen. You ready?"

Tristan nodded. His dark skin and hair were hidden by the cloak he had fashioned out of the driver's curtain. He pushed the button to open the door, waved a quick goodbye to Emery and turned toward Gray with his hand out. "Thanks for getting us this far."

Gray grabbed his hand and pulled him in for a quick hug. "It took all of us to get this far." He released Tristan and looked him in the eye. "Be careful. No heroics. Just see if it looks like Thomas is still there. If you're not back in two hours, we're coming after you."

Tristan stepped back and raised the hood over his head. With his face shadowed, his eyes gleamed. "If I'm not back in two hours, get her to safety." He motioned to Ginger. "Then come back for me."

Gray started to argue, but Tristan turned on his heel and stepped through the open door of the hovercar into a swirl of blowing sand. Gray watched his retreating back until his makeshift cloak blended in with the blowing sand of the desert.

CHAPTER FORTY-SIX

Tristan wiped the sweat and sand off his forehead and peered through the glare of the sun. He was lying flat on his stomach near the edge of the oasis, hoping his cloak offered enough camouflage to protect him from detection. But detection by whom? So far, despite lying in the sand for what seemed like an hour, he had seen no one. He glanced at the sun, trying to determine how much of his two hours he had left. He would need to head back to the hovercar soon if he didn't want to be left behind.

He wiped the sweat out of his eyes again and slowly rose from his hiding spot. No shouts of alarm came from the oasis. He was pretty sure the place was deserted. His eyes scanned the area in front of him; the small pond of water rippled in the slight breeze. Nothing else moved. He heard no sounds other than the wind. Glancing once more at the sun, he moved toward the water to look for any sign of Thomas.

His steps were quiet in the sand but seemed to echo in the vastness of the desert. He stopped to refill his canteen, figuring that it was better to do it now in case he had to flee into the desert. But all of his training was telling him there was no one here except him. He capped his canteen and started toward the hidden room in the dunes. It seemed the most likely place for Sarge to keep Thomas.

When he arrived at the dunes, a large, undisturbed pile of sand covered the entrance to the hidden room. There was no way anyone had used that room to contain Thomas. Tristan returned to the main part of the oasis, his eyes scanning high and low for any sign that the young boy had been here. He held his hand over the coals in the fire pit, searching for any sign of warmth but found none. As he rose back to his feet, he noticed a cut on the palm tree across from him. He crossed to the tree and smiled. Carved into the bark were Thomas's initials. The resourceful boy had managed to get something sharp to leave evidence that he had been there. Tristan leaned closer. There were marks under Thomas's initials. He squinted to try to read them. Was that an E?

Something sharp poked Tristan below the ribs in his back. Slowly, he raised his hands and turned his head to find the source of the weapon.

"Elton?"

"Don't move."

"Or what, you'll skewer me? Where is everyone else?"

Tristan's eyes quickly took in Elton's ragged appearance, his sand-covered clothes and unwashed face. What worried him most was the feral look in Elton's eyes. "How long have you been out here?"

Elton poked him with the stick whose point he had honed to a razor sharpness. "I'm asking the questions. Turn around."

Careful not to catch himself on the end of the stick, Tristan slowly turned around, keeping his hands in the air.

Elton licked his lips. "How did you get here? You should be dead."

"I'm harder to kill than you thought. But why are you the only one here? Where's Thomas?"

Elton spat. "Thomas," he sneered. "I should have killed that little brat. Who knew she would take such a liking to him?"

Tristan wrinkled his nose in confusion. "Who took a liking to him? Maeve?"

Elton laughed. "Not Maeve. She's dead now anyway." Tristan winced. He hoped Elton was just speculating and not speaking from actual knowledge. "Arabella. Treated the kid like her long, lost relative."

Tristan inched forward and lowered his hands slightly. "Where did she take him?"

"To Palumbra for her triumphal entry. Where else?"

Elton looked in the direction of Palumbra as if he could see it from where he stood. Tristan lost no time taking advantage of Elton's mistake, grabbing the pointed stick and turning it on Elton. Elton put up a feeble resistance but was no match for Tristan's superior strength and training. Tristan poked Elton lightly with the stick.

"How long ago did they leave?"

Elton stared at the ground, and Tristan thought he saw tears forming in the corners of his eyes. "Yesterday."

"Why are you still here?"

"She left me behind to watch for you." His shoulders slumped. "But, really, I think she just left me behind to die. Maeve warned me she would turn on me when I was no longer useful."

"You should have listened to Maeve." He poked

Elton again. "Let's go."

"Where are we going?"

"To rescue Palumbra."

"No way." Gray stood in front of the door to the hovercar with his arms crossed and his legs braced as if daring Tristan to try to move him. "We are not taking him with us."

"Gray, be reasonable," Tristan said in a calm voice. "We can't leave him here."

"Sure we can. He sold us out. Left us to die. Why should we save him?"

Gray felt a hand on his shoulder. He turned his head and focused on Emery. "Because you're better than him."

Gray straightened his shoulders. "What if I'm not?"

Tristan's serious gaze bored into Gray's defiant one. "I know that you are. Maeve knows that you are."

Gray's gaze faltered. He turned his eyes to the sky and swallowed slowly before returning his gaze to Elton. "Does it matter? His actions most likely killed her."

"No!" Emery jumped down from the hovercar and stood in front of Gray. "You can't think like that. We have to believe she's still alive."

Gray's shoulders fell, and his eyes glistened. He swallowed again. "I just don't know how she could have made it. By now, half of Palumbra could be dead." He stared at Elton. "And it's all his fault."

Elton took a step forward, fell to his knees in the hot sand and bowed his head. "I don't have an excuse. I wanted the power Arabella offered me, and I didn't care what it cost. I can't change what I did, but I am sorry."

"Maeve might be dead, and you're sorry? How is that supposed to make anything better?" Gray turned and put one foot in the hovercar. "Leave him here to rot."

Tristan stopped Gray with a hand on his arm. In a voice that only Gray could hear, he said, "What do you think Maeve would want you to do?"

Gray's knuckles whitened where he gripped the door frame. Finally, he said, "Fine. Bring him along." He whirled and looked down to where Elton still knelt in the sand. "But one wrong move, and I'm tossing him out."

"Agreed." Tristan grabbed Elton roughly by the arm and pulled him to his feet. "Get in the car. Sit down and keep your mouth shut."

CHAPTER FORTY-SEVEN

Maeve carefully placed one foot on the ground, letting her weight travel from the heel to the toe in an effort to be as quiet as possible. The others were spread out in a line to her right and left as they approached the plagoran grazing in the clearing. She could see the yellow tag on its ear, but even when she squinted, she couldn't read the number on it. She gave a silent snort. Did she really think the plagoran that she had helped would remember her? And would it care if it did?

She glanced over at Amelia who kept her gun trained on the plagoran but gave Maeve a quick wink. On her other side, Private Campbell had her gun trained on the plagoran with her finger on the trigger. She glared at Maeve. They had left Rufus in the trees at the edge of the clearing, fearing he would spook the gigantic creature.

The plagoran raised its head; its nostrils flared as it sniffed the air. Private Campbell raised her gun to take aim at the plagoran's head, and Patrick motioned with his head for Maeve to take the lead. She gave Private Campbell a hard look, which Private Campbell returned with a sneer. Maeve shifted her focus back to the plagoran, rolled her shoulders and took another step into the clearing. The plagoran sniffed the air again and swiveled its head until its gaze landed on Maeve. It let out a roar, and Maeve froze. The plagoran took a thundering step toward Maeve and roared again. Maeve scanned the opposite tree line with her eyes, looking for the plagoran's mate. They might be able to deal with one plagoran, but she was pretty sure that two would mean the end of their little group.

Despite Maeve's earlier bravado in front of Patrick and the others, her knees were shaking. She swallowed to keep what little breakfast she had eaten in her stomach and wondered briefly if her insistence on not killing the plagoran to get the venom would end in both her and Emma's deaths. She shot a glance at her empty hands and wondered at the wisdom of not carrying a weapon. The plagoran took another earth-shaking step toward her while Maeve stood frozen to the spot. She could hear the rustling of the others behind her as they sought the best shot without moving from their positions. The plagoran let out another roar; this time an answering roar echoed from the trees on the other side of the clearing. The sound spurred Maeve into action.

Slowly, she walked toward the plagoran who eyed her warily with its large, yellow eye. With every step she took, the plagoran roared, and its mate answered. Each time the answering roar was louder. Maeve thought she could feel the ground begin to shake, but she continued to walk slowly toward the plagoran, her arms at her sides, trying to appear unthreatening. Her hands shook.

When she was about 20 feet away, the plagoran let out a mighty roar and lowered its head to look her in the eyes. Its egg-shaped, yellow eyes met Maeve's in an unblinking stare. She didn't dare move despite her feet itching to run back the way she had come. She stared back into the plagoran's strangely haunting gaze without blinking. Her heart raced, and her breath came in short, quiet pants, making it impossible to catch her breath. Sweat rolled down her spine. Carefully, she held her hand out, palm up, like her father had shown her to do with a horse. She didn't think a plagoran had much in common with one of the government's plow horses, but it was all she could think to do. What was she thinking? She didn't have any experience with animals. They should have sent Private Thompson out first.

The plagoran looked left and right as if counting how many were in their group. Maeve heard Amelia shift behind her. Slowly, the creature lowered its head toward Maeve until she could read the number on its tag – 56823. It ignored Maeve's outstretched hand and brought its face toward her own, stopping just inches from her nose. Maeve was nearly blown over by the force of its breath, which smelled of grass and acid. She could see chunks of whatever it had eaten for breakfast caught in its many sharp teeth. The long teeth in the front held the venom, and she fleetingly wondered if she could just grab the tooth and run. Instead, she held her breath and didn't move. The plagoran shuffled backward slightly then lowered its head even more so its eye was looking directly into Maeve's.

"Hello." Maeve's voice cracked. She tried again. "Hello."

The plagoran cocked its head as if trying to place Maeve's voice. She raised her outstretched hand toward its nose, causing it to shuffle backward. She dropped her hand to her side.

"OK. It's OK. We're not going to hurt you."

The plagoran opened its mouth, and Maeve stifled the urge to step backward. In a barely audible voice and without taking her eyes off the creature in front of her, she said to Amelia, "Hand me the container." Amelia placed a small vial in her outstretched hand. The plagoran's eyes followed her every move.

"Remember me?"

The plagoran blinked again as if it understood her.

"I helped you, remember?" Maeve took a step forward. "I fixed up your wound."

The plagoran stood still, watching Maeve. She took another step toward it. The ground beneath her feet began to shake.

"There are about to be two of them," Private Thompson said from somewhere behind Maeve. "Finish making friends with it, so we can get what we came after and get out of here."

"I don't have a lot of time," Maeve said to the plagoran. "I need some of the venom from your tooth to help my friend. We don't want to hurt you."

She took another slow step in the plagoran's direction, continuing to speak as she moved closer. "How long have you been out here? Did Arabella put you out here, hoping to keep anyone from Palumbra from heading toward The Hub?" She kept up a stream of chatter as she finally got close enough to touch the plagoran. In what seemed like slow motion, she raised her shaking hand toward the plagoran's nose. It growled low in its throat, and the ground under Maeve's feet continued to shake with the steps of the plagoran's approaching mate. She held up the vial in front of its eye as she placed a hand on its nose.

"Be careful, Maeve." Amelia's quiet admonishment

drifted to Maeve's ears.

The plagoran's large, yellow eye gazed into Maeve's brown ones and blinked. Maeve took that as acceptance and placed the vial against the plagoran's long front tooth. The vial seemed tiny against the tooth. Nothing happened. She took a closer look at the tooth and noticed a bump at the top of the tooth against the gumline. She moved the vial to the bump and pressed it against the creature's gums. Clear liquid began to drip into the vial. The plagoran stood unblinking as Maeve filled the vial. When it was full, she removed her hand from the creature's nose and stepped back.

"Thank you."

The plagoran blinked again and stepped back. Maeve began walking back to the others when a furious roar split the air. The plagoran's mate had arrived.

"Maeve, hurry!" Patrick shouted.

Maeve sprinted toward the tree line, careful not to drop the precious vial. Gunshots rang out and an unearthly scream rose from behind her. She turned to see the plagoran and its mate fall to the ground, and she stopped in disbelief. Fury rose inside her, bubbling into a froth of anger waiting to be released on whoever had pulled the trigger. She let out a scream of her own and turned to run back to the plagoran when hands grabbed both her arms and pulled her into the treeline. Maeve struggled, kicking and biting the people who refused to release her.

"Maeve." Patrick's voice broke through her fury.

"Who? Who did it?" Anger dripped from every word.

"It wasn't us," Amelia said. She pointed into the clearing. "It was them."

CHAPTER FORTY-EIGHT

Gray scanned the area in front of the hovercar, trying to find the source of the unearthly scream that had just split the air. Emery rushed to the front and peered out the window. The vehicle continued to glide just above the ground as Gray maneuvered it through the trees. They were so close to Palumbra, so close to help for Ginger. Another scream split the air.

"What do you think it is?" Emery asked, swiveling her head from side to side, trying to find the source.

Gray shook his head as he carefully steered the hovercar around a large oak tree. "I don't know." He looked over his shoulder at Ginger's motionless body and pale face resting on Tristan's leg. "But we don't really have time to stop and find out."

"I know you're right, but whatever that is sounds like it's in a lot of pain."

Gray took one hand off the controls and squeezed Emery's shoulder. "We can't save everyone, Em. We have to focus on getting Ginger some help."

Emery nodded but continued to scan the area. Her forehead wrinkled and she pointed off to the right. "Gray? Is that a hovercar?"

Gray slowed the vehicle and squinted in the direction Emery pointed.

"I think it is. What is a hovercar doing this close to Palumbra?" He brought their hovercar to a stop and strode to the back of the car where Elton sat.

"Did Arabella have a hovercar when she left you behind?"

Elton had said nothing since they had entered the hovercar and had kept his gaze firmly settled on the floor. When Elton tipped his face up toward Gray, his red eyes gave away the fact that he had been crying. Gray didn't care. "Yes. She had soldiers with her when she left."

Tristan gently moved Ginger's head from his lap and joined Gray. "What was her plan?"

Elton sat up straighter. "Why should I tell you?" All traces of his earlier remorse had morphed into defiance.

Gray wanted to shake him. "Are you kidding me? She left you behind to die in the desert. I thought you were sorry for what you did. Why wouldn't you tell us what you know?"

"Maybe she was going to come back for me." Elton sounded as though he was trying to convince himself.

"You aren't the brightest, are you?" Tristan sneered. "She tried to kill all of us. What makes you think you're special. Arabella uses people, then she discards them. We're your best hope for survival, but only if you tell us what you know."

"We can always just leave you out here by yourself." Gray renewed his original threat.

Elton looked from face to face, all united in their dislike of him. "I'm sorry." His shoulders slumped and he hung his head. "I knew what she was, but I thought I was smarter than her. She lured me in with promises of power and never being hungry again."

"Then she left you to starve." Gray said without compassion. "Arabella only cares about Arabella. Now, tell us what you know."

"I don't know the whole plan, but she was going to let the virus weaken the population of Palumbra, then a few days later she planned to attack."

"Did she really have an army to use?" Tristan asked.

Elton shook his head. "No. She had a hundred soldiers or so, but she figured that would be enough."

"Against an entire city of people?" Gray looked bewildered. "That's insane."

Elton twisted his wrists against the rope restraints. "You didn't see the way the virus ripped through Bellus. So many people died. It would have been easy to overpower Bellus with just a handful of troops. She's betting the same thing happens in Palumbra."

Tristan returned to the bench where Ginger lay and looked out the window where he could just make out the other hovercar. His gaze lingered on the shallow rise and fall of Ginger's chest. "Why would they stop out here? It doesn't make sense. There's no strategic value to these woods."

"How many soldiers did she have with her?" Gray asked Elton.

Elton shrugged. "Maybe 10? She sent most of the other soldiers on ahead of her to stake out positions outside Palumbra, but nothing was supposed to happen before she was here to oversee the attack."

Gray pointed out the window. "Why would she

stop here?"

"I have no idea. That wasn't part of the plan, as far as I know."

"What are we going to do?" Emery asked. "Ginger still needs help."

Gray pondered their options. Ginger had to be their first priority, but could they just leave the enemy hovercar without investigating it? What chance did they have if it was Arabella?

"We should press on into Palumbra and get Ginger the help she needs. We can let Cleo know that we think Arabella is out here."

Tristan nodded, but Emery objected. "What about those screams? We should at least get close enough to make sure no people are in danger."

Gray raised his eyebrows at Tristan in a silent question. Tristan once again studied Ginger's still form then nodded his head slightly at Gray.

"OK, Emery. We'll get as close as we can."

Maeve's mouth dropped open. Across the clearing, wielding a gun and looking triumphant next to a hovercar stood Arabella. She motioned to the guards next to her, and they warily approached the now silent and still plagorans. Maeve closed her mouth and fisted her hands in anger that Arabella had gunned down the creatures she had tried so hard to keep from harm. Once more, Maeve started toward Arabella.

"Maeve, you can't go out there." Amelia grabbed her arm, but Maeve shook her off and kept walking. Amelia hurried to catch up.

"What are you doing? You can't let her know we're

here." Amelia pulled on Maeve's arm again, digging in her heels and forcing Maeve to stop.

"She killed them. She killed them for no reason."

Patrick jogged up to them. "She had a reason. It's the same reason we wanted them."

Maeve turned to him. "She wants their venom? Why?"

"She probably needs it for a vaccine. Can't have her troops catching the virus by accident, can she?" Patrick grabbed Maeve's other arm. "But you still can't go out there. We have to get that venom back to Palumbra."

Before Maeve could respond, Amelia dropped her arm and twisted to look back into the clearing. "What is she doing?"

"Who?" Patrick asked.

"Private Campbell. Why is she crossing the clearing?"

The three of them watched as Private Campbell got halfway across the clearing then shouted something to the guards around Arabella. The guards parted and Arabella stepped forward. She said something that Maeve couldn't hear, and Private Campbell continued across the clearing, stopping to speak to Arabella when she reached the other side. Private Campbell gestured toward the tree line where they were standing, and Maeve, Amelia and Patrick shrunk back into the shadows.

A guard handed something to Arabella who raised it to her mouth and began speaking. Her magnified voice echoed through the clearing.

"So, Maeve, you somehow survived. Too bad it won't be for long." She let out a cackle that sent shivers down Maeve's spine. "I'm going to need you and your friends to come out of those trees."

No one moved. As long as Arabella and her guards couldn't see them, she couldn't shoot them.

"Tsk. Tsk." Arabella's voice rang through the clearing again. "Are we really going to play this silly game? Come now, Maeve. We all know I hold the key to making you do whatever I want." Arabella reached behind her and pulled someone forward. One of her guards pointed a gun at the person's head. "Do you want him to live?"

Maeve rushed into the clearing. "Thomas!" she screamed. "Don't hurt him, Arabella!"

"Tell your friends to come out of whatever hole they're hiding in."

Maeve gave an apologetic look at the tree line as Patrick, Amelia and Private Thompson emerged from the trees with their guns raised over their heads. Patrick shot her a murderous look as he moved to stand next to her.

"Great strategy," he muttered as Arabella directed them to put down their weapons. They threw their guns down in front of them.

"I couldn't let her kill Thomas."

"She's not going to kill him, Maeve. He's her only leverage over you. That would be a stupid move. You gave up any advantage we had."

Maeve said nothing. Patrick's words made some sense. Arabella was clearly holding onto Thomas for a reason, and she wouldn't get rid of him until he had served his purpose. She replayed Patrick's words in her head. Something didn't make sense. Arabella thought she was dead, so she didn't need Thomas as leverage over her; that was just a happy coincidence for Arabella. What else could she need Thomas for?

"What do we do now?" Amelia asked. Private Thompson stared at the ground, and Maeve looked around for Rufus. Where had he gone?

"I guess we wait to see what she does next. Be ready to run when I say so."

CHAPTER FORTY-NINE

Gray stopped the hovercar in the trees on the opposite side of the clearing from the other hovercar. Arabella's voice rang through the air, but he couldn't make out her words.

"Can you see what's going on?" Gray asked Emery who was perched on the seat next to him.

She shook her head. "They're too far away." She squinted then pointed slightly off to the right. "What is that?"

Gray followed her finger and saw a large shape loping through the underbrush toward the hovercar. It was large and dark, and Gray hoped it wasn't another genetically engineered creature for them to fight. As the shape came closer, Gray's hand hovered over the controls.

"It's Rufus!" The cry came from Tristan who had twisted around to look out the window with Ginger's head still cradled in his lap.

Gray hit the control to open the door and clambered out of the hovercar, closely followed by Emery. Even Elton lifted his head to take in the scene. Rufus jumped up and put both paws on Gray's shoulder, licking his face.

"Hey, boy." Gray rubbed Rufus's ears. "How did you get out here?"

Rufus dropped to all four paws, then tugged on Gray's sleeve and started pulling him forward. "What is it? Do you want us to follow you?" Rufus continued pulling on Gray's sleeve so hard that the fabric began to rip. Gray gently pried Rufus's mouth off his sleeve, and said, "OK, boy. We're coming." He turned to look over his shoulder. "Emery come with me. Tristan, can you have the hovercar ready to go?"

Tristan nodded. "Be careful."

Emery and Gray followed Rufus, who had picked up the pace when he realized they were following him. He ran ahead of them, doubling back when they fell too far behind. Finally, they reached the edge of the clearing, and the sight in front of him left Gray feeling both horrified and relieved. Maeve and some other people were standing on the side of the clearing waiting for Arabella's guards to cross the clearing to them. Arabella stood in the doorway of the hovercar with a tight grip on Thomas's shoulder.

With Arabella's guards fast approaching, Gray motioned to Emery and Rufus to stay where they were. Emery grabbed Rufus's collar and told him to sit. Gray crept forward until he reached the edge of the tree line, careful to remain hidden in the shadows.

"Maeve," he said in a loud whisper.

She started but didn't move otherwise.

"I'm behind you. We have a hovercar. We can make it back there, but you're going to have to move now."

Maeve's head bobbed slightly to let him know she had heard him. He saw her take a deep breath, then she and the others sprinted for the tree line. Bullets rained around them. The man on Maeve's left stumbled as they reached Gray, but Maeve grabbed his arm and pulled him along. Emery and Gray sprinted with them, Gray taking over Maeve's spot helping Patrick. Rufus ran to the tree line, then back to Gray, whining, then sprinted off into the woods.

"Rufus!" Maeve cried. She started chase after him.

"Maeve," Gray said sharply. "We can't. Follow Emery. We have to get back to the hovercar."

A bullet plunked into the tree next to him, underscoring the urgency.

Maeve looked sadly in the direction Rufus had run but nodded to acknowledge Gray's words. The hovercar came into sight, and Gray heaved Patrick's arm over his shoulder and urged him onward.

Emery reached the hovercar first and scrambled into it, followed by Private Thompson, Amelia and Maeve. Maeve turned to help Patrick and Gray through the door. Gray hit the button to close the door as a black streak came flying out of the woods and into the car.

"Rufus," Emery exclaimed. She threw her arms around him and buried her face in his fur.

Gray rushed to the front of the car and traded places with Tristan, pushing the car to its limits of speed and maneuverability to get them away from Arabella's guards. "Get down," he yelled as bullets plunked the side of the car. Gray worked the controls and pulled away from the guards following them. No one spoke as they huddled on the floor, heads below the windows. After several minutes, the plunking sound stopped, and the only noise was the hum of the hovercar engine.

Gray turned his head to see Maeve climbing to her

feet and making her way across the car to stand next to him.

"Hi," she whispered.

Gray took a careful look at the landscape in front of the hovercar, then pulled her into his embrace before dropping his lips to hers. He could feel her sink into him and relief swept through him that she was alive and back in his arms. Reluctantly, he pulled away from her but kept his arm wrapped around her waist as he turned back to the hovercar controls. She leaned into his side and looked around for the first time since they had entered the vehicle. Her eyes widened when she saw Ginger's still form on the seat, her head once again cradled in Tristan's lap. She pulled away from Gray and took a step toward Ginger. Gray held his breath as her eyes landed on Elton. She turned back to him, disbelief written across her face.

"What is he doing here?"

Elton raised his head, and his tortured eyes met Maeve's. The silence lengthened. Maeve clenched her fists and looked back at Gray. "Why is he here?"

Gray opened his mouth to answer, but Tristan spoke first. "I found him at the oasis when we stopped to look for Thomas. Arabella left him behind."

"So what?" Scorn dripped from Maeve's every word. "You took pity on him and brought him back with you? He didn't show any concern for us when he was turning us over to Arabella."

Gray placed a hand on her arm. "It's not ideal, but Arabella betrayed him, too."

Maeve shook off Gray's hand and marched over to stand directly in front of Elton. "You killed Shalara. You almost killed Emery and me. Emma is still sick, and if we don't get this," she held up the plagoran venom, "back to Palumbra soon, she will die. Thomas is still with Arabella. And you expect me to feel sorry for you because Arabella abandoned you after she had no use for you?"

Elton refused to meet Maeve's eyes and instead stared at the floor. "I'm sorry. I don't have a good excuse. I was so caught up in my own issues that it never really made much difference to me what happened to anyone else. As long as I was safe, everything seemed justifiable."

He shook his head. "I know that's not enough, and it never will be."

"You're right. Nothing you do will ever be enough." Maeve turned her back on him and took the two steps across the car to where Ginger lay unconscious in Tristan's lap. She watched as he gently stroked Ginger's hair and tucked a wayward strand behind her ear. The gentle look in Tristan's eyes made Maeve wonder if there were some unexplored feelings between the two. She fell to her knees next to Ginger and asked, "What happened to her?"

Tristan explained how she had fallen off the cliff, and how Gray had rescued her. "Do you know where her injuries are? Do we have any medical supplies?"

Tristan nodded his head in the direction of Ginger's leg. "Her leg is broken, but she might have internal injuries, too. We did the best we could to splint her leg. We're just trying to keep her warm until we can get back to Palumbra."

Emery settled on the floor next to Ginger. "Can you help her?" she asked.

"I'm not sure there's much more I can do for her than you guys did without any kind of medical supplies.

Let me look at her leg."

Tristan pulled the blanket back. Ginger shifted restlessly, but Maeve couldn't tell if it was from pain or from the dissipating warmth now that the blanket had been lifted. Gently, she examined Ginger's leg, then motioned for Tristan to pull the blanket back into place.

"You guys did a decent job. There's not much more I can do for her until we get her back to Palumbra."

"Is that where we're going?" Patrick asked in a pained voice, and Maeve turned her attention to him. Private Thompson had used his shirt to bandage Patrick's leg.

"Can I look at it?" she asked.

Patrick shook his head. "It's fine. The bullet didn't hit anything important, just grazed my thigh." Maeve took another look at the bandage and noted that the bleeding seemed to have stopped, so she moved back to Gray. Despite their circumstances, he smiled down at her and pulled her back up against him as if he needed to touch her to make sure she was real. "Want to introduce me to your friends?"

Maeve made the introductions, then Patrick limped over to Gray.

"What's your plan, soldier?"

Gray looked up, a question on his face, when Patrick called him soldier. "Even if I didn't know Maeve, I would know who you are. There are lots of questions about why you and he," he pointed at Tristan, "went AWOL. Lots of rumors that you were on some top secret mission, which apparently turned out to be true."

"I guess so, sir," Gray replied.

"So," Patrick reiterated. "What is your plan?"

Gray glanced over his shoulder before returning his gaze to the terrain in front of him. "We need to get Ginger some medical help, and we need to turn Elton over to the authorities, so we're heading back to Palumbra. There's also the matter of that venom." He looked at Maeve. "Can you tell me what's going on? You said Emma is sick."

Maeve nodded. It took her a minute to answer Gray as she choked back her guilt and worry. "She got too close to me. John had seen this virus before, and he found one dose of the cure in the New Government's storage." She closed her eyes and swallowed. "Emma insisted that he give it to me." Maeve couldn't continue. A huge lump clogged her throat when she thought of the sacrifice Emma had made to keep her alive.

Patrick picked up the story. "We can make more of the cure, but we needed plagoran venom. Maeve is the only person who has seen a plagoran recently, so she joined our group to find them. We got the venom, but then Arabella showed up and killed the plagoran. One of my soldiers betrayed our hiding place."

"A Palumbran betrayed you to Arabella?" Tristan asked. "Why?"

"Because Arabella either has something to hold over the soldier's head or she promised them something they couldn't resist." Elton's quiet voice answered the question. All heads turned toward him. "It's how she works. She got Maeve to do what she wanted by threatening her friends. She got me to do horrible things because she understood my need for safety and power. She'll use any form of threat or manipulation to get her way. That's why she's dangerous."

No one spoke, but Elton's words lingered in the air. The thought that maybe Elton had learned a lesson flitted through Maeve's head, but she pushed it aside. She noticed the view outside the hovercar had changed from the hilly land outside Palumbra to more closely resemble the woods that ringed the city. The hovercar came to a silent stop.

"Why are we stopping?" Patrick asked, turning to look out the window in front of Gray.

"I think this is as far as we can go," Gray said, pointing at a line of soldiers ahead of them. They were far enough away that the soldiers hadn't seen them yet, but they could tell that these weren't Palumbran.

"Anyone interested in a return trip to the tunnels?" Gray asked with a wry smile.

CHAPTER FIFTY

Maeve looked at the battered group assembled around the old well. They needed to get into the tunnels before they were caught by Arabella's troops, but as her gaze scanned from Patrick and his wounded leg to Tristan carrying Ginger's limp form in his arms, she wondered how they would all get down the ladder.

"I'll go down first and make sure the tunnels are clear," Gray said. "Send Emery down next."

"I should go first," Patrick said. "This is supposed to be my mission."

Gray motioned to the blood now seeping through the makeshift bandage on Patrick's leg. "You're wounded, and we don't know what's down there. I'm familiar with the tunnels, and I'm all in one piece."

"Which is a change from the last time we did this," Maeve said. The edges of Gray's lips twitched upward. "But how are we going to get Ginger into the tunnels?"

"I'll carry her over my shoulder," Tristan said. "Probably not the best thing for her leg, but it's the only way."

"We need to get her some real help soon." Maeve chewed on the side of her thumb, trying not to let her concern for Ginger overwhelm her. She didn't want to worry the others, but the longer Ginger was unconscious from fever, the more troubling her condition became.

"What about Rufus?" Emery asked. "How do we get him in the tunnels?"

Maeve saw Gray wince at the question. She had already asked Gray that question before they abandoned the hovercar. She didn't like the answer either. Gray crouched down so he was eye level with Emery and put his hands on her shoulders. "I don't like this any more than you're going to, Em, but we can't take him into the tunnels."

Emery began to shake her head, her hair flinging from side to side. "You can't leave him out here. What if they find him?" Her voice shook, and she blinked her eyes rapidly. Maeve moved to Emery's side and pulled her into a hug.

"I know it's hard, Emery, but Rufus is smart. He saved me, and he can survive out here until we can come back for him."

Emery looked up at Maeve with shining eyes. "You promise we'll come back for him?" Maeve squeezed her into another hug.

"Of course, Em. That dog's a hero. We'll come back."

Maeve knelt next to Rufus and stroked his head. She thought his brown eyes looked resigned as if he knew what was about to happen. Emery dropped to her knees on his other side and brought his face around until they were nose to nose. Rufus licked her nose, and Emery giggled. "Be good, Rufus. Go and hide. Don't let them find you." She kissed his nose and stood up.

Maeve stroked his head again, and echoed Emery. "Don't let them get you, Rufus. We'll be back. I promise."

She would have sworn Rufus nodded, then turned his back on them and trotted into the trees. Maeve sniffed once, then squared her shoulders and turned back to Gray. "Let's get moving before we get caught."

He gave her a quick nod, then disappeared down the well. Everyone peered into the darkness, listening for any sign of resistance when Gray reached the bottom.

"It's good." His voice rose out of the darkness. "Send Emery down, then Tristan with Ginger, then Patrick. Let's get the most vulnerable down here. The rest of you keep watching for Arabella's troops."

Emery scampered over the rim of the well, and Maeve held her breath when Tristan hoisted Ginger over his shoulder and slowly descended into the darkness. Patrick took one last look around and followed Tristan. Maeve scanned the horizon in the direction where they had seen Arabella's troops but saw no movement.

"Your turn, Maeve," Amelia said. Maeve gave one last look in the direction that Rufus had gone and swung her leg over the edge of the well.

"Move it," Private Thompson said, pulling his gun to a position where he could fire it and pointing it in the direction where they had last seen Arabella's troops.

"What is it?" Amelia asked.

"Movement over there." He motioned with the tip of his rifle. "Move it, Maeve."

Maeve scrambled down the ladder and waited at the bottom for Amelia's feet to appear. Gray took in her furrowed brow and worried look and rushed to join her. "What is it?"

Amelia's feet finally appeared on the ladder. "Arabella's troops are headed this way."

"What?" Gray asked. "Why? They should be headed toward Palumbra, not back toward us. Is Private Thompson coming?"

"He was supposed to be right behind me." Amelia twisted her hands together. "I don't know why he's not already on his way down." They tilted their heads back, eyes focused on the place where the ladder extended up into the meager daylight.

"Where is he?" Amelia asked.

"Where is everyone else?" Maeve asked Gray as it registered that they were the only three at the foot of the ladder.

Gray never took his eyes off the ladder. "I sent them down the tunnel to find supplies and to find a place for Ginger to rest."

It seemed to Maeve that an hour had passed, but she knew it was only a few minutes, when Private Thompson's feet finally appeared over the edge of the well. He pulled the cover over the top of the well as he quickly descended the ladder.

"What took you so long?" Amelia demanded.

"I was trying to see where Arabella's troops were going. It looks like they're retreating."

"That's the best news of the day," Gray said.

"But they were headed into the woods where Rufus went."

Maeve's face fell, and she began to chew on her thumb once again. Gray gently pulled her hand away from her face. "He'll be fine. Let's get into Palumbra to get Ginger some help and the venom to Emma. Then we can come back and find Rufus. If Arabella's troops are retreating, that means that the Palumbra troops are driving them back. She'll be on the run. That's good news."

Maeve lifted her troubled eyes to Gray's. "But what about Thomas?"

Gray gave her a grim smile. "One problem at a time, Maeve. One problem at a time."

###

"Do you think we can get her to swallow it?" Tristan held out some ground willow bark to Maeve. She and Gray had found the others in a room just down the tunnel from the well entrance. Ginger lay on a cushion of blankets with another blanket covering her. Patrick sat in a chair, wincing as Amelia peeled the makeshift bandage from his leg.

Maeve turned her attention back to Tristan. "Mix it in some water and get Gray to help you hold her up. Just don't let it choke her." She shifted her head toward Patrick. "I'm going to look at his wound."

For the next 20 minutes, Maeve checked everyone's wounds, binding up Patrick's leg with a better bandage and helping Gray and Tristan force willow bark water down Ginger's throat. She wasn't sure how much Ginger actually drank, but something was better than nothing. She stroked her hand over Ginger's hot forehead while Emery held her sister's hand. Maeve leaned close to Ginger and said, "Come on, Ginger. Hang on for just a little longer."

Emery watched her every move. "Is she going to be OK?" Her voice sounded small and unsure. Maeve stood and walked around Ginger's makeshift bed and pulled Emery to her feet, wrapping her in a strong hug. "I hope so, Em. I really do." She stepped back, placing her hands on Emery's shoulders and leaning down to look her in the eyes. "We're going to do everything we can to help her get better, OK?" Emery nodded and bit her lip. "And that means getting back to Palumbra so we can send help here. I'm going to go talk to Gray. Keep wiping her forehead with a cool cloth."

Emery grabbed the scrap of fabric they were using as a cloth and placed it on Ginger's forehead, and Maeve joined Gray and Tristan as they examined a map on the wall. Gray's eyes lit up despite the serious nature of whatever they were discussing. He took her hand and pulled her into his side, and Maeve leaned into him, happy to once again have the option to touch and talk with him, happy that the kiss they had shared in Arabella's company was not the last one they would ever share.

"We need a plan," she said.

"That's what we're working on." Gray gestured toward the map. "Look familiar?"

Maeve smiled in spite of herself. "That's the map of the tunnels we used last time."

"Yeah. Not much has changed."

Tristan pointed at a black line on the map. "It should be a pretty easy walk to get into Palumbra. This tunnel comes out right in the city center."

"What are we waiting for?" Maeve asked. "Let's get going."

"I think you should stay here." Gray's serious blue eyes bore into hers. She was shaking her head before he finished talking.

"Maeve, listen to me. You're a nurse. We're leaving wounded people here. They need you."

Maeve continued to stubbornly shake her head. Tristan tapped Gray on the shoulder and said, "I'm going to go check on Ginger."

"I'm going with you." Maeve stood with her feet spread apart and her hands on her hips, ready to do battle. Determination blazed in her eyes.

"That doesn't make sense. You can be much more useful here."

"I already dressed Patrick's wound. He'll be fine. There's nothing more I can do for Ginger. She needs help from Palumbra. Emery and Amelia can keep her comfortable until we get back. Please, Gray. I don't want to be separated from you again. Not knowing what had happened to you was worse than anything Arabella could do to me."

Gray closed his eyes as if in pain. "Don't you think I know what that feels like? I thought you were dead. I can't bear the thought of putting you in danger again."

"Am I really any safer here?"

"Yes! This part of the tunnels is deserted. No one uses these anymore, but the closer we get to the city center, the more likely it is that someone in The Resistance remembered they were here and decided to use them in the fight against Arabella's troops. That means some of Arabella's troops could have followed them down."

Maeve placed a finger on Gray's lips. "That doesn't even make sense. If the troops have found the tunnels, I wouldn't be any safer here than I would be near the city center." She took her finger from Gray's lips and traced a line on the map. "They're all connected." She took a step toward him. "You can't just tuck me away so I'll be safe, Gray. We have a job to do."

She didn't say anything else but held Gray's tortured gaze with her own. She was going with him. She was just waiting for him to acknowledge it. She watched the emotions flit through his ice blue eyes: fear, determination, anger, and finally, resignation. He blew out a breath, warming her cheek.

"Fine. Just be careful." He paused and lifted his hand to cup her cheek. She leaned her face into the palm of his hand, relishing the feeling of being near him again. He closed his eyes and drew in a deep breath before he whispered, "I don't know what I'd do if I got you back only to lose you again."

CHAPTER FIFTY-ONE

Maeve, Gray, Private Thompson and Elton walked briskly through the dim tunnels. Gray had found a forgotten gun and some ammunition in one of the tunnel rooms, and Private Thompson carried his army-issued weapon. Gray had found another gun for Maeve, but she had once again refused to carry it. Gray relented only when she had tucked a small knife into her belt, but Maeve had no plans to use it, either. Elton walked with his hands tucked into his pockets, weaponless, in front of them. Private Thompson watched him warily, but Elton had made no move to escape.

Maeve took a few quick steps to catch up to him. "Elton?" He raised his head and raised one eyebrow in question but said nothing. "Was it worth it?"

Elton's brow furrowed in confusion, but he remained silent.

"The few fleeting moments of power you had when you turned us over to Arabella. Was it worth it?"

Elton shrugged. "Look at where I am now. I'd say no."

"Would you make the same choices again?"

Elton kicked the dirt on the ground as he walked

with his shoulders slumped. He stared straight ahead as he answered. "I wish I could say no, but it all sounded so good. I would never go without anything again. No worries about safety or food or shelter. That's what she offered me, and when you don't have any of that, you'll do whatever it takes to get it." He turned his head to look at Maeve. "I know you think I'm a terrible person, and I'll be the first to admit that I did terrible things. But I didn't do it because I'm evil. I did it because I thought it was the only way to have those things. I wish I could say I wouldn't do it again." He paused for so long that Maeve thought he might not say any more. In a voice barely above a whisper he said, "But I just don't know."

Before Maeve could answer, Gray had pushed between them and flattened himself against the dirt wall, his gun at the ready. He motioned for them to do the same. Private Thompson leaned slightly out from the wall and whispered around Maeve and Elton. "What is it?"

Gray didn't take his eyes off the tunnel ahead of him as he whispered back, "Voices."

In the quiet, Maeve strained to hear any sound. A low murmur made its way through the tunnel. She leaned her face close to Gray's ear and said in a voice that was more breath than sound, "They're coming this way."

Gray nodded and looked up and down the tunnel. They were in a stretch of the tunnel that was simply tunnel, no rooms branching off to the side, and Maeve tried to remember the last time they had seen a room or another tunnel branching off. "Should we go back?"

Gray kept his eyes trained on the tunnel, and Maeve thought she could make out a pinprick of light. Gray shook his head. "There's a room just up this tunnel.

Hopefully, they're going there. We'll sneak past once they've entered."

Maeve bit her lip but said nothing. If she squinted, she could see a door nearly 100 yards down the tunnel. She prayed Gray was right because that didn't leave them much time to escape back down the tunnel if he wasn't. She shifted toward him again, but as she leaned toward him, he raised a finger to his lips and motioned for her to settle back against the wall. She held her breath as the light grew bigger and brighter. She thought she could make out several figures trailing behind the light. She sucked in a breath as one voice came carrying through the darkness.

The light turned and disappeared into the room, leaving the tunnels once again shrouded in a dim light. Maeve waited until she heard the door shut before breathing again.

"Why is Arabella in the tunnels?" Gray asked her.

"I may have told her the plans for the laser weapon she wanted were in the tunnels."

"Why would you say that?"

Maeve shrugged. "It was the best I could come up with at the time. I was trying to save your life."

She took a step forward, but Gray's arm barred Maeve from moving. She was intent on getting revenge on the woman who had taken Thomas and could have already been the cause of Emma's death.

"We can't," Gray whispered in her ear. "We have to get that antidote to Emma and help for Ginger. She's on a wild goose chase that will keep her busy for a while. We can send troops back to capture her."

Maeve settled back against the wall and shot a look at Elton, catching him giving the door a thoughtful look.

"Don't even think about it," she growled.

Elton shook his head vehemently. "I wouldn't. She left me to die in the desert. I would never trust her again." He paused as if weighing his words. "But we could end this right now."

Gray leaned away from the wall and pinned Elton with his fierce gaze, his blue eyes like chips of ice. "Our job is to get this antidote to Emma and to find help for Ginger. We're not going to risk our friends' lives by waltzing into that room with no idea what we're up against."

Elton wilted under Gray's authority, holding up his hands in surrender. "OK. We'll do it your way. But what if we never get another chance at Arabella? What if Thomas is in that room?"

Elton's words made Maeve pause. Would they be sacrificing Thomas if they walked by that door without going in?

"Gray's right," Private Thompson spoke up. "Our mission is to deliver the antidote and find help for Ginger. We're going to have to wait until we have more support to attack Arabella."

Gray moved away from the wall and stood in front of Maeve, holding her gaze with his. Maeve knew he could see the conflict in her soul reflected in her eyes. How could she choose between her friends?

"We'll get him back, Maeve, I promise." Gray's eyes had changed from the ice chips directed at Elton to a warm, blue filled with resolve for Maeve. "Even if we have to trek across the desert into The Beyond. We *will* find him."

Maeve held his gaze for a moment longer, then

squared her shoulders, stepped forward and placed her hand on his cheek. "I'm holding you to that." Gray covered her hand with his and nodded. She adjusted the pack on her shoulders and motioned for him to lead the way. "Let's go."

Gray adjusted his own pack and began jogging down the dimly lit tunnel, taking care to make as little noise as possible. The rest of them followed. Private Thompson had just cleared the door when it slammed open, causing everyone to freeze for a split second. Maeve frantically swiveled her head from side to side looking for somewhere, anywhere, to hide, but the long expanse of tunnel provided no cover. Gray shoved her behind him, and Private Thompson did the same with Elton. Both Gray and Private Thompson trained their guns on the door as they quickly shuffled backward down the tunnel, putting as much distance as they could between themselves and the door without turning their backs.

"Run," Gray whispered to Maeve, but instead of running, she grabbed a handful of his shirt to let him know she was staying. Elton was already five steps down the tunnel when he looked back at Maeve with pleading eyes, begging her silently to run down the tunnel with him, but after a quick glance at him, Maeve kept her fist wrapped in Gray's shirt and her eyes trained on the door. She heard Elton's footsteps pounding in the dirt behind her. Her body stiffened when Arabella stepped through the door.

"Oh, hello again," she said. Gray's finger tightened on the trigger, and Maeve hoped he wouldn't pull it. They still didn't know where Thomas was, and as much as she hated Arabella, she didn't want Gray to have to kill anyone.

Despite her troops having been in a pitched battle, Arabella looked as if she had done nothing more strenuous than wash her face. Maybe that *was* the most difficult thing she had done today, Maeve thought. It's not like she led her troops into battle.

"What a delightful surprise to find you here." Arabella tapped her blood red lips with a matching fingernail. "Did I say surprise? That would be a lie. We've known you were here since you turned that corner." She pointed to the ceiling. "Cameras. The New Government installed them. We just borrowed the feed for a bit." Two guards stepped into the hallway behind Arabella, pointing their guns at Gray and Private Thompson. Maeve saw a bead of sweat roll down the side of Private Thompson's face and wondered if he had any actual experience against a live enemy.

"Well, that should work in our favor since the New Government can see what's happening here," Gray said with a quick upward glance to the camera.

"Oh, silly boy, we blocked their access when we took over the feed, and it's unlikely they're watching the tunnel cameras closely enough to notice when one camera goes offline. They do have some battles still to fight above us."

Maeve felt Gray tense at Arabella's words and realized he had been hoping that help would come.

"Why don't you just hand over the plagoran venom that you took, and you can be on your way?" Arabella held out her hand as if she really thought Maeve would just hand it over. Maeve moved to stand beside Gray. He shot her a warning look and motioned for her to step back, but Maeve ignored him.

"Why would we do that? And why would we trust you to keep your word?"

"Because you have no other choice, Maeve." She motioned down the tunnel. "If you take one step down that tunnel, my guards will shoot you and your friends. There's nowhere to hide." She wiggled her fingers. "So, come on, now, hand it over."

"Where's Thomas?"

Arabella stretched her lips into a smile that didn't reach her eyes. "Oh, don't you worry about him. He's somewhere safe. I have big plans for him." Her smile got wider. "He's my own flesh and blood, you know. I'll take good care of him."

Maeve sucked in a breath of surprise, and her eyes widened at Arabella's statement. She felt Gray startle beside her.

"What do you mean your own flesh and blood?"

CHAPTER FIFTY-TWO

"You should have done your homework, Maeve. He's my sister's son." She schooled her face into a false impression of sorrow. "Unfortunately, she died fighting for The Resistance. My brother was raising him, but I think it's my turn now. I do so need an heir to mold into the next ruler of Palumbra since Elton was such a huge disappointment."

Maeve never took her eyes off Arabella.

"Enough chit chat." Arabella snapped her fingers impatiently. "Hand over the venom."

Maeve started to move forward, but Gray's hand on her arm stopped her. "Again, why would I do that?"

"Shoot the tall one."

Maeve was never sure exactly what happened next. With a mighty heave, Gray thrust her behind his back and pushed her down the tunnel away from Arabella. She hit the ground knees first and scrambled to her feet as Gray propelled her forward. Bullets bit into the dirt walls and ground around them, and Gray turned periodically to fire back. "Stay low, and move," he yelled. "Don't look back."

Maeve's heart pounded, and she could feel every muscle as her feet hit the floor in a full-out sprint. Ignoring

Gray's order, she glanced over her shoulder just in time to see Elton fall to the ground, blood blooming from his chest. Maeve hadn't even known he came back. His eyes met hers for a split second, and she imagined she saw peace in them before he sprawled face down in the dirt. She looked for Private Thompson and found his motionless body on the ground just feet from where Elton had fallen. She wanted to stop. Her chest hurt, not just from the running but for the sacrifice that had just been made. Her face was wet, but she didn't remember crying. Gray tugged on her arm as they rounded a corner of the tunnel, silencing the barrage of bullets for a moment. She tried to stop, but Gray was relentless.

"Keep moving, Maeve. We have to lose them and get back to the city."

She kept her feet moving through a sheer act of will. Her heart felt heavy in her chest. "Why? Why did you let them do it?" Her words came out choppy as she gasped for enough breath to move, speak and mourn.

"I didn't know, Maeve. I didn't." Gray turned them down another tunnel. "I heard whispering, but I didn't know Elton had returned. I thought he took off." He glanced down at her, his face drawn and his eyes filled with sorrow. "Private Thompson shoved me out of the way and yelled at me to run at the same time that Elton charged Arabella."

"Why didn't you fight?"

"I couldn't, Maeve." They came to a fork in the tunnels, and Gray didn't break stride as he chose the left branch. "We were sitting ducks in that tunnel. I had to get you away. If one of us doesn't make it back to Palumbra, then Emma, and probably Ginger, will die."

"So, we sacrificed two other lives?"

"We didn't do it Maeve." Gray's voice was quiet, reverent. "They did. All we can do is decide what to do with the chance they gave us."

Neither spoke again, but tears continued to roll down Maeve's cheeks until they reached a wide spot in the tunnel where a wooden ladder was dug into the dirt wall.

"This is our exit." Gray pointed up to a circular opening in the tunnel ceiling. "You first. Wait for me at the top before you remove the cover."

Maeve stood in the shadow of a brick building in the center of Palumbra. For a city that had just begun to rebuild from the revolution, the sight was disheartening. Piles of rubble lined the sidewalks where bricks and wood from the storefronts had been demolished in the new fighting. The street itself was pockmarked where bullets had dug up the street. It was eerily quiet. Besides Gray, Maeve saw no one out on the streets. In the distance she could hear sporadic gunfire, but it seemed the bulk of the fighting was over.

"This way." Gray took her hand and began to jog toward the government building at the heart of the city. Its shiny glass surface towered over the rest of the buildings in Palumbra, but as they neared, Maeve could see that the first few floors had taken a beating from the fighting. Much of the first-floor glass lay shattered, and burn marks showed near the doors. As they approached, a Palumbra soldier stepped forward and pointed his gun at Gray.

"Identify yourself."

Gray dropped Maeve's hand and slowly raised his own. Maeve followed suit.

"Gray Cantwell." He tipped his head toward Maeve. "This is Maeve Jackson. I'm a soldier, and she's a nurse. We have something that Cleo wants."

The soldier pulled a communicator from his belt and said something Maeve couldn't hear.

"Got any ID?"

Gray rolled his eyes at the soldier. "Do we look like we're just out for a stroll?" Maeve hadn't paid much attention to their appearance until Gray made that comment. She took in his torn shirt, muddy pants and dirt-smudged face. She hadn't fared much better. The elbow of her shirt was ripped, her pants were covered in mud and dust and plagoran saliva, and she was sure her face was as dirty as Gray's.

"Tell Cleo we're here," Gray said. "She knows us."

The soldier spoke into his communicator again then lowered his gun and motioned for them to follow. They entered the building, and Maeve noted the destruction inside. What had once been the reception desk was tipped on its side and split down the middle. Glass, concrete and paper were strewn across the entryway. Debris crunched under their feet as they made their way to the stairs. They climbed to the third floor where the damage was less noticeable, a chunk of wall missing in a few places or the occasional hole in the ceiling or floor. They reached a double wooden door, and the soldier knocked twice. Maeve heard Cleo's voice call out, "Bring them in."

The soldier pushed the door open, and Maeve and Gray entered a large conference room. Cleo stood alone at the window on the other side of the room, staring out. Maeve could see smoke rising in the distance. Without turning, Cleo said, "Join me, and tell me what you see."

Maeve and Gray walked over to the window and flanked Cleo. From this vantage point, they could see the Palumbra troops driving back the meager forces Arabella had brought, thinking the people of Palumbra would be too sick to fight.

"It looks like we're winning," Maeve said, then immediately wanted to pull the words back into her mouth. Was it winning when people were dying?

"They're not fighting," Gray said. "At least not very hard."

Cleo nodded. "You're right. I don't know if it's a trick or if they really are done fighting. We've cut off their escape back to The Hub, and we've offered to accept the surrender of those who no longer want to fight. I don't know where they're going."

"I'm sure Arabella has a back-up plan," Maeve said.

Cleo nodded and turned to face them.

"You two look like you've had a time of it. Did you get what we need?"

Maeve nodded, dug in her pack and pulled out the plagoran venom. "It should be enough for the antidote to save Emma."

Cleo took the venom then closed her eyes for the space of two heartbeats. When she opened them, the sorrow they reflected shattered Maeve's world.

CHAPTER FIFTY-THREE

Maeve clutched her stomach and fell to her knees, her head bowed as she gulped for air. She had suffered so much and worked too hard for this to be how it ended. She felt Gray's hand grip her arm and pull her into the embrace of his muscular arms. She laid her head on his chest and waited for Cleo to speak. Maybe she was wrong. Maybe Cleo wasn't about to tell her the worst news.

"I'm sorry, Maeve." Cleo's quiet voice caught on the last word. "Emma died this morning. She wasn't alone; John was with her. It was peaceful."

Maeve wanted to cry. She did. She wanted to let out a wail of misery and mourning, but the pain was too deep, the wound too new. Her eyes refused to fill with tears. Her mouth refused to release a sound. But her heart did not refuse to break, and an all-consuming emptiness filled her, the knowledge that one of the few people in the world that knew her and loved her was gone. The emptiness became an ache. She hurt. It was as if her body was being ripped in two by the pain.

She knew Gray was rubbing her arms and speaking, but her ears could not make out the words. He spoke to Cleo over her head. Whatever he said had Cleo rushing out of the room, but Maeve was numb to it all. Emma was gone. Emma had been her rock, her source of wisdom, the grandmother she never had, and one of the few people in the world that she trusted completely. When her parents had betrayed her to the WG, their relationship had broken, perhaps irreparably so, but Emma had stepped into the gap and become the parent she needed. What would she do without her?

Gray leaned down so his eyes were level with hers. He continued to rub her arms in warm, even strokes. "Maeve, I know how it feels." Maeve blinked as she took in his words. "When Night died, the pain was unbearable – even more so because we thought he had betrayed us." Maeve blinked again and remembered how she had comforted Gray in the weeks after his uncle's death, which left him without any family. "It's going to hurt." Gray shook his head. "The pain may never go away completely, but it will get better. You'll figure out how to live without her."

Maeve shook her head in denial. Gray pulled her back into his chest and wrapped his arms around her. She felt him kiss the top of her head. "I know it doesn't seem like it now, but you will. And you'll go on to live a life Emma would have been proud of. Because that's how you honor her."

Maeve pulled back from Gray and looked up into his face, wondering whether she dared to voice the words that had been floating in her head since Cleo delivered the life-changing blow. "But it's my fault she's dead."

Gray started to protest, but Maeve stopped him. She had to speak the words.

"She got the virus from me. If I had just refused to

come back to Palumbra. If I had just stopped in the forest and died, she would still be alive."

"But you and Thomas would be dead."

"So, you're saying you would trade Emma for me and Thomas?" Maeve pushed herself out of Gray's embrace, but Gray caught her by the wrist and gently pulled her back toward him.

"No! I wouldn't trade any of you." Gray cupped her face in his hands, forcing her to look him in the eyes. "But, Maeve, you made that decision because you were trying to save Thomas. Arabella told you she would kill him if you stopped before you got to Palumbra. What other choice could you have made?"

Maeve's shoulders slumped. "Why is there always a cost? Why does it always seem that when I make a choice someone dies?" She stepped back again and raised her tortured eyes to Gray's face. A tear dripped from the corner of her eye.

"This choice wasn't yours, Maeve. It was Emma's."

"I got her sick."

"She chose to get near you after you told her. She chose to give you the antidote." Gray's words were calm, measured, as if he was choosing each one carefully. "This was her choice, her sacrifice. Don't take that on yourself. It's a burden you weren't meant to carry."

Maeve thought back to her last conversation with Emma. *"Maeve, if I don't make it, remember, I made a choice, too. And I know it was the right one."*

Another tear tracked its way through the dirt on her cheek. "She told me that. She said it was her choice." Tears were falling freely now, and she rested her forehead on Gray's chest. "I just wish we had made it back sooner."

Gray closed his arms around her, his tears joining hers, and whispered. "Me too, Maeve. Me too."

CHAPTER FIFTY-FOUR

Maeve opened her eyes and took stock of her surroundings. Her head was pillowed on Gray's chest where they were stretched out on a couch in the hospital wing of the New Government headquarters. The ache in her chest that had begun three days earlier when she learned of Emma's death hadn't lessened; she had just learned to put one foot in front of the other in spite of it. She shifted to a sitting position, careful not to wake Gray, and looked over at the hospital bed where Ginger lay. Maeve sighed. She settled back on the couch, gathering her courage for another day of waiting for Ginger to wake up. Her gaze traveled over the hip-to-ankle cast, noted the line dripping medicine into her vein, took in the bruises on her arms and stopped on Ginger's blue eyes – her open blue eyes. Maeve jolted to her feet.

"Ginger!"

Ginger lifted one hand in a weak wave. "Hi."

Gray's eyes popped open at Maeve's shout. He shot to his feet, his soldier's training taking over as he scanned the room for a threat. Finding none, he turned to Maeve, "What are you shouting about?"

Maeve pointed at Ginger who repeated her weak

wave and greeting.

"Ginger!" Gray grinned. "Nice to have you back."

"Nice to be back." Ginger's voice was scratchy from lack of use. She coughed to clear it, and Maeve handed her a glass of water. "Where are Emery and Tristan?"

"Sleeping," Maeve said. "We've been taking turns staying with you."

"What happened? Last I remember, Gray and Emery were stealing a hovercar."

Maeve barked a short laugh. "There's a lot to tell you."

Gray and Maeve pulled chairs up next to Ginger's bed and filled her in on everything that had happened to them. When they got to Elton's death, Ginger said, "I guess he was making up for Shalara."

Maeve shrugged. "Maybe. I think in the end he truly wanted to do the right thing. I just wish the right thing hadn't been dying."

"You guys got the venom back here and they made the antidote, so everything is OK? Is Emma coming to see me later?"

Maeve and Gray shared a long look. "Do you want me to tell her?" Gray asked. Ginger's head swiveled from Gray's face to Maeve's, understanding beginning to sink in.

Maeve shook her head and swallowed. She thought she had cried all the tears she had to cry in the past three days, but she was wrong. Her eyes filled once more.

"We didn't make it back in time. Emma died three days ago." Maeve's voice broke, and once again tears spilled onto her cheeks.

Ginger sniffed, and Maeve watched the tears track

down Ginger's face, mirroring her own. Gray squeezed Maeve's hand, his own eyes glistening. After a moment, Ginger wiped the tears from her eyes with the hand not attached to the medicine line.

"So, we didn't get the antidote back in time. Surely they caught Arabella? And what about Thomas?"

Maeve opened her mouth to answer, but a light knock on the door interrupted. Tristan peeked his head around the door, his eyes widening when he saw Ginger talking with Gray and Maeve.

"You're awake!"

No sooner had he spoken than he was pushed aside, and Emery hurtled through the door. She flew to Ginger and was about to hurl herself onto her sister's bed when Tristan caught her from behind. "Leg, remember?" Emery nodded and moved as close to the bed as she could get.

"How come no one came and got me?" She glared at Maeve and Gray.

"That was next. We were filling Ginger in on what happened while she was unconscious."

"Em," Ginger said. "You OK?"

Emery nodded, then sniffed and wiped her nose with her sleeve. "I'm fine. It's you we were worried about. I'm so glad you're going to be OK. You wouldn't wake up." Her voice became whisper soft. "I was scared."

Ginger gave her hand a weak squeeze. "We're going to be fine. I'm going to be fine. You can't get rid of me that easily." She gave Emery a watery smile and turned back to Maeve.

"Tell me what happened with Arabella and Thomas."

They all stared at the floor until Maeve gathered the courage to speak. "She got away, and she took Thomas with her."

Ginger stared at them in horror, her gaze moving from face to face as if willing one of them to say it wasn't true.

"How?"

Tristan came to stand next to Emery. "She was gone when the soldiers Cleo sent went looking for them. They never came by the room we were hiding in so they must have gone out a different way."

"Do you guys have any good news?"

Gray nodded. "Well, the good news is that she doesn't have much of a following left. Most of her troops chose to surrender when they realized they weren't going to just waltz in and take over. Just a few of her troops scattered into the desert, but we don't know how many were left in Bellus. We cut off their ability to get back there, so their only choice is to take their chances in The Beyond."

Maeve took over. "The other piece of good news is that with the plagoran venom, we have plenty of antidote and the ability to make a vaccine against the virus, so she can't just try the same tactic again."

"But no Thomas?" Ginger asked.

Maeve shook her head, unable to speak. Gray took her hand and squeezed. "We're going to find him. I don't know how, but we will."

CHAPTER FIFTY-FIVE

On the day they buried Emma, the sun turned the sky a brilliant pink as it slowly descended below the horizon. It was as if the heavens were giving Emma one last taste of the beauty the earth could offer. Maeve stood on the hill, leaning against the well as the sun said its final farewell. She held a sheet of paper filled with Emma's familiar handwriting that John had given her during the funeral and told her to find a quiet place to read it. Alone on the hill with the sun saying a brilliant goodbye, Maeve opened the note.

My courageous Maeve,

You were the daughter and the granddaughter I never had, and I couldn't have loved you more if you had truly been my own. I know that you will blame yourself for my death, but this was my choice, Maeve. I knew this could happen, and I know you did your best to save me. Let that be enough, Maeve. Don't carry any guilt over my death. My choice. I chose to lay down my life for you because I love you. And I know you would have done the same for me.

Don't mourn too much for me. I had a long life,

and so much of it was good. I know it might not have seemed like it, but I loved two wonderful men, both for far too short a time. But those loves were sweeter for not having had much time. I fought a good fight, and though the battle may seem lost, the war is not yet over.

Be brave, Maeve. So much has been asked of you in your young life. Stay strong. Keep your friends close. And never lose who you are. Stand your ground and do what is right.

And know that my love will always be with you. It never dies.

Emma

Maeve smiled a small smile and folded the note. The ache in her heart was still there, but after reading Emma's note, she found peace there as well. She would let go of the guilt and honor Emma's sacrifice while wrapping herself in the love that Emma had given her.

Light footsteps climbed the hill behind her until strong arms wrapped around her waist. She leaned back into Gray's embrace, tilting her head up for a kiss. His lips brushed hers, and she sighed as a tingle ran down her spine at the contact. She wondered if that would ever go away. She hoped not.

"Did you read it?"

Maeve laid her hands over his, the note trapped between them, and nodded. "Do you want to read it?"

"Only if you want me to."

Maeve tucked the note into his hands. "She would have wanted me to share."

Gray kept Maeve tucked against him with one arm as he read the note. When he finished, he said, "What do you think?"

"I think she's right. I can't take responsibility for a choice that she made. We all have to make choices. I can only be responsible for my own. Sometimes our choices are hard, and there may not be a good one, but they define us and change us. We have to embrace that."

Gray squeezed her tight. "I knew you would get there."

She patted his hands, which were once again clasped in front of her. "This doesn't mean I want to pick up a gun again, though. I can't do that again."

She felt Gray nod where his chin was propped on her head. "It's your choice."

They stood in silence, watching the sun slip lower and lower. When the last rays spread out over the hillside and the day had turned into dusk, Maeve turned in Gray's arms. Gray leaned down and kissed her, and Maeve felt a piece of her heart begin to mend.

"I love you," Gray said when he lifted his head. "I should have told you before now. I kept waiting for the moment to be perfect."

"I know, but it's nice to hear it. And what moment could be more perfect than this one?" She looked him in the eyes. "I love you, too."

She rested her head against his chest and without looking up asked, "What do we do now?"

"Read the rest of your letter."

Maeve peered up at him in the gathering darkness. "The rest of it? I read it all."

"Look on the back."

In the increasingly dim light, Maeve took the letter from him and turned it over. In small script near the bottom of the page, Emma had added a postscript.

P.S. John put a tracker on Rufus.

Maeve gave Gray a puzzled look. "Why is that important?"

"We haven't found Rufus."

"I know. Emery and I have looked every day."

"Think, Maeve. Where would Rufus have gone?"

Maeve drew in a sharp breath. "He would have followed Thomas."

Gray smiled and nodded. "Let's go see John."

Find out what happens next in The Lost Boy, *available soon.*

If you liked The Lost City, *please consider leaving a review on Amazon or Goodreads.*

Read Emma's story for free in The Time Capsule *by signing up to receive my newsletter at booksbyfairchild.wixsite.com/ldfairchild*

About the Author

L.D. Fairchild lives in one of the only big cities in Kansas with her husband, two daughters and two dogs. When she's not dreaming up new ways for the world to end, she loves reading, creating things and spoiling her dogs.

Since she spends her days in imaginary worlds, she loves meeting people in the real one. Be sure to look her up on Instagram and Facebook or drop her a note at booksbyfairchild@gmail.com.

booksbyfairchild.wixsite.com/ldfairchild

Made in the USA
Monee, IL
30 March 2024

55422961R00236